OMEGA DAYS

AN OMEGA DAYS NOVEL

JOHN L. CAMPBELL

BERKLEY BOOKS, NEW YORK

THE BERKLEY PUBLISHING GROUP
Published by the Penguin Group
Penguin Group (USA) LLC
375 Hudson Street, New York, New York 10014

USA • Canada • UK • Ireland • Australia • New Zealand • India • South Africa • China

penguin.com

A Penguin Random House Company

Library of Congress Cataloging-in-Publication Data

Campbell, John L. (Investigator)
Omega days / John L. Campbell.
pages cm. — (An Omega Days novel ; 1)
ISBN 978-0-425-27263-3 (pbk.)
1. Zombies—Fiction. 2. Horror tales. 3. San Francisco (Calif.)—Fiction. I. Title.
PS3603.A47727O64   2014
813'.6—dc23
2013046999

PUBLISHING HISTORY
Berkley eBook edition / June 2013
Berkley trade paperback edition / May 2014

PRINTED IN THE UNITED STATES OF AMERICA

10 9 8 7 6 5 4 3 2 1

Cover images: Omega symbol © Morphart Creation / Shutterstock; Oakland Bay bridge ©
Sigurcamp/Shutterstock; Texture © Sanexi/Shutterstock; Zombie © TsuneoMP/Shutterstock.
Cover design by Diana Kolsky.
Interior text design by Laura K. Corless.
Title page art © iStockphoto.com/trigga.

This is for my boys:
Harrison, Fletcher, and Daniel

And for Linda, always

ACKNOWLEDGMENTS

Special thanks to the following: Charles Liebener, USN, for his inside views of a secret world; my editor, Amanda Ng, and the talented folks at Berkley, for being captured by San Francisco zombies and giving a newcomer a shot; and my agent, Jennifer DeChiara, who believes and who broke her arm at a red-carpet affair. And to all those relentless, ravenous, and wonderful readers who devour zombie fiction with an insatiable appetite, many thanks.

UNCLEAN THINGS

ONE

Xavier Church sat on a bowed, secondhand sofa while a window fan pulled evening air into the tiny living room. The apartment was small and furnished from thrift shops, but it was clean. Jesus stared down from every wall, featured in the Last Supper, his moment of crisis in the garden, and many other scenes. Crucifixes and ceramic Virgin Marys were everywhere.

He sipped at a glass of lemonade, listening to Mrs. Robles puttering and stalling in the kitchen. Across from him an eighties-era television sat silently on a metal stand, reflecting his image in shadow tones. Staring back at him was a once-handsome black man in his middle forties with close-cut, graying hair, wearing the black suit and white collar of a priest. The collar seemed at odds with his boxer's build and the cruel pink scar that split his dark brown face. It started above his left eyebrow, snaking down the side of his nose and across his cheek before hooking back in to end at his chin. Not handsome anymore. Not since he was seventeen, when LaRay Johns caught him outside an Oakland 7-Eleven.

Mrs. Robles finally returned to the living room cradling something wrapped in a dish towel in both hands and set it gently on the coffee table in front of the priest. Though only in her thirties, she looked twenty years older, worn down from a hard life here in the Tenderloin neighborhood of San Francisco. She was still in her work clothes, a cleaning company uniform, one of her three jobs.

"I find this in his room, Padre," she said. She perched on the edge of a chair and clasped her hands tightly in her lap, watching him with eyes red from crying.

Xavier lifted the edge of the towel, revealing a black, short-barreled revolver. "Did you ask him where he got it?"

Mrs. Robles nodded. "But he no tell me. He curse at me, tell me to mind my business. But I know he get it from those boys."

The woman didn't need to tell him who those boys were. It could only be 690K, the Latin gang that controlled this part of San Francisco. The 690 represented an address, supposedly where their founding member—a gangster now long dead himself—had made his first kill, an apartment building that his followers had turned into a shrine and where no one dared live. The K stood for killers. They were as ruthless as MS-13 and dreamed of one day rivaling the size and reach of that infamous gang. Recruiting young was their specialty, the random murder of an innocent their initiation. Xavier knew them well.

"Has he been going to school?"

She shook her head.

Xavier let the dish towel fall back over the pistol. Years of running the parish youth center and providing counseling for inner-city families had taught him many things. One was that by the time a gun came into the house, it was usually too late. He hated the idea, hated the pessimism that had steadily crept into his life, tainting his views on everything and souring his belief in the goodness of people. He prayed for strength, but the thought that mankind as a whole was happy in its race toward damnation, content to abuse and destroy one another, had taken hold and grown in him. He hated his own weakness most of all, his inability to fight back against this cancerous attitude.

He forced a smile at Mrs. Robles. "Let me talk to him."

She smiled back and came to him, taking his hands in hers and squeezing them, then left the room. Xavier saw the gratitude in her eyes, the belief that he would actually help her son, and he felt like a fraud. Voices in Spanish came from the other room, one soft and the other sharp, angry. Then a fourteen-year-old boy slouched into the room, head down with his hands in his pockets, being prodded along by his mother. He dropped into an armchair across from the priest, crossed his arms, and looked away. Mrs. Robles stood in the kitchen doorway, nervously smoothing her uniform apron.

"Hey, Chico," Xavier said, using the boy's nickname. "I haven't seen you around the center for a while. You don't like boxing anymore?"

A shrug.

"You should come by Saturday night. The fight's on pay-per-view, and we're all going to order pizza and hang out." No reply. "Your friends miss you."

"They're not my friends," Chico said. "Just a bunch of losers."

"You've got some new friends now, huh?"

Chico crossed his arms tighter, still not looking at the priest.

"Is that where this came from?" Xavier gestured at the lump under the dish towel. "Want to talk about it?"

The boy glanced at the table. "Not really."

Xavier looked at the boy, a skinny adolescent in need of a haircut, trying desperately to grow a mustache. He wore baggy jeans and a long-sleeve, plaid flannel shirt buttoned to the neck and down to the wrists. Some styles never changed. The priest noticed that his left sleeve was dark and reddish just below the elbow. "What happened to your arm?"

Another shrug.

"Roll up your sleeve for me, Chico."

He hesitated, then unbuttoned the cuff and slid the flannel up past his elbow, wincing. A blood-soaked bandage was wrapped around his arm, and at the sight of it his mother gasped and crossed herself.

"What happened?" asked Xavier.

"I was coming home from school." He looked at his mother and curled his lip. "I *did* go today, I wasn't lying. I cut through an alley and got jumped by a homeless guy. Crazy fu . . . guy bit me."

Xavier saw that the boy was sweating. "Take a ride with me to the ER, Chico. We'll get it looked at, just to be—"

The apartment door crashed open, wood splinters flying, banging hard into the wall and smashing the glass frame of Jesus ministering to children. Two men rushed in, not much older than Chico. One was bigger, his head shaved bald, the other more stocky with slicked-back hair. Both had "690K" tattooed in small black characters at the corners of their left eyes, and both held black automatic pistols at arm's length, turned sideways.

Mrs. Robles screamed and moved toward her son, but the man with slicked-back hair pistol-whipped her across the face, sending her to the floor. Xavier started off the couch, but the gangbanger turned the automatic on him and shouted, "Sit the fuck down!"

Chico Robles swore and charged them, but the bald one punched him hard in the side of the head, knocking him to his knees. He straddled the fallen boy from behind and took a fistful of his hair, jerking his head back. "So you a little bitch, huh?" he hissed.

Chico cried out as the bald man twisted his hair.

"You was supposed to meet Chato," he said, jerking a chin at the man with the slicked-back hair. "Let him watch you do someone, show me you had balls. That was two days ago."

"I was gonna do it, I swear!" Chico cried.

"Yeah, sure you was." Another jerk of the hair, another cry. "You pussied out like a little bitch."

"Do him, Perro!" Chato yelled, keeping his pistol pointed at the priest.

Perro shoved his gun against the back of Chico's head. "Ain't gonna be no bitches in my set."

Xavier held up his hands. "Wait. Take a second, Perro, think about it."

The gangbanger looked at him and raised an eyebrow. "Bitch, no one gave you permission to use my name."

"Yeah," said Chato, taking a step closer, prodding the air with his pistol.

"He's just a kid, man," said Xavier, glancing at Chato's gun. The opening of the barrel looked big enough for a train to come out of it. "You made your point; he's not good enough for you. Why not split?"

"Shut up, *Padre*," snarled Perro. He gave Chico's head a rough shake and leaned in close to the boy's ear. "After you I'm gonna do the priest, and then your mama. Me and Chato both gonna fuck her first, though."

"Do him, Perro," yelled Chato. "Do him!"

Perro clicked back the hammer of the automatic. "Good night, bitch."

An all-too-familiar rage boiled inside the priest, and Xavier did nothing to hold it back. His hand shot out, snatching the revolver out of the dish towel. It came up quickly and he pulled the trigger twice, knocking Chato against the wall. Perro looked up in surprise and swung his automatic toward the priest, firing, as Xavier turned the revolver on him. The crash of Perro's gun was deafening, the white of muzzle flash at close range blinding as something whispered past the priest's ear. He pulled the trigger of the revolver, once, twice, three times, four, and clicking. Perro was still firing, and something hot kissed Xavier's cheek. Then the bald gangbanger was falling backward, tipping over the TV and going down with it in an explosion of glass and plastic.

Silence then, with only the thumping of his heart in his ears. Xavier was standing, didn't remember getting to his feet, and his nose burned with the scent of cordite and the sharp tang of blood. He stood with his arm outstretched, blinking, the revolver hot in his right hand, suddenly heavy. He let it fall to the floor and stared at his hand, while something warm and wet ran down his cheek and neck.

Chico cried and crawled to his mother, taking her in his arms and stroking her hair, yelling for her to wake up. The frightened faces of neighbors appeared in the hall beyond the open doorway, voices speaking urgently in Spanish as in the distance sirens began to wail.

Father Xavier Church felt his legs give out and he collapsed back onto the couch. He couldn't stop staring at his hand.

Red and blue lights flashed in the street in front of the apartment building, squad cars and ambulances packed in tightly, uniformed officers warning away the curious. The ambulance carrying Mrs. Robles and her son, who refused to leave her side, had already left. Near the steps of the building, an old man with white hair and a Windbreaker zipped up to his priest's collar stood with two inspectors, one a black sergeant and the other a Hispanic lieutenant, who had just finished telling him what had happened.

The older man was Monsignor Wellsley, the senior clergyman in Xavier's parish. He glanced over to where Xavier was sitting at the back of an ambulance, a medic applying a bandage to the side of his face where a bullet had carved a red furrow. "The men he shot?" he asked.

The sergeant jerked a thumb at the apartment building. "Both dead," he said. "He got one in the chest and the throat. The bigger one caught a single round in the forehead. The other shots went wild."

The lieutenant gave his sergeant a look. "Thanks for the graphics, Tommy. Father, they were both known gangbangers, and it looks like they came here to execute the boy. Your priest got them first."

The monsignor looked again at Father Church, who sat quietly, staring at nothing. "What happens now?"

The inspectors looked at each other. "We're in pretty strange territory here, Monsignor," the lieutenant said. "It looks like a clear case of self-defense, or going to the defense of another. But a priest as the shooter is a new one for me."

"Is he going to be charged?"

The lieutenant shrugged. "I can't say what the DA will do with this, Father, but I really don't want to book him tonight. We've got the weirdest calls coming in, and we're pretty busy. I'd just as soon release him to you, if that's okay."

The sergeant nodded beside him.

"I don't see him making a run for it," the lieutenant said. "If the church will take responsibility for him tonight, and make sure he comes in tomorrow morning to make a statement, I don't see any reason why he can't go with you."

Wellsley shook their hands. "Thank you, Lieutenant. We'll be available for whatever you need."

The cops nodded and moved away quickly, in a hurry to be off on other business. The monsignor walked over to the ambulance, where Xavier just looked up at him and shook his head. Wellsley thanked the paramedic, who told him it wasn't a serious wound and to treat it with Tylenol. He put an arm around his priest and guided him through the emergency vehicles.

"Let's get you home, Xavier."

Monsignor Wellsley had produced a Valium from somewhere and ordered Xavier to take it before he went to sleep in his room at the rectory. Xavier's dreams were dark, twisting corridors filled with gunfire and screams, and several times he came to in the night, groggy and disoriented, certain he heard helicopters overhead and screaming outside his window. Sleep quickly pulled him back down each time.

A headache was waiting when he awoke, daylight filtering through the curtains and turning the small, simple room a faded yellow. The memory of last night was waiting too, and he immediately tried to pray, as he had every morning since his late twenties, searching for an answer, some understanding, not daring to ask forgiveness.

He couldn't do it. The words sounded false, and he had the unshakable feeling that he was praying to a God who had already turned away. Instead, Xavier sat on the edge of the bed for more than an hour, the headache making his eyes hurt, replaying the scene in the apartment. He heard the gunfire, could smell the blood, saw it splattered on peeling wallpaper and soaking into cheap carpeting. He sensed that he had walked off a cliff from which there could be no return.

And just like that, he knew he wasn't a priest anymore. He waited to feel the great emptiness that would come with that knowledge, the void left in the place of his faith and vows, but there was nothing. That was even more frightening, for it suggested that his faith had left him long ago and made him wonder if it had ever really been there at all.

Xavier put on jeans and sneakers, then pulled on a black sweatshirt with fading letters that read *St. Joseph's Boxing*. On most men it would have been baggy, but on Xavier it could not conceal his broad V shape of wide shoulders, back, and chest muscles. He visited the hallway bathroom, the mirror revealing bloodshot eyes and a face that looked aged overnight. Three Tylenol later, he went downstairs.

The rectory was quiet and empty, and even the secretary was not at her usual post, a desk near the front door. On the dining room table was a note from the monsignor, asking him to please stay in the rectory and not use the Internet or answer the phone until the bishop and the archdiocese could be consulted.

The beat of a helicopter close overhead made him look at the ceiling and think about his dreams. He went to the kitchen, where he found Father Frye standing at the sink and looking out the window. The smell of coffee filled the room, and he poured himself a cup. Frye, a man in his eighties, didn't look away from the window.

"Where is everyone?" Xavier asked, adding a packet of Splenda and stirring.

The old man waved a hand. "Some sort of emergency. Been gone since last night." Frye was all but retired and too old to go out much.

"What kind of emergency?"

A siren yowled in the distance, and the old man shrugged. "Can't say. I couldn't find the TV remote, and I'm too old to figure the damn thing out without it."

Xavier smiled over his coffee and switched on the small flat screen mounted to a wall in the corner of the kitchen. The volume was down. A reporter was saying something on-screen and gesturing at a tank in the background. Then the tank fired silently, making the reporter duck as the camera jerked to the right. A crowd of people a block away was surging up a smoky city street, backlit by burning cars. Xavier joined the old man at the sink. "What are you looking at?"

"Sister Emily," he said. "I think so, anyway. My eyes aren't so good anymore."

A small, walled garden separated the rectory from Sisters of Mercy, the convent next door. Out on the grass, in front of a flower bed, a small, stooped woman in a pale-blue-and-white nun's habit was standing wearing gardening gloves, facing away from them. On the grass nearby was a basket with rose shears sticking out of it. The nun's arms hung limp at her sides, and she was swaying back and forth.

Father Frye squinted. "I don't know if she's praying or just day-dreaming, but she's been that way for a while now. Lord, I hope it's not a stroke."

Xavier looked at the old nun. She didn't look natural. "Maybe—"

The *BOOM* of an explosion rolled over the yard, and both men jumped as a cloud of black smoke rose from somewhere beyond the convent. Sister Emily's head snapped up at the sound.

They both started toward the kitchen door but stopped short when they saw the images on the silent TV screen. A shaking camera showed a San Francisco street filled with police cars and military vehicles stopped at odd angles while a trolley car burned in the background. A crowd of people was moving toward a small cluster of cops and National Guardsmen, who were firing into them. Only a few people fell to the gunfire before the crowd pressed forward. The cops and troops began backing up as they neared, and on the left side of the screen a single officer was suddenly jumped by people who bore him to the ground and began tearing at him with hands and teeth.

Xavier stared at the images, disbelieving, and was slow to notice Father Frye going out the back door. "Sister Emily?" the man called. "Come inside, dear."

The younger priest tore his eyes from the screen and followed him out. Father Frye was walking across the grass toward the nun. Sister Emily turned at the sound of his voice, and Xavier saw at once that the front of her habit was soaked with blood, one of her cheeks torn nearly away and dangling by a flap of skin. "Dear God," he whispered.

"Sister!" Frye saw the wound and ran to her, and she reached for him as he arrived. She growled, gripped him by the arms and sank her teeth into his face. The old man screamed as the smaller nun took him to the ground and bit him again, this time in the throat, her hands clawing at his arms as he tried to fend her off.

Xavier sprinted toward them and grabbed Sister Emily by the

waist, pulling her off. A piece of Father Frye's throat came away in her teeth and she snarled, trying to twist around. The old woman was nearly weightless in his powerful arms, and he flung her high and far. She landed with a crunch of brittle bones and rolled as the old man lay on his back on the grass, pawing at his throat and gurgling as jets of blood sprayed into the morning air. Xavier went to him, dropping to his knees, but already the blood was losing strength and the old man stiffened, staring at the sky with empty eyes.

A growl came from behind, and Xavier turned to see Sister Emily on her feet once more, stalking toward him, a rib jutting out of her side and her head hanging awkwardly on a fractured neck. Her eyes were milky and her hands were raised, fingers clutching as she chewed a piece of skin that still had whisker stubble on it.

The bang of a wooden gate made him turn, and he saw more nuns entering the yard through a stone archway from Sisters of Mercy, half a dozen of them, each covered in blood and horrific wounds, one missing an arm, another most of her face. A hand clutched at his shoulder and he jumped away a second before Sister Emily's teeth snapped at the air. The arriving nuns gave out a collective moan and moved toward him.

With a last glance at the man on the ground, Xavier ran back to the kitchen door, slamming it behind him, fingers fumbling to turn the lock in the knob. Moments later the nuns were at the door, thumping against it with fists and bloody palms, streaking the glass, moaning and glaring at him.

Xavier Church had seen dead before, in hospitals and tenement fires, in drug overdoses, in the destruction left by drive-by shootings, and in the small apartment of a poor Hispanic woman and her son. He knew it when he saw it, and though it was impossible, he was seeing it on the other side of the kitchen door. That moment of disconnection from reality pushed over into the realm of madness when Father Frye appeared behind the cluster of nuns, his throat open to reveal a torn larynx, eyes cloudy. Frye moaned with the rest of them and crowded against the door.

Xavier backed into the kitchen, unable to take his eyes off the people—*if that's what they are,* he thought—on the other side of the glass. On the TV behind him, a news image showed Red Square in Moscow, as rows of troops fired into a mass of people that moved relentlessly forward. The Kremlin was burning in the background.

Father Church turned and ran through the rectory, to the corner of the front room where the secretary's desk sat. Behind him came the sound of breaking glass, followed by enraged snarls. He looked at the row of hooks where the keys for the rectory's vehicles were kept. The hooks were empty. The sound of cracking wood came from the back of the house, and Xavier bolted out the front door, into the street, and into a world quickly coming apart.

TWO

It was August 13 and the fall semester would begin in three days. The morning sky was bright blue, and although it was still early, already the campus of UC Berkeley was buzzing with activity, nowhere as much as in and around the many housing facilities as thirty-five thousand students prepared for the new school year. Outside Cunningham Hall, one of Berkeley's newer, high-rise dorms, parents and students flowed across sidewalks and lawns, carrying boxes and trunks and mini fridges, laptops and luggage, moving back and forth from the parking lot like worker ants. Families took breaks under the spreading trees, excited kids chattering and apprehensive parents trying to put on brave faces.

Skye Dennison was eighteen, pretty, and eager for her parents and sister to head back to Reno, Nevada. It wasn't that she especially resented her mom's fussing or her dad's constant warnings and advice, or even the never-ending barrage of questions from thirteen-year-old Crystal. She loved them, but she was ready to be on her own. She was an adult now.

"You're coming home for Christmas, right?" Crystal was walking beside her pulling a wheeled suitcase, chewing her bottom lip as she did when she was anxious. She wore a blue-and-yellow T-shirt showing Oski the Bear, Berkeley's mascot, a present from her big sister.

"Of course I will," said Skye. She was dressed in shorts and a tank top cut low enough to make her father scowl, her long blond hair pulled into a ponytail tucked under a baseball cap. "Don't be dumb." Her own arms were filled with a Rubbermaid tote of desk supplies. Somewhere behind them, Dad would be grumbling about "all this crap" she needed for the dorm, wishing aloud for the thousandth time that he had brought his hand truck. Mom would be rolling her eyes and telling him to lighten up.

"Aren't you going to be lonely?"

Skye knew this was Crystal suggesting that *she* would be lonely now that her sister was a freshman away at college. She gave the girl a gentle elbow. "I'll miss you."

"Really?"

"Yeah, really. But we'll Skype, and I'll be home before you know it. You'll barely know I'm gone, and you won't have to complain about sharing the bathroom anymore."

Crystal shrugged.

"Besides, you're going to be busy. Starting high school's a big deal."

Her sister shrugged again, but this time she smiled.

They set their loads down not far from the doors to Cunningham Hall and plopped onto the grass to wait for their parents. Both immediately went to their iPhones, Skye texting her best friend, Kate, who had gotten into Rutgers. After a few minutes she noticed a frown on her sister's face. "What's up, snot?"

"Don't call me snot." She didn't look away from the screen. "Something's happening in San Francisco."

"What?"

"I don't know yet. Fires or a riot or something."

Skye looked to where the city would be across the bay but couldn't see it through the campus buildings. Cotton balls for clouds drifted overhead, and it was hard to believe anything bad could happen on a day like this.

"It's a big city," she said, "there's always something going on there." Kate texted her back to ask if California guys were as cute as New Jersey guys. Her thumbs blurred. *Definitely. Cuter.* Their parents arrived a moment later, her father setting a footlocker down with a grunt.

"Almost done," said Mom, dropping to the grass beside her daughters and falling onto her back with an exaggerated groan. "You girls will have to carry me upstairs." They all laughed.

Dad swung his arms like a track star warming up and puffed a few quick breaths. "Okay, two more bags," he said. "You want to start getting this stuff upstairs? I'll be right back."

"Once we're done with our nap," Mom said, making the girls laugh again.

"I'll give you a nap." He shook a fist and winked at Skye. "See you in a minute." He headed back to the parking lot.

Skye watched him go, glanced at her mother chatting with Crystal, and was suddenly not in such a hurry to see them leave. She slipped her iPhone into a hip pocket and eyed the pile of stuff on the grass, strategizing what to take up first. She looked at her mom, then past her. Dad had almost reached the lot when a man in a hospital gown staggered out from between two cars. Dad stopped and held out a hand to him, but if he said anything he was too far away to hear.

The man in the gown jerked toward her dad, grabbed his arm, and bit his shoulder.

"Dad!" Skye exclaimed, springing to her feet as her mother and sister looked around in alarm. Off to their right, people suddenly began screaming. Ahead, her dad went down with the hospital patient on top of him.

Skye ran toward them, ignoring her mother's shouted questions. She didn't know who this person was or what kind of problem he had, but he was hurting her dad and Skye was going to kick his ass. Dad was hammering at the crazy person with his fists, but now the man's face was buried in her father's neck, and she saw those fists suddenly open, fingers shuddering and clawing at the air.

"Daddy!" Legs pumping, Skye crossed the distance and kicked the crazy person in the ribs as hard as she could. He didn't even react. There was blood everywhere, and one of her father's legs was sticking out straight, twitching in a way that made her want to be sick. The crazy person was snarling and ripping at her father's neck with his teeth.

She kicked him again, then beat at his back with her fists. "Get off! Get off! Get off!"

Another scream from behind her, and she recognized Crystal's voice. She spun to see her little sister standing with her hands over her ears, shrieking as she watched two people tearing at their mom on the ground. Skye started sprinting again, back toward her sister, and then a screaming, fast-moving shape rushed at her from the right. She stopped and leaped back as a campus police car roared across the lawn in front of her, spitting up grass, siren wailing. The squad slid to a stop, tires digging furrows in the turf, and a paunchy cop struggled out of the driver's door, holding his pistol.

"Help them!" Skye pointed to her mom and sister. The cop didn't. He charged toward the entrance to Cunningham Hall, where dozens of students and parents were shoving and trampling one another, trying to get inside. Behind the mob, half a dozen wounded and bloody people were pulling down stragglers, biting and snarling.

Skye ran around the back of the police car but then stumbled to a halt as she realized the people on top of her mother were *eating* her.

A scream of her own rose in her throat. The rapid *POP-POP-POP* of the campus cop's pistol got her moving again, and she grabbed Crystal by the arm.

"Run!" Skye shrieked.

Not waiting for a reply, she pulled at her sister and started running across the tree-covered lawn, away from their mother, away from where a cluster of snapping figures were pulling the campus cop to the ground as he wailed like a hurt child. It seemed everyone was running, and everyone was screaming.

The ones who weren't running were the worst, however. Slumping and stiff, flesh ripped and dangling, heads tilted and twisted, they moved steadily toward knots of cowering people, students trapped in doorways and parents cut off between parked cars. Skye heard pleading and attempts at reason from frightened voices around her, and she heard the terrible tearing of flesh, the thud of bodies hitting the ground.

With Crystal's arm clenched tightly in hand, Skye hauled her along, dodging piles of luggage and plastic totes, weaving around bodies with *things* crouched over them and pulling them apart. She batted aside the outstretched hands of a staggering man in a janitor's uniform, pulled Crystal past a bloody parent who was savaging a teenage boy against a tree. The boy was screaming, *"No, Mom, no!"* She didn't know where they were going, only that they had to keep moving.

A loudspeaker was blaring something she couldn't understand, and there were sirens off to the left. She took them between two build-ings, finding another grassy area with another parking lot and more buildings beyond. Skye had visited the campus only once and didn't know her way around. She turned them left toward the sirens. Screaming seemed to come from every direction, people running toward and away from them, sometimes into the arms and teeth of shuffling figures. Over in the parking lot she saw a woman with a shrieking toddler trapped between two cars as bloody figures closed on her and her child from both directions. Skye almost stopped, almost turned to help, but then glass exploded above on her left.

She jerked her sister back just as a body slammed to the sidewalk in front of them with a crunch of bone. The body lifted its pulped face, one side of its head flattened, and hissed at them through broken teeth. It began crawling forward using its arms to pull its shattered lower half.

Crystal screamed and Skye pulled them away, across the grass. Ahead, in a building across from them, a woman in a dark-blue-and-gold tracksuit was standing at an open doorway, looking left and right. She waved at the girls. "C'mon! Hurry! Hurry!"

They did, and a moment later they were in some kind of ground-floor office. The woman pulled the door closed and locked it, staring out through its small window. The room had a couple of desks and a long table ringed with chairs, and the walls held dry-erase and bulletin boards. An open door led to a hallway.

"Thanks," Skye breathed, but the woman at the door ignored her, muttering to herself.

Crystal started to cry, her whole body shaking. "Mommy."

Skye pulled her close and started to cry too, once more seeing her mother being devoured, her dad's twitching leg, a dozen other horrors. They held each other, trembling and sobbing. In the hallway beyond the door, someone was moaning.

The tracksuit woman kept muttering, "Got-to-got-to-got-t-t-to . . . P-police . . . Got-to . . ." She didn't leave her place at the tiny window, just wrapped her arms around herself and pressed her nose to the glass, looking left and right and back again. Skye saw the rip in her tracksuit pants then, high on her inner thigh, and realized the woman was standing in a lake of blood. She and Crystal had run straight through it, leaving skidding, red footprints on the tile floor.

"Hey," Skye said softly, "you're really hurt. You should sit down."

Crystal pulled at her sister. "What's happening? Is Mommy going to be okay?"

Skye pulled her close, pressing her sister's face against her shoulder. The moaning in the hallway came again, followed by a metallic bang that Skye recognized. It was the sound of someone bumping against a metal fire extinguisher hanging on a wall. It happened all the time in high school, usually when kids were running or screwing around. The sound was followed by a kind of whispering, but a *wet* whispering.

"Got-to-got-to-g-g-got-to . . ." The tracksuit woman paid no mind to the two girls or the spreading pool of blood. Skye put an arm around Crystal and walked to the hallway door, peeking outside.

About twenty feet away, a girl Skye's age wearing jeans and a San Francisco Giants jersey was moving slowly toward them on stiff legs. One of her feet was turned inward, and her head lay on her left shoulder as she stretched out one arm, pawing at the wall. Half her face was a red, ragged wound with one eye dangling from the socket, and her belly had been torn open. Ropy intestines hung down and trailed behind her, through her legs, making a wet, whispery sound on the tile floor.

The girl saw them and bared her teeth in a growl, then picked up the pace.

Crystal screamed as Skye hauled her inside, slamming the door, finding a snap bolt and turning it. The top half of the door was a window crisscrossed with safety wire, and the girl appeared there a moment later, pressing her destroyed face against the glass and smearing it. One hand thumped at the door, and her mouth opened and closed.

They backed away. "She can't be alive like that," said Crystal.

"I know," Skye said. It was something from a movie, something that couldn't be real. The dead girl in the hall thudded rhythmically against the door.

The tracksuit woman made a soft "oh" sound and slid to the floor, lying slumped against the door. She stayed that way for a second, then fell onto her side in the red pool. She was pale and her eyelids fluttered. "Oh," she said again, staring past them, and then she was still.

"Hello?" a voice called from the hallway, muffled through the door. "Can someone help me?" It was a girl's voice, and at the sound of it Skye saw the dead girl's head snap left, and then she moved in that direction. A moment later there was a scream, a high wailing abruptly cut short. Skye squeezed her eyes tight and held her sister close, wishing to be back in her bedroom, in their safe little house in Reno, with Mom and Dad laughing in the kitchen. She wished it all away, wished it to be a nightmare from which she would scream herself awake, then sit in her bed shaking with nervous laughter.

She opened her eyes to see Crystal looking at her hopefully, so she stopped her wishing and tried the phone on one of the desks. Every available line was lit. She dug the phone out of her back pocket and dialed 911. A recording informed her that all operators were busy with other calls, but to hold the line and not hang up.

Crystal walked to the hallway door as Skye redialed, looking out through the smeared glass. "I don't see her anymore," Crystal said.

"That doesn't mean she's not there," Skye warned. The recording came on again. "Don't open the door."

"I'm not stupid." Crystal strained to look left and right.

Skye shook her iPhone. She didn't know anyone in California, had no one to text. She thought about calling her mom or dad's cell, hoping that maybe . . . She didn't, knowing that hearing their cheery, recorded greetings when they didn't answer would drive her to tears again.

"Is someone going to come for us?" said Crystal. She had stopped crying, at least for now, and for that Skye was grateful. When Crystal cried, *she* wanted to cry, and then she couldn't think. Death was all around them, and the killing was still going on. If she stopped think-ing, they'd both end up like the woman in the tracksuit or, worse, like the girl in the hall.

"We're going to have to take care of ourselves for a while, snot. We have to be smart and quiet, and if we move, we move fast. Got it?"

"I got it. Don't call me snot."

Skye smiled at her and went back to the iPhone, looking for a directory. There had to be half a dozen police departments in the area, and they all must have phone numbers other than 911. She sat on the edge of a desk and tapped at the small screen.

Outside, a distant siren wailed and there were more shots, like faraway firecrackers. The screaming was more infrequent now, and Skye tried not to think about what that meant. A few minutes later the dead girl was back thumping against the hallway door, her face wet with fresh blood. Already Crystal had lost her initial fear—a childhood bombarded by gory movie and video game images had quickly transformed the ghastly to mundane—and she watched the girl's jerky movements with curiosity.

Skye found the campus police number. Busy. She dialed the California Highway Patrol, the sheriff's office, the Berkeley Police Department, all resulting in variations of "please stay on the line" mes-sages. The muffled honking of a car alarm sounded from outside.

"I think if we—"

Skye looked up at her sister's voice to see the tracksuit woman standing behind her with glassy eyes. Before she could even speak, the woman sank her teeth into the thirteen-year-old's neck. Crystal screamed, and the woman grabbed at her, raking fingernails across her cheeks.

Skye rushed her, crying her sister's name, and punched the woman hard in the face, breaking her nose. The woman growled, released the neck, and bit Crystal in the back of the head. Skye ripped the woman's hands off her sister and pulled them backward, retreating to the far end of the office. The woman followed, reaching and stumbling against the long central table.

Crystal was wailing, curling into a ball on the floor, holding her head and neck, blood escaping in jets through her fingers where the artery had been torn. Skye stood over her, facing the oncoming creature. She spotted a pencil cup on the nearby desk, the black handles of scissors poking out of it, and she snatched them up, holding them high.

The corpse came on, eyes glinting, and Skye let out a snarl of her own as she lunged forward, stabbing with the scissors. The tip plunged into the woman's eye and the blades sank to the handle. Instantly, the dead woman stiffened and then collapsed, the weight of her fall pulling the scissors from Skye's hand. The body didn't move.

"Skye?" Behind her, Crystal was pale, her voice soft, her body no longer trembling. Her Oski the Bear shirt was soaked red, her hair wet and matted, and her eyelids drooped. Skye knelt and gathered her into her arms.

"It's okay, snot. You're going to be okay." Tears burned in her eyes.

Crystal smiled at her. "Don't call me snot." Then she died.

Skye cried her name over and over, holding her limp body close, rocking her, sobbing. They stayed that way for some time, one sister holding the cooling body of the other, as a dead girl in the hallway thumped against the door.

Then Crystal moved in her arms.

"Snot?" Skye pulled back and looked at her sister's slack, ashy face. Cloudy eyes flicked her way, and Crystal made a raspy sound deep in her throat. Then she lunged, teeth snapping, just missing Skye's face.

Skye screamed and shoved her away, scrambling backward like a crab as her little sister struggled to crawl after her. The brown eyes that had looked up to her as a hero were now dark and malignant, all traces of warmth replaced with a predatory need. Skye backed over the tracksuit woman, her own voice coming out in a long wail, and she found her feet.

Crystal let out an enraged howl as Skye reached the outer door, snapped the dead bolt back, and yanked it open. A moment later she was running. Dozens of maimed figures lurched among the trees and emerged from dorms, and they turned toward her with a rising, collective moan. It made her run faster.

A parking lot was ahead, and beyond the first row of parked cars stood a tan, camouflaged vehicle, a Humvee with a long antenna and a man poking out of the top next to a big machine gun. Others in uniform moved around it.

"Help!" She raced toward the vehicle. "Help me!"

One soldier, a young man close to her age carrying a rifle with a scope, spun at the sound of her voice, seeing her running at him.

"Help me!"

The soldier snapped the rifle to his shoulder, aimed at Skye, and fired.

THREE

Peter Dunleavy was thirty-seven, a hundred million short of being a *billionaire*, and was about to go to federal prison for forty years. So his lawyers told him, a pack of overpaid parasites—supposedly the best legal minds money could buy—who couldn't seem to manage something as simple as fraud and tax evasion. Worthless.

He sipped an iced tea and sank further into the wide leather seat, looking out the oval-shaped window beside him. The parasites assured him the jury would find him guilty either today or tomorrow, despite their best efforts. They were confident of a reversal on appeal. Dunleavy did not share their enthusiasm and had no intention of waiting around for appeals. Or even convictions, for that matter.

The only successful thing the parasites had accomplished was to arrange for his release during the trial. A frustrated federal prosecutor had made passionate but unsuccessful pleas to the judge, pointing out that Dunleavy had plenty of reasons, and more than sufficient financial means, to be a flight risk.

"Goddamn right," he murmured, swirling the ice in the glass, the luxuriant main cabin of his G6 surrounding him. Next stop, his mountain villa in Venezuela. It was a country politically at odds with the United States and uncooperative with extradition. Sizable payoffs to top government officials ensured it would remain that way, at least with regard to Peter Dunleavy.

Now, however, the viability of that exit plan was in doubt. The G6, and according to the pilots *all* air traffic, had been grounded. Dunleavy's first thought was that his plan had been discovered, and he spent the first hour staring out the window of his plane, expecting to see vans of U.S. Marshals racing toward him across the tarmac. When that didn't happen, Peter's fright turned to annoyance. The pilots said that no further details had come from the tower, only the instruction to hold position.

On the table in front of his seat rested a Bible, a pair of tablet computers that had been shut off, and a hardcover copy of his latest best seller. On the dust jacket was Dunleavy, smiling with perfectly white teeth and wearing an expensive Italian suit, arms raised as the sun rose majestically behind him. *Finding Your Inner Savior* stood out in big silver letters at the top, and at the bottom, also in silver, was *Reverend Peter J. Dunleavy*. Like the five that had gone before it, the book was a major hit.

Now they wanted to take it all away from him: the estates, the yachts and private jets, the portfolios and bank accounts (the ones they knew about, anyway), the Dunleavy Bible College in Missouri, the Sunday TV show and televised fund-raisers, the stadium events, the merchandising . . . his entire ministry. Tax agents and federal accountants were poised like jackals awaiting the fall of a wounded zebra, ready to freeze and seize his empire the moment a conviction was handed down.

He sipped the tea. It needed more vodka.

Parasites, every last one of them: the federal prosecutors, his wife in Jackson, his mistresses scattered across the country, his global congregation of followers, even his loyal staff. Everyone wanted a piece of Peter Dunleavy, and despite their endless stream of sickly sweet platitudes, every one of them was salivating in anticipation of his fall. He swallowed more tea and thought about the handgun in the compartment beside his seat, the big Glock that felt heavy and good in his hand. He wasn't going to prison, he wouldn't cry for forgiveness on TV like Jim Bakker had, wasn't going to watch as they stripped him of everything he had sweated and bled to build. And he would damn sure take some of those phony, smiling faces with him when he went.

One of those faces was moving up the aisle toward him, passing half a dozen highly paid secretaries and aides as he returned from the cockpit. Anderson James was his closest advisor, a true believer with a quick, capable mind who had been with Dunleavy since his humble beginnings, and who had devoted his life to the reverend and the ministry. After being forcibly removed from his first career (he didn't even like to think about that), Dunleavy had sought solace at a Pentecostal tent revival. Despite his belief—scattered and directionless as it had been—he failed to connect with the messages of the snake-handling, fast-talking preachers. It just seemed ridiculous, certainly nothing God would endorse.

It was there in that sweltering tent, watching the joyful and righteous quake and shriek and open their wallets, that he realized he had been a fool. God cared nothing for zealots, did nothing to spare them from ridicule and torment, and was likely amused at their suffering. Dunleavy watched a woman fall down with holy vigor, then crawl to her hands and knees and offer her open pocketbook to a smiling young man on stage. Yes, God looked kindly upon the clever and strong. These people were sheep, and God favored the shepherd.

During the revival he met Anderson, a man his age, bright and well connected, with a mind for finance and an understanding of show business. He lacked the charisma and self-confidence to stand in the spotlight himself, but he was committed to the faith and in desperate need of someone in whom he could believe. Here was someone Dunleavy could use. They would begin a friendship that would elevate the young minister to the pinnacle of wealth and influence within the televangelist community, and Anderson would become his most faithful servant.

Dunleavy sipped his tea and imagined blowing the man's head off with the Glock.

Anderson sat down across from the man known worldwide as Brother Peter. "The tower is saying it's an FAA grounding, and not just here, across the country," Anderson said. "The only thing in the air is military, and all airborne civilian traffic is being ordered to land."

"Another terrorist attack?" Dunleavy asked. Wouldn't that just figure. He should have flown out last night.

The young man shrugged. Dunleavy had forbidden any of them to use any electronic devices, no phones or tablets, for fear the feds were tracking him and would discover he was at the airfield. As a result, they were cut off from any information. "They're not saying, but they did tell us to prepare to taxi back to the private terminal." Dunleavy's G6 had been on the tarmac, fourth in line for takeoff, when the tower closed every strip at Oakland International.

Dunleavy said nothing, only swirled his ice. Return to the terminal? Not a chance. He wasn't going to get this close to freedom only to give up and surrender to the heathens. He'd take the Glock to the cockpit and order the pilots into the air. The thought of hijacking his own jet made him let out a little giggle.

The inappropriate noise and the look in the reverend's eyes made Anderson James more than a little uncomfortable. He wondered, as he had begun to do more and more often since his friend's ordeal began, if a breakdown might be coming. It wouldn't come as a surprise. The man was under incredible stress, and Anderson's heart ached for him. He shifted in his seat. "I'm sure it's only temporary."

Dunleavy looked at him, picturing his brains splattered across the

cabin's white bulkhead, wanting to scream, *Everything is temporary!*
Life is temporary! Instead he nodded and looked back out the window.
They were at the part of the taxiway that curved into the runway itself,
and he could see three jets lined up ahead of them: a big United, a
smaller JetBlue, and a Southwest. The sparkle of white landing lights
glowed in the sky far out beyond the airport, an inbound jet.

How would his inner circle, his faithful followers at the front of
the cabin, react when he took the plane at gunpoint? They'd probably
be too shocked to do much of anything. Anderson would try to talk,
of course, to reason with him. Dunleavy would kill him in front of
the others. That would keep them quiet and in their seats.

Outside, a man shuffled across the asphalt wearing ear protectors
and a bloody gray jumpsuit, his arms hanging limp. Brother Peter stared
at him as the man tripped and fell over a field light, as if he hadn't seen
it poking out of the ground. He landed hard on his face without even
putting up his hands to stop the fall, then climbed slowly to his feet and
wandered away in an entirely new direction. Dunleavy shook his head.

The sparkling lights grew larger, eventually resolving into the
shape of a 747, which suddenly began to tip to one side. The reverend
watched in amazement as the big aircraft seemed to turn sideways,
nose over, and drop out of the sky. It hit with a silent, red bloom of
fire, and a moment later the thunder of the impact rolled across the
runway, making the G6 shudder. Plumes of blazing fuel and pieces
of wreckage sailed into the air as the fireball tumbled at an angle,
across grass and asphalt, and slammed into a distant part of the terminal. Fiery rain dripped from the sky, and debris arced down in
smoking lines, hitting with smaller explosions.

As his followers cried out and pressed their faces to the glass,
Brother Peter sagged back into the leather seat and drained the last of
his vodka iced tea. The burning wreckage was strung in a long line
across the runways. The G6, hijacked or not, wasn't going anywhere.

FOUR

Alameda

Filming went long, starting before the sun rose and not wrapping until late morning. Cell phones had been switched off and everyone was so involved in the process that no one really noticed the pillars of smoke across the bay, or the increased helicopter traffic. The frequent sound of sirens was distant but, considering their proximity to Oakland, not unusual.

The Naval Air Station at Alameda had been closed for twenty years and was now a perfect location for the segment they had just filmed. This was due in part to its being a military backdrop and a rich source of history, but mostly because of the deserted, wide open spaces of its long runways. Alameda Island sat on the southwestern edge of Oakland, the small city of Alameda filling the eastern half, the western end occupied by the former military base. All of San Francisco Bay spread out before it, with the city a glittering jewel across the water.

Their guide had waved good-bye and locked the main gate behind them, driving off in his jeep. Bud Franks, a fifty-year-old former deputy sheriff, drove the black van through the Alameda streets, bound for the bridge that would take them off the island, onto I-880, and then home to Sacramento. The truck carrying the film crew was behind them.

In the passenger seat sat the star of the History channel reality show, Bud's niece Angie West. Twenty-seven, with hard good looks and incredibly fit, she had often been compared to Linda Hamilton's character in *Terminator 2*. She was wearing a tight black T-shirt with the History channel logo over the left breast, jeans tucked into high boots, and expensive, circular biker sunglasses. She liked the whole Linda Hamilton image, respected the hard work the actress had put in to carve and shape her body, and so she herself worked hard in the gym to stay fit. Her producers loved it, and the fans ate it up. Right now, however, she was staring out the windshield wearing a frown, unconcerned with her physique or TV image. Her cell phone kept giving her an "unable to connect" message.

"It's a bunch of BS, Ang," said her uncle, slowing as the traffic thickened near the bridge. "Some kind of hoax and people are buying it. Probably more of that flash mob nonsense, only this time those jackasses are getting themselves shot."

Angie nodded and redialed. As soon as they got in the van they had heard the special news reports. It was surreal. The living dead? Really? No one seemed to be joking, and regularly updated reports of death tolls were rising. According to the news, it was everywhere.

That included Sacramento, where Angie's husband, Dean, and their two-year-old, Leah, would be waiting for her.

Nothing but brake lights ahead, a river of stopped cars that traveled well beyond the flashing lights of a police car in the distance ahead. Her uncle Bud cut the wheel to the right, bounced over a sidewalk corner, and headed down a side street. The GPS announced,

"Recalculating." The truck with the film crew followed. They cut down to Buena Vista and headed south to where the GPS showed them Lincoln Avenue would curve into the second of four bridges off the island. More brake lights waited, cars and SUVs, bumper to bumper.

Bud turned again, driving deeper into Alameda, the inbound lane mostly clear but the outbound packed with traffic. He reached Central Avenue and turned south, the film crew still following as he zigzagged through the streets. The GPS indicated it would be a while before they reached the next bridge approach. While they were stopped at a light, an orange-and-white Coast Guard helicopter roared low overhead, making them both jump.

Angie still couldn't get through, and each time she tried to text she got a "network unavailable" signal. The last text she had gotten from Dean was time-stamped 7:12 A.M. and simply said, *R U OK?* It was an unusual question; he knew she was working and where she was. There had been nothing since. Her uncle's cell phone was similarly out of service. She looked out the window and chewed at a thumbnail, watching a neighborhood slide by where people were hustling to vehicles carrying luggage and coolers and pets.

"Dean's smart," she said, and her uncle didn't wonder whom she was trying to convince. "If there's real trouble, he'll gear up and get Leah out in the Suburban."

"That's right," said Bud. "He'll take good care of her, no question."

Angie looked at her uncle. "This can't be real, right? It's a flash mob thing, like you said. Maybe some sort of chemical spill, hell, even aliens. But zombies? No way."

The High Street Bridge was not going to be an option. Traffic for the approach was backed up a dozen blocks, so Bud muscled the van through the clog, ignoring shouted curses and angry horns, and continued south, the film crew truck so close it rubbed their bumper a couple of times. They would reach Fernside Boulevard and curve along the southern tip of the island, toward the Bay Farm Island Bridge, the last route off Alameda and the path to Oakland International Airport. They had already decided that if driving out wasn't going to happen, they'd leave the van in long-term parking (a huge liability and highly illegal, considering what was inside, but fuck anyone who complained) and fly out, going private charter if necessary. They pulled onto Fernside, the airport visible across the water, and quickly found two lanes of stopped traffic.

On the radio, the news reported the FAA grounding of all non-military flights, and Bud and Angie looked at each other. Soon after, the long tone of the Emergency Broadcast System blared from the speakers, followed by a monotone voice announcing that the federal government had declared martial law, and all citizens were ordered to get off the streets, with more information to follow.

The message hadn't even finished before the fireball climbed over the distant runway.

They stared at the rising cloud as people in the cars ahead of them got out to look and point, many holding up phones to capture video. Bud saw the cameraman jump out of the truck behind them and walk over the low concrete median, pointing his camera at the explosion.

"We're not getting off Alameda," Angie said quietly.

"Not today, anyway," said Bud.

Something rapped hard against Angie's window, and she turned to see her producer, Bruce, standing outside, a pudgy guy her age in a stocking cap, trying to grow a beard. She rolled down the window.

"Are you hearing this stuff on the news?" Bruce asked.

Angie nodded. Ahead of them, the cameraman was walking forward slowly, panning across the lines of stopped cars and gatherings of people looking toward the airport. Over the producer's shoulder she saw a teenage boy with long hair hanging in his eyes and wearing a backpack, walking sluggishly out from between a pair of houses, moving toward the road. A moment later several more people emerged from the same place, a mixture of men and women, different races and ages. They all moved with the same shuffling gait, and all in the same direction. It didn't look right.

"We're not going anywhere, so we're going to leave the van here." Bruce looked back at it. "We'll go ahead on foot." He didn't notice that Angie wasn't looking at him. "We just can't pass on an opportunity like this. There's going to be great footage."

The kid with the long hair and backpack stumbled off the curb and lurched toward the lanes of unmoving cars, the mix of people following. Closer now, Angie could see that the kid was injured, his shirt soaked red and his face badly torn, one ear completely ripped away, as if he had gone down on a motorcycle at high speed and the asphalt had skinned off one side of his head. The others were bloody too, and they moved as if in a daze, bumping into one another, arms limp at their sides, like accident victims in shock.

"Bruce . . ." she started.

The producer turned and stared. The long-haired kid turned toward him and shuffled faster, letting out a whining noise.

"Hey, kid, you're really hurt!" he called out.

A woman's scream split the air from farther up the line, and Bud saw the cameraman jog out of sight in that direction.

"Get in the van, Bruce," Angie said, opening the door. The producer stood there as the kid got closer. "Get in the goddamn van, Bruce!"

The kid's skin was ashy, his eyes a milky white, and now that he was closer she could see that huge chunks of flesh had been torn from both his arms, revealing white bone in places. They were the kinds of wounds you just didn't walk around with.

"Bruce!"

The producer jumped as if startled awake, but by then the kid was lunging, catching him by his shirt and hauling him in close. Bruce screamed as the kid bit him in the face, pulling him away from the door, their bodies thumping along the side of the van. The mix of people staggered into the road, among the cars, reaching through open windows or going after those who had left their vehicles to watch the fire.

Angie slammed the door shut and locked it, buzzing up the window. Uncle Bud, who in twenty years as a deputy had learned to leave half a car's length distance in stopped traffic so there was room to maneuver in an emergency, cranked the wheel left and gunned the van up and over the concrete median in a tight U-turn.

Angie saw the people in the road being pulled down by the dead.

"Ang . . ." Her uncle's voice was tight. She was already out of her seat and moving into the back, steadying herself as the vehicle swayed and her uncle accelerated.

Their time slot was between a show about storage container auctions and another about pawnshops, but hers was by far the most popular. It (like the other programs) was much more scripted than most people suspected, especially the staged arguments and special guests who conveniently just happened to be available for the show (booked upward of six months in advance). A lot of it was pretty corny, but the audience loved it, the contracts paid them all ridiculous amounts, and she got to do what she loved.

Both sides on the exterior of the black van featured the promo shot for the show, a photo of her standing in front of her husband, uncle, and father, all of them dressed in black with their arms folded, wearing serious expressions. The History channel logo was down in one corner, and above it all in big letters was *Angie's Armory. Family = Firepower.*

The van owned by the family of professional gunsmiths was customized, filled with shelves, tool drawers and locking cases, bolted-down grinders and reloaders. Rows of assault weapons, shotguns, and hunting rifles were mounted in racks along both walls. Angie selected an evil-looking black automatic shotgun with a collapsible stock. She opened a locker and pulled out a canvas bag of heavy magazines, slamming one into the weapon as she moved back to the front. She had to climb over a long, black, hard plastic case strapped to the floor, the Barrett fifty-caliber sniper rifle that they had been demonstrating during the morning's filming.

Bud swung the van down a side street and planted his foot on the accelerator. "Not a hoax," he said. "We put down anything that's a threat."

Angie planted the weapon between her knees and nodded, already anticipating the familiar recoil. Her thoughts were a scatter of questions, disbelief, and her daughter's face.

FIVE

San Quentin was California's oldest prison and had the state's only death row for male inmates, the females being shipped off to Chowchilla. "The Q" had used the gas chamber all the way up until 1996, when the little room had been shut down in favor of lethal injection. Squatting on a finger of land that jutted out into the bay, its imposing concrete walls and miles of high double fencing topped with razor wire housed 5,200 inmates, well over capacity.

Now it was on fire.

Bill "Carney" Carnes and his cellmate, TC Cochoran, sat next to each other inside the transport van, both wearing bright orange coveralls, both in leg and waist shackles. Carney was forty-four and rock-hard, with a severe gray crew cut. His coveralls did little to conceal his broad build but served to hide the colorful mosaic of tattoos across his back and chest and down both arms. He had seventeen years in on a twenty-five-to-life bit for double murder.

TC had just turned thirty-one, a former meth head who had used his time away from the destructive effects of the pipe to transform his body into something even bigger and stronger than his friend. He was also covered in ink and was proud of his thick mane of blond hair. A lifetime of drugs, theft, and violence had seen him inside state walls more often than outside, and he was eight years into a life sentence for robbery-homicide after shooting a Korean convenience store clerk in the face without provocation.

Six other inmates shared the van with them. They had all been roused early and given a chance to quickly clean up before being herded into the van for the drive to San Francisco. All had appearances in court this morning, Carney for yet another hearing in his pointless appeal process, TC to face arraignment for allegedly slashing another inmate's face with a piece of sharpened plastic over a cigarette debt. Truthfully, there was no *allegedly* about it, and TC had been aiming for the man's throat, not his face. The van had just reached the Richmond–San Raphael Bridge when it was stopped at a California Highway Patrol roadblock still being hastily set up. The correctional officer who was riding shotgun had spoken with a helmeted Chippie for a few minutes, and then they were turning around, heading back to the Q.

The gates were in view when the prison siren went off, and the van pulled quickly onto the gravel shoulder. Now they sat and watched pillars of black smoke rising behind the high walls, overhearing the COs up front behind their steel mesh divider talking on the radio and listening to frantic chatter.

"What's happening, Carney?" TC asked.

"Like I know."

"Is it a riot?" His younger cellmate craned his muscled neck to get a better look out the windshield, over the heads of the COs. "Man, that's my luck to miss it. The perfect chance to shank that motherfucker LeBron." Freddy LeBron was an inmate who had twice disrespected TC in front of others, and TC owed him a death. Carney elbowed the younger man hard and whispered for him to keep his voice down, but the COs hadn't seemed to hear the comment. TC looked at his cellmate with a hurt expression. "You didn't have to do that."

"Shut the fuck up," said Carney, "I'm trying to listen."

Cochoran, physically more powerful and infinitely more violent than the older man, looked out the side window and pouted.

"Hey, CO," called another inmate. "What's going on?"

"We'll let you know when you need to know," said the driver, not looking back. The inmate flipped him off below the seat, where the officer couldn't see it.

As the flat, single-tone siren blared through the morning air, Carney expected to see California Highway Patrol and Marin County Sheriff's cars go racing past them toward the prison. The road was empty. Ahead, he saw thick columns of smoke blowing out into the bay, and then came the far-off crack of a rifle. Everyone in the van stiffened.

There was fast, panicked chatter on the radio now, and although most of it was unintelligible, the word *breach* came through clearly. The driver immediately put the van into a U-turn and headed away from the prison.

"C'mon, CO, what the fuck?" yelled the same inmate. The others were demanding answers too, all except Carney, who sat quietly and watched the two officers. They were tense, anxious, and something bad was happening. Frightened, armed men in charge of chained, helpless men was not a good combination.

The van drove for a mile and then turned onto a side road, traveling through hilly country of short pines and August-brown grasses. Carney read a blue road sign as they passed it: *California DOC Tactical Training Facility ½ mile.* The COs stayed quiet.

Within a minute the van arrived at a turnoff and a gate set in a high chain-link fence running off in both directions into the pines, topped with razor wire. One of the COs spoke into the radio, and the gate rattled open, allowing them to drive into a small parking lot occupied by one dirty Ford Taurus. The gate rattled closed. At the edge of the lot stood three single-story cinder-block buildings with dark green shingled roofs. On the other side of them, a gun tower—identical to those at the Q—rose into the blue sky.

When the van stopped, the COs turned in their seats and looked at the inmates, who had fallen silent. The radio still crackled nonstop in the background, but they had turned it down. It was the driver who spoke, the senior man. "Listen up. The Q is in lockdown. You're all going to be held at this facility until the situation is resolved. It is not designed to hold inmates, so we're making accommodations. However, that does not mean you get the opportunity to fuck around. Fucking around will have severe consequences."

Technically, the COs were not supposed to curse at them, although it happened. The driver's tone, and more the look in his eyes, told the inmates that the rules had changed, and *he* was not fucking around.

"We're going to exit you from the van in a minute," he continued, "where you will line up in close single file. Don't get out of line. Then we're going to all take nice little shuffle steps to the middle building, to that green metal door." He pointed out the windshield so every inmate could make no mistake of where he meant. "Another officer will open the door and you will file inside. You will cross the room and sit down on a long bench against the far wall. It's the only one in there, so you can't miss it. Once you are seated, you will each be handcuffed to a bar."

A few of the inmates began to grumble. The CO in the passenger seat lifted a shotgun and racked it.

"Understand this. If you deviate from my orders in any way, it will be considered an escape attempt and you will be shot. Are there any questions?" the officer finished.

There were none. Several minutes later the line of men in orange was shuffling across the lot, the two officers walking slowly on each side watching them, shotguns ready. No one got out of line. The green metal door opened as promised, and an overweight CO in his fifties and wearing khaki, also armed with a shotgun, motioned them in. Soon, all eight inmates were seated on a bench in the main room, a classroom of some kind, each with his right wrist hand-cuffed to a bar bolted into the wall. Their waist and ankle chains had not been removed, and the position was both awkward and uncomfortable.

With the men secured, all three COs moved to a corner of the room and started speaking quickly and quietly. At the far end of the bench, Carney strained to hear but was unsuccessful because of the constant complaining of the other seven men seated beside him. He looked around the classroom instead. There were bulletin boards covered with official-looking documents, notices of upcoming athletic and shooting competitions, colored flyers announcing picnics and family outings, and a few photographs. Some flip charts leaned against walls, and posters with silhouettes of weaponry and statistical data were mounted to others. On the wall near the officers someone with at least a little artistic talent had painted a cartoon of a ridiculously muscled guy in a corrections uniform, with the words *NO PAIN, NO GAIN!* stenciled over it. The rest of the wall was covered in a detailed diagram of San Quentin and the surrounding area.

"Man, I just know someone is gonna get to LeBron before I do," whispered TC. Carney ignored him, watching the officers closely. The two COs from the van looked pissed, and the fat guy just looked scared. He was some kind of put-to-pasture caretaker, certainly not one of the buff, aggressive tactical officers who trained here. Carney had a good idea they were all busy up at the Q. There was some sort of brief disagreement, which the van driver seemed to win. All three then approached the inmates, who quieted down again.

"Officer Zimmerman is going to watch over you for a while," said the senior man, indicating the fat caretaker. "We'll be back when things settle down. In the meantime you will remain on the bench, without exception."

The inmates started moaning. "What if we gotta go to the john?" one of them asked.

"Yeah, I got to go right now," said another.

"Then you'll have to piss yourself," said the driver, "but you'll stay on the bench. Officer Zimmerman will use deadly force on anyone who gets out of line." The driver and his partner left the building to cries of "*Fuck You!*" Zimmerman went into another room, where Carney could hear another official-sounding radio talking.

He was almost certain he heard gunfire in the background of the transmissions.

SIX

Napa Valley

He was supposed to be the new Jack Kerouac. He was supposed to write the next great American road novel, and had in fact handwritten two-thirds of it in the notebook he kept in his old Army surplus backpack. Now, as Evan Tucker looked out the window of the tiny efficiency cabin he was renting, he realized his dream of becoming the novelist of his generation might have to be put on hold for a while.

The cabin was right on the edge of the road, the first of six in a row along a tree-lined dirt drive, gold-and-green rural Napa wine country spreading out like a postcard in each direction. A blue 2002 Harley Road King sat just outside the door, dusty and heavy with miles but still dependable, saddlebags mounted behind the seat. Evan wore faded Levi's over black work boots, and a gray T-shirt bearing the image of a fish skeleton and an advertisement for Captain Hobbs Ale. He was average in height and build, with blue eyes and black hair that hung to his collar, twenty-five and not bad looking. He shoved his hands in his pockets and leaned against the window frame.

Yes indeed, it did appear that a book about his experiences on the roads of America had just become irrelevant.

There was an intersection out in front of the cabin with a blinking yellow light suspended by crossed wires overhead. Squealing brakes and a crunch of metal had brought him over to the window, and he had now been here for thirty minutes watching it all unfold. A bread truck had broadsided an older Taurus station wagon at high speed, right where the two roads crossed. His first thought had been to call for help, but the cabin didn't have a phone, and Evan didn't own a cell. He had stepped out onto the little porch, intending to jog over to see if he could help, but quickly changed his mind. A man in some kind of fast-food uniform—who was missing one of his arms—staggered into the intersection and over to the open door of the bread truck, where the driver was alive but pinned behind the steering wheel. The fast-food man began hauling on the driver's leg, ripping away his trousers and tearing into the flesh with his teeth.

The scream reached all the way to the cabin, and the biter clawed his way up and tore open the driver's belly, backing away with a fistful of intestines stringing out between them. The screaming stopped. When three more people arrived, all moving in a lurch with torsos held at odd angles and crowding in to feed on the bread truck driver, Evan stepped back inside and closed the door, going back to the window. Two of them moved toward the station wagon and crawled inside through broken windows. The vehicle rocked, and there was more screaming.

A jacked-up black pickup appeared at the intersection, rumbling to a stop as a young man in boots and a cowboy hat jumped out, talking into a cell phone as he ran toward the station wagon. He stuck his head through a window, and then Evan saw his legs jerk as the cowboy was pulled into the car.

He knew he should try to help, try to do something, but the survival instincts he had developed after four years on the road were on high alert, warning him that being a Good Samaritan right now would get him killed. He stayed put, feeling guilty about it, but too afraid to do anything but watch.

Sirens began to wail off to the left. Soon a green-and-white sheriff's car pulled to a stop at the intersection, an ambulance right behind it. As the cop stood at his car door talking into a radio, two medics jogged past.

One paramedic went down at the bread truck. The other got yanked into the Taurus by one arm, started screaming, and then stumbled backward, without the arm. He staggered a few steps and fell, and a moment later one of the bread truck eaters reached him and fell on his body. The cop walked forward, firing as he went. Bullets hit the ghoul kneeling over the medic, but it only twitched from the impacts, not giving up its meal. Only when one of the cop's rounds hit it in the head, blowing a pink puff into the air, did it fall and lie still.

Head shot, Evan thought.

It was too late for the medic, however. The cop dropped an empty magazine and slapped a new one in just as another bread truck ghoul took him down from behind, finishing him quickly. Then it was just sparkling emergency lights and the crackle of official radios in the quiet morning countryside. No other vehicles approached the intersection.

Evan didn't feel guilty anymore about not going out to help. He lit a cigarette, ignoring the *No Smoking* sign screwed into the back of the door, his hand shaking. Outside, things got worse.

The two ambulance attendants and the cop were all back on their feet now, shuffling around the accident scene despite their mortal wounds. The disemboweled bread truck driver jerked in his seat, still pinned. The people who had crawled into the Taurus had crawled back out and wandered away, followed by the cowboy, missing his hat and most of his face. A little girl in a bloody pink jumper, gore matting her blond hair to her head, crawled out next and just stood at the edge of the road, facing the cabin. Her mother, the driver of the Taurus, tried to climb out her own window, but she was a huge woman and became wedged. Now she hung half in and out, flabby arms with hunks of flesh bitten away reaching outward, fingers grasping.

Evan smoked and watched the little girl. She swayed gently from side to side and seemed to be looking at him. He knew she couldn't possibly see him at this distance, not through the glare on the window, but he still didn't like it.

I don't like a dead girl looking at me, he thought. *Imagine that.*

The madness of it all didn't paralyze Evan Tucker the way it would many people that August morning. He was bright and blessed with a vivid imagination and an adventurous personality; he had always been able to quickly adapt to new situations. This, however, was something of a stretch. To himself, he admitted that it might take some time to accept that the dead were walking and feeding on the living. But he knew he couldn't take too long to wrap his head around it, not if he wanted to survive.

What did he know? He couldn't stay here, that was easy. Half a can of Pringles and a bottle of Diet Coke wouldn't last long. He'd need to find food and water. He'd need to get on the move. If this was widespread—and he had the feeling it was, although he couldn't say why—then the authorities would try to put together crisis centers, like Red Cross shelters. He'd try to find something like that. He had a big folding knife, but that wouldn't do. He'd need something more effective, because he would need to protect himself.

Evan Tucker had been in only a few fights in his life, most of them in school, and only one as an adult, where he and his opponent had been outside a bar in Ocean City, Maryland, both of them so drunk their wild swings had failed to connect ninety percent of the time. This would be different, and he wondered if he could do it, wondered if he could hurt, or kill, one of them.

Them. What were they? People? They looked that way, certainly had been, but they had changed. They killed without hesitation, and those they killed soon rose to join their ranks. The mathematics of that quickly processed, and the word *legions* popped into his head. They could be put down, however, as the cop had demonstrated. They looked slow, which meant they could be outrun or evaded. Were they all slow? He wondered if they could think, perform simple tasks, or use tools and weapons. Could they run, climb, problem-solve? How strong were they? What else could kill them? How did they pass along the infection, if that was what it was?

Many more questions than answers. He had no doubt he would learn what he didn't know, and at least he had a start. Across America in those first days of the apocalypse, few people would ever get the chance to discover what Evan did in that half hour. Most would not survive first contact, and would only swell the numbers of the dead, just as he envisioned.

There were a few things Evan was going to need.

He shoved his few belongings in his Army backpack, making sure his notebook was nestled in the bottom. Relevant or not, it was four years of work and he wasn't about to leave it behind. Although the weather was too warm, he pulled on a denim jacket and shrugged into his pack. The Harley's tank was three-quarters full, and he made sure the keys were secure in the left front pocket of his Levi's. He checked the window once more before stepping onto the porch, and was glad he did.

Mr. Adelman was walking past the cabin, on his way to the road, wearing a bathrobe and boxer shorts. Evan had met the man a few days ago, a middle-aged, paunchy restaurant manager recently thrown out of his house by his wife, holing up in this place until he could settle into something better. Adelman was short and balding, a nice enough guy who showed interest in Evan's writing, assuring him he would buy a copy when the book was published. He was also dead. His right leg had been gnawed down to the bone, and he dragged it behind him through the dirt as he shuffled past. Evan felt bad for him as he watched the middle-aged corpse wander by, but he stayed inside until the man was out of sight, and only then went onto the porch.

The bloody little girl in the jumper started toward him at once.

Evan jogged toward her and the intersection, gauging her speed and movement, giving her a wide berth as he passed. Mr. Adelman had his back turned and was heading for the bread truck. Evan picked up speed, running past the two smashed-up vehicles and swinging wide around the reaching arms of the fat woman in the car window.

The cop and ambulance attendants shifted toward the sounds of his boots and moaned. Two of the ghouls near the accident reached for him across the hood of the Taurus, and Adelman turned. Evan kept moving. He reached the police car and yanked open the passenger door, kneeling on the seat and looking inside. Nothing. He dashed around to the driver's door and reached in for the trunk release. It popped, and he looked up to see the cop and medics heading toward him. Two of the bread truck feeders and Mr. Adelman appeared around the back of the truck.

Evan found what he was looking for in the trunk, a pump shotgun with a dozen red shells pushed through nylon hoops along its sling, the weapon cradled in a metal floor rack. A rack with a keyhole. A locked rack.

"Shit." The dead were closer, feet sliding over the asphalt, their moans rising and falling. He eyed the cop's belt, expecting to see keys dangling there. They weren't. Had they fallen off when he was attacked? Then the smell of exhaust and the sound of the idling motor made him curse again. He went back to pull the keys from the ignition, just as the first of the dead men bumped into the police car's hood.

In seconds he was back at the trunk, flipping through keys, looking for one that might fit. He heard scraping feet along the side of the car. His fingers jammed a small silver key into the bracket, turned, felt resistance, and then it moved. The shotgun came free and years of duck hunting with his father were put to good use as he quickly checked to see if it was loaded, saw that it was, and racked a round.

One of the medics let out a wailing sound as it rounded the corner of the car, reaching for him. Evan leaped back as it grabbed and snapped, and then backpedaled down the road, gaining distance, putting the stock to his shoulder and sighting on the medic's slack face. He saw a wedding ring on one of those grasping hands, and though his finger tensed, he didn't squeeze.

The thing that had once been a man lurched toward him, gaining ground, a gurgling coming from its torn throat. It moved its tongue as if to speak, but Evan thought it might just be reflexive, hungry jaws working and pulling back lips. He took more steps back as it came on. Did it have a worried family waiting somewhere? Its gurgle turned to a frustrated snarl.

The medic's partner, the cop, and the others were moving steadily, all passing the sheriff's car, focused on Evan as he continued backing up, weapon still raised. They gasped and made mewling sounds, like hungry children or animals. A distant moan came from the right, and Evan glanced over to see three more stalking toward him across a field.

He sighted on the medic again but still couldn't pull the trigger. It had seemed so simple before: assess the situation, come up with a course of action, exploit opportunities, and eliminate any opposition. Sure, if he'd been some guy in an action movie this would have been no problem. The action hero probably could have gotten himself laid in the process. But Evan wasn't that guy. These were people, and he couldn't kill people, could he?

The dead didn't stop, kept coming on and backing him up, and the figures in the field were getting closer. He decided there would be a better time and place to assess his sudden attack of morality, when he could berate himself for being stupid. He had to stay alive to get to that point, though.

Evan started moving right, toward the field and the edge of the road, and was pleased to see his stalkers angle in his direction. Once they had moved sufficiently to one side, Evan bolted left, swinging wide around them and running back toward the intersection. Arms reached and angry moans came from behind him as he sprinted back to the open trunk of the deputy's car. He had seen a small first-aid kit and a long black flashlight held to the deck by Velcro straps, and he slung the shotgun across his chest as he grabbed both.

Then he was running again, back to where the fat woman was still wedged in her car window, croaking and gnashing her teeth at him. Evan stopped again where the deputy had dropped his automatic when he'd been attacked, and he shoved the handgun into a jacket pocket before racing back toward his cabin.

The Harley was waiting, sitting there with the midmorning sun gleaming off its chrome. He was almost to it when the little girl in the pink jumper lunged out from the narrow, weed-choked space between the cabins. She made a high-pitched growl as she caught hold of his left leg and went in fast with her teeth.

Evan screamed and twisted, bringing the flashlight crashing down on her head, trying to pull away. She hung on and bit hard, but her teeth only sank into the seam of his Levi's. Evan swung again at the top of her head, dragging her little shape with him as he tried to escape, hitting again and again and again.

Her hands loosened and she sagged away, eyes rolling up, mouth open. Evan smashed her with the flashlight again, and the lens and bulb shattered as her head caved in. She slipped facedown into the dirt, and Evan realized the shrieking he was hearing was his own as he used his boot to stomp the head flat.

He dropped the flashlight, stumbled a few steps away, and threw up.

Breathing hard, bent over with his hands on his knees, he stared at the red gore covering his boot, and a fresh surge of vomit came up.

He coughed and wiped the sleeve of his jacket across his mouth, looking behind him with watery eyes.

They were coming.

He shoved the first-aid kit and the cop's nine-millimeter handgun in the saddlebags, then used bungee cords to secure his backpack to the tail. The powerful engine came to life, and he was moving. He leaned forward and throttled past the knot of corpses at the end of the dirt road, gunning it through the intersection. There were more now, coming across the fields. Evan Tucker left them behind as he accelerated south, putting Napa behind him.

SEVEN

Berkeley

Skye screamed and tensed for the bullet as the soldier fired. Something thudded to the ground behind her, and she looked down to see a hand inches from her foot.

"C'mon!" the soldier yelled, waving her over.

She just stared at him.

"Move your ass!" he yelled.

She did, closing the distance to the soldier and the other men in camouflage as they piled into the Humvee. A couple were firing their rifles in different directions, the sharp pops startling this close up. The young soldier yanked open a back door of the vehicle and shoved her in. Two other college kids her age were already inside. One was a boy in an Affliction T-shirt, the other a girl in shorts and a pink blouse, both of them tucked into tight balls in a space in the very back, hugging their knees. They stared at her with fearful eyes and said nothing.

A moment later the soldiers were in as well, squeezing her between them as they stuck their rifles out open windows and the vehicle leaped forward. There were five of them, one soldier standing in the middle, sticking his body out through a circular hole in the roof, where the machine gun was.

"Hold this," he shouted to Skye, handing his rifle down to her.

Skye stared at the thing. Of course she had seen them on TV and in video games, but she had never actually held a real gun in her life. She didn't touch it.

"C'mon, honey, take it!" he insisted again.

"Do it." The soldier who had saved her, crammed in on her right, spoke softly. He stood the weapon on its stock and guided her hand to the barrel. "Just hold it like that, between your knees. Jay needs to work the sixty."

Skye didn't know what a sixty was but learned a moment later when the soldier who must be Jay, standing in the circular hole, opened up with the M60 machine gun mounted to the turret. He fired the thirty-caliber weapon in short, choppy bursts, and Skye cried out first from the noise of it, then from the rain of hot, empty shell casings bouncing down into the Humvee. All the other soldiers, with the exception of the driver, were firing out their windows as well.

The driver was moving fast, the heavy vehicle swaying as he dodged stopped cars and staggering figures. From the middle of the rear seat, Skye would have had a good view out the windshield were it not for the machine gunner standing in front of her. Something thumped against the front of the Humvee.

"Try not to hit them," said the soldier in the front passenger seat.

"Why not? It saves us rounds," the driver, a man with the name *Martinez* on a patch over one pocket, responded.

"'Cause if they go under and jam up the axle, it's gonna fuck up my truck, Corporal, that's why not."

"Copy that, Sergeant."

Out the right window Skye saw trees and campus buildings passing, the road lined with cars. Beyond them, people were moving stiffly across lawns, wandering in all directions. Everyone she saw wore torn and bloody clothing. And then she saw one moving much faster than the others, a young man with dreadlocks flying as he sprinted and wove among the dead, waving his arms at the Humvee.

"Live one on the right," Skye's soldier called out. She had to think of him that way; he had gotten her out of there, and she didn't know his name.

"Got him," said the sergeant, and the vehicle slowed. Skye saw the machine gunner shuffle left, and then his weapon started barking again. Brass rattled on the metal decking around her feet.

Skye saw the slow-moving people taking hits, bullets smashing into them. Some were knocked down, others spun in different directions, and one collapsed onto the grass when his legs disintegrated beneath him. Most kept moving, and the one without legs just crawled after the running man, pulling itself along by its hands, just as the corpse had when it fell out the window and landed in front of her and Crystal. Just as she noticed all this, the gunner, whom her soldier had referred to as Jay, shouted down from the turret.

"They're not going down, Sergeant!"

"I can see that, Hayman! Keep up your fire!" the sergeant said.

The man with the dreadlocks reached the Humvee, and Skye's soldier—as he turned she saw the name *Taylor* on a patch over a chest pocket—climbed out and told the man to get in. Dreadlocks scrambled inside, wedging up tight against Skye with a muttered, "'Scuse me."

Taylor had his rifle to his shoulder and did a half-circle sweep of the area. There were lots of people moving slowly toward them, but no more runners. "That's it," he yelled, climbing in. The Hummer started moving before he'd closed the door.

Skye heard the sergeant speaking into a handset, a mix of common language flavored with the kind of numeric, military lingo she'd heard in movies. The radio answered back in the same language. She heard words like *sweep, tangos,* and *sector,* and none of it made much sense, but she clearly heard him say, "Four civvies on board." That had to be her, the kids in the back, and the dreadlocks man.

They left the campus behind and were quickly in the surrounding community, the vehicle turning and the corporal steering around objects in the road as he had been instructed by his sergeant. He banged on the horn and swore repeatedly, and sometimes there would be a crunching noise against the grille. Each time that happened, the corporal grunted, "Fuckers."

In the back, the girl started crying and the boy held her. The soldiers fired sporadically, and every once in a while the machine gun made a harsh ripping noise. The vehicle kept moving, accelerating, slowing, then accelerating again.

"Ain't this some pretty shit?" Dreadlocks asked of no one in particular. He shook his head and looked at the floor. "Ain't this some shit?"

Skye suddenly remembered Crystal's cloudy eyes as her sister snapped at her, and she forced the thought away. She made herself focus instead on the weapon she held upright before her. The barrel was smooth and cool against her palm, and she ran her eyes down its length. Games, movies, and television had given her more of an education in the structure of an assault rifle than she realized, for she understood a lot of what she was looking at, even if she didn't know what it was called. The barrel and the muzzle were easy enough, and the opening at the end was smaller than she would have expected. A rubberized grip under the barrel was there to steady it, and this was a scope on top, with a red lens. Did that mean you could see in the dark with it? She didn't know. There was where the clip went in, and behind it was the trigger and the pistol grip. She hefted it, surprised that it didn't weigh more.

"Six point three six pounds," said Taylor.

Skye glanced at him. She hadn't realized he was watching her. "It's light."

"Not so light when you have to grip it by the barrel and hold it extended at arm's length. Then it gets heavy awful fast."

"Why would you have to do that?"

Taylor shrugged. "Mostly in basic, as punishment for being a screwup."

The sergeant turned in his seat, and Skye saw that his name patch said *Postman*. "Private Simpkins, you good to go?" Postman asked.

The soldier to Skye's left gave his sergeant a thumbs-up without looking back.

"And on the topic of screwups, Taylor," Postman said, "quit flirting and keep your eyes on your sector." The young soldier grinned at Skye and went back to watching out his window.

Skye looked at Taylor. He was handsome, not Abercrombie-model handsome, but with a rugged appeal. She decided he was maybe twenty. Then she went back to looking at the rifle, no longer afraid of it and curious. There were a couple of small levers near the clip—the *magazine*, she corrected herself—which would probably be a safety, and a way to take out an empty magazine. The whole rifle had a smooth, solid feel to it, despite being made mostly of plastic. Could she handle it if she had to? She decided she could, if she had someone to teach her. She glanced at Taylor's profile, and then the image of her dad being pulled down hit her hard. Guilty tears burned in her eyes, and she committed to herself that she *would* learn how to use it, so she could kill them. Kill them all.

The radio spoke, and Sgt. Postman responded. He told the driver to turn left ahead, checked a plastic-coated map he was holding on one knee, ordered a right and then another left. He pointed. "Right there. Right in the intersection."

The Humvee came to a smooth stop, and the call of "Security out" had doors opening. Postman, Taylor, and Simpkins exited the vehicle, leaving Corporal Martinez at the wheel and Jay Hayman in the turret. The dreadlocks man tried to get out too, but the driver looked back. "Stay put," Martinez said.

The man glared at the corporal and then sat back, sighing dramatically. "Ain't this some pretty shit?" Skye decided she didn't like him. She didn't know why.

Out on the pavement, Private First Class Taylor stood next to his sergeant. The intersection was free of vehicles, but they quickly saw that an accident up ahead had backed up cars behind it. Doors stood open, the vehicles abandoned. Somewhere beyond them something burned, making a column of dark smoke. The side streets held only cars parked along the curbs.

"Morning rush," said Taylor. "There should be more cars in the streets."

The sergeant nodded. "Yeah, but other places are jammed so tight you can barely walk. Why should any of it make sense?"

"Copy that," said Taylor.

Three blocks to their right, a military truck with six wheels and a canvas cover—a "six-by"—sat in an intersection of its own, men in camouflage moving around it.

"That's First Platoon," said Postman. "They're setting up blocking positions."

Taylor looked at him with a raised eyebrow. "Blocking positions? Does the brass think these things are going to mount some sort of offensive? They're scattered and completely disorganized."

"Do you see any stars on me, Taylor? I don't know what the fuck they think. Our orders are to hold here and watch for civilians until we get instructions." He nudged the PFC. "But the next time the generals sit me down and ask me how to run their wars, I'll be sure to voice your concerns."

"Good. Don't forget." Taylor's eyes crawled over parked cars and doorways, then up to rooftops. They were now in a more commercial part of Berkeley, an older neighborhood with ground-floor shops and apartments above. "What do we do with civvies if we find them? We're full up."

Postman pointed toward the green truck. "We send 'em down to First Platoon."

Taylor used his rifle scope to look down that way. Lots of doorways and alleys, plenty of places for the dead to hide. Those three blocks would be a long walk. "We going to send these guys down there?"

The sergeant glanced at the Hummer, then at the distance to First Platoon. "Not just yet. Let's see what happens."

The radio summoned Sgt. Postman back to the vehicle, because they were only a Guard unit and weren't equipped with the personal-headset and throat-mic radios issued to regular units and troops overseas. He returned a couple of minutes later and moved around to the hood, snapping his fingers to get his squad's attention. "That was Sergeant Rodriguez," Postman said. "Second Platoon is engaged to the east." They all glanced to their rear, as if expecting to see soldiers fighting.

Postman looked at his men. "Remember your briefing, and what we've seen. We need aimed, single shots, so shooting on the move is going to be pointless. We'll conserve ammo." Pvt. Hayman made a sour face, his big, lethal toy no longer of much use. Machine guns were not precision weapons. He reached down and took his rifle from Skye's hand, then started turning in a slow circle, looking for trouble. "Rules of engagement remain the same," Postman continued. "Fire on a freak only if you're certain it's not a wounded person walking slowly."

"They got to get too close for that!" said Simpkins from the opposite side of the vehicle.

"You'll just have to work it out." The sergeant turned to cover his own sector.

Taylor watched an empty street. And why was that? he wondered. All the streets of Berkeley had at least a few freaks wandering around. Had this neighborhood been evacuated already? He doubted it. The one civilian evacuation plan he had heard of had been a clusterfuck that quickly turned into a buffet for the walking dead.

The radio squawked with requests for situation reports and several demands for medical airlift. One panicked call for an artillery fire mission made them all glance at one another. A distant crackle of gunfire drifted on the air, along with a far-off siren and the thump of rotor blades. It was coming from behind them, where Second Platoon was supposed to be. Sgt. Postman moved closer to listen to the radio, as Taylor caught movement at the edge of his vision. He snapped the rifle up and tracked the scope in that direction, moving it over cars, over sidewalks, even up across second- and third-story windows.

He saw curtains and blinds moving, pawing hands and dead faces pressed against the glass. Taylor shuddered. How many were trapped inside these buildings? How many were still *alive*, afraid to leave the safety of their locked apartments? What would happen to them? So many, so fast . . . His National Guard unit in Richmond had been mobilized at four A.M. that morning, and after a quick briefing at the armory, where they drew their weapons and gear and learned the rules of engagement, they were rolling. Information was sketchy and incomplete, most of it beyond believing, but here it was all around them. They had been told only that the freaks (no one had come up with a catchy name for them yet, but Taylor had faith in his military brethren) may or may not be contagious. There was some talk about a fever, speculation about biological warfare, and some completely crazy nonsense about the infected actually being the walking dead. That last part was quickly determined to be true.

The numbers of the dead were steadily increasing, spilling into the streets. Civilian police were being overrun, and the few scattered military units in the area were overwhelmed. Those with Internet access stated that it was everywhere. Taylor heard a captain outside the armory speaking softly with another officer, saying the situation had already passed the point of control.

More movement, on the street now, about midway up the block: an old man, shoulders hunched, shuffling out between two cars. He was bald and wore a gray sweater, and dragged one foot as he walked. Taylor sighted on him. Through the magnification of the sight he searched for blood on the old man's clothes. He didn't see any. *Hell,* he thought, *his spine could be dangling exposed or the back of his head chewed away and I wouldn't know it from this angle.*

More staggered out from doorways and between buildings, men and women, a couple of kids, a wide variety of races and ages. *Zombies, the ultimate diversity group,* Taylor thought. There were more than a dozen, all of them torn up, and they followed the old man into the street. He shuffled on toward the Humvee, head down.

Taylor put his sight directly on that bald head, searching for a torn ear, a fleshy rip, something. And then the old man lifted his head, and Taylor saw his eyes, bright and wide, his face pinched with effort as he tried to shuffle faster. He looked over his shoulder at the horde coming after him and let out a little cry.

"Oh shit, he's—"

A single rifle shot cracked over Taylor's head, and he saw the old man take the hit in his stomach. He winced, grabbed his belly, and fell to his knees. "Got him!" Hayman yelled from the Humvee turret.

"Hayman, he's alive!" Taylor started in that direction, still using his sight. A rising groan came from the street as the horde caught up to and swarmed the kneeling man, tearing him apart.

"Mother*fuckers*!" Taylor opened up, planting his feet and squeezing off rounds into the crowd. Bullets thumped harmlessly into shoulders and chests and thighs and necks, until Sgt. Postman smacked the back of Taylor's helmet and yelled, "Head shots, goddammit!" Taylor took a deep breath, sighted, fired. A woman's head popped a little pink cloud behind it, and she collapsed like a marionette whose strings had been cut.

Hayman began firing again and shouted, "Action rear!" On the far side of the Hummer, Simpkins went to the back of the vehicle to add his fire. The dead were approaching in the direction from which the soldiers had come, a crowd as wide as the street, bodies at the edges bumping along parked cars. They came on slowly but didn't even hesitate when one of their number went down to a head shot. The dead walked over the fallen, and a couple out front moved faster than the rest, in a sort of sidestepping gallop, arms flailing.

"Action left!" Corporal Martinez called out, stepping from the driver's seat, sighting his rifle down the new avenue and opening up. Soon, all five soldiers were firing, shifting direction as more and more creatures moved into the street, bloody parodies of people.

Inside the Hummer, Dreadlocks whipped his head left and right, looking at the scenes playing out beyond the windows, his hands beating a nervous tattoo on his knees. "Shit, shit, shit," he whispered, again to no one but himself. Skye edged away from him. In the back, where there were no windows, only the closed, curved rear hatch, both the boy and the girl were crying now.

Without warning, Dreadlocks jumped out of the vehicle. Skye saw him run to the right and disappear near the back of the Hummer where the firing was constant now, and then a moment later he appeared again, running left, his head still whipping in every direction. Through the windshield Skye saw him sprinting up the street with the traffic accident in the distance. A scattering of lurching figures jerked toward him all at the same time and started to move faster, and Skye was reminded of the way schools of fish all changed direction at once. Dreadlocks slid to a stop, looked left and right, and then darted left, out of sight between two buildings.

High-pitched screams came from there a moment later.

Skye discovered that panic is infectious. She bolted from the Hummer, seeing Taylor and the sergeant each kneeling and firing single shots, one after another, into a growing crowd. Bodies fell, but not enough. Their numbers swelled as new arrivals slid in from every direction. As Dreadlocks had done, she ran to the rear, where Simpkins was firing into a wall-to-wall mass of the dead, surging forward. Cries of "Reloading!" came from all around.

Up in the turret, Hayman heard a strangling screech to his right and looked down to see Corporal Martinez on his back near the driver's door, covered in half a dozen growling freaks. "Sergeant!" He turned and fired down into the new swarm, shell casings spinning through the air and peppering Skye. She didn't notice. She was frozen in place, arms hanging limp like the creatures that were steadily approaching, now less than thirty yards away. Her stare was fixed on one shuffling figure, its chest open, exposing torn organs and a broken rib cage.

Skye's mom locked eyes with her daughter, groaned, and started to gallop.

EIGHT

Father Xavier stood in the shadows inside a hair and nail salon, watching the front window through which he had entered. Or, where it had been. It now sparkled in fragments on the tile floor, mixed with bottles of hair care products from overturned displays and larger wedges of shattered mirrors. He wasn't the vandal; he had found it this way. Photos of beautiful African American and Latina women stared down from every wall, with overdone eyes and red pouting lips, wearing a variety of styles and braid arrangements. The place smelled of burned hair.

It was only a little past noon, and already the power was failing. Xavier had seen entire blocks blacked out, traffic signals hanging dark over intersections. Fires had begun, as had the looting, and the experience of a life lived so close to the street assured him that some of the gunfire and screaming had nothing to do with the walking dead. People could be equally predatory with their own kind.

The cop had proven that.

Xavier found him a couple of blocks from the rectory, an SFPD patrol car engulfed in flames only yards away. The cop had been stripped of his weapons and hung by the neck from the arm of a streetlight. The priest assumed it had been done *before* he changed into what he now was. The undead cop dangled and jerked, fists clenching and unclenching, eyes rolling and mouth gaping in a long, continuous gasp.

Behind him in the shadows of the salon, someone sneezed. Another voice hissed to "Shut up!" which was answered by, "Go fuck yourself, pal." A girl whimpered, and someone lit a cigarette. Xavier glanced back at the people crouched behind the chrome-and-vinyl swivel chairs. Most looked at him with an emotion with which he was all too familiar: hope.

He shook his head. "You've got the wrong guy," he murmured, looking back out the front. A pair of old African American ladies shuffled past the window, the kind of ladies who never missed church and tried to sit as close to the front as they could. Except one of them had a big bite of meat missing from her cheek, and the other's scalp was peeled back all the way from her eyebrows, hanging on her neck like a grisly ponytail.

They had almost moved past when they shuffled to a stop, both tipping their heads back at the same time. They swayed, turning their heads this way and that, and then rotated their bodies until they were facing the broken window of the hair salon.

Xavier froze. The sharp smell of cigarette drifted past him, and he tensed, watching the old women. They swayed, heads still lifted and twitching slightly. Then they started crawling through the window.

A woman's scream in the street outside made them stop and turn their heads, and then they were crawling back out, heedless of the broken glass cutting their knees and palms. They shambled off in the direction of the screams.

Xavier let out a held breath. He turned to the people hiding behind him, his voice a harsh whisper. "I think they smelled the cigarette. Put it out."

"What?" asked a large man in a checked shirt. He was squatting near a sink, a cigarette dangling from his lips. He had a beefy face pocked with old acne scars and the blown blood vessels of a heavy drinker.

"You heard me," said Xavier. The man glared at him for a long moment, then crushed it out. The priest returned to his watch.

It had all gone so fast, and the all-powerful authority everyone assumed would take care of them in a crisis folded quickly, replaced by anarchy. Since leaving the rectory, Xavier had seen only a handful of moving emergency vehicles, and only at a distance. Sirens echoed off buildings, and the occasional, unintelligible babble of a public address system floated through the streets. Most of the police cars and ambulances he saw were vacant, doors standing open with no one in sight. There had been no sign of the military, and the beat of helicopter rotors came from above without the aircraft ever coming into view. Plenty of civilian cars, minivans, and SUVs had been moving at first, but they were quickly abandoned as streets and intersections clogged. Fires burned unchecked, entire buildings ablaze and putting off heat so intense it drove people away.

There were so many people, all of them running: groups and families, singles and pairs, headed in every direction and none appearing to have a sense of where they were going. He saw no checkpoints, no uniformed people with bullhorns directing people to safety, no organized evacuations. Car horns sounded, fires roared, and glass broke as looters took advantage of the chaos. On a few relatively clear streets he saw cars tearing along recklessly, at high speed, scraping parked cars or plowing into others, slamming into hydrants that popped and erupted in great plumes. A big red Coke truck pushed unstopping through crowds of screaming refugees, its horn blaring as bodies disappeared under its front bumper. The driver wore a crazed grin and pounded the wheel as a Kenny Chesney tune bumped at max volume from the cab. There was gunfire and screaming. Lots of screaming.

And there were the dead. They seemed to be everywhere, monstrous corruptions of the human form relentlessly pursuing the living, who were often too slow or panicked and allowed themselves to be cornered. They were pulled down, savaged, and killed, and within minutes arose as freshly made ghouls. Their numbers multiplied with every passing hour.

Father Xavier went straight to St. Joseph's, only blocks from the rectory, and found only the janitor, a man named Raul who spoke no English. Xavier's Spanish was passable, but despite this the man couldn't be made to understand what was going on. Or perhaps, the priest thought, it was simply too horrible to accept.

"*Sí, sí,*" the man repeated, nodding his head and smiling nervously. Xavier grew frustrated. Could Raul at least understand that there was a crisis, and he had to find safety? The janitor nodded faster and started backing away. Xavier took a deep breath and held up his palms. He hadn't wanted to frighten the man. He had come here thinking the people of the parish might have been drawn to St. Joseph's as a sanctuary, but that had not been the case.

Xavier's parish—it wasn't actually *his* parish, it was Monsignor Wellsley's, Xavier was just a priest—sat in the middle of the Tenderloin, serving a San Francisco neighborhood not far from downtown, Union Square, and the financial district. Despite its proximity to those upscale addresses, however, it might as well have been another planet. The Tenderloin was hell.

More than forty-four thousand people lived in its one square mile, packed together in a soup of crime, drugs, homelessness, prostitution, and heartbreaking poverty. It was a place of vermin-infested hotels, liquor stores, thrift shops, pawnshops, and XXX video stores. Vagrants (San Francisco had a reputation for having the most aggressive vagrants in the United States) slept lined up on sidewalks, huddled against buildings in nests of plastic bags, cardboard, and piles of filthy clothes. A functioning shopping cart, the vagrant's home on wheels, was prized above all else and savagely defended against would-be cartjackers. Xavier had once heard two women in designer coats and shoes, standing in line at a boutique coffee bar, talking about the city's vagrant population. They speculated that they were worse than the New York homeless, because the weather here wasn't as hard on them.

"At least the bums in New York have the decency to die off in the winter," one had said, and they both laughed.

It turned out that the homeless died off in San Francisco in August, by the thousands, and now roamed the streets as never before, giving a new definition to the word *aggressive*.

Xavier told the janitor to go with God and headed to the youth center next, moving cautiously along the streets. When he saw the dead he ducked out of sight to let them go by, and when he couldn't do that, he sprinted past them. He didn't try to join any of the running knots of people he encountered, and most veered away when they saw him, a muscled black man on his own with a frightening scar. He decided he was lucky no one had shot at him.

The kids at the youth center called him "Father X" and liked the fact that he had grown up in the tough streets of Oakland, never losing touch with what that was like. They were drawn to his imposing size and fearsome appearance, paired with a gentle and understanding nature. He was a sanctuary in a bad neighborhood, fearless and protective of his kids. He was someone who would never lie to them, who would listen but also be real with them, calling them on their bullshit but never making them feel small. They respected him, loved him, and more than a few managed to leave the neighborhood to find a better life, returning years later to thank him and tell him he was the reason they had made it out.

Xavier was only able to get within view of the center, a squat building of dirty red brick with rusting mesh bolted over the windows. Lifeless figures teemed in the streets around it, and within the chain-link-enclosed basketball court and playground he could see dozens more, drifting into each other or hanging on to the fence and making croaking noises. Even from his point of concealment behind a Dumpster across the street, he recognized some of them: Davon and Cleon; the little kid Marcus with the enormous Afro; Little P, who had trouble with shoplifting; Charmaine, the twelve-year-old girl who had nearly been raped last January; Kiki and her little brother, Troy, who had a speech impediment. Boys and girls who came to play ball or box or just to hang out someplace away from the dangers of the street. Xavier saw others he knew, people from the parish, mostly mothers and old people.

When he saw the toddler, he knew God had abandoned them. She was facedown on the asphalt, a little Hispanic girl still buckled into an umbrella stroller and dragging herself across the ground by her hands. The rasp of hundreds of shuffling pairs of feet filled the air, but the metallic scrape of that stroller and the tiny, determined snarls of the dead thing pulling it threatened to drive him mad.

Too late for his kids at the center, for the people of his parish and the city as well. Too late for them all. Xavier stumbled away, unable to look any longer, his eyes burning with tears. He had ducked into the salon a few minutes later to avoid a trio of dead homeless men, and found these people hiding within.

"We can't stay here," he whispered, turning back to the group.

"And go where?" demanded Barney Pulaski, a union pipe fitter, the one who had been smoking.

"Yeah," said the teenager, a girl named Tricia, blond with too much makeup, whose constant crying had made her look like a raccoon. "It's not safe out there. That's why I came in here. I'm not leaving."

Next to her, a man in his forties with a gaunt face in need of a shave, wearing khakis and a button-up shirt, just shrugged. A twelve-year-old in a gray hoodie clutched a skateboard and stared. Xavier stared back at them. He didn't want this, didn't want the responsibility. He had failed so many already, not the least of whom was God. Saying "we" a moment ago was a slip, and they would be stupid to follow him. He was a murderer, whether his victims had been vicious gang members or not, and he had broken a sacred oath, hadn't been there for his parish or his kids when they needed him.

"The city's too dangerous," he said. The math of more than forty thousand people packed into this neighborhood, rapidly turning into those creatures outside, was overwhelming. And that was just here. What about all the other neighborhoods?

"And go where?" the pipe fitter repeated, speaking slowly, as if to a child.

Xavier looked at him, then away.

"Who put you in charge, anyway?" Pulaski lit another cigarette.

"I'm not in charge." And that was that. He was getting out. They could stay if they wanted to. Perhaps God would take mercy on them, but he doubted it. Xavier knew he was beyond salvation.

"That's right," said the pipe fitter, blowing smoke at him and glaring.

The gaunt man stepped past Pulaski and stuck out his hand. "Alden Timms. I'm a high school teacher. I was on my way to work . . ." He shrugged.

Xavier shook his hand and gave him his name. He didn't tell him he was a priest.

Alden nodded, glancing out the front windows. "You said we need to get out of the city, and I agree. It's just a matter of time before they come in here. We're pretty exposed." He was pale and looked tired. "I'm scared to go out there, but I think we have to. How do you think we could get out?"

Xavier ignored the look Pulaski shot him. "I saw traffic jams and hundreds of abandoned cars. We'd never get a vehicle through it."

"What about bikes?" the skateboard kid asked, looking hopeful. "They can get through tight spaces, and we could carry them over cars if we had to."

The priest was relieved to see they were thinking, and not just paralyzed, waiting to become a meal for a walking corpse. He still didn't care for the whole "we" thing, feeling as if he were being pulled into their world against his will. "I think those things would just snatch you off if they got close enough. You'd be better on your feet."

"If we walked," said Alden, "we'd have to cross a bridge. If the roads are clogged, wouldn't they be too?"

Xavier nodded.

"There's the BART tube."

"Yeah, and it's probably full of dead things," said the skateboard kid. "Forget that."

"I'm not going into a tunnel with those things!" Tricia's voice was shaking, getting louder with each word. The group shushed her, except for Pulaski, who muttered, "Bitch is gonna get us killed."

"What about walking south, toward San Jose?" said Alden. "No bridges, no tunnels."

Xavier shook his head. "It's basically just one big urban sprawl between here and there. Lots of population. Lots of those things."

"Well, you've got all the answers," sneered Pulaski.

"No," said Xavier, "just more problems. Look, I don't have the answer. You can all do whatever you want, and you can stop looking at me to solve the problem." He pointed at the pipe fitter. "Like he said, I'm not in charge."

Alden Timms pressed on as if he hadn't heard. "So we're on foot, and staying together sounds safest." He looked at the boxer. "Where should we start?"

Tricia's voice, humming right at the edge of panic, came again. "Someone's going to come for us. The police. The Army. Someone. They'll know what to do."

Pulaski snorted.

"We should just wait right here for them. Stay quiet and wait right here," Tricia insisted.

"And get eaten," said the skateboard kid, climbing to his feet. "I'm going with you."

"I'm not staying here alone!" she shrieked. Everyone ducked, and Xavier's eyes snapped to the broken window.

"Fucking shut up, you crazy bitch!" Pulaski's voice was a hiss, and his eyes were murderous.

Tricia covered her face with her hands and made a whimpering noise. Nothing approached the window, though on the other side of the street a pair of ghouls lurched past one another and bumped shoulders without reaction, heading in opposite directions. Xavier looked at his "flock." They'd probably all be dead within the hour. He held out his hands in a calming gesture he'd often used to defuse angry young men on the basketball court. "Alden's right, it's safer to be together. If we start moving"—*now I'm saying it,* he thought, disgusted—"we might find the police or some kind of organized evacuation, and then we won't have to worry how to get out of the city."

"Right," Pulaski said, curling his lip and crushing out his cigarette. "The police."

Alden touched Tricia's shoulder, and she flinched. "That's just how it's going to happen, Tricia," he said, his voice soft. "We walk together for a while until we find the authorities, and then they'll take us right out of here."

She slowly lowered her hands. "You think so?"

"Absolutely."

Tricia wiped her nose on a sleeve. "Do you promise?"

"I promise." The schoolteacher said it with a smile and without hesitation. Xavier liked him for that. Alden looked at the priest. "So, since we're walking to find help, what direction would you suggest?"

"We could go to the police department," offered the skate-board kid.

"Maybe," said Xavier. "We could check it out on our way. I was thinking we'd head for Eighth Street, follow it under I-80, and then come up toward AT&T Park. There's marinas there."

Alden nodded. "A boat. Sounds good."

"We wouldn't need roads then," said Xavier, "and they couldn't get to us. They don't look coordinated enough to swim." He had no idea if this was true. For all he knew it was their element of choice, but they appeared as if they would sink to the bottom or, at best, bob like corks. A boat might be just what they needed. If they could find one.

Pulaski stood with a groan. "This is so cozy, I think I'm gonna puke. All your plans don't amount to shit, because we're gonna get eaten the first time we run into those things, which should take about a minute or two."

Tricia started crying again and hid back behind her hands. Alden shook his head at the pipe fitter, and Xavier faced him. "Your attitude isn't helping."

Pulaski was taller than the priest, heavier but not as broad. He looked Xavier up and down. "What are you gonna do about it, tough guy?" His voice was dangerous, like the warning shakes of a rattle-snake, and Xavier wondered how many poor souls had heard that tone in barrooms just before Pulaski put their lights out. They would be smaller guys, of course, for that was how men like him operated. Xavier thought about how it would feel to have this jerk in the ring. Then he shook his head. *Falling away from the calling faster and faster, aren't we? Murder last night, brawling today? What's next?*

The priest held out his hands again. "I'm just asking that you stop upsetting the girl."

The pipe fitter snorted again. "Sure."

"You can stay here if you like," offered Alden.

"Not a chance." He poked the priest in the chest with an index finger. It didn't yield much. "Understand something. I'm not taking orders, and I'm not taking chances." He looked at them all. "I wasn't kidding. We're gonna run into them, no way around it. What are we gonna do then?" He looked back at the priest. "I want a way to protect myself. That comes first."

The schoolteacher touched Xavier's forearm, and his voice was soft, almost apologetic. "We need to find a pharmacy too. I have a heart condition." He rubbed at his chest without realizing it. "My meds are in my apartment, but it's too far away."

Pulaski rolled his eyes. "That's fucking great."

Alden shook his head. "I know what I need, it will only take a few minutes, and we don't need to make a special trip. We can find a pharmacy on the way."

Xavier smiled at him. "We'll get your meds."

"And I want a weapon," Pulaski said. "You got an answer for that, great leader?"

The priest looked at the floor for a long moment, and then nodded, sighing. "I know a way to take care of that too."

NINE

Berkeley

Taylor nearly pulled Skye off her feet. "Get in the truck!" Gripping her arm, he hauled her to the rear door and shoved her inside. The floor was a carpet of rattling brass casings. In the turret, Hayman finished off the ghouls that had torn Martinez apart, and Simpkins popped open the broad rear hatch of the Humvee before joining Sgt. Postman in dragging the man's body to the back and lifting it up and in. The two college kids skittered to one side as the limp body was pushed in next to them, and the boy started crying.

Without all of them firing, the streets at all four points of the intersection were rapidly filling with the dead, moving steadily nearer, the group with Skye's mother the closest, only a dozen yards away. The moaning rose from all directions.

"What the hell, Sarge, he's dead!" Hayman said, slapping a new magazine into his rifle.

The sergeant slammed the hatch closed. "No one left behind. Start that sixty up and give us some breathing room."

Hayman swore and handed his rifle back down to Skye, then began raking the M60 across the nearest crowd, his mounted weapon jumping as he tried to steady its aim, searching for heads. Some shots hit the mark, and bodies dropped. Most thudded harmlessly into cold flesh. Doors slammed as the squad climbed aboard, Sgt. Postman now driving. Skye found herself next to an open window, with Taylor sitting shotgun in front of her.

Damaging the Hummer no longer seemed to matter to Postman. He spun the vehicle hard right and gunned it, heading for First Platoon, smacking the grille into a handful of moving bodies, the big tires thumping over them and cracking bones. Skye searched for her mother, praying she wouldn't see her. She didn't.

"Keep up your fire!" the sergeant yelled, and at their windows Taylor and Simpkins snapped off single rounds, cursing wild shots as the vehicle bounced and swayed.

Above her, Skye heard the machine gun stop as Hayman shouted, "Reloading!" To her left, Simpkins cried, "Last mag!" and slapped in his final full clip.

"Honey," Postman said, risking a glance back over his shoulder while the Hummer drove over four shuffling bodies, "I need you to reach back over the seat. That soldier back there has some Velcro pouches with magazines of ammo in them. I need you to get as many as you can, and distribute them between Simpkins and Taylor. Can you do that?"

Skye said she could and set down Hayman's rifle, kneeling backward on the seat and looking into the rear. The boy and girl were useless, holding one another and sobbing. She shook her head. She had just seen her dead *mother* coming at her in the street, and *she* wasn't going to pieces. She leaned over, ripping open pouches attached to a harness the man wore, finding the magazines. She grabbed as many as she could, nudging Pvt. Simpkins's back and giving him half. She pushed at Taylor's shoulder and handed him the rest. He gave her a smile and a wink.

The Hummer banged into a stumbling woman in a yellow housecoat, sending her flying to bounce off a telephone pole, and then the sergeant was accelerating. Through the windshield she could see the Army truck now only two blocks away, the street between here and there filled with an obstacle course of abandoned cars and walking corpses. The Hummer's hood and windshield were streaked with gore.

"Outstanding, honey," Postman said. "Do it again, look for more magazines, and this time bring his rifle back with you. Be careful, though."

Skye reached back again. She found three more magazines and gripped his rifle by the strap, pulling it over the seat. The dead corporal lifted his head and looked at her with milky, yellowing eyes. Then he snapped his head to the left, seeing the college kids, and a second later he was on them, snarling and tearing at flesh. Screams filled the vehicle as Skye jerked back, a jet of arterial blood first streaking across the side of her face and then spraying up across the roof like a red sprinkler.

"Simpkins, deal with that!" the sergeant shouted.

Pvt. Simpkins pulled his weapon in from the window, twisted in the seat and aimed, then froze. He watched his friend push the dead, glassy-eyed boy to the side and scramble after the girl, sinking teeth high into the thigh of one kicking leg.

"Simpkins!"

The private squeezed off three quick rounds, one of them catching the corporal in the back of the head. New blood pumped across the interior of the vehicle as the girl's torn femoral artery shot it out in long gouts. She sighed and sagged against the wheel well, hands fluttering uselessly at the wound. It was over quickly.

Up front, the sergeant cursed steadily as the vehicle slalomed up another block, and Hayman's M60 began chattering again, for what little good it was doing. Both Taylor and Simpkins were firing out their windows again, so Skye set the extra magazines she was holding on the seat beside her and held both the dead corporal's and Hayman's rifles.

Crystal had come back. Mom had come back. The soldier, the woman in the jogging suit. They bit you and killed you and you came back, you . . . Skye jerked forward as grasping hands came at her from the rear, the boy and girl crawling over the seat. The girl grabbed Pvt. Simpkins's head from behind and bit off his left ear. The boy dragged himself over, took Hayman by the waist, and sank his teeth into the soldier's hip.

Both soldiers shrieked, and Skye screamed for the sergeant to stop. He did, stomping the brakes and throwing them all forward. Hayman dropped from the turret only to have the boy grapple with him, pulling him down and biting his face. The girl had a firm grip on Simpkins and was working on his neck. The soldier's arms and legs danced in erratic twitches.

"Out! Out!" Postman and Taylor piled out their doors, and Skye followed, still gripping the rifles. On the left, the sergeant exited so close to a pair of corpses that he had to hit them in the face with his rifle butt just to clear some room to bring it to his shoulder. He shot them both in the head, then looked inside the Hummer at his two men. They were gone. "Move to First Platoon's truck!"

Taylor was already jogging that way, rifle held to his shoulder, tracking everywhere his head moved. He squeezed off rounds as the dead stumbled out of doorways, between cars, and emerged farther up the street. Skye stayed close behind him, the rifles in her arms like pieces of firewood.

"Keep up with me, Postman!" Taylor yelled.

"I'm at your six," came the reply, boots pounding behind Skye. The three of them ran like that the last block and a half, both soldiers firing as they went, Postman often walking backward to drop targets approaching from the rear. As they approached the intersection with the truck, there were no more ghouls coming at them, only motionless bodies in the street. When they got there, however, they could only stand and stare.

The olive-green, canvas sides of the truck were splashed with blood. Thousands of shell casings littered the pavement, rifles lay on the ground where they had been dropped, and the still bodies of people in civilian clothes were everywhere. The walking dead, killed a second time. No one else was here, not a single body in uniform, walking or otherwise. Silence blanketed the intersection.

"Where are they?" Taylor whispered.

"Hell if I know," the sergeant whispered back. The big truck sat in the center of the intersection, and he walked slowly around the front and looked in that direction. There were only abandoned cars, fallen bodies, and a building burning in the distance. Nothing moved.

Taylor touched Skye's shoulder, and she jumped. "Sorry," he said, smiling. "Will you stay right here and keep watch the way we came? In case some of the ones we shot were only knocked down? They'll head this way."

Skye looked. She could see a couple in the street, but they were a good distance away, beyond the last intersection, little more than heads moving behind cars. "Sure."

Taylor nodded and turned away, then looked back. "What's your name?"

"Skye Dennison."

He smiled. "Skye. I like that." Then he moved off, rounding the back of the truck. The street in that direction looked the same, empty except for a couple of moving figures far off.

"Taylor."

The soldier answered his sergeant's summons, coming up to stand beside him on the far side of the truck. Postman pointed up the last street. Two blocks away, a mass of bodies was swarming over another deuce-and-a-half cargo truck and a pair of Humvees, while more crawled on their hands and knees, tearing at whatever was on the ground beneath them. The dead were a mix of civilians and people in camouflage.

"Overrun," whispered Taylor.

Postman nodded. "Radio said First Platoon put together a collection point for refugees, remember? What do you bet that's what they're feeding on?"

"Which means there'll be more of them in a few minutes." He shook his head. "We need some high ground."

"Copy that," Postman said. "Let's gather ammo, look through the truck"—he jerked a thumb at the big vehicle—"and seize one of these rooftops."

Taylor began ejecting magazines from rifles he found on the ground, shoving them into a shoulder bag. Sgt. Postman moved around to where Skye was still standing watch. "Hey, Taylor's girlfriend, you've been doing good."

She blushed. "It's Skye."

"Okay, Skye, we're going to need your help, and we need to move fast. We've got a whole mess of tangos . . ."

"Tangos?"

"Targets . . . T for *tango*, bad guys. There's a bunch of them a couple blocks that direction, and we want to be gone before they decide to come this way." He asked her to climb into the truck and throw down anything that looked like it was medically related, and anything marked *MRE*.

"Meal, Ready-to-Eat," he said, then left to rummage through the cab. Skye set the rifles on the ground and climbed up into the cargo area of the big truck. Right away she found a heavy, green plastic box with a red cross on it. The sergeant said to throw things down, but she didn't think that would be a good idea with this, and spent several minutes figuring out how to drop the tailgate. Then she climbed out and lifted the box down, carefully setting it on the street.

She went back up inside and resumed her search, and a couple of minutes later Postman joined her. He had a new, olive-green bag hung across his chest now. "There," he said, pointing to a stack of cardboard boxes. "Toss those out."

Skye saw they were indeed stamped *MRE*. "It won't hurt them?"

The sergeant picked up a pair of heavy, rectangular metal containers stenciled *5.56mm* and shook his head. "Nope. The damage comes *after* you eat them."

Soon they had a small pile at the back of the truck. Taylor rejoined them, his shoulders heavy with belts of Velcro pouches, a pair of rifles on his back, and a long, padded case. He unzipped the case and showed the contents to Postman. To Skye it looked like a science fiction hunting rifle with what looked like a long, black can at the end of the barrel. Postman nodded. From the back of the truck the sergeant produced three camouflaged backpacks. He hung one on Skye's back and began packing it with individual MREs from the cardboard boxes. Each looked like a brown plastic bundle about the size of a paperback.

"That's food?" Skye raised an eyebrow.

The soldiers both shrugged. "So they tell us," said Taylor. He and Postman stuffed medical supplies and more MREs into their own packs, then unsnapped their body armor and let it fall to the pavement.

Taylor saw Skye's question before she asked it. "They're not shooting at us. It's unnecessary weight."

Skye nodded, nearly staggering under the weight of her own pack and one rifle. Then she looked at these men, especially at Taylor, who was close to her own age. They were carrying extra rifles, ammo pouches, helmets, even metal cans of what she figured were extra bullets, and both bore it easily, without complaint. Skye decided she was going to have to toughen up.

"High ground," said Postman, nodding at Taylor, and the younger man led off, motioning for Skye to follow. He took them down the street left of where the undead civilians and soldiers were swarming, his rifle pointed ahead and sweeping from left to right and back again as he advanced. Skye stayed close, paying attention to the way he moved, how he placed his feet, how he handled his weapon. When Taylor and the sergeant spoke, she listened to their brief, clear way of communicating, picking up on what had sounded like slang at first, but to them was a language unto itself: *Tango* meant target. Directions were expressed in terms of the face of a clock, *your six* meaning "behind you." Letters were expressed in words: *alpha* for A, *bravo* for B, and so on. They spoke in *meters* and *klicks*, kilometers, and it made her wish she had paid more attention to learning the metric system, beyond knowing the size of a two-liter bottle of soda.

It didn't take Taylor long to find what he wanted. Without warning he angled from the center of the street and headed to the sidewalk. A Starbucks with some metal chairs and umbrella tables outside occupied the ground floor of a building next to a flower shop, and between them was a door with a frosted glass window, the street address stenciled on it in gold numbers. Taylor moved to the door, found it unlocked, and led them inside.

They were in a small foyer with black-and-white tile on the floor, facing another door with a frosted glass window. One wall held a row of built-in mailboxes with name labels stuck to each. The interior door was probably the kind that had to be opened by someone in an apartment above by pressing a buzzer, but since the power was out, Taylor simply forced it. He then led them up a stairway into a hallway lined with doors that a battery-powered emergency light showed was empty. Stairs on the left led upward, and the soldier climbed, moving on the toes of his boots, rifle aimed high as he crept up the steps.

Another hallway, another stairway. Taylor led them up quickly. On the next landing they heard something snarling down the hallway, and both soldiers moved in next to each other, rifles pointed. Skye tensed, waiting for the crack of their weapons, but whatever it was must have been inside one of the apartments. Nothing moved in front of them.

Skye stared down the gloomy hall as something banged hard against wood. She was almost certain she saw a door rattle in its frame not far away, and didn't notice Taylor ghosting past her. Sgt. Postman gave her a gentle nudge and gestured at the younger soldier, who was climbing the next flight of steps. Skye followed.

The top of these stairs ended in a metal door with a simple crash bar and opened onto a flat tar roof with a two-foot-high wall running all around the edge. The buildings to their left and right were one story lower, and at the back of the roof the top of a fire escape ladder curled over the little wall and dropped into an alley below.

"Secure that door," Postman said, and Taylor looked it over for a moment before producing a folding tool from one pocket. Skye recognized it as a Leatherman, a multipurpose tool just like the one she had gotten her dad for Christmas a couple of years ago. Taylor turned it into pliers, wedged it into the seam low on the door where it met the metal frame, and then used his helmet as a hammer to drive it in tight. He next produced a small, curved metal box with folding legs and set it about six feet from the door, wrapping a wire around the doorknob and running it back to the box, where he carefully twisted it down onto a connector.

"Skye, come here," Taylor said.

She joined him, and Taylor pointed at the little box. "That's a claymore mine. It will go off if the door is opened and kill anything in its path. Please keep away from it."

Skye said she would.

They shed their packs and extra weapons in the shade of an

air-conditioning unit, then walked to the wall overlooking the street out front and took a seat on the edge looking down. A handful of corpses were shuffling among the cars, some dragging crooked feet, others with necks craned forward as if walking were an effort. A few were in uniform. Columns of smoke rose in all directions beyond the surrounding rooftops, and distant sirens wailed. Ghostly, sporadic gunfire echoed in the distance. From here they could see part of the bay, and San Francisco beyond, hazy at this distance. Heavy smoke rose there too, and the tiny shapes of aircraft floated above it.

"The radio is in the Hummer," said Postman.

Taylor nodded. "And it's gonna stay there. Too far."

"Maybe. I'll think about it."

Skye pulled out her cell phone to check for a signal. Still nothing, and her battery level was down to half. The screen saver was a close-up of her and Crystal, faces mushed against each other and laughing hysterically. Her eyes began to burn.

"Someone's going to come looking for the platoon," said Taylor. He squinted back toward the intersection with the deuce-and-a-half truck in it. A pair of corpses in uniform wandered past the truck.

"Maybe," said Postman. He looked at Skye. "How are you doing?"

She shrugged. "I'm scared." Her lip trembled. "I miss . . ." And then the tears came. Taylor reached for her but she pulled away, running across the roof to the air-conditioning unit, dropping to the other side of it with her back against the metal, not wanting them to see her. She gripped her cell phone in both hands and cried, head down, shoulders shaking with the sobs. It all poured in at once, her family, her life, the world. She let it come, burying her cries in an arm, not wanting to wail, powerless to stop it, and the anguish carried her away like a riptide.

An hour later the tears were gone, leaving her hollow and drained. She couldn't remember being this tired, wanted simply to drop onto her side and let the black nothingness of sleep take it all away. She didn't. She feared the dreams that might come.

A boot scraped at the tar roof beside her, and she lifted her head to see Taylor crouching there, arms resting on his knees. She must be something to see, she thought. It had been an ugly, snotty cry. The young man didn't look at her with disgust or contempt, and he wasn't giving her the fake pity face people used at funerals when they didn't really care about the deceased. It was a matter-of-fact face.

"You okay?"

She wiped an arm across her nose and rubbed her palms into her eyes before she shrugged. "I guess."

"Good. There's not enough of us." He touched her elbow and guided her until she stood. "The sergeant says it's time to turn you into a shooter."

TEN

There were eight of them now: Dunleavy, five staffers, and the two pilots in their starched white shirts and striped shoulder boards. The G6 was well behind them and they were moving as a group, out in the open, crossing a grassy area and heading toward a squat, concrete structure painted in red and white checks. A bristle of antennae was fastened to its roof.

A door stood open in one side of the little building, and this small promise of shelter was what drew them. Staying in the open was a death sentence, as they had quickly learned, and the terminal was no longer an option.

Dunleavy and the others had still been sitting in the private jet, everyone staring at the fire and talking at once, when the second plane went down. It was a fat Lufthansa jumbo and had probably been in a holding pattern circling high above Oakland. The plane appeared without warning, a white mass streaking out of the sky like a missile, engines screaming as it dove straight into the main terminal of

Oakland International. The blast rocked the G6, and the bloom of fire was so intense it made everyone flinch back from the windows. Burning jet fuel turned the terminal into an inferno.

Anderson stood in the aisle. "Everyone needs to stay calm. I think we need to leave the plane and get off the airfield."

No one moved, except Dunleavy, who shoved the Glock into his front waistband and pulled his shirt down over it. It was clear he would not be expected in court today, or any day for that matter.

Anderson went forward to confer with the pilots, and that was when everyone noticed the big United on the tarmac ahead of them. A door high on its left side popped open, and a second later an inflatable yellow slide ballooned outward. The G6 went silent as they all stared and waited, but no one came out. Almost a full minute passed before a fat man in a dark business suit appeared at the opening, tie undone and shirt pulled open to reveal a hairy chest. He bumped into the door frame and then didn't exit so much as he fell out backward, onto the slide and quickly ending in a heap at the bottom. His arms and legs kicked for a moment, like a pudgy turtle on its back trying to right itself, and then he slowly got to his feet. The businessman stood there, arms hanging at his sides, swaying as if dazed.

A young woman in a flight attendant's uniform leaped through the opening, her mouth open in a scream they couldn't hear, and slid right into the businessman at the bottom. He fell on her and tore her apart.

No one else came out of the plane.

Even steady, calm-under-pressure Anderson couldn't keep the staffers from panicking then, and screaming filled the cabin until from the back their spiritual leader yelled, "Oh, shut the fuck up!" It startled them to silence. The reverend looked past a shocked Anderson and at one of the pilots standing in the cockpit doorway. "Get me off this bitch."

The pilot did, opening the hatch and lowering the stairs to the asphalt. The minister shoved his Bible into an expensive leather carry-on, pushed his way up the aisle past his loyal followers, and climbed down. They followed.

And there had been nine of them. Until one of his staffers (a twat from Kentucky who'd repeatedly refused his offers to come to his hotel room) ran whimpering toward the emergency slide of the United flight, as if she could somehow save the fallen flight attendant. He had never considered the girl terribly bright, and this proved it. The businessman took her down the moment she arrived.

Now down to eight, the little band neared the airfield outbuilding. The businessman, the flight attendant, and the Kentucky twat lurched across the grass behind them in pursuit. On the inside of the door was a bloody handprint, the building a single room filled with long gray circuit breaker panels. In the center, a set of concrete stairs with yellow-painted metal handrails descended into a dimly lit tunnel.

The group hesitated. The minister shoved through, checking the door handle to find that it automatically locked once closed. "Get in," he ordered. When they didn't immediately respond, he grabbed the arm of a young male staffer and propelled him forward. "Get *in*." He pulled the door firmly shut once the last one was inside, then moved through the small crowd and started down the stairs. He stopped when he realized no one was behind him.

"What are you waiting for?"

One of the staffers, a pretty blonde, began crying. Another woman backed away from the stairs, shaking her head. "I can't go down there. *They* might be down there."

"I'm sure of it," Dunleavy said.

The man whose arm he'd grabbed started whimpering. "What's happening?"

Anderson looked at his boss with concern. "Pete, are you okay?"

The televangelist looked at his right-hand man. "Pete? Oh, no, no, no." He pulled the Glock from his waistband. "It's Brother Peter from now on. Even to you, Anderson." He smiled. "Call me Pete again and see what happens."

The man stared at the gun.

Peter looked at the others. "It's the End of Days, children, and only the faithful shall survive the onslaught of Satan's minions. Only they shall be lifted up in the Rapture." The words flowed easily, the same kind of rhetoric that had served him so well in his ministry.

No one spoke.

"You must believe in me as you believe in almighty God, and obey my word, for He speaks through me." They simply stared. He cocked his head and gestured at the door with the pistol. "Or, you could take your chances and go out there, get eaten like little Miss Kentucky." He had already forgotten her name. It didn't matter. "Of course if you touch that door, I'll blow your heart out through your ass."

With the exception of the two pilots, who quietly stepped away from the door (Peter liked that, liked pragmatic men), the rest of his followers didn't move. This couldn't possibly be the man to whom they had pledged themselves, who had baptized them and raised their spirits with his powerful sermons, had lifted their hearts in times of sadness with a gentle touch. Before them now stood a man the media proclaimed was not only a fraud, but an unscrupulous asshole. The media had been right.

Brother Peter gave them all the same angelic smile that romanced the camera and drew in followers worldwide, the smile he used for his book covers, tent revivals, and television interviews. The difference was that now it was a genuine smile, for he was feeling an unexpected inner peace growing within himself. He suddenly realized that this serenity was the understanding that God was more than a scheme used to attain power and wealth. Peter *was* special; God was real and had a plan for him in this new world. A feeling of freedom came with this knowledge, for he now knew that God would forgive anything he said or did. He was also excited, knowing there were more mysteries yet to be revealed.

"I am God's chosen voice," Peter said, believing the words for the first time, "His beloved shepherd, and you are my flock. We will gather others unto us. I will watch over you and protect you." The smile grew. "Now get the fuck down here."

The reverend trotted down the stairs, not looking back to see if they followed. He knew they would. As for what awaited them underground, he had no fear. It wasn't just the Glock; that was a mere tool. It was his memories of another time, his vast experience with the tunnels of the Underworld. Creatures of fire and destruction slept there, and Peter Dunleavy knew them well.

ELEVEN

Alameda

"We're going to get stuck," Bud said as he hit the brakes and ran the van up onto a sidewalk, clipping a plastic real estate flyer box and sending it spinning. Cars were jamming the intersection ahead and he bulled the van around them, taking a right and scraping a fender along the side of a landscaping truck.

Angie gripped the shotgun between her knees and watched out the window. "We need a bunker."

"We're a long way from the ranch," Bud said. He suddenly stomped the brakes, making Angie brace herself against the dashboard as the van shuddered to a stop to avoid a group of people running into the road. They carried luggage and a Playmate cooler, and close behind them a girl of six or seven, arms badly bitten and clothing soaked red, followed in a lunging gallop, mouth hanging open.

Bud punched it once the group was past, and Angie watched in the side mirror as the group tried to jam itself into the doorway of a

UPS supply store. The little girl caught a straggler and climbed his back, seizing his head in her hands. Then the scene was gone.

Angie looked forward.

North of Sacramento, the Franks family ranch sprawled across fifty acres deep in the foothills outside Chico, good land with its own water source, private and remote. A sturdy fence ran all the way around the property. Angie's mother and father lived there full-time, and there were ranch hands to tend the horses and livestock. That was where Dean would be taking Leah, her husband driving the Suburban hard north with their little girl strapped into her car seat in back, a loaded nylon emergency bag on the seat beside her. Dean's ten-millimeter would be riding on his hip, and a shotgun much like the one she was holding would be in a fast-release dashboard mount on the passenger side. He wouldn't stop, wouldn't take chances, and wouldn't let anyone get between them and safety.

She should have been with them. They had never seemed so far away in her life.

The ranch was more than a house and stables; it was a sanctuary. Her great-grandfather Titus Franks had bought the property in the thirties, and her grandfather Earl had begun the first of many improvements during the fifties when a nuclear war with Russia seemed inevitable. Grandpa had built his first bomb shelter there, and it still stood, though now her mother used it as a vegetable cellar. Her father had carried on the family tradition and built a five-chamber underground concrete dwelling. It had power and ventilation and plumbing, tapped into a well, and was stocked with food and supplies. In addition, because of the nature of the family business, it had enough firepower locked within its rooms to arm a third world country. They weren't really *preppers*, at least not like some of the silly rednecks featured on that other reality show. But they all understood that the world could be a dangerous place: war, economic collapse, plague, superstorms, civil disorder. . . . If a person had the means—

and Angie's family certainly did—why not take out a little insurance against disaster? *This* type of apocalypse hadn't been considered, of course, but the ranch could probably weather that as well.

Most people would have thought them a bit mad if they knew, so they kept it a family secret, nobody's business. To the rest of the world it was merely a Northern California ranch. Dean and Leah would get there, she was confident of that. They might even be there already.

Right. They also might be wandering Sacramento's streets, a walking dead father and his shuffling corpse toddler, mindless and unknown to one another, drifting apart in search of prey.

Angie bit the inside of her cheek hard enough to draw blood, willing the tears not to sting her eyes. No, they had gotten out, and Angie and her uncle Bud would find a way to join them.

The streets were tightening up with more and more traffic, all of it going nowhere, but remaining in its neat lanes as instinctive driver's habit demanded. *The world is falling apart, and I'll bet people are still using their turn signals,* Angie thought. Bud, unfettered by driving courtesy, muscled the van around most of it, but they were still slowing. People were everywhere, swarming down sidewalks and across the pavement, carrying children and pets and bags, moving in all directions. Car alarms whooped and sirens came from everywhere, and both uncle and niece tensed each time they heard the sporadic crack of gunfire.

The news on the van's radio was a confused mess, on-scene reporters trying to describe fires and car wrecks and carnivorous horrors only to be cut off by an urgent bulletin, an official warning for citizens to remain in their homes, just as frequently followed by a different authority instructing people to report to this high school or that stadium for evacuation or medical treatment. Sometimes a report would announce that the aforementioned "safe area" had been compromised, and that people should stay away. There was all manner of speculation about viruses and contagion, most of it vague or outright guesswork.

The warning that these animated corpses were both dangerous and infectious, and were to be avoided at all costs, was the only consistent message. "Don't get bitten," was the repeated caution.

Shapes were running in the streets, and the dead surged among them. Bitten and torn, hobbling after screaming people, they fell upon the slow and cornered and fed. Angie stared in disbelief as lives were ripped apart before her, scenes of impossible horror flashing by the windows as her uncle Bud struggled to get the van through the increasingly impassable streets. She wanted to help, to do something, but they were gone in seconds, replaced by new nightmares.

She noticed it as Bud drove past. "Stop! Back up, back up!" she exclaimed.

Bud reacted, jamming the brake pedal to the floor and throwing the van in reverse.

"A firehouse," Angie said, pressing her face against the side window and looking back. "The bays are open and empty. Pull right inside."

Bud backed up until he was even with a three-story redbrick building, something from the early twentieth century, with two high, open garage doors standing side by side. He drove in on the right side and stopped.

"You get the doors, I'll cover," Angie said as she jumped out and locked the shotgun to her shoulder while her uncle moved toward the doors. She swung the muzzle left and right and behind as he found the switch. They rumbled down.

"Power's still on for now," he said, his own automatic in his hand. He looked back into the long, empty bays. "We need to make sure we're alone."

Angie nodded.

A car horn blared outside the closed bay doors, and they turned toward the narrow horizontal windows to see an eighties-era Cadillac, a well-maintained white classic with lots of chrome. It sat at an angle in the short driveway, and four people were climbing out, the driver an older black man in a blue, vintage bowling shirt wearing a backward Kangol hat. They ran toward the bay roll-ups.

A door between the garage and the firehouse banged open, and a man stumbled out. He wore the blue trousers and shirt of a fireman's uniform and had a bloody bandage wrapped around his left forearm. The fireman's skin was an ashy shade, and his pale blue eyes appeared almost frosted. Fresh blood smeared his gasping mouth and stained the front of his shirt, and he groaned as he staggered toward them.

"We saw you!" shouted the Caddy's driver from outside, banging at the window. "We saw you go in!"

The fireman's lips peeled back in a snarl, and he reached. Angie unloaded the twelve-gauge at ten feet, the *boom* like a cannon going off in a closet, and hit him center mass. The corpse flew back against a wall, half its chest blown away, shredded organs and ribs exposed. It gnashed its teeth and tried to get to its feet. Bud fired three, four, five rounds, all hitting, all doing nothing but make it jerk a bit. Angie chambered another shell and blew its head off. The fireman's body slumped and didn't get back up.

More banging at the door. "Don't shoot! We ain't like them!" Faces pressed against the glass. "Open the door, don't leave us out here! We got a child with us!"

Bud looked at Angie, who hesitated before nodding. He hit the switch and the segmented panels rumbled upward. Angie aimed the shotgun at the newcomers as they ducked in, freezing once they saw her with the big weapon. "Stop. Let me look at you."

"We ain't bit, ain't like them," the Caddy driver repeated. The other three, a twenty-something black girl and an Asian woman with a little boy who didn't appear to be hers, shifted nervously in the open garage door as if they had to pee, casting fearful glances over their shoulders.

Angie didn't see any wounds or blood. "Come in," she said. Bud had the door rolling down as soon as she said it.

"Thank you, miss," the Caddy driver said, smiling. He appeared to be in his sixties and had a gold-capped front tooth.

Angie nodded. "We haven't even checked this place, don't know what's in here." She gestured at the fireman's body with the barrel of the shotgun. "Wait here while we check, okay?"

The new arrivals nodded, standing close together. The Cadillac driver looked out the window as a man in mechanic's coveralls, his bottom lip and chin dangling in a red flap, pawed his way along the Caddy's side, leaving wet, rusty smears. "Just had that washed," the driver said.

Bud locked the van and it made an electronic chirp as he and his niece surveyed the bay. It ran the length of the building, front to back, and looked like it could hold four trucks, parked behind each other in pairs. Identical garage doors at the back would allow vehicles to pull straight through, and both were down. Racks for hoses and equipment lockers lined both walls of the bay, and a small door opened into a storage room with a big generator and attached fuel tank. The only other exit was the door through which the dead fireman had come.

Something bumped against the front rolling doors.

Angie and Bud walked back to see that the group had moved closer to the van, except for the Caddy driver, who stood at a window, face to face with a dead man. The mechanic was bumping repeatedly against the door, milky eyes searching.

"Yeah, you an ugly motherfucker, all right. Ugly like my sister's husband!" the Caddy driver said with a short laugh. "And I ain't gonna let you in no matter how hungry you are." He turned and smiled at Angie and Bud, the gold cap a sharp contrast to teeth that were so perfectly straight and dazzling white that they had to be dentures or implants. "We'll be fine. You do what you got to do. We ain't gonna let them in."

Angie nudged Bud, and they went into the firehouse to begin their search. It took a half hour, and they found another fireman, this one dead near a tipped-over chair and a big radio set, who'd had his throat torn away along with one side of his face. He was a fresh kill, obviously the victim of the first fireman they'd met. The rest of the building was empty of occupants, living or otherwise, and within those thirty minutes they decided Angie's instincts had been good. The firehouse would make a decent bunker, at least for a little while. It wasn't the family compound, but it would do.

When they returned to the first floor they found the dead fireman standing and swaying near the radio. He turned and growled. Angie put him down without hesitation, a single blast to the face.

Other than the two sets of garage doors, they found several other ways into the station. A rear door—metal with an interior crash bar—opened to a small parking lot out back, filled with cars. It was tightly shut and could be opened from the outside only by using a key. A glass door in a front foyer was concerning, but it locked with a thumb-turn latch. Could those things break through a glass door? They decided that if they stayed, they would have to find a way to barricade it. Stairs led to a flat roof, which was empty except for an ashtray can and a couple of lawn chairs, and a fire escape led down from second- and third-floor windows on one side. The ladder was pulled up out of reach from the ground. All the windows on the ground floor were reinforced with crisscrossed wire.

The firehouse had a dormitory room of bunks, toilet and shower facilities, a large kitchen and pantry, a couple of small offices, and the room with the radio. Sporadic voices floated from it, and they both had to resist the urge to stop and listen.

"We can hold here for a while," said Bud, putting an arm around his niece's shoulder. "Good pick."

"We're not staying long," she said.

"I know. We'll get to the compound."

"That's right, we will." Her face was strained, and Bud knew comforting words wouldn't get her to stop thinking of Dean and Leah. He was worried about them too, worried about his brother and his sister-in-law as well, but knew they were safe in Chico. Angie's family was on the road and wouldn't be safe until they were behind the fences of the Franks ranch. He *hoped* they were on the road.

They walked through a long room with folding banquet tables and stacks of chairs. Balloons were tied in clusters, and a big banner at one end read, *HAPPY 50th SCOTT!*

"I'm . . . I wish I knew . . ."

Bud gave her shoulder a squeeze. "They're safe, honey. Count on it."

She nodded, not believing it and hating herself for it. She should be with them, keeping her family safe. If only the production schedule hadn't called for the Alameda segment, or if it had been a week later, then they'd all be together. *Angie's Armory* had been such a whirlwind, an excited fever of fame and money, a chance for her family—now fourth-generation gunsmiths—to really build for the future. Contracts and photo shoots and parties, financial worries evaporated overnight, celebrities to meet . . . it fed her ego as well as their bank account. Now it was like ashes in her mouth, a meaningless pursuit of vanity and greed that had separated her from her daughter and the man she loved at a time when they needed her most.

They heard the electric whine and metallic rattle of a garage door opening.

Bud swore and bolted ahead, Angie right behind him, and they burst into the truck bay to see both front doors still down. At the back, the Cadillac driver stood at the switch, the left door raised three feet, motioning as a trio of people ducked inside, a young woman and two little kids.

"Thank you!" the woman exclaimed, hugging the Caddy driver as he grinned and lowered the door. She looked at the others, holding the kids close, a pair of girls five or six. "They were just wandering out there, crying. They're not mine. I thought we were going to . . ." She trailed off.

The girls stayed close together, wiping at their eyes. "Where's Mommy?" one said.

"I saw them in the parking lot," the Caddy driver said, "hiding between cars. Couldn't let them stay out there."

Bud Franks moved to the narrow windows and looked out. A pair of corpses were walking slowly between the cars. The Cadillac man had saved three lives, but Bud realized they were going to have to come to some kind of understanding about opening doors. Angie knelt in front of the little girls and spoke quietly with them, and her uncle eyed the older man in the Kangol hat. He stuck out a hand. "Bud Franks."

"People call me Maxie," the Caddy driver said. His handshake was firm and dry.

The others introduced themselves. The Asian woman was Margaret Chu, and the boy with her was Denny. She had pulled him away from where two ghouls were eating someone with long hair, while the boy stood by screaming, *Stephanie!* The young black girl was Tanya, and the woman with the two girls was Sophia Tanner, a real estate agent. The girls she had rescued were apparently sisters, who didn't give their names and hadn't spoken since one of them asked about their mommy.

"I'm going to get everyone settled," Angie said, gathering the new arrivals and herding them into the main firehouse, leaving Bud and Maxie in the bay.

"For now," said Bud, "let's at least agree not to open any more outside doors unless we have some weapons ready, okay?"

Maxie gave him a gold-capped grin and lifted his bowling shirt, revealing the butt of a silver revolver shoved in his waistband. "Got that covered already."

Bud wasn't sure if that made him feel better or worse. His cop's eye inspected the man, wondering, *Felon?* Maxie lit a cigarette, sent a cloud at the ceiling, and looked right back at Bud. "Y'all mind if I smoke?" Maxie asked.

Outside, something was now thumping against the rear garage doors.

TWELVE

Zimmerman, the heavy correctional officer and their only guardian, had turned on a TV in the corner of the big classroom. He sat in a chair staring at it, the shotgun on the table beside him, massaging his chest as news images of the impossible rolled across the screen.

There were fires, ambulances lined up outside emergency room entrances, acres of traffic jams and devastating car wrecks, scenes of uncontrolled looting, roadblocks where tanks stood alongside police cars, images of people in yellow biohazard suits putting quarantine notices on doors and loading body bags onto flatbed trucks. There were boulevards packed with refugees on foot, pulling luggage and pushing strollers and shopping carts loaded with possessions. Other streets were vacant, littered with discarded bags and coolers, abandoned bicycles, prowled by stray dogs. Bodies fell from skyscrapers. There were scenes of boats, all shapes and sizes, swarming across the San Francisco Bay and heading out to sea, and high-altitude footage shot from a helicopter of Oakland International Airport awash in a sea of flames centered on the wreckage of a Lufthansa jumbo jet. People wore painter's masks and latex gloves. Soldiers were seen in full chemical gear, looking like aliens with goggled faces. Talking heads droned about infection and transmission, arguing that the plague was passed on by the bite, others disagreeing, claiming the true threat was death by any cause. Politicians spoke of calm and promised an effective response.

The dead were everywhere, filling the streets and hunting down the living. Troops and cops fired at them, military helicopters gunned them down from above, and the cannons of armored vehicles smashed buildings and abandoned cars. They kept coming.

The CO repeatedly tried his cell phone, got no answer each time, and grew increasingly flushed and agitated. He would slap the device down on the table, only to pick it up a moment later and try again. Eight men in orange jumpsuits, handcuffed to a wall, sat quietly and watched. The radio in the other room was now emitting only static. Carney watched the officer, not liking the way he rubbed at his chest.

"CO, you okay?" Carney called.

The officer ignored him. Once Carney had broken the silence, the others joined in.

"Hey, CO, I gotta take a piss."

"CO, is this shit for real?"

"When we gonna eat, man?"

"Hey, CO, what's going on at the Q?"

"I wanna call my lawyer."

"Can you turn on TMZ?"

Zimmerman didn't even look back. He tried his cell phone again, slammed it to the table, muttering something they couldn't hear. Then he stood, took a few steps and froze, grabbing at his chest, his face a grimace. He crashed to the floor.

The inmates exploded, shouting, jerking at their handcuffs,

hurling questions and obscenities at the fallen man. TC looked at his cellmate, and Carney shook his head slowly. "Stay cool."

The officer did not respond to any of the shouting, didn't even move, and across the room Carney could see a small pool of blood where the man's face had hit the floor. *Dead,* he thought, *and we're chained to this bar.* At the other end of the row, two inmates, one black and one white, began arguing, shoving one another and making threats, their voices rising.

On-screen, the image shifted to show troops setting up medical tents in a Kmart parking lot. Then it cut to a split screen of a man in a lab coat talking, while on the other side computer graphics displayed microscopic particles bumping together and consuming one another. The president came on, calling for order and assuring everyone that the government had the crisis under control.

The arguing inmates were about to come to blows when the CO climbed slowly to his feet across the room. There was silence then, broken only by the scuff of the man's boots on the tile floor. He walked a few steps in one direction and stopped, then turned and shuffled back, lifting his head and moving it in short jerks. He faced a wall and stood there with his arms at his sides.

"Damn, CO," called an inmate, "you went down hard, man."

The officer turned, revealing a nose crooked from where it had broken against the floor, his skin pale and his eyes filmed over with a creamy glaze. His head twitched. He looked like the things they were seeing on TV.

When the CO started around the table and began moving toward the bench, the inmates panicked. They yelled and tugged at their handcuffs, pulling at the rail. Then the CO was on them, and with a snarl he took a bite out of an inmate's arm, the black guy at the far end who had been arguing. The man screamed and tried to punch at him, but the CO clawed for a better grip, biting again, ripping away an ear.

The man beside him pulled away, pressing against the next man in line, straining to get as far away from his handcuff as he could. Leaving the black inmate shrieking and holding the bloody tear where his ear had been, the CO went for the next man in line, seizing the extended arm and biting deep. Everyone was screaming, except for Carney.

"Hey, fuckface!" He stood, hopping up and down with a rattle of chain. "Fuckface, over here!"

The CO tore at his victim's arm, crunching on bone, flesh parting as his fingers ripped at tendons and muscles. He growled deep in his throat, and his prey's eyes rolled up as he passed out.

"Carney, what are you doing, man?" TC asked.

Carney ignored his cellmate, pulled off one of his canvas slip-on shoes, and threw it at the corpse. It hit the CO in the side of the head, and he pulled away from the arm to look. "That's right, fuckface, over here! C'mon, over here, come get me!"

"What the fuck?" shouted TC. "Don't bring him over here!"

"Shut up and be ready." Carney kept yelling and jumping, and the CO started toward him, moving past the other inmates as they cringed away and tucked into balls. "Keep coming, keep coming . . ." He glanced down at TC. "Trip him when he goes by."

The dead CO lunged for Carney, and TC's leg shot out. The thing stumbled, and as it fell forward Carney leaped back. It hit the floor face first again, snarling, but before it could start back up, Carney had slipped off his other shoe and was jumping with both feet, coming down on the back of its head with his heels. TC was on his feet at once and began stomping too, an animal growl of his own coming through clenched teeth. They kept at it, slipping in blood and pulling themselves up, landing blows with their feet until they heard the crunch of bone, and then kept at it still. After two minutes the uniformed body was motionless, its head a flattened mess.

The inmates cheered. Carney used his feet to pull the body close, then stretched an arm and unclipped the keys from its belt. A few minutes later he and TC were free of their cuffs, their waist and leg restraints in a pile next to the body.

"Hard-core, man!" The inmate next to TC lifted his handcuffed wrist. "Me next."

Carney shoved the keys in his jumpsuit pocket and dragged the corpse away from the bench, searching it. TC retrieved the shotgun. The other inmates shouted demands, and the maimed man at the far end wailed to be taken to a hospital. TC cradled the shotgun and grinned at them. Carney examined the diagram of the prison and surrounding area, finding the facility where they were being held in a box in the lower right corner.

"Let's go," he said.

TC motioned with the shotgun. "What about these guys?"

"Not our problem." Carney left the room. TC grinned at the cuffed and screaming inmates again, then followed.

The building had a locker room next to a weightlifting gym, and here they swapped their orange jumpsuits for the black ones worn by San Quentin's tactical officers. Bloody feet were wiped down and soon wore black combat boots. They found some bottled water and a few granola bars, and Carney discovered a heavy folding knife, which he slipped into a pocket. TC kept the shotgun close and stopped often to listen in case the other COs returned. He had no intention of returning to his cell.

A sound that was part roaring and part screaming floated through the building, and when they went to the classroom door to look, TC poked the barrel of the shotgun through first. On the bench, the two inmates who had been mauled by the CO had turned. The one without an ear moaned and strained against his handcuff, as the one beside him with the mangled arm fed upon the inmate next over. The man's belly had been torn open and pulled out, and he was slumped with his head back, dead eyes staring at the ceiling.

As they watched, this corpse suddenly twitched, and the head came up slowly. The other creature stopped feeding at once and tried to reach for the next inmate, beyond his newly risen brother.

Dominoes, Carney thought, looking at the remaining men in orange. They pleaded, prayed, babbled, tried to pull away. Carney felt nothing for them and wasn't about to release them. They were killers and animals, not to be trusted. He trusted only TC, and only so far. Carney watched the slaughter a bit longer, though, learning.

TC nudged his friend. "Let's boogie. You got the CO's keys, right? That's got to be his Taurus in the parking lot."

"Yeah, but I want to check something first," Carney said.

TC followed him across the room and out into the sunlight. "We got wheels and a piece, man. What else do we need?"

Carney stopped, rested a hand on his cellmate's big shoulder, and pointed. Two people were standing at the chain-link gate to the facility, an older man in torn overalls and a teenage girl in a bloody tank top. As they watched, a black woman in a floral-print housecoat shuffled up to the gate, tugging on the fence.

"Things are different now, TC. There's more to worry about than cops. You get that?"

TC looked at the corpses rattling the fence, thinking about what they had seen on TV and on the bench inside. "It's the end of the world, man," he said, smiling. "No more rules."

Carney shook his head. "Wrong. The rules are just different, and if you break them, you die." He pointed. "Or worse."

The corpses moaned in agitation.

"I need you to listen to me, and do what I tell you."

The younger man saw another corpse, this one in bloody pajamas and bare feet, make its way from the road to join the others at the gate. "Those COs aren't coming back, are they?"

Carney watched the pajama corpse grab the chain link and shake it. "I don't know, but stay ready. I think they've got bigger problems, though." He looked in the direction of the prison, where the thickening smoke still climbed into the air. "If they're even still alive."

They watched the corpses for a while. "What now?" asked TC.

Carney led them to the third cinder-block building, using the dead CO's keys to get inside. He found what he'd expected, and the keys opened that as well: the armory. Inside was gear the tactical officers used for both training and actual crises, and more weapons than he could count. The fact that it was untouched only confirmed his suspicions about San Quentin, that it had gone down too fast for an organized response. The armory was a gift. What they found next exceeded his wildest hopes.

It sat in a garage near the armory, a huge, bright blue armored truck with *CALIFORNIA D.O.C.* stenciled on the side. Carney ran his fingertips across the metal, over the letters. "What's up, Doc?" he whispered, his tone reverent. It was a Bearcat, an armored vehicle used by law enforcement during riots, a monster on four big, hardened, off-road tires, with armored glass viewports, a tank-style hatch in the roof, and a ballistic windshield covered in steel mesh. Double doors at the rear gave access to a compartment where a dozen men in full riot gear could sit across from each other on benches.

"It's a nasty mother," said TC, "but what about the Ford? This thing's going to draw attention."

"I don't think that matters anymore," said Carney. To him the Bearcat was more than freedom. In the world he had seen on TV, it meant survival. "Let's get to work."

The Bearcat had a full tank of diesel. They spent an hour loading it with gear, weapons, and ammunition, and they each took the time to pull on a full set of cell extraction body armor. Carney reminded his cellmate of how the things killed, and so they both donned black, heavy plastic shin, knee, and forearm guards. They finished with mesh-reinforced biteproof gloves, a standard in America's prisons, where inmates often chose that method to assault officers.

They broke open a pair of vending machines and emptied them of soda, bottled water, and snacks. TC left for a few minutes, then returned to report that all six men on the bench had turned.

By the time the Bearcat rolled into the afternoon sunlight, Carney at the wheel (it took some adjusting, since he hadn't driven in seventeen years and never something this big), nearly twenty of the walking dead were gathered at the gate. Three of them wore orange San Quentin jumpsuits, and that answered any questions about the prison's fate. Carney pictured thousands of the dead wandering the cement halls and tiers, drifting through the exercise yards and across the manicured lawns of the administration buildings. COs would be among them, their adversarial role now moot in this new reality.

Carney hit the gate at forty miles per hour, blowing it open and sending bodies flying or crunching under the big tires. The massive steel push bar on the front of the Bearcat handled it easily, and after a short drag the gate fell away and they were rolling. When they reached the main road and turned left, away from the prison, they saw what Carney already knew: corpses in orange shuffling over the asphalt. The Bearcat drove over them.

Soon they were at the entrance to the Richmond–San Rafael Bridge and what was left of the highway patrol roadblock. A couple of cruisers sat with their rooftop lights flashing, a yellow sawhorse standing between them. The outbound, northwest lanes were completely blocked with stalled traffic, car doors standing open, but the lanes heading toward the urban sprawl were clear. Bodies moved sluggishly among the vehicles, and near the roadblock a corpse in a highway patrol uniform walked to the armored truck and beat its fists against TC's door. Out over the bay, a pair of fighter jets streaked by, wings flashing in the sun as they banked and headed south.

"Brave new world," whispered Carney.

TC grinned and waved at the dead cop, then lit two cigarettes from a pack he had found in a locker, passing one to his friend. "Where we going, brother?"

Carney put the Bearcat in gear and started pushing one of the patrol cars out of the way. "Mexico."

THIRTEEN

San Francisco—The Tenderloin

Father Xavier and his group learned fast. Single file and quick was best, moving between cover and keeping out of sight, Dumpster to doorway and down alleys. They slipped into unlocked buildings when they could, standing still and holding their breath until the dead passed. Silence was their ally. By the time night settled over the city, they had traveled a total of six blocks. They had seen no indication of an organized evacuation, no military or police activity, and only heard the occasional helicopter without actually seeing one. A jaded voice within the priest suggested that any evacuation would take place in the upscale neighborhoods, and the dregs of the Tenderloin, as usual, would have to fend for themselves.

As they went, they watched and learned about the dead, an easy task because they were everywhere. Xavier paid close attention. Generally, they were slow and seemed to have a short attention span, frequently wandering with no apparent sense of purpose. At times they were motionless, standing still, maybe swaying a little, sitting on bus benches or propped against walls, staring at nothing.

The priest knew now what the absence of a soul looked like. Though he understood they were dangerous killing machines, his heart ached for them, and for the lives they had lost and would never regain. He couldn't think of them as evil.

Their balance was poor, and they were prone to trip over curbs or obstacles in the street, falling and slowly getting back up. There didn't seem to be any communication among them. When prey was around, however, their lethargy vanished, and Xavier's group had witnessed up close the horror that followed, powerless to do anything to stop it. A young woman in a miniskirt and bare feet, her legs badly bitten from her ankles to her thighs, stumbled out of a doorway and into the street, dazed. She stood in the open, crying, hands pressed to her ears and eyes squeezed shut.

It attracted attention.

Corpses fifty feet away did not immediately react to her presence, which told the priest their range of vision was probably short. Her crying, however, caused creatures up to a block away to immediately turn toward the sound and start moving. Their clumsy gait seemed to improve, and they moved faster, a few even breaking into a sliding gallop. *Hearing more acute than vision. Speed and coordination improves when pursuing prey.* The girl didn't even put up a fight.

Other events drew them: fire, gunshots, loud noises, car engines. Xavier suspected that whatever passed for instinct in them interpreted these stimuli as belonging to live humans and, thus, food. As for their feeding, he couldn't begin to understand what benefit eating had for a dead, and likely decomposing, body.

They could climb a little—over low obstacles like abandoned cars—and could manage stairs, though not swiftly. Xavier had seen one struggle up a lowered fire escape stairway, then stop and lose focus, bumping its hips against the railing until it tumbled back down. The resulting fractured leg didn't prevent it from walking, just exaggerated its limp. He had seen others use doorknobs but had not seen any other tool use, and for that he was grateful. They were weapons all by themselves.

The most fascinating thing they learned, and perhaps the most helpful, was that the dead both were relentless and did not react to injury or pain. No matter how badly maimed their bodies were, they kept on coming, and there were plenty of limbless corpses moving through the streets to validate this. In one case, a dead woman made her way down the sidewalk, arms extended and probing ahead of her, while her head was twisted *backward* from some hideous accident. She made frustrated grunting noises.

They had seen this relentlessness in action from concealment at the mouth of an alley, looking out at an intersection where a city bus had slammed into the side of an orange municipal dump truck. A handful of passengers were trapped on board, their screaming muffled behind glass as the dead encircled them, hammering at the sides and making the bus shake. It started slowly, with one or two detecting movement or noise from within, and in a short while handfuls were gathering. When the people inside started screaming, the dead appeared in droves, and soon there were more than a hundred pressing in on all sides. Someone on board had a pistol and slid open a window to fire into the swarm. Six shots went off at point-blank range, and only one of the dead went down. Xavier strained to see what had been different about that one, but at this distance he couldn't tell.

Someone on board couldn't take it any longer and opened the door in an ill-conceived escape attempt. The dead poured in, and it ended quickly.

Now, as an evening chill came on with a light fog, Xavier and the others stood in the darkness of a mom-and-pop dollar store that had been trashed by looters, a fact that made a couple of them shake their heads at the irony. The street outside was filled with wrecks, broken glass, and moving figures. They were little more than silhouettes in the fog, drifting silently among the cars. At the end of the block a lone streetlight was on, but no others. There were no lights in any of the block's ground-floor shops or apartment windows above.

Pulaski stood beside the priest, holding a tire iron. "We've wasted all our daylight. You better be right."

Xavier hoped he was. Directly opposite them was a four-story brick building with graffiti-covered walls. The ground floor, once a store of some kind, was boarded over with weathered plywood and covered in spray-painted tags, the most prominent of them a big, black *690K*. To the left, the street-level doorway that would lead to the apartments above stood open like the black mouth of a crypt.

"You've been here before?" Alden whispered, joining them.

"Never inside," said Xavier, "only out front."

Pulaski looked at him. "Then you don't really know."

Xavier shrugged. "This is one of their places, so it's likely. I told you earlier I wasn't making any promises."

"Yeah," the pipe fitter continued, "but you sounded pretty damned confident. Enough to take us six blocks in the other direction from where we wanted to go. Enough to keep us from checking out that police car we saw up on the curb."

The priest looked at him. "That was a death trap. You would have drawn them the moment you stepped into the street, and then what would have happened if you'd reached the car and found nothing?"

"Someone probably already took the shotgun," Alden added. "You would have gotten killed for nothing."

Pulaski snorted. "So I got to spend more hours creeping like a rat to get killed here instead."

"It's still our best bet," said Alden, patting the priest's shoulder. He hadn't said a word about detouring for his medication. They'd seen only one pharmacy, and it had been on fire.

"How will we even know where to start looking?" said Pulaski.

Xavier gave him a sideways glance. "You're assuming we live long enough to get into the building." He saw the man swallow hard and tried not to take pleasure from it. "We'll probably have to go door to door. First we need to get there."

Alden nodded and moved away, returning a moment later with three plastic water bottles three-quarters filled with gasoline, a rag stuffed into each. The skateboard kid, whose name turned out to be Ricky Hammond, though he insisted on being called Snake, had siphoned the gas from an abandoned car with a length of garden hose.

"I'm less worried about them," Xavier said, indicating the dead.

"Why?" Pulaski asked.

"Because 690K doesn't play around, and they'll blow you away without even thinking about it." He pointed to the building across the street. "What worries me is that some of them might still be alive and holed up in there. If they are, your tire iron isn't going to do much good. They pack serious heat."

Pulaski scowled. "That's why we're here, isn't it?" The bluster was gone from his voice.

"We don't have a choice, do we?" said Alden.

"Of course we do. We can pull out of here and follow our original plan, try to get to the marina."

"We're lucky we made it this far," said Pulaski. "No way we cross half the city and live if we're unarmed."

"We could still go check that police station," Xavier offered, "avoid this place entirely."

"Except anyone who's still alive and trying to get out will go there," said Alden. "We'd find it empty, or get ourselves shot by other survivors. Not many people know about this place, do they?"

Xavier shook his head. "No one stupid enough to risk going up against these guys."

"Stupid like us," Pulaski muttered.

"You don't have to go."

"I'm going."

"Then like we discussed," Xavier said. "Ricky . . . sorry, Snake. You throw two of the bottles as hard as you can toward the streetlight. It should draw them off, and we wait until that happens. The rest of you stay here and out of sight while Pulaski and I go in."

They all nodded.

The priest looked at the twelve-year-old again. "You watch that doorway. When you see us in it again, if they've moved back into the street, you throw the last bottle in the other direction to draw them that way. We'll cross when it's safe."

Snake smiled and shook the bottles.

Xavier gripped Alden's shoulder. "Give us thirty minutes. If we're not back, get them out of here and head for the marina."

The schoolteacher's eyes announced the doubts he had about being up to that task. "Make sure you come back."

A minute later, Pulaski lit the bottles with his Zippo, and Snake crept onto the sidewalk. Two balls of fire arced through the night. The kid had an arm, because both hit the pavement almost directly beneath the lone streetlight, pools of fire erupting and throwing the shadows of cars and moving figures on nearby walls. The dead moaned and moved toward the small blaze, and two shapes slipped out the storefront and scooted across the street, shadows in the fog.

Xavier and Pulaski moved fast, sprinting behind the backs of the shuffling ghouls and reaching the doorway. Silence and darkness awaited them, and they plunged inside, the thin light from outside lost in seconds. They climbed a stairway, Pulaski going first with the sharp end of his tire iron. A landing gave a choice of more stairs going up, or a hallway. At the end facing the street, pale light from outside came through a dirty window and created a bluish glow, not enough to see by. Pulaski lit the Zippo.

In their small circle of light they could see that the hall was littered with trash and empty beer bottles. Every door, every inch of wall, and even the ceiling was covered in graffiti. The pipe fitter looked at the priest and raised an eyebrow. Xavier looked at the doors, then pointed a finger at the ceiling. They climbed to the next floor.

The thumping came as soon as they reached the next landing, where there were no more stairs, only another hallway like the one below, complete with trash and more graffiti. They froze. It came again, something heavy, *bump, bump*. It was coming from the right, so they moved left, toward the back of the building.

As he had told the others, Father Xavier had been here once before, nearly two years ago, although he hadn't shared the details. The building was one of the places where gang members crashed, and he had come for a meeting on behalf of a young man named Manny Lovato. 690K was drawing the boy in, seducing him with the promise of easy money, sex, drugs, and little responsibility. Manny was the son of a woman in his parish, a bright boy who got decent grades and had a chance at a higher education, an opportunity to escape the dead-end life of the Tenderloin. Father Xavier had come to meet with the leader of 690K, at the time a twenty-five-year-old thug named Smiles. He had come to plead for them to leave the boy alone. They met on the sidewalk out front.

"He's mine," Smiles had said, shrugging. "His life, his ass. They're mine. You're too late, Father. I already claimed his soul." The words were spoken without malice or anger, just matter-of-fact. The gang leader smiled and nodded politely at everything the priest had to say, hearing him out. And then another shrug. "He's mine." Xavier had gone away defeated and frustrated. Three weeks later Manny Lovato was killed by police after a high-speed chase, following a drive-by shooting. He was sixteen.

That was the moment Xavier realized how naïve he was and began to see the futility of his efforts to turn people away from the lure of sin. It was the start of his slide into doubt and bitterness. And now he was back at the scene of his failure.

They began searching rooms, tensing every time they opened a door. Pulaski's lighter revealed squalid crash pads containing filthy mattresses, piles of dirty clothes, overflowing ashtrays, discarded liquor bottles, and used condoms. The reek of stale marijuana clung to everything, and obscenities in Spanish were spray-painted on the walls. They investigated room after room and found neither the walking dead or live gangbangers. They also didn't find the object of their search.

Their watches showed the minutes draining away.

In the hallway once more, they looked at the only door on the floor they hadn't searched, the one from behind which came the thumping. They both knew what that sound meant but didn't know how many the sound represented. On the door, someone with some artistic talent had painted a winking, yellow smiley face wearing a jeweled crown, with *690K* beneath it in script. Xavier tried the knob and found it locked. He pushed on the door, and it rattled just a bit, cheap pine.

"Ready?" Xavier whispered.

Pulaski shook his head, scowling. "We know what's in there." He raised his tire iron. "You said it, this won't be enough."

"This room is the best bet. Get ready." Without waiting for agreement, Xavier threw his broad shoulder hard against the door. It didn't pop open; it exploded with a sharp crack of wood and came off its hinges. They charged in.

The curtains were pulled back from the room's single window, letting in enough light from the street so they could see. Even without the image on the door, it was immediately apparent that this was the gang leader's crib. Leather couches faced an enormous flat-screen TV, and a big bed covered in satin leopard-print sheets stood in a corner. On the walls hung framed posters of Pacino in his *Scarface* role. A granite-topped coffee table sat between the couches and the TV, covered with DVD cases, cigarette packs, and empty champagne bottles.

Smiles wasn't here. The zombie bumping around the room was a heavyset Puerto Rican girl in lingerie, her skin ashy and her eyes a cloudy gray. The long wounds of her slit wrists were clearly visible as she reached and stumbled toward the two men, making a thick gurgling sound.

Xavier leaped left, up onto the bed, where he discovered the sheets were tacky with blood, a sticky box cutter lying near a pillow. Pulaski froze, staring at the girl with his mouth hanging open as she closed on him.

"Kill it!" Xavier yelled.

Pulaski dropped the lighter, grabbed the tire iron with both hands, and drove the sharp end into her belly. The girl grabbed at him, getting a fistful of his hair and pulling herself forward. The pipe fitter shrieked and jerked away, but she didn't let go and stumbled after him, the tire iron poking out of her.

Xavier came in from the side, throwing a hammer blow of a punch at the side of her head, then three more. The dead girl's head rocked to the side and she fell against the TV, knocking it over, but not releasing Pulaski's hair, dragging him down as he yelled, "Get it off me!"

Xavier was about to land another punch, but she turned her head and he faced snapping teeth. Instead he jumped back, looking around as his shoe crushed a plastic bong lying on the floor.

The girl got her other hand knotted into Pulaski's hair, and she pulled.

"Ah, Jesus, Jesus, *Jesus!*" Pulaski strained back against her, trying to pry her fingers loose, but she was a big girl, bigger than him, and now she was bringing those snapping teeth to his face.

Hanging on a wall near the corner was an Aztec calendar with a ferocious-looking face at its center, crossed spears behind it. Xavier darted that way but ignored the spears (he figured they were cheap replicas) and snatched something off the floor beneath the calendar. He came up with a red obsidian statuette of an Aztec fertility god with a gigantic, curving penis. It was solid and heavy, and he raised it over his head and brought it crashing down on the girl's skull.

There was a crunch, and her fingers jerked open. Pulaski fell backward. Xavier hit her again in the same spot, grunting with the force of the swing, and her head caved in. The girl's body slumped against the wall and slid over onto the floor.

Both men were breathing hard, and neither spoke for a moment. Finally Pulaski approached and yanked the tire iron out of her belly. "The head," he gasped.

Xavier swallowed hard and nodded. "The head." He tossed the fertility god onto a leather sofa.

"I thought I was gonna piss myself," Pulaski said, looking at the priest. "But I was so scared, I don't think I could have squeezed a drop if I wanted to."

Xavier checked the front of his jeans. "I thought I did piss myself."

They stared at each other, laughing like two crazy people, and then looked at their watches in the glow from the window. "We're out of time," Pulaski said.

They searched the room quickly, neither wanting to go through all this and leave empty-handed. They were rewarded. In the closet, hidden behind stacks of sneaker boxes, they found a combat shotgun, a pair of automatic handguns, and a big, snub-nosed .44 Bulldog revolver. Inside several of the shoe boxes they found boxes of ammo for everything. A Timberland boot box held half a dozen loaded magazines for an assault rifle.

They found the AK-47 concealed in a cutout hollow in the bed's box spring.

"Satisfied?" Xavier asked.

Pulaski grinned, loading the shotgun.

They tore apart the closet until they found a pair of nylon gym bags, putting the handguns and magazines in one, the boxes of ammo in the other. Xavier checked the Bulldog, found it loaded, and slipped it into a pocket of his jeans. He slung the AK-47 over a shoulder, and they went back downstairs, stopping again in the doorway.

The fire had gone out, and once again bodies moved slowly through the fog. There were more of them now.

"Use your lighter," Xavier said. Pulaski lit it, holding it high and moving it up and down, like a nightclub owner signaling a stand-up comic that his time was almost up. There was no response from the darkness of the looted dollar store. Xavier checked his watch. They had been gone for forty minutes.

"Do it again." Xavier said.

Pulaski did, and then they waited. Nothing. "They're gone. The teacher did what you told him and took off. We're on our own," Pulaski said, nudging the priest with his elbow. "Let's find a back way out of here."

Xavier stared at the dark shop across the street, imagining Alden trying to get the two teenagers out of the city alive, knowing the man wouldn't make it. The list of people Xavier had failed just added three more names.

A small shadow emerged onto the far sidewalk, and there was a glimmer of fire. A second later there was a whoosh as the Molotov cocktail sailed through the fog, away from the streetlight. Flames spreading across the hood of a car got the dead moving in that direction, an eerie keening rising from the shuffling figures. Within minutes the street was clear, and the two men hustled back to their group. There were smiles of relief all around.

"I'm sorry it took so long," Snake said, grinning at the priest. "I forgot that you guys had the Zippo, and I had to dig through the counter back there to find another lighter."

Xavier shook the boy's hand. "You did great." He hefted one of the gym bags, and Pulaski showed them the shotgun. "We all did. We'll figure out the weapons later. Right now we should get out of here, find a place to hole up until morning." He dug a few magazines out of the bag and shoved them in his pockets, then slipped the Russian assault rifle off his shoulder.

Pulaski pointed his chin at it. "You know how to use that?"

The priest inserted the magazine, snapped back the arming bolt, and thumbed the weapon to safe. His face turned grim. "Yes." Then he led them out the back.

FOURTEEN

Berkeley

It was close to midnight by the time they finished up, and Skye thought she might just collapse right where she was and sleep on the tar roof. Everything ached; her knees and thighs burned from holding the same position for hours, her right shoulder felt like someone had been hitting it with a hammer, and her arms were iron bars. Were it not for the soft, yellow ear protectors Taylor had given her, she knew she would also be deaf.

"You did well for a first-timer," Sgt. Postman said. "It's about repetition and discipline, but talent plays a part. You're not afraid to pull the trigger, and that's important. And you listen, even more important. Practice will make you better."

Skye smiled, gathering from Taylor's expression that the sergeant didn't hand out many compliments.

"We're almost done," Postman said.

"Almost?" she asked. Was he kidding?

"You're not finished until you clean your weapon, lady." Postman produced a cleaning kit, informing her it was an extra and hers to keep. Apparently he had been planning this for a while. Then the two soldiers spent an hour teaching her how to break down the M4 and how to clean, oil, and reassemble the weapon so that it was ready for action. This was all done by the glow of a flashlight.

"I'll clean the sniper tonight," Postman said, "but only this once." He threw her a wink.

Taylor walked with her to the other side of the roof, where he had spread a poncho out on the tar. "Use your pack for a pillow," he said.

She eyed the lumpy camouflage backpack, filled with MREs and spare magazines. It sure wasn't the pile of down pillows on her bed back in Reno.

Taylor chuckled. "You'll be asleep so fast you won't even notice it."

But she wasn't. Her tired body was loaded with adrenaline from the evening's shooting, and now that she had time to sit and really look around, she was too awed by what she saw to close her eyes. Berkeley lay in darkness, vast stretches of black punctuated by tiny pockets of light, generators or perhaps patches of the power grid that hadn't gone down yet. None were close to them. Fires burned in the night, some as small as a lone, burning vehicle, others wild infernos as entire blocks burned unchecked. The air reeked of smoke.

The bay was a flat black field with only the occasional pinpoint of light, a small boat maybe, or buoys, and the great city beyond was burning. The Bay Bridge, normally a ribbon of light, was nothing but a silhouette, and she couldn't even see the Golden Gate. Some aircraft flew high above, their blinking lights no different than on any other night, and there were helicopters buzzing over San Francisco, though fewer than had been there when the sun was up. Nothing flew over Berkeley. A light fog was coming in, and soon the city across the water would be masked.

A ghost town, she thought.

She watched Taylor and Postman break down their own weapons

and begin cleaning them, hands moving with practiced efficiency. She had been clumsy and wanted to be able to do it with their speed and confidence.

Skye had learned so much today, and aching more than her muscles was her head, trying to remember and process the day's many lessons. Sgt. Postman was a good teacher, direct and patient, but also quick to correct with a stern voice or firm grip when ignorant hands did something wrong. Very different from the weary, soft, and even bitter teachers in high school. The sergeant knew his job well and insisted that you learn, without excuses.

He had started with the assault rifle, the M4, explaining the basic structure. She learned how to load a magazine, how to load the magazine into the rifle ("It is not a *gun*, lady"), and how to arm it with the charging handle. Each magazine held thirty rounds, and the rifle had an effective range of five hundred meters. She was shown where the spent brass was ejected, how to "safe" the weapon and eject an empty magazine, and how to switch from single-shot semiauto to a three-round automatic burst. He told her full auto was a waste of ammo, and told her if he ever caught her switched to "rock and roll" she would do push-ups until her arms turned to Jell-O. She spent an hour "snapping in" with the unloaded rifle, as Postman showed her how to hold it, how to fit it into the hollow of her shoulder, and where to rest her cheek. He taught her about safety, *Lord* how he went on about safety.

"Tell me about the scope," Skye said.

He shook his head in disgust. "That is a sight, an ACOG sight to be precise. It's a combat sight designed for quick use."

She looked through it. A pair of radiant green chevrons seemed to float in the air, points used to mark the target, and not unlike a video game. "Does it see in the dark?" He said it did not.

The M4 didn't kick as much as she expected, and after the first magazine she barely noticed it at all. Postman put her right to work on targets in the street below, and she spent more than two hours killing zombies. It was a total rush. She also learned that a head shot was not an easy thing to make, and Skye sent more than her share of bullets whining off pavement and brick buildings, or *thunking* harmlessly into chests and arms and legs, which didn't bother the tangos one bit.

"The human head is only about five point nine inches wide to begin with," the sergeant explained. "The farther away from it you are, the smaller it gets."

She missed a lot. She hit a lot of dead flesh to no effect. The *kills*, however, those were the *real* rush. Seeing one of the walking dead stiffen and collapse as one of her bullets found its mark, that puff of pink mist and gray matter that popped when her shot went where it was supposed to, that was worth every ache and pain.

"Understand that hitting a target from a stationary position is much different than from a vehicle—"

"Which is almost impossible," Taylor added.

"—or while walking."

She nodded at the sergeant. "I want to learn that too."

The soldiers looked at each other and laughed. "Well, Miss Dennison, I was kind of hoping we'd link up with our troops and get you someplace safe before we had to teach you the advanced stuff."

Skye blushed. She didn't *want* to be shipped off like some refugee. She wanted an M4 in her hands all the time, to be a hunter, not a victim.

Postman had worked with young soldiers for many years, not only at home but in both Afghanistan and Iraq. Those soldiers were boys who had seen friends killed, whose childhood was quickly stripped away by the brutality of war. He saw something in the girl's eyes he knew well, something he appreciated as a professional, but also found a little sad. "Back to work."

The late-summer sun took its time going down, and they had

enough light to use the assault rifle until around nine. Then the sergeant introduced her to the M24. "The fancy name for this is the M24E-XM2010. Got all that?"

"Not a bit of it," she answered.

"Wiseass. Doesn't matter, it's just an improved variation of the basic M24 sniper rifle, very different from the M4." And he was right. Everything about it was different: longer, heavier, harder to handle, and with a completely different balance. It had a snap-out bipod to keep it steady ("But a sandbag or a pack as a shooting platform is best") and carried only five big .300 bullets in a stubby magazine. At the end was a long suppressor designed to reduce noise and flash and keep the recoil manageable. This rifle did have a scope, Postman explained, which could be swapped out for another capable of night vision.

The sergeant went through all the same procedures as with the assault rifle: loading, proper grip and sighting, and more safety. In the last of the light he had her fire five rounds, and she discovered that it kicked like a bastard. She missed with three; grazed a hip, which succeeded in spinning the corpse in a half circle; and blew off an arm with her last bullet. Not a head shot among them.

Postman spoke about curved trajectories, minute of angle, vectors and fractions of gravity, range, crosswinds, and leading the target. It was an incomprehensible jumble, and not understanding made her angry since she had always thought of herself as a fast learner.

The sergeant saw her frustration and said, "Our snipers go to school for months just to learn the fundamentals. Don't expect to pick it up in a couple of hours."

That helped a little.

"Just remember some basics," he continued. "The farther away from the target you are, the more the bullet drops, so the higher above the mark you have to aim. Fire a little bit in front of moving targets, where they're *going* to be when the bullet gets there. The rest is Kentucky windage."

"What?" she asked.

He smiled. "Guessing. Shooting and adjusting until you get it right."

"Why didn't you just say that first?"

"Because it burns through your ammo. Remember to steady your breathing and let it out slowly as you fire. Don't forget to relocate. That's one of the most important lessons a sniper learns."

Taylor was watching her face and saw her eyebrow go up. "Changing position after a couple of shots," he said. "The longer you stay put, the easier it is for your targets to find you. Movement equals life."

They were words she would remember.

"But we've been shooting from the same place for hours," she said. "They keep coming."

Postman looked at the street. The fog didn't reach this far in from the bay, and there was a half moon above. It revealed hundreds of corpses congregating below, all facing the building from which they were shooting, steadily pressing forward. "Yeah, I noticed. They seem drawn to the gunfire."

"So explain why that's not bad, if movement is life."

"Well, for one thing they can't shoot back. And I don't really think they're smart enough to figure out how to get up here." He gestured out at the town. "We didn't see a single freak on a rooftop, did we? They're more like cattle." He snapped on the night scope and gave her back the rifle. This time Skye scored four hits, including a head shot. That one just disintegrated from the neck up.

"Holy shit," she whispered.

"Yeah, holy shit," Postman said, laughing. "At short range, with that caliber bullet, you could blow the head off a cow."

Skye looked at the big rifle in her hands. Its power was humbling.

Now, as she stretched out on the poncho, her M4 loaded and resting beside her, she looked up at clouds tinted silver by moonlight, stars darting in and out of them high above. It was the same sky that had been there last night, but tonight the world it looked down upon was very, very different. Had it only been this morning when everything changed? Her mom and sister laughing on the grass in front of the dorm, Dad grumbling good-naturedly about carrying luggage . . . It felt like a lifetime had passed since then. Thoughts of her family carried her off to sleep.

She had a nightmare.

An explosion. Snarling. Gunfire.

"Skye! Skye, get out!"

Not a dream. The dead surged through the rooftop door, which had been shredded by Taylor's claymore, spilling out in a tumble, scrambling to their feet, still more pouring out behind them. Sgt. Postman was buried beneath thrashing shapes, his legs kicking as a dozen corpses tore at him. Taylor was ten feet away and on one knee, firing and dropping shapes in the doorway. Not enough of them.

"Move!" he screamed. *"Skye, move, move!"*

Bodies fell, only to have more stagger over them. Taylor dropped an empty magazine, reloaded, and started firing again. "Get off the roof!" he shouted. Snarling shapes slammed into him, bringing the young soldier down with an angry yell. Teeth and hands tore at him, and in seconds his yelling turned to a thick gurgle.

Skye was on her feet. Postman had stopped moving, and she couldn't even see Taylor under the pile of hungry fiends. More corpses stumbled through the door, looking around, spotting Skye. She snatched up her rifle and grabbed the pack she had been using as a pillow, racing across the roof and throwing it over the side. She threw the rifle strap around her neck as the dead pursued her toward the drop-off.

With one hand she grabbed the arched top of the ladder and swung over, her sneakers slipping on the rungs, and she hurried down. Arms shot down at her over the low wall, a fist catching some of her hair. She screamed and fought to pull free as another hand groped for a hold of its own. Skye gripped the sides of the ladder and swung her legs out, letting her full body weight drop. Hair came loose with a ripping sound, and she screamed as she clutched at the metal rungs, stopping her descent before she could free-fall. Moans came from above as she descended, feet moving fast.

The alley would be filled with the dead, she thought, standing and waiting for her. They would pull her off the ladder and tear her apart. When her feet hit the asphalt she spun, gripping the rifle and bringing it up quickly, determined to take as many with her as she could.

The alley was empty in both directions.

She found her pack and pulled it on, slinging the rifle strap properly around her neck as she had been shown, taking the weapon in both hands. At the top of the ladder, agitated shapes still clawed at the air. She wanted to go back up there, to kill the things attacking the men who had saved her life, knowing it was too late. Tears sprang into her eyes and she wiped at them savagely, shaking her head. No more, she told herself.

Skye put the rifle to her shoulder, switched off the safety, and jogged into the night.

FIFTEEN

Air Lieutenant Vladimir Yurish was lean and tall, almost too tall to be a helicopter pilot, even in the Russian Federation. He kept his knobby head shaved bald, and with his flattened nose, broad lips, and protruding ears, he looked like something from a medieval fairy tale. Something that lived under a bridge. His colleagues back home affectionately called him the Troll.

It had never bothered him and hadn't kept Anya from loving him as a husband for fifteen years. Their three-year-old, Lita, had often taken his face in her small hands and said, "handsome," then kissed him on the forehead. Both were gone now, lost in an automobile accident four years ago, during a simple trip to buy groceries. It still hurt, and he thought about them every day. Seeing what the world had become, however, made him quietly grateful that they had not lived. Losing them was devastating, but he couldn't imagine the pain of knowing they had turned into what was down there.

No, the Troll would never be one of the handsome faces on the recruiting posters. He was, however, an exceptional pilot, and that was why he was here in the United States. The Federation was purchasing a hundred UH-60A Black Hawks, and Lt. Yurish and several others had been sent here to qualify as instructors for the new machines.

He liked the Black Hawk, liked the high quality with which it was manufactured and the relative ease of maintenance (at least compared to Russian birds). He liked the United States even more: its prosperity and opportunity, the friendly people and smiling faces, the availability of anything a person could ever want. A week ago if someone had told him he would be flying over a U.S. city with a door gunner firing down into crowds of Americans, he would have said they were drunk or insane. But then, the shapes down there weren't really Americans anymore, were they?

"Lieutenant, orbit right, got a cluster at three o'clock." The door gunner's voice came through the intercom.

"Copy," Vlad said. He worked the antitorque pedals and the cyclic between his knees and moved the helicopter into a slow orbit to the right. The machine gun mounted in the open right door chattered. Sixty-four feet long and seven feet wide, five tons unloaded, the Sikorsky UH-60 could carry eleven troops with full gear (more if it had to) while blasting along at 183 miles per hour, and had a ceiling of nineteen thousand feet. It was a comfortable aircraft to fly, but despite the relaxed look on Vlad's unfortunately shaped face, it—like all helicopters—required constant control and correction, especially during combat operations. No one was shooting at him, but he was flying low over an urban area, and a mistake could put him and his crew on the ground in seconds. He had no desire to be down there.

"Get some, fuckers," his gunner said, letting off short bursts.

Vlad's co-pilot, an American (Vlad was the only Russian), looked out the right window and said, "There's more up the block, RJ. Coming around that school bus."

Between bursts the gunner grunted, "Got it."

Groundhog-7, the call sign for Vlad's Black Hawk, was circling Thomas Jefferson High School in the suburbs of Fresno, the streets and buildings passing one hundred feet beneath them. A late-summer evening was coming on, the sky a riot of streaking pink clouds and skies fading through blue into navy and purple, a ten-knot wind coming in from the distant Pacific. Vlad held a steady orbit as his gunner—he had only one, who shifted back and forth between the port and starboard weapons as needed—provided cover for the operation below. Groundhog-7 was the only bird assigned, the only one that could be spared. They actually had more aircraft than pilots, which was why Air Lieutenant Yurish had been given command of this ship.

"RJ," the co-pilot said, a second lieutenant named Conroy, "you missed all the freaks and just lit up the bus."

"It ain't as easy as it looks," RJ replied.

The co-pilot snorted. "Hell, didn't you play video games?"

"You're welcome to pop back here and take over the trigger, el-tee. I'll sit up front and help the Mad Russian fly this pig."

"Nyet!" Vladimir barked. "This is complex machinery and it requires more than a grammar school education, RJ. Lieutenant Conroy has already discovered this, much to his dismay."

"Copy that," RJ said, laughing. Conroy grinned as Vlad watched his instruments and kept the bird in a perfect, lazy right-hand circle. The fenced football field of Thomas Jefferson was being used as a refugee collection point, and a single company of National Guardsmen was trying to maintain its perimeter, handle the civilians at the gate, and protect the growing line of them stretching out well into the high school's parking lot. It was a slow process, made so because every refugee had to be checked for bites before being allowed to enter. Those bitten were escorted off by MPs, and Vlad tried not to speculate on what happened to them. It was necessary, though. The same type of operation had been tried up and down the coast, and failure to check for bites, letting the infected inside the perimeter, had ended in disaster.

"Got a side street with lots of targets," RJ called.

Vlad slowed and hovered for a moment while the gunner chopped into them, then resumed his orbit.

Trucks waited in a row on the fifty-yard line, and they would serve as transportation to get the refugees to Lemoore. Naval Air Station Lemoore was a much more secure facility, Vlad's assigned base since the crisis began, and could handle the mass of fleeing civilians. At least it would put more secure fencing between them and the freaks, as the Americans had taken to calling them. The problem below was immediately obvious. A thousand people wandered and waited on the football field, with close to a thousand more lined up at the gates. There were only twenty trucks.

RJ was switching out ammo boxes in the back, and Conroy was on the radio relaying the status of the operation back to base. As twilight fell and a deepening gloom descended over the streets, the only way to distinguish live refugees from the dead was the speed of their movement. The National Guard had erected generator-powered lights on the field— the only source of illumination in this part of blacked-out Fresno—and loudspeakers blared a repeating message that all civilians should immediately make their way to the high school. It was working to some extent, as fleeing people raced through the streets from all directions, almost exclusively on foot since the roads were blocked by fields of abandoned cars. The problem was that the dead were drawn not only to the running figures, but to the sound of the loudspeakers as well.

The gunner's M240 woke up as he unleashed long lines of tracer ammo down into the gloom. Several minutes later Vlad heard him curse. "Troll, we got a problem," the gunner said. Vlad enjoyed the nickname, had taught it to his new comrades, and someone had even painted it on his flight helmet. "This isn't doing a damn bit of good. The freaks aren't going down."

"Are you even hitting them?" Conroy asked. "I can barely see them down there."

"Yes, *sir*, but it just chews them up. A few fall, maybe one in ten, but the rest just keep coming. It's almost impossible to make a head shot."

"Stay on it," Vlad ordered.

"Roger that."

Both pilot and co-pilot could see that the gunner was right; the automatic fire was having minimal effect. On the ground, the guardsmen were engaging "leakers" that had made it through the Black Hawk's suppression fire. There were plenty of them, coming down side streets and across parking lots, piling up against the football field's fence. The civilians drew closer to the trucks as the vastly outnumbered guardsmen fired at the fence. At the main gates, panic erupted.

The line to get in was five to six people wide and nearly fifty yards long, creeping forward imperceptibly as refugees were slowly cleared to enter. One platoon of guardsmen was strung out along its length on both sides, looking outward. When slouching corpses began coming through the cars in the lot and closing on the line as rifle shots started to light off like strings of firecrackers, the refugee mass began to scream and push forward.

When the first of the undead blundered into the line and took down an elderly man, all remaining order disintegrated. People began shoving each other out of the way, trampling those unfortunate enough to fall. Hands gouged at faces and fists were thrown, and the shrieks of frightened children in their parents' arms added to the chorus of fear.

Vlad saw it happening and brought the Black Hawk into a low hover off to the left of the mob, while RJ poured fire into the shapes appearing out of the dusk. His bullets chopped into windshields, hoods, dead flesh, and asphalt as he tried to keep the dead away from the line. Through the windscreen, Vlad saw a young officer waving his arms frantically as his men struggled to close the gates to the field.

"Call this in," Vlad ordered, and Conroy started speaking to Lemoore.

The crowd surged against the closing gates, and farther back the line came apart as people realized their sanctuary was being cut off. They scattered and ran back into the neighborhood.

The dead pursued them.

"Weapon dry," RJ shouted, unclipping from his safety line and scuttling across to the M240 in the port opening, clipping back in. Vlad twitched the cyclic, and the big bird slid sideways, over the heads of the crowd, putting RJ's gun in position. The gunner went to work, tracers flashing in undulating lines.

Out on the football field, truck engines fired and headlights came on as the big vehicles began to roll into a column, each packed beyond capacity with refugees. Many more tried to climb onto rear bumpers, hoods, and grilles, a few falling to be crushed beneath unstopping tires. The trucks grumbled toward the gates, where determined civilians who had succeeded in pushing their way in now scattered to avoid being run down. Guardsmen backed away from the perimeter, forming up around the moving vehicles.

"Groundhog-Seven, Ranch House," the controller at NAS Lemoore said in Vladimir's earpiece.

"Seven copies," Vlad responded.

"Groundhog, Echo transport is pulling out and will return to base in convoy."

"Ranch House," Vlad said, "we have already reported that there are not enough trucks."

"Affirmative, Groundhog. The rest will have to follow on foot. Echo Company will remain on the ground as security and walk them in. You will provide air cover as long as possible."

Vlad shook his head. The trucks had a long run through Fresno and the surrounding open country before reaching the base. That would leave, what? About two hundred men? To protect a thousand civilians as they traveled on foot, through an overrun city, at night, with one ineffective Black Hawk above. Insanity. Vlad asked for

Ranch House to repeat its orders, and got the same reply. He muttered something in Russian that his co-pilot and gunner couldn't interpret but understood well enough.

"Confirm, Groundhog-Seven."

"*Da, da*, Groundhog-Seven confirms." More Russian then, a hot string of it intended for the controller, who didn't reply.

The trucks passed through the open gates and out into the parking lot, as people poured after them. Guardsmen paired up and stayed well out to the sides, as fearful of what the panicked crowd might do as they were of the dead, and within minutes they were engaging targets with their rifles. The trucks picked up speed, and as their taillights vanished into the neighborhood, leaving the refugees on foot behind, a cry of despair went up that briefly drowned out the moans of the dead.

Vlad stayed overhead, RJ doing his best to chop away at stiff shapes limping toward the flow of people. Scattered riflemen fought desperate battles on all sides, quickly depleting their ammo as the huge group moved slowly, the dead coming at them from all sides, snatching victims and dragging them into the shadows.

An hour later RJ reported that both his weapons were dry, and the gauges up front showed that the Black Hawk's gas tank was soon to be in the same condition. Vlad informed Ranch House that he was bingo fuel, and base ordered him home. He did as ordered. He would not be allowed to refuel and go back out.

Back at Lemoore, Vlad sat on a crate near the main gates, chain-smoking and waiting. Sixteen of the twenty trucks arrived four hours after leaving the football field, the drivers staring out their windshields with haunted eyes. The thousand refugees traveling on foot and the company of men assigned to guard them didn't show up until two days later.

When they did, they were dull-eyed corpses rattling the fence.

SIXTEEN

The great ship turned and put the vast Pacific to her stern, making her way toward the mouth of the bay. The helmsman didn't need landmarks; the complex navigational gear knew where it was going, but they were overdue to meet up with a tug to guide them and a harbor pilot to safely take them into the bay. The absence of lights on the Golden Gate Bridge was an unusual sight. Fires burned there instead, lines of stopped cars lighting off one by one as gas tanks exploded. It was surreal, but few aboard were in a position to notice.

Lieutenant (junior grade) Doug Mosey stood with a radio microphone in his hand, calling the hangar deck, the last place the XO had reported his position. There was no answer. Throughout the bridge, enlisted men and women tried to remain calm at their stations and weren't doing a very good job of it. They took their cues from the only officer on deck, a twenty-seven-year-old JG left to conn the greatest warship in the world, a job for which he had not yet passed qualifications.

"Lieutenant," called a petty officer wearing a headset, "combat reported in the aft machine shops, and in starboard enlisted berthing."

Mosey nodded and ran a hand over his dry lips. Combat had been reported in so many areas of the ship, and these were just the latest. Many sections did not respond to requests for situation reports and hadn't been heard from after their first, frantic calls. Several times the petty officer reported hearing gunfire in the background, indicating the presence of a security team, but most of the time there had just been screaming.

As the USS *Nimitz* approached the bridge—a San Francisco icon— the navigation computer automatically relinquished control to manual conning, assuming, as it had been programmed to do, that a qualified harbor pilot who knew the bay was aboard. A young woman in khaki, a quartermaster second class or QM-2, reported the change. Mosey didn't acknowledge her, so she repeated it. The officer was staring out the bridge windows. Tiny, flaming objects were falling from the Golden Gate and vanishing into the dark waters below.

"Lieutenant," she said firmly, "we are on manual navigation and the helm is awaiting orders."

"Slow to one-third," he said. "Maintain present course."

The bridge crew glanced at each other.

"Try CINCPAC again," Mosey said. The last order from Commander-in-Chief, Pacific, had been for *Nimitz* to steam into San Francisco Bay and drop anchor, in order to provide assistance to both civilian and military authorities attempting to control an unspecified "civil uprising." There had been no further orders, and *Nimitz* had not been able to reach them since.

After a couple of minutes, "CINCPAC does not respond, Lieutenant."

Of course. No one was responding. And now the ship that had been sent to provide protection was in need of rescue. Mosey looked out the bridge wing down onto the massive deck, lit by whatever landing and work lights they had been able to switch on. In the light and shadow he saw two men in purple refueling shirts—"grapes," they were called—running past the number one catapult, a crowd of sailors limping after them.

Nimitz began to pass beneath the Golden Gate. A pair of flaming bodies dropped out of the sky and slammed onto the deck. After a moment, one of them began to drag itself away.

Coming back from a Far East tour, *Nimitz* had first stopped in Hawaii for two days before heading east, and then up the West Coast. Her support ships dispersed, and the air group had flown off to their home port in Seattle, leaving the cavernlike hangar deck empty of aircraft except for the ship's helos.

"Combat reported in the reactor spaces," said the petty officer.

Mosey spun to look at him. "Did you hear any weapons fire?"

"Negative, sir." The young man swallowed hard. "Only . . . only moaning."

Midway up the California coast, things had gotten strange and then quickly stepped over the line into madness. It had been those SEALs they brought on board. A lone helo carrying a team of special operators had flown in from Los Angeles, reporting casualties on board. The eight men had been mixing it up in some kind of "civil disturbance" and were pretty badly torn up, having to be taken off the helo on litters and whisked down to the medical facilities. Mosey heard scuttlebutt about *bite wounds*, of all things.

The attacks started in sick bay, and then spread. Within an hour, what looked like a full-blown mutiny was under way. A mutiny? On an aircraft carrier? Ridiculous. But in the midst of it the admiral had been killed, the captain went missing and was presumed dead, and the executive officer had taken command of the ship.

"Sir," said the quartermaster, "the nav gear indicates we need to come right." She was nervous. None of them had ever entered San Francisco's waters before—there hadn't been an active naval base here for many years—and this was unknown territory. The regulations required that a knowledgeable harbor pilot take command of the bridge to guide them in. They should have remained offshore until one arrived.

More bodies were slamming onto the deck from the bridge above, several of them burning. Most started moving again after impact, and Mosey couldn't take his eyes away from the sight. There was no sign of the grapes who had been chased across the deck a moment ago.

"Lieutenant, we need to reduce speed and come right."

Mosey rubbed at his lips again, still staring out the window. The fighting was everywhere, seemingly in every compartment, and cries for help choked the intercom, frightened voices shouting over each other. The XO had put Mosey, the only officer around, in command and left to lead a large security detail in an attempt to retake the ship. That had been two hours ago, and it was twenty minutes since he had last called in.

The quartermaster appeared beside Mosey and gripped her senior officer's upper arm tightly, her voice coming through clenched teeth. "Sir, we are going too fast, and if you do not maneuver this ship, we are going to run into Alcatraz. Do you read me, Lieutenant?"

Nimitz cleared the Golden Gate, and the city came into view on the right. The ship's bridge went silent as everyone stared. San Francisco was blacked out. Heavy smoke rose in pillars visible against the lighter evening sky, and fires raged within the city. One skyscraper's top dozen floors were ablaze, making it look like a giant birthday candle. The steep boulevards and the sweeping Embarcadero, normally lined with headlights, were black, and the famous pier that usually glowed like a carnival was a silhouette sprinkled with small fires. The blinking lights of a lone helicopter drifted high above the city.

"It's dead," Mosey whispered.

Nimitz sliced through the choppy waters at one-third its max steaming power, throwing a powerful wake from its steep, razored bow. An alarm went off, and another young man yelled, "Sir, we have a collision warning left at zero-four-zero degrees."

The quartermaster ran to her terminal. "Lieutenant. *Lieutenant!*" She swore and turned to the helmsman. "Come right fifteen degrees. Slow to seven knots."

The young man spun his tiny wheel—a chrome disc the size of a dinner plate, something that always shocked visitors to the bridge of such a massive vessel—and the great ship began to turn, although slowly. The collision alarm kept sounding. Before the order to slow could be executed, the hatch to the bridge banged open, and Mosey spun around. "Why isn't that secured?" he demanded.

Two men came through, the younger one in bloody blue camouflage with a rifle over his shoulder, half carrying, half dragging an older man in red-soaked khakis. Mosey immediately recognized the XO, who was trying to raise his head. A sailor standing the port watch with a big pair of binoculars around his neck looked through the open hatch and saw the passageway filled with stumbling, bloody sailors, groaning and coming toward the opening. He slammed the metal hatch and dogged the handle, engaging the mechanical device that would secure the door.

"I thought he was dead," the security man said, his voice shaking. "Thought I lost him in the passageway, but he's moving again. He's hurt bad."

Mosey saw that the younger sailor's sleeves were hanging in tatters, the flesh of his arms ragged with bites and bleeding. He was pale and barely finished speaking before he lost his grip on the XO and sagged against a bulkhead, sliding to the floor and bleeding out. His eyes were open, but glassy and far away, no longer seeing. The lieutenant ran to the XO and dropped to his knees beside him, turning him over.

The helmsman's maneuver hadn't been quite enough, and as *Nimitz* passed the fabled prison island—much, much too close—it scraped its port-side hull across a ridge of sunken rock. More warning bells sounded, and the red general quarters bridge lights cast them all in a hellish glow as the warship shuddered, hard enough to throw several people off their feet. *Nimitz* turned away, a sixty-foot gash torn in her outer hull, which immediately began to fill with seawater.

The XO let out a gasp as Mosey turned him onto his back, revealing a torn throat already congealing with blood, eyes turned to a cloudy gray. He grabbed Mosey's head in both hands and pulled him down, biting off the younger officer's lower lip and a chunk of his chin. The lieutenant screamed as the XO's next bite tore out his jugular, spraying the nearby helmsman.

It went quickly after that. The XO, soon accompanied by the sailor who had carried him here, finished off the unarmed bridge crew in minutes. A few tried to escape, caught at the secured hatch while they struggled to open it. The female quartermaster managed to dodge reaching arms and snapping teeth, yanking the hatch open only to be pulled to her death by the corpses waiting on the other side.

Within five minutes the bridge was manned by bodies that shuffled and bumped against one another, oblivious to the many warnings coming from consoles and the blaring alarms of loudspeakers. *Nimitz* pushed on through San Francisco Bay in a slow turn to the right, its helm unattended. On several of the lower decks, automated watertight doors closed in response to the hull breach, trapping the living and the dead together in dark spaces. The compartmentalized design of the outer hull prevented the flooding from spreading, but the damaged section took on so many tons of water that the aircraft carrier began listing forward and to port, pulling it slowly away from its former heading.

In its journey across the bay, *Nimitz* scraped the long side of a drifting freighter crewed only by the dead, ripping off protruding radar domes and gun mounts. Still in a slow right arc, the carrier rounded the tip of San Francisco and headed for the Bay Bridge. Treasure Island, a former naval base turning into a trendy community of condos, passed close on the left, and without a pilot to steer clear, the warship ran across shoals at roughly the same point in its damaged hull, tearing it open further. More seawater poured in, and the vessel pulled left. The same side of its flight deck rubbed against one of the massive concrete and steel supports of the Bay Bridge, shredding metal and rubberized decking, dragging the ship even more sharply to port.

The ship's computer reacted to the new damage—and lack of response to its warnings—by shutting down forward propulsion. *Nimitz* was adrift, now turned almost due east by the latest impact and the weight of the incoming water. Slowing, but momentum still carrying it along at eleven knots, the monstrous ship was an unstoppable force. A fifteen-foot sailboat holding a dozen refugees who had managed to get out of Oakland (none of whom knew how to crew a sailboat) blundered helplessly into the shadow of the looming aircraft carrier. The sailboat snapped in half and was pulled under in seconds.

Nimitz drifted toward the western tip of Oakland and finally found a large enough shoal to stop it, grounding in a frightful squeal of tearing metal and grinding rock. Silt and mud sucked at the hull, creating a vacuum and holding the ship tightly to the shallow bottom. As before, seawater rushed in and filled whatever space it could before the engineering design allowed it to go no further. *Nimitz* came to rest a half mile off shore, listing on an eight-degree angle to port.

Without the appropriate responses to its queries, the master computer shut down one reactor and reduced power on the other so that it could run internal systems only. There was power but no propulsion. Scattered, desperate battles flared in isolated spaces of the ship and then died out. Bodies thumped against metal bulkheads or floundered in flooded compartments; feet dragged across decking and stumbled up and down stairways, low croaks and moans echoing throughout miles of passageways.

America's greatest naval weapon was now a ship of the dead.

FREE FALL

SEVENTEEN

For most, questions about how and where the Omega Virus started, how it managed to spread so fast, and why no one was prepared to deal with it ceased to matter. It was here, it was a pandemic, and for most it was an extinction-level event. For those who cared, the generally agreed-upon outbreak date for OV was mid-August. The first weeks of the plague, and the devastation that came with it, forced the remaining survivors to wonder if life had moved into its final act.

For many of them, that question was swiftly answered.

Bakersfield

Dr. Charles Emmett walked slowly up a fire stairwell, pushed open a door, and stepped out onto a gravel roof. Beneath him, Francis Miller Presbyterian Hospital was coming apart.

The news had begun calling it the Omega Virus, OV, before all broadcasting ceased. Their declaration was echoed by many of his colleagues: If you were bitten by the dead, you perished and turned.

The media liked it simple. Dr. Emmett knew there was something more complex and far more sinister at work. It took him nearly two weeks before he was certain, and by then, communication beyond the hospital walls had ceased to exist. He had attempted to use the military radios of the troops standing guard at sandbag and barbed-wire perimeters around the building, but he had first been told they were restricted to military traffic only, and then been assured that even if he could use the equipment, he would only achieve company-level communication.

They had all learned a great deal that first day of outbreak, however. It was an experience he was sure had been repeated up and down California and across the country. Francis Miller and Bakersfield General, only a few miles away, had quickly swelled to capacity with the sick and wounded, and both hospitals were soon forced to turn patients away. Most of these people, with no place else to go, just waited in the parking lots. Those who had been bitten but not killed outright by the walking dead ended up sharing the crowded hallways and lobbies with patients suffering gunshot wounds, burns, and injuries from traffic accidents. People with broken bones, severe cuts, heart attacks, and pregnancies come due waited among the bitten. Every available bed, gurney, and wheelchair was filled.

Fatigued staff tended to the worst cases first as best they could, but still people died of their injuries in the crowded corridors without ever being seen. The deceased rose within minutes, and those same corridors turned into slaughterhouses with no way out. If the Army had not arrived in several trucks when they did, little more than a platoon's worth of soldiers, the hospital would have been overrun. As it was, more than half of the Francis Miller staff and three-quarters of the patients died in the resulting melee. Bakersfield General received no troops and folded.

Two weeks of examining both deceased and heavily restrained zombies, combined with exhaustive lab work, revealed that it was actually two viruses at work, not one. Emmett nicknamed the infection carried by the walking dead the Corpse Virus or CV, determining that not only was it carried in the fluids of the dead, it appeared to be most concentrated or virulent in the corpse's mouth. An unbitten person could still be infected by fluid contact, like a blood-borne pathogen, but not always. Even direct exposure through an open wound or orifice wasn't guaranteed to transmit every time, but a bite was a death sentence. A bite guaranteed transmission of CV one hundred percent of the time. CV brought on the horrible fever that killed within twenty-four hours and had so far proven completely immune to any medical attempts to stop or slow its progression. CV was an efficient, determined executioner.

It wasn't turning victims into the walking dead, however.

Dr. Emmett knew the few troops guarding the hospital couldn't hold forever. He took off his white coat and stethoscope and let them fall to the gravel as he made his way to the edge of the roof atop the six-story building, stopping at the narrow concrete lip. Muffled cries came from below, along with the sound of breaking glass. He looked over the side to see what appeared to be hundreds, perhaps thousands of the dead moving across the parking lot and lawns, slamming into the sandbag defenses. More of the dead shambled out of the hospital, attacking the soldiers from behind. Gunfire and screams filled the air.

Only this morning, as he had stared bleary-eyed at his files and lab reports, did he realize the mistake he and everyone else had made. There was a second virus, the *true* Omega Virus. Each of his test subjects, including himself, was hosting the dormant Omega Virus, which appeared to be localized in the brain. His realization also explained the need for massive brain trauma to stop one of the dead, or prevent turning in the first place. If the brain was destroyed, it couldn't support OV.

OV lay dormant, waiting patiently for a trigger. Death was that trigger, whether brought on by the fatal Corpse Virus, a broken neck from a fall, a gunshot wound, or old age. And the virus waiting to turn its host was within everyone he had tested. Dr. Emmett was so shaken by the hopelessness of it all that he couldn't even speculate at its origins, its abrupt appearance. Did it matter? Death was the one condition from which no one could escape, and *this* was what the next life held. In the end, it wouldn't make a difference if *anyone* learned of his discovery.

He looked at the sky and took a deep breath as the rooftop door banged open behind him with a chorus of snarls. Stepping off, leaning forward, he hoped he would land on his head.

The loss of hospitals was a scenario repeated across the state. By the end of August, streets throughout California were crowded with walking corpses dressed in scrubs, lab coats, and hospital gowns.

Long Beach

Hank Lyons lived in a two-story apartment complex not far from the industrial parks and shipyards. A single man in his fifties, he watched the news until he could stand it no longer, and then shoved as much canned food as possible into a piece of rolling luggage and headed out in his Ford Escape. Baxter, his Jack Russell terrier, rode in the front seat beside him, eyes bright and stubby tail wagging at the adventure.

The airport was shut down, the roads were rapidly jamming with panicked motorists, buildings were burning. At one point a bullet punched through his back window.

"Screw this," he told Baxter. The dog barked in agreement. Hank headed for the docks, thinking he and his dog might get aboard a ship—any ship, it didn't matter—that could carry them to safety.

He wasn't the only one with that idea. Three blocks from the port, the Escape became trapped in a sea of unmoving traffic, people streaming between the cars on foot. He snapped on Baxter's leash and joined them. Within minutes, the dead poured out of Long Beach and into the traffic jam, and people started running, dropping their bags and possessions and fighting to move faster, pushing and trampling the slow to move. Hank ditched the rolling luggage, lifted Baxter into his arms, and ran with them.

What few ships there were, tankers and freighters and car carriers, had already raised their gangplanks and were casting off. People shouted and waved, pleading for them to come back, and many even leaped into the oily water to swim after them. The dead slammed into the crowds packed along the edges of the piers. Hank sped away into a maze of long steel containers, still carrying Baxter.

The dead were in there too.

Cut off on all sides, he climbed to the roof of a forklift and hurled his dog onto the top of a rusty blue cargo container, then jumped after him. Both man and dog made it. Baxter barked in approval, and Hank discovered with relief that although several of the dead managed to climb onto the forklift, they weren't coordinated enough to make the jump and tumbled off into the gap.

Once the hordes were done with their victims on the piers, they wandered, and soon discovered two meals trapped on top of the container. By the end of the day there were more than a thousand of them surrounding the long metal box, groaning and reaching. They didn't go away, and no one came to the rescue.

Hank Lyons lasted four days in the open before lack of water claimed him. Baxter, dying of thirst himself and barely hanging on, nervously licked Hank's dead face for five minutes, until his master groaned and climbed slowly to his hands and knees. The Jack Russell danced around him happily, and then leaped into outstretched arms.

After Hank ate Baxter, he wandered to the edge of the container and fell off into a crowd that no longer cared about him.

U.S.-Mexico Border

The defense of the crossing from Tijuana, Mexico, lasted four days. The Mexican side fell first and thirty thousand corpses pushed north, both using the main road and stumbling across the shallows of the Rio Grande. Even supplemented by Army units, U.S. Border Patrol officers simply didn't have the firepower to hold them back, and the fences couldn't withstand the relentless shaking and pressing weight.

A new kind of undocumented visitor crossed the border.

Chula Vista, California, was rolled up the next day, the ranks of the dead increasing as the wave surged north. By the time it reached San Diego, the city was already on its knees. The Mexican swarm finished it off.

Riverside

Buck and Stuart stood on a mound of earth, latex-gloved hands shoved in the pockets of their FEMA Windbreakers. They wore goggles and surgical masks to shield them from the stench and the lime. The medical experts said with confidence that it was not airborne, but both men knew there wasn't yet enough research to prove that. The goggles and masks were of little use, regardless. The corpses reeked, and the lime made their eyes burn. The grumble of a nearby bulldozer forced them to shout.

"I think they just finished the new trench," Stuart said, pointing across the soccer field toward a yellow bucket loader. It huffed diesel as it rotated on its tracks, swinging its jointed arm. A line of flatbed military trucks was waiting a short distance away from the digger, cargo decks piled with bodies.

"It's going to fill right up," Buck said.

A hundred yards behind them, a helicopter sat at one end of the soccer field, its blades turning slowly. Soldiers in full chemical gear, looking like googly-eyed insects in their green chemical suits and protective hoods, relaxed as they walked in pairs around the field, rifles slung. The fighting was farther west, and this was a secure area. They were happy not to be up on the line.

The trench in front of the two men had quickly filled. A hundred feet long, it was stacked end to end with bodies covered in white powder. Several were still moving. The bulldozer was pushing earth back into the trench at the far end. Closer to the mound where Buck and Stuart stood, two men from the World Health Organization were moving along the trench, both in full white hazmat suits with plastic face shields and oxygen tanks. One carried an electronic tablet, the other a long metal probe attached to a handheld black box. He would stop at the edge, probe one of the bodies, say something to his colleague, who would tap in some data (Buck wondered how he managed to work a digital tablet in those bulky gloves), and then they would move farther down the row.

"Bet those suits are uncomfortable," Stuart said.

"Worse for the grunts." Buck nodded at a nearby pair of soldiers. "The WHO guys probably have little air conditioners in there."

They watched the men in white suits work, not even a little curious about what they were testing. Both were exhausted, dark circles under their eyes, unwilling to do more than stand on this hill of dirt and watch. Not that there was much for them to do. FEMA had sent them to organize disposal, which they had done. Their only job now was to wait for instructions and go where the chopper took them next.

They looked out at the field. "Still plenty of room for more," said Stuart.

The park was a beautiful green expanse of trees, bike trails, and sports fields at the east side of the L.A. suburb. Heavy equipment had turned it into a mass grave, and this trench was the fourteenth dug and filled since daybreak.

Plenty of room. Stuart nodded slowly. It was a physical act just to keep his eyes open. They both knew there probably wouldn't be a chance to dig and fill more trenches. The Army reported that the line was holding, but the two men had been through this yesterday in Compton. The skinnies would start slipping through the perimeter, compromising the line, and the Army would fall back or even be overwhelmed in places. It would be no different here; the only question was when. The dead were pouring out of L.A. by the tens of thousands.

Buck grimaced. "Skinnies" was a term the Army had used to refer to the local population during its ill-fated adventure in Somalia twenty-plus years earlier. Now everyone used the term, including civilians. It had gone viral, so to speak, and wasn't that just hilarious? He supposed it was appropriate, though. As many of the walking dead decayed, they shed much of their fluid (not all, he cautioned himself—they were still juicy enough to infect you) and grew emaciated, rotting skin drawing tight against their bodies and features. It was as good a name as any.

The man with the long probe stopped to jab his device toward one of the lime-coated bodies, one that was struggling to pull itself out from under other motionless corpses. The edge of the trench suddenly collapsed, and the man tumbled in on a cascade of crumbling dirt, dropping his tool, arms flailing. His buddy ran in the other direction, waving at two of the patrolling soldiers.

Buck and Stuart didn't move, didn't call out. They just watched.

The man started crawling back toward the edge, his movements slow and uncoordinated in the bulky suit. The ghoul in the lime pit caught hold of one of his legs and used it to pull itself free of the other bodies. Then it scrambled onto the man's back and began tearing at the suit. Within moments the bright red of blood splashed across the white fabric, and the man rolled onto his back in an attempt to fight off the creature. It straddled him, ripping away his mask, and then worked its face in past his raised arms, getting at the exposed flesh.

Two soldiers trotted up to the edge of the trench, raised their rifles, and fired, hitting the powdery ghoul in the head. It slumped over, and the man turned to start climbing again. One of the soldiers shifted his weapon and fired again, blowing out the back of the WHO man's head. The bulldozer didn't stop working.

Stuart yawned. "How much longer, do you think?"

Buck pulled away his goggles and rubbed at tired, stinging eyes. The soldiers had resumed their patrol, and the other WHO worker had not returned to the trench. "Probably tomorrow," Buck said. "Depends on how long it takes to put the equipment on the trucks. The line should hold that long, at least."

"North?"

"Or farther east. L.A. is done."

They watched as a teenager covered in lime and missing an arm tried to claw its way out of the trench. The bulldozer buried it.

"I heard they might pull us back to Denver," said Stuart.

Buck looked at his colleague. Had the man not been listening during the morning briefing, or was he just too tired to remember they had been told Denver was already gone? He was about to remind him when he saw men scrambling out of the cabs of the distant flatbeds, followed by the driver of the bucket loader. They all ran to the right. A moment later a Humvee came tearing across the soccer field, a soldier in the turret facing backward unloading a long stream of fifty-caliber rounds.

The dead had arrived. They came out of the trees to the left, surging through a playground and across a baseball field, an endless line of them, a thousand, ten thousand, more.

"Oh shit," Buck said. "C'mon." He tugged his friend's sleeve and they began to run for the waiting helicopter, its turbines winding up in a loud hum, the rotor blades spinning into a blur. The FEMA men waved their arms as they ran, shouting, an army of the dead behind them.

The chopper lifted off while they were still fifty yards away and banked out over Riverside. The WHO man in the helicopter's doorway took off his white hood and waved at the two running figures until they were out of sight.

Redding

Many considered Redding to be California's last population center of any significant size before the Oregon border. Stephen Farro, Redding's mayor for the past six years, stood on the sidewalk outside the small regional hospital next to his grim chief of police. A line of school buses was pulled to the curb and waiting at the entrance while hospital staff helped patients board.

"I don't see what else you can do, Steve," the chief said.

Farro didn't reply. What else? He had wrestled with that question and come up with this answer. These people had all been bitten, yet not killed by their attackers. They were infected and suffering from the fever to different extents, but there was no way to reverse it. They would soon become dangerous, a threat to the citizenry. He had a responsibility to the town.

"I've got one of my boys waiting," the chief said.

"Only one? Can he handle all this? Why not more?"

"It's Andy Pope."

Mayor Ferro looked away. He had never cared much for Andy Pope, a sly weasel of a cop who skirted right on the edge of abusing his police powers and had an obsession with both guns and violent movies. The perfect man for this job.

"He'll do fine. And I can't spare any more, not since the Army didn't show up like they promised. We got sightings not only on the edge of town, but inside as well."

The mayor looked at his chief. "We're not contained?"

"Hell no, we're not contained. Robbie Morris called in that he'd seen a mob of 'em coming down the off-ramp of I-5, then went off the air and didn't respond to calls. Derrick Link went out to have a look, and we haven't heard from him either."

Farro looked back at the buses. The patients were being told they were being moved to a quarantine area. Instead they would be driven out to the gravel quarry where Andy Pope was eagerly waiting with a scoped assault rifle. Most were likely too weak to put up much of a fight or run very far, so it wouldn't take long.

A woman in her forties and a girl of fourteen, both flushed and sweating, wearing pale blue hospital gowns, were about to climb the steps of a bus, and stopped when they saw Farro. "Steve?" the woman called.

The girl said, "You'll come to see us soon, right, Daddy?"

The mayor looked away.

Sacramento

Luther and Wanda, both dressed in the light purple scrubs of orderlies (now splashed with blood), sprinted down the sidewalk, Sacramento Memorial Hospital burning behind them. Flaming bodies were walking stiffly out of the inferno and into the street. A rifle cracked several times and then went silent. Luther carried a long-handled screwdriver and Wanda a fire extinguisher, both dripping with red and gray. The orderlies were wiping madly at their faces, rubbing their eyes. That last fight in the fire stairwell had been messy.

Corpses shuffled ahead on the sidewalk. They darted right, down the cracked cement driveway of a three-story house converted to apartments, a shabby thing sagging on its foundations. The weed-choked backyard was empty, and they bolted up the rear steps and through an open kitchen door, slamming it behind them.

The dead passed by. The orderlies found towels and scrubbed at their faces over the kitchen sink, thankful that the water was still working, gargling and spitting, rubbing some more. Then they crept upstairs, made sure it was empty, and hid in a bedroom. There was no talk about what they would do; they were too exhausted, not just from the running and fighting, but from the previous forty-eight-hour shift without sleep. Wanda passed out on the bed. Luther propped a pillow against the bedroom door and leaned back against it. He tried to sleep, but it eluded him.

He knew about the bites, about the virus and how it was transmitted. He knew about the life expectancy, and what happened after clinical death. It was the *slow burn* that frightened him now, the term the doctors used to refer to the condition following exposure to infected fluids, usually by way of the eyes, nose, mouth, or open wounds.

The zombie in the stairwell, the one wearing a security guard uniform . . . his head had *exploded* when Wanda hit him with the fire extinguisher. They both caught a face full of gore, and it had gotten into their eyes.

Slow burn. Symptoms appeared within the hour and mimicked those of an OV bite: fever, nausea, chills, delirium. It ran for twenty-four hours, the last twelve of which left the victim in a near-comatose state. A vulnerable state. At the end of the twenty-four-hour cycle, fifty percent of victims died and reanimated within minutes as the walking dead. The other half, however, awoke weak but alive, their immune system managing to fight it off.

The docs couldn't explain it, and some proposed that the virus was somehow weakened when exposed to air, as opposed to the full dose that invariably came from fluid-to-fluid contact, as in the bites. They were excited nonetheless. Not only did it mean at least some of the infected could pull through; it gave a glimmer of hope for a possible cure. Of course, none of those excited doctors were alive anymore at Sacramento Memorial. Walking around, maybe, but not alive.

The fever came on fast. Luther threw up on himself a short while later, then began slipping in and out between the sweats and shivering. Within hours he was seeing and talking to people who weren't there, and some time between the six- and twelve-hour marks, he fell onto his side, eyes closed, his breathing shallow and ragged.

In the bed, Wanda went through it all as well.

Nothing entered the house to disturb them for the next twenty-four hours.

Luther awoke groggy, his mouth dry and pasty. He needed water, and he had a cramp in his shoulder from lying on it for too long. He blinked and struggled back into a sitting position. He thought he might pass out from the effort, and when he didn't, he looked around, wondering at his surroundings. It came back quickly, and he sighed, nodding slowly. He had survived the slow burn. *Thank you, Jesus.*

Wanda snarled and lunged off the bed.

Stockton

Things couldn't be better for Vince. No more of his girlfriend whining for him to get a better job, no more of his asshole boss yelling when he was late, no one to tell him he was a fuckup. The world was his for the taking, and he was taking.

A bright yellow drop-top Corvette sat idling at the curb, and a pair of chromed .45s hung under his armpits in twin shoulder holsters. He had taken the guns and the car from a rich asshole in his garage. The man had been so busy loading groceries into the car that he hadn't seen Vince creeping up behind him with a long-handled shovel. *Whang!* The asshole went down. Half a dozen more hits to the head made sure he wasn't getting up again.

He'd burned a couple inches of rubber off the Vette's tires tear-assing around Stockton, screeching to a stop when he saw a skinny. He'd then hopped up onto the back of the seat and blazed away with the twins until it went down. He wasn't worried about ammo. The rich asshole had boxes and boxes of it in a bag behind the driver's seat. No cops hit him with lights and sirens, no one yelled for him to stop, to quit being such a fuckup. Stockton was a ghost town. It was his town.

A trip to a jewelry store and a smashed case put gold around his neck and diamonds on his fingers. Now for the big score. He faced a pair of glass doors, grinned, and shouted, "My town!" as he heaved a cinder block through one of them. Vince stepped into the Bank of America and flipped off the cameras as he strode across the lobby carrying a handful of empty pillowcases and a crowbar.

"Will you be making a withdrawal today, sir?" He hopped the counter. "Why, yes I will, fuck you very much." The cash drawers gave little resistance, and soon he was filling the pillowcases with tightly wrapped bundles of joy.

Vince held a strap of hundreds up to one of the cameras. "My town, fuckers!"

The purple dye pack exploded six inches from his face.

Screaming and blind, Vince clawed his way over the counter and stumbled toward the brightest point of light he could make out, the front doors. His noise drew attention, and the skinnies caught him on the sidewalk.

He never saw it coming.

Malibu

Claire Mercer was twenty-two, Hollywood beautiful (tucks, Botox, and implants that had healed nicely) and on her way to becoming a star. *Midnight Beauty* was red-hot: gorgeous, pampered, twentysomethings filled with angst falling in and out of love and danger with equally hip vampires. After coming in midway through the season and getting smash reviews, she had been signed as a regular for next year and handed a fat contract. Those first paychecks had made for a nice down payment on the beach house.

Her agent was already talking movie deals, maybe a perfume line.

The flu (the real flu, not that other crazy shit that was going around) had kept her in bed and out of touch with the world for days. She had turned off her cell, disconnected the house phone, and spent her time on the edge of the tub, puking into the bowl, or curled up and shivering under the blankets. She felt like dying, and didn't want to talk to anyone. Out of touch was what she got, and she missed some important news.

Now she stood in her living room, an impressive view of the beach and the Pacific beyond rows of tall windows, wearing vomit-stained pink pajamas and holding a butcher knife. The dead were smashing their way through all that glass, moaning and tumbling into the house. Claire stood and screamed.

Her agent would have been proud. It was a horror star's scream.

Palm Springs

Gloria tried to steer and fight off her husband at the same time, stomping the brakes and cranking the wheel hard to the left, into their driveway. Gravity threw him and his snapping teeth away from her (and threw her snarling teenage son across the backseat) long enough for her to crash the Volvo into the side of the house.

The air bags deployed, saving her from a spinal injury, and pinning her undead husband against his seat.

Gloria fumbled for the handle and fell out onto the driveway, her nose broken and bleeding from the air bag, and ran for the house, sobbing. Her husband and son managed to get out too, and lurched after her, but she made it inside and slammed the front door, locking it. They pounded the wood, flinging their bodies against it, as Gloria backed into her front room, hands over her mouth and shaking her head.

All they had wanted to do was stock up on groceries and bottled water, but the supermarket parking lot was like an asylum, people wrestling carts away from each other, pushing and hitting. It was like hell's version of Black Friday. Then those two *things* tried to crawl through the open side windows and tore into her boys. Gloria got them out of there in the Volvo, but they died on the way home. For a while.

Father and son groaned and hammered at the door, and Gloria sat down to cry.

An hour later a pair of rifle shots rang out from the street, and the pounding stopped. A bullhorn voice echoed through the neighborhood. *"This is the United States Marines. All civilians are being evacuated to Twenty-Nine Palms. Come to the sound of my voice, and wave something white over your head. Any persons not waving white will be shot. This will be the* only *evacuation of this neighborhood."*

Gloria heard a line of trucks rumbling past but made no move to go outside. When they were gone, she got out her photo albums and spent an hour looking through them, crying softly. Then she drew a warm bath and placed a razor blade on the marble edge before getting undressed.

Madera

Their skin was brown to begin with, but years of working in the sun, moving between orchards and farms and being outside in all sorts of weather, had turned it to creased leather. They were people with little interest in their political status, other than avoiding deportation, which was no longer a concern. For them there had been only work and family.

There were seven families, more than fifty people, and they kept to the rural roads, fading into the fields at the first sign of a vehicle or *los muertos*. They knew how to hide, how to stay quiet. They moved like ghosts.

Ricardo and Miguel walked in the lead, their wives and children in the group behind, everyone keeping up and no one complaining. Theirs had always been a life of labor, a hard life doing the work the *gringos* didn't want to do. They had little and thus had little to lose, so this new life was simply another obstacle to overcome.

When *los muertos* couldn't be avoided, Ricardo and Miguel and the other men swiftly fell upon them with machetes, putting them down fast without drawing attention. Many of the women also carried machetes, spades, and knives as well, for they had children to protect. Like their men, they did not shy away from hard work.

The town of Madera was behind them now, and the group moved across a tall bean field that they or people they knew might have planted. Staying in single file, they walked quietly down the long rows. Soon they would turn south, their only plan to return to their families and whatever homes awaited them in Mexico. That was as much tomorrow as they considered. They gathered food and water as they went and packed themselves into drainage culverts at night to sleep, posting guards at each end, moving again at dawn. In the evenings the women prayed the rosary, asking the Blessed Mother to watch over their families.

Ricardo came to a fence and motioned his brother forward. US 99 cut across in front of them, with more fields beyond. Word was passed back that they would be crossing. Ricardo pointed down the road, and Miguel peered around the edge of a beanstalk to see a bright blue Saab fifty yards away, off on the shoulder. It was up on a jack, a tire lying flat on the asphalt nearby.

Even at this distance they could hear the woman screaming inside. One of *los muertos*—the woman's husband?—was beating at the windshield with his fists. Another dressed in overalls pounded at a passenger window.

Miguel used wire cutters to clip the fence, and the two men pulled the barbed strands well back, tying the ends to posts. Then they readied their machetes and eased out onto the pavement, motioning for the others. Fifty men, women, and children slipped silently past them and trotted across the road, vanishing into the field on the other side. Ricardo and Miguel watched the corpses carefully, but they were so intent on getting into the vehicle that they hadn't noticed all the potential prey passing a short distance behind them.

When the last of the group was across, the two brothers followed. There was never a thought of going to the woman's aid, even though the two corpses could have been easily dispatched.

The *gringos* were not their people.

Los Angeles

From the floor-to-ceiling windows of his thirtieth-floor office, Lou Klein watched Los Angeles fall. He wore an expensive Italian suit without a tie and stood on the rich carpeting in bare feet. Grey Goose swirled in a tumbler and he sipped, taking pleasure in the burn as it went down. He preferred it with ice, but there hadn't been any of that in a long time. The hand holding the glass sported a five-carat diamond pinkie ring.

Lou was alone on this floor, perhaps even in the building. Samantha had gone to the roof and jumped to her death hours ago. He pressed his balding head against the glass and looked down, wondering if she was now dragging her shattered body through the street.

"Are you still there?" he asked his cell phone. It was the only piece of technology in his office still working, and only because he always kept a spare battery in his desk. The flat screens, the tablets and iPods, the refrigerator and air-conditioning vents, all were silent. He missed the iPod. He would have liked to hear Morrison's haunting voice singing about "The End."

There was a long pause, and then a woman's voice said, "Still here."

It was laughable. He had tried to use the phone for seven days, the length of time he'd been trapped here, without making a single connection. In desperation he had finally called his ex-wife and gotten through immediately. He sipped his Goose and decided that Fate had a twisted sense of humor. Lou Klein was one of the top record moguls in L.A., and all that his wealth and influence might have provided— airborne evacuation, a team of mercenaries with armored vehicles to drive him out of the city—was out of reach. There was only Aggie.

"Are you sure she's gone?" his ex said. There was no trace of sarcasm or smugness, no reproach.

"Yes. I saw her fall past the window."

Another pause. "I'm sorry."

Lou believed her. Even after all the anger and scandal, and despite the fact that Samantha had been the reason for their divorce after twenty years of marriage, Aggie was capable of compassion. She had always been a good woman. Far better than he deserved.

"She said she couldn't do it anymore. The waiting, knowing how it would end. I don't blame her." When things began falling apart, Lou arranged for a helicopter to meet them on the roof and carry them to Santa Monica. From there a chartered sea plane would pick them up and take them to a little island he owned in the South Pacific, where they would wait out the crisis in comfort and safety. The helicopter never showed. By the time they decided it never would, L.A. was too dangerous to risk going out on foot.

"You loved her," Aggie said. "It's hard, I know."

Lou didn't agree or disagree. For the last two years he had been

questioning if he really did love Samantha, or if it had been something else. A change? Excitement? Passion? Sam had been all those
things. But love? He looked down on streets packed with abandoned
cars and an overrun military convoy, as well as tens of thousands of
walking corpses. The black-and-white of an LAPD squad car could
still be seen in an intersection, the dead flowing around it like a stone
in a stream. Its rooftop lights had flashed for a full day before the
battery died.

"I was thinking about Ireland," he said. "Remember that trip?"

"Of course." He could hear the smile in her voice.

They had been newly married, and one of the groups he had signed
had gone platinum, his first success of that magnitude. Flush with
cash, they took a spontaneous trip to Ireland as a celebration. It rained
every day, but they went out in it anyway, holding hands and laughing
like fools, sitting on stone walls and making out in the downpour like
teenagers as the locals drove by, frowning in disapproval.

"That was a good trip." Lou drank his Grey Goose.

"It was." A long silence. "We were different then."

"Tell me again that you're safe."

She hesitated, and that told him all he needed to know. Aggie was
alone in the big house on Cape Cod, where a wall of glass overlooked
the dark Atlantic. Lots of glass. She said there was food in the house
and fuel in the generator. "I see people on the beach," she said. "Well,
not people, but none of them have come up here."

Lou looked at the carpet. August on the Cape? It would be packed
with summer tourists, which meant it was now packed with the dead.
"Stay away from the windows," he said. There was no reply, and another
long silence.

"Are you okay?" she asked.

"I think the building is on fire. I've been smelling smoke for over
an hour."

"Can you get out?"

He looked at the half-empty tumbler. "I wouldn't last five minutes down there."

They said nothing for a long time, and Lou began to wonder if he had lost the connection. He stared out the window at the mobs in the street, at the fires sending up a charcoal blanket to cover an already hazy city.

"Do you want me to go?" Aggie said at last.

He bit his lip and his chest hitched. "No. Please stay on with me . . . as long as you can."

"I'll stay on."

Lou finished his drink. If he had any balls he would go up to the roof and follow Samantha out over the edge. He knew he wouldn't, though. Too much of a coward, and no one knew that better than the woman at the other end of his phone.

"I love you, Aggie."

He heard the smile again, three thousand miles away. "I love you too."

THE DEVIL'S
ASHES

EIGHTEEN

Napa Valley

The time Evan had once filled with scribbling notes for his future novel or sitting quietly, deep in thought, had now been replaced by the new demands of survival. He spent two weeks leaving the Napa Valley on his Harley Road King, partly because he was being especially cautious, avoiding the dead whenever possible and taking his time scavenging. His real reason, however, was the desire to put off getting close to heavily populated areas for as long as possible.

He traveled by day, spending half his nights in businesses or stores, the other half in private homes, preferably those set back from main roads with lots of open space around them. These he scouted carefully before entering, circling and peeking in windows. Twice he had approached houses thinking he would sleep there in safety, only to turn back when he caught a glimpse of a corpse or two wandering through the rooms inside. One time he turned up a long dirt lane toward a Spanish villa resting on a hillside, surrounded by vineyards, but rifle shots (he assumed they were warnings because he wasn't hit) came from the house and drove him away.

The houses provided him with the basics: food, a plastic flashlight, first-aid odds and ends from medicine cabinets, a handheld can opener, fresh socks and clean underwear. No firearms, and no ammunition.

Evan spent a night at a winery, first taking an hour to scout the exterior, then another inside to ensure he was alone. That night he drank wine by candlelight, vintages he never could have afforded, toasting a farewell to the world. It earned him a crushing hangover the next morning, and he spent another day there trying not to move around too much and nibbling crackers, hoping to keep them down. He wrapped two good bottles in bubble wrap and tucked them away in his saddlebags.

A visit to the Napa County Airport revealed that half a dozen small planes were still present, tied down and covered in tarps. The place was deserted, except for a handful of the dead, but it was of no use to him. Evan didn't know how to fly, though he briefly considered trying his luck in a cockpit. He quickly dismissed the idea as he pictured himself lifting off, only to slam nose down in a fireball seconds later. Surviving this thing and then dying from dazzling stupidity would be an affront to every good person who hadn't made it.

The dead were everywhere, at least by rural standards, he supposed. Mostly they were lone wanderers or little knots shuffling along a road or across a parking lot, some walking out in fields or trying to untangle themselves from where they had gotten mixed up with a barbed-wire fence. They were scattered, and easy to keep away from out in the open. A few times when he had no other choice, he accelerated and drove the Harley right through them, hunching low over the handlebars and tucking his elbows in to avoid reaching arms.

In the time since the outbreak, he had seen only two survivors. He didn't count whoever shot at him, because he didn't see them. The first was a man in a straw hat driving an ancient Chevy pickup, heading in the other direction, his bed filled with cardboard boxes and metal drums. He threw a wave as he passed but made no effort to stop, and Evan didn't turn to follow him. He didn't want to get shot at again. The other was a woman in her thirties wearing sweatpants and what looked like a fireman's coat, carrying a golf club. As soon as she saw Evan and his Harley she ran off the road and disappeared around the back of a house. Evan sat astride his silent Harley on the broken yellow line for an hour, waiting to see if she might come into view again, but she never came back.

Still making his way slowly south, he took a trip into the outskirts of American Canyon, a burg below Napa. There he filled up at a quiet gas station, using a hose and a hand pump to draw the fuel from an underground tank. He had never done anything like that before and was proud of himself for pulling it off. Snacks and sodas from inside went into his saddlebags and pack to supplement the canned goods he had found in the houses, and he sat for a while on a big trash can drinking a warm Coke and looking at the empty road and silent buildings, listening to the wind. A hawk floated high above in a lazy circle, unconcerned with the demise of the human race below.

A quarter mile into town, just off Lincoln Highway, he found a Big Grizzly Tackle Shop. The front windows were broken and the power was out, just like everywhere he had been. He left the Harley out front and went in with his police shotgun.

The corpse was on him the moment he stepped inside.

Snarling and grabbing with filthy, blood-encrusted nails, it lunged from behind a postcard spinner, knocking it over. A man about his size dressed in khakis and a button-up shirt, it gave off a green stench, its flesh rotting and turning black around savage wounds. Evan yelped and shoved at it with the butt of the shotgun, its teeth grating at the stock and one hand pawing at the metal. He reversed the weapon, pushed the barrel into its belly, and blew a hole in it.

The thing fell back on its rear and then climbed to its feet, blackened organs and a loop of intestines drizzling out through the fresh hole. Evan choked down a surge of bile, aimed at its head, and pulled the trigger.

Nothing.

Cursing, he took a step back, racked a shell into the chamber, and tried again. This time the thing's head disintegrated, the blast leaving Evan with ringing ears.

Hands shaking and heart pounding, Evan ejected the spent casing and fed two more shells into the weapon, pumping the slide so that it was ready to go. He tracked the barrel around the dim interior of the store, trying to control his breathing, trying to listen. There was no more sound, no more movement. He looked at the corpse at his feet. Stupid. Mistakes like that would get him killed.

Give yourself a break, he countered. *This was your first.*

No, that wasn't right. The little girl back at the cabin, she had been his first. This was the first he had killed with the shotgun, and he had almost botched it. Smart and careful, those would be his rules. Otherwise he would end up like the thing on the floor.

Zombie. The word was just too Hollywood. He'd have to come up with up something better. He was a writer, after all. Words flipped through his mind as he searched the tackle shop.

Creeps?

Ghouls?

Shades? They were certainly shadows of their former selves, but the word sounded insubstantial, and they were real enough.

Trolls?

Cadavers? No, too many syllables. *Look out, it's a cadaver!* Too formal.

Stinkies? Too cutesy; might as well call them Smurfs.

Moldies? Again too cute, but in a few weeks it would certainly be applicable.

Drifters? That one had potential. He had seen the way they wandered without any apparent purpose. *Drifters* was a contender.

Evan had no interest in fishing rods, reels, or lures, didn't care about nets and tackle boxes. And he'd be damned if he'd get caught wearing one of those *On Golden Pond* hats. Near the back of the shop, however, he found a section dedicated to camping, and although it had been rummaged through and picked over—someone else had the same idea, he guessed—careful looking uncovered a few treasures. A large, good-quality backpack would strap nicely to the Harley's handlebars (though he'd hang on to his old Army pack; they had seen a lot of miles together). He picked out a rain poncho. A new all-weather sleeping bag would replace the ratty and no longer waterproof roll he had used for years. No sentimental value in that thing, and it smelled vaguely funky.

Slugs?

Skunks?

Flesh monkeys? That was just stupid, but it made him laugh. And there was no doubt a garage band out there somewhere that was already using that name. Or at least they had been. He found waterproof matches and some cans of Sterno cooking fuel; a bigger and better flashlight than his pilfered, plastic version; three packages of batteries; and a big canteen with a shoulder strap. It all went into the backpack. Under a pile of boxes containing air mattresses he discovered a sturdy yellow folding shovel but cast it aside. Too bulky.

Rotters?

Biters? He liked that one almost as much as *drifters*.

In a small stockroom—he let the muzzle of the twelve-gauge go in first—he found a hatchet with a leather cover snapped over its head. He liked the weight and saw that the cover was designed to slide onto a belt. He put it on immediately and promised himself to practice with it. It was definitely an up-close weapon, a whole lot closer than he ever wanted to get to them, but it would do well in an emergency and it would save bullets.

Thugs?

Moaners?

The Damned? Perhaps they were, but it only worked as a plural.

On a low shelf was an assortment of the dehydrated food packets backpackers used, self-contained meals that only required water and were both light and compact. He suspected they tasted like shit, but if food grew scarce they would be gourmet cuisine. He took enough to fill half the pack, and then added a charcoal-colored fleece and a heavy green sweater. It wouldn't be summer forever.

Wogs?

Trogs?

Jabberwocks?

There were no firearms. There had been, an empty rifle rack behind the cash register was evidence of that, as well as a couple of bare shelves under it that had no doubt held ammunition. It was too much to ask for, he supposed. He couldn't complain; the shop was a real score.

Drifters. The word came back to him, so he decided that was the one. He headed back out to the Harley and found one—a drifter—angling toward him across the street. It was an old lady in a nightgown, one chewed breast exposed and big bites taken out of her batwing arms. She groaned and quickened her pace.

Evan thought about the new hatchet. It would be quiet, wouldn't attract more like this one, and he needed to practice. She was an old lady, right? He caught himself. She had *been* an old lady, and that didn't mean this creature coming toward him retained even a shred of her former physicality. Now she was a predator, and might she not be just as strong as the others?

Be careful, be smart.

"Fuck it," he said, and blew her head off with the twelve-gauge. He motored out of town without waiting to see what else the shot had summoned.

Evan took another full day heading slowly east on American Canyon Road, weaving around wrecked or abandoned vehicles, speeding past slow-moving drifters and genuinely enjoying the solitude of traveling alone through beautiful country. For him it was the best aspect of riding, and for a little while it was just the road, the hum of the engine, and the pines and hills sliding by. He lost himself in it.

He spent the night in a log home constructed and furnished like a hunting lodge, building a fire in the big stone hearth and cooking up a pot of stew. Warm beer from the kitchen pantry washed it down, and he stayed up late wrapped in a Navajo blanket staring into the fire and thinking about a dead world. It was being reborn, he knew, but as what was something yet to be understood. He questioned his direction of travel. It was taking him to areas that had formerly been packed with people, something he knew he should avoid. North would have been better, less populated, and he could scrounge on the move. So why head into a nightmare?

Because he had to *see* it, he admitted at last. He had to bear witness to what had become of this crowded, high-speed world where humans had been so arrogant as to call themselves the dominant species. It wasn't smart, he knew, but he also knew that if he didn't see it, he would be haunted by unanswered questions. And there was always the chance that some sort of organization remained. He thought it unlikely, but part of him, despite his choice for a solitary life on the road, longed for the company of others.

He would still be careful. Just have a look, and if it was the wasteland he suspected, he could always fade back into the sticks, his curiosity satisfied. Evan slept in a king-sized bed upstairs, buried in pillows. As he faded off, he wondered if it might be the last night he ever enjoyed such comforts.

They were camped in the southbound lanes of I-80, right at the top of the on-ramp, a cluster of pickups with campers, minivans, and an honest-to-God VW bus with a peace symbol painted on its face between the headlights. Evan was on top of them before he realized it. A bearded man in denim and a woven, hooded pullover (a "drug rug") stepped out from behind a panel van and pointed a lever-action Winchester at him. He almost put the bike down, braking hard and sliding, the rear tire threatening to slip out from underneath him, but he managed to stop without crashing. A woman with a headband and a long braid appeared pointing a double-barrel shotgun. His own was slung on his back, and he knew he'd be dead before he got his hands on it.

"You be cool, we'll be cool," called a man's voice. Evan looked up to see a guy in his fifties standing on top of the VW bus, wearing camouflage shorts and hiking boots, a denim vest over a bare chest, and an Australian outback hat with a feather in it. A black assault rifle hung around his neck on a sling, and his hands were draped over it. A pistol and a big knife were belted at his waist, and a grenade hung from a thong around his neck.

Evan raised his hands slowly. "I'm cool."

The man on the bus had a scruffy beard and wore round sunglasses. "If you don't bring aggression, you won't find any here," he said. "What's your name?"

"Evan Tucker."

"Are you scouting for a bigger group?"

He shook his head. "I'm on my own."

The guy with the drug rug approached and looked him over closely. "I don't see a radio," he said.

The leader slid off the bus and approached. The other two didn't lower their weapons, and Evan saw more people peering at him from around the ends of vehicles, men and women, kids too. It seemed everyone over the age of ten was armed.

"So, Evan Tucker." The leader stopped in front of the Harley. "Who were you before nature decided to take it all back?"

He shrugged. "Just traveling. I'm writing a book. I was."

"Tourist guide? Self-help?" He raised an eyebrow. "Cookbook?"

Evan grinned and blushed. "Road stories, my thoughts and phi-losophies. Like Kerouac, I guess."

The man's face split with a smile. "The rogue of the road!" He extended a hand and Evan shook it. "Welcome," he said. "Poets are most welcome. I'm Calvin. This"—he swept an arm—"is the Family." When Evan's face betrayed a sudden worry, Calvin laughed and leaned in. "Not cult family or any Manson nonsense, dude. Good family. And lots of us actually are related."

With their leader accepting of the newcomer, the people who had been hiding and watching came out to greet him, and Evan was more than a little surprised at their warmth. After introductions were made (he knew he'd never remember all their names, although he had heard an "America," a "Sunshine," and a "Little Bear"), about a quarter of the adults went back to stand watch at positions set up in a ring around the little camp. Evan was reminded of settlers in the Old West circling the wagons.

He had an opportunity to wash up and fill his canteen, was given something to eat—beans and canned tuna—and guided to an empty lawn chair where a circle of seats had been set up around a small stack of wood. Calvin pulled a camp stool up next to him and offered a small ceramic pipe shaped like a skull. Evan accepted, enjoying the smooth draw of high-grade smoke.

"I made that," Calvin said, taking the pipe when Evan passed it back and firing his own hit. "I'm a potter. I used to follow the Dead . . . can you choke down that irony, man? I sold these out of my van in the parking lots during the concerts. When Garcia passed I followed Phish for a while, but it wasn't the same."

"It's nice," Evan said, admiring the simple design. Blue eyes bulged from the little skull's sockets.

Calvin handed it back. "It's yours. I've got boxes of them."

As the afternoon drew on, the wood at the center of the ring was lit, and the evening meal prepared in Dutch ovens, a ham and potato dish. Evan's mouth watered. Sentries were changed and everyone had a chance to sit and eat. More names were given. "River" and "Mercury," "Sympathy" and "Starlight." Calvin explained that he and the Family had been something of a traveling commune, nomads crisscrossing Northern California, renting farms for periods of time, staying with friends who had land, even squatting in state forests. Everyone who could work did odd jobs to keep the group going, and for years they had lived their lives relatively free of the restrictions and conformist demands of mainstream society. They gave their children fanciful names and smoked their reefer and dreamed of a better world. Evan felt like he had discovered a lost tribe long believed extinct. Although probably less so in California, he granted.

Calvin was a self-proclaimed "combat hippie," as strong a believer in the Second Amendment as he was in all other personal freedoms. "Better living through chemistry," he said, "but peace through superior firepower." Everyone in the Family knew their way around firearms, and the caravan picked up and tucked away whatever it found, including some military hardware scavenged from overrun Army units.

Evan was introduced to Calvin's brother Dane, a slender, blond man three years younger with a master's degree in botany. He was the Family's resident expert on all things herbal, both medicinal and recreational. Faith, Calvin's wife, was thin and tattooed, weathered from the sun, her hard appearance offset by lovely blue eyes and a warm smile, one of those rare women who made you feel instantly welcome. She and Calvin had five children, ages ten to nineteen.

"And they're all alive and with us," Faith said. It was clearly a source of parental pride for her and, Evan realized, no small feat considering what was happening in the world.

They asked him how he had come to be here, where he had been when it all fell apart. Evan told them about his cross-country travels, about his writing, and what he had seen in Napa. He even spoke a little about his reasons for coming down out of the hills.

Calvin gave him a gentle smile. "Being on your own has advantages. You can move faster, you only have to worry about yourself, and there's no arguing with the simple joy of solitude. It gets lonely, though, and it's nice to have someone to talk to." He squeezed his wife's hand. Evan couldn't disagree.

Calvin spun the wheel on a silver Zippo depicting the Aztec calendar, lighting another bowl as the sky passed through the darker shades of blue and plum, and embers from the fire danced up and away. "We were in a campground in Rockland Hills, just north of here. We didn't want to leave, not with what we were hearing on the radio, but the food ran out and we had some medical concerns." He snapped the lighter shut. "We figured to head east, hook up with I-5, and go north to Oregon. Fairfield was burning, and I mean the whole city. . . . It was like looking through a window into hell." He held out the pipe. "We moved through as fast as we could."

Faith took it from him and reloaded. "Not fast enough."

Calvin nodded, staring into the fire. "We lost folks. Lee and Ukiah, one of their kids."

"Drifters? The dead, I mean."

The aging hippie nodded again. "We've been calling them *The Lost*. A little flowery, I know. I like *drifters* better. Certainly more appropriate."

Several people around the fire bobbed their heads in agreement. Evan noticed that they all watched Calvin closely and didn't speak when he was talking, only listened.

"We got as far as Vacaville before we had to turn back. Couldn't get the vehicles through the traffic jams, and there were too many damned drifters. A hundred thousand at least, moving like a river down the highway, headed west."

Faces around the fire turned inward as people relived it, and a few looked over their shoulders, out at the darkness.

"We headed for Travis, the air force base."

"Against my principles and judgment," Dane added.

Calvin smiled. "Dane ran for mayor of a small town once and lost. Ever since then he's had a hard-on for anything having to do with the Establishment." Calvin made quotation marks in the air with his fingers.

"I almost won."

Calvin choked. "It was a blowout, man!"

"They voted for a fascist because they're sheep."

Calvin laughed. "They voted for him because he was a Republican, and you're an angry, dope-smoking anarchist." He slapped his brother's leg as Faith handed over the pipe. Dane took it, grinning.

There were some chuckles around the fire, and then silence. Calvin was looking into the fire again. "I was hoping we'd find shelter there. You'd expect that from a military base, right? I wasn't crazy about it either—I knew they'd want our guns—but it's spooky out here. Dangerous. We've got kids with us, you know?"

Evan nodded. Some of them were right here, sitting on the pavement and leaning against the legs of their parents.

"It didn't matter. The base was crawling with drifters, and the jet fuel tanks were burning merry hell. We had to turn back again." His voice became a whisper. "We lost three more friends to that little side trip."

Evan saw that Calvin carried that responsibility like a weight and wished he had words for the man. Instead he asked, "Why are you out in the open like this? Why not head back into the countryside; there's fewer of them. You could stay on back roads."

"We're heading south," Faith said, "to a ship."

"That's right," said Dane. "We're going to sail off into the sunset."

Evan looked at each of them. "What ship?"

Faith leaned forward in her chair. "We took a CB from a tractor-trailer. There was nothing but static for a couple of days, but then we connected with a guy who said there was a big medical ship at the docks in Oakland, guarded by the Army. They're taking on refugees, and then they're sailing for Alaska."

Heads nodded around the fire.

"It's only going to be there for a little longer," she said, "so we have to keep moving if we're going to catch it before it leaves."

Calvin smiled at his wife, but Evan didn't see the same look of hope there as he did on Faith's face. It sounded sketchy to him as well, but he wasn't about to argue with her. And who was he to say? He'd been isolated, and there might well be a ship. But Oakland? Evan had a vision of urban canyons, of tight, impassable streets and armies of the hungry dead.

"The cold is gonna suck," said Dane, "but at least there won't be as many drifters to deal with."

Calvin looked at Evan. "I'd prefer to stay in rural country myself, for the reasons you gave. But if it is a medical ship . . . Some of the Family have special needs: high blood pressure, trouble with a thyroid. My two youngest kids are diabetic and take insulin. We have a cooler in the bus that runs off the battery so it doesn't go bad, but our supplies are running low, and if we run out of fuel the cooler will go too." He attempted a smile and almost made it. "We have to try."

Evan smiled back at his host.

Calvin sighed and seemed to shake it off, leaning over and giving Evan's knee a friendly squeeze. "You really are welcome here. Stay as long as you like, travel with us, split in the morning, whatever suits you. We don't judge."

"Thank you. I probably will head back to the hills. I just think . . ."

"No worries, man. But if you decide to hang out for a day or two, I'd be honored if you'd let me read what you've written so far. I know writers get touchy about their rough stuff, but I may never meet another poet."

Evan laughed. "You can read it. Just go easy on me, okay?"

Calvin nodded solemnly and put a hand over his heart. "Gentle, I promise."

A figure appeared out of the darkness behind the man, placing a pair of slender hands on his shoulders. The man's face brightened at once and he reached up to grip the hands, tipping his head back and smiling. A woman of nineteen or twenty with long black hair gave him a kiss on his forehead. Evan's breath caught and his heart sped up. She was the most beautiful woman he had ever seen.

"Evan, meet my daughter Maya."

The girl turned a pair of curious, sapphire eyes on her father's visitor, and the corners of her mouth went up just the tiniest bit.

Evan Tucker fell all at once.

NINETEEN

Alameda

"Move your ass!" Angie shouted, bracing her elbows on the flat surface of a stone trash can and snapping off rounds, shifting fire right and left. She was using one of her favorites from the van, a Galil, the standard-issue Israeli assault rifle. Made of wood and black steel, it was based on the AK-47's globally respected design but was chambered to fire 5.56-millimeter NATO rounds. It featured a stubby barrel and a folding wire stock and could be outfitted with night or daytime optics, silencers, and laser pointers. The Galil was not only her personal favorite but the weapon of choice for many military professionals around the world.

The Galil kicked out brass as bodies fell, heads blown apart. The grocery store parking lot was quickly filling with the dead, and they were getting closer. Angie pulled the trigger on an empty magazine, ejected it, and drew another from a pouch on her vest. The Galil cracked again a moment later.

"Almost done," shouted Margaret Chu. Ten feet behind Angie,

Margaret and Tanya along with two other men were emptying a pair of shopping carts into the open back hatch of a big Ford Excursion.

"We still need the water." Tanya ran back into the store with one of the men. The other, a lawyer named Elson, retrieved a shotgun from the front seat of the SUV and started firing at corpses shuffling in from the other direction.

Angie dropped another mag and reloaded, stepping away from the trash can and walking several yards into the parking lot, where she would have a broader field of fire. She dropped to one knee and the Galil bucked. A man in black jeans. A man in torn khakis. A woman wearing a baseball cap. A guy in mechanic's coveralls. Weeks of decay had turned their bloodstains a rusty color and blackened their wounds. Whatever swelling decomposition had caused had leaked out of the older ones, leaving skin sagging and gray. Some were fresher kills, bloated and green. When one of her rounds found the torso on the swollen ones, they blew open like bags of wet spinach. The dead didn't notice and lurched forward. Flies buzzed in clouds around most of them.

She shot a teenage girl in pajamas, a fat man wearing only boxers, a woman in a business suit and skirt. Not every round was a successful head shot, but she was patient and adjusted fire, hitting the mark with the next squeeze of the trigger.

Three clips emptied. She inserted another. "We need to go!" she yelled.

The lawyer's shotgun was silent, and Angie pivoted on her knee, aiming in his direction. The man was leaning against the hood of the SUV, fumbling fresh shells into the weapon. A pair of corpses ten yards from him broke into a gallop, arms swinging.

Angie sighted.

Trigger squeeze.

A body fell.

A tick of the sights to the right.

Trigger squeeze.

The round punched through the second creature's throat, and it kept coming. The lawyer saw it, cried out, and dropped a handful of shells to the asphalt.

Slow breath.

Trigger squeeze.

The side of its head blew off and it collapsed.

"Calm down and collect your shells, Elson," she said, turning back toward the main parking lot. Angie had found the lawyer during one of her solo scouting trips three days ago, hiding in the back of a corner market. She brought him back to the firehouse like a stray, one of many she had collected over the weeks since the outbreak, and it turned out the man had a little experience with skeet and clay pigeons. That made him a shooter. Not a particularly skilled one, but at least he had handled shotguns before. She had armed him with a twelve-gauge Remington from the van.

"I'm loaded," he called, reappearing at the hood of the SUV.

"Slow and steady," she said between her own shots. "Aim and squeeze, keep count of your shells."

He nodded and fired, blowing a corpse's leg off at the knee. It immediately started crawling. His next shot was to its head.

"How are we doing, Margaret?" Angie asked.

"They're still inside," Margaret answered. She stood at the open SUV hatch, rubbing her hands and looking back and forth between the parking lot and the entrance to the store. Margaret wasn't a shooter, but she was relatively fit and willing to go out, so Angie tasked her as a field worker. Everyone had a job. There were others back at the firehouse she didn't dare allow into the field, like Sophia Tanner, who was afraid of everything and didn't *want* to go outside but was great with the kids. An elderly couple—the man afflicted with MS and his wife who couldn't be far from an oxygen bottle—sat at windows as lookouts. And there was a rotund, balding man in his fifties named Jerry who wheezed when he climbed the stairs. Angie didn't know how he had stayed alive the six days it took for him to discover the firehouse as a safe haven, but he did, and with his sense of humor intact. Jerry was a work-at-home programmer by day and an amateur stand-up comic on the weekends who often apologized to Angie for his lack of useful skills. She had decided he would learn how to strip and clean weapons.

Her uncle Bud wasn't allowed to leave either. Someone strong needed to remain behind to keep the firehouse secure, and she also wanted a person she could trust to keep an eye on Maxie.

The rumble of a metal U-boat platform truck came from behind her as the other man in their group, an insurance adjuster named Mark Phillips who had joined them only yesterday, emerged from the store with stacked cases of water in gallon jugs. He and Margaret started loading it at once, filling every available space in the back of the Excursion.

"Where's Tanya?" Angie asked as she slapped in a new clip and collected her empty magazines, shoving them in vest pockets.

The insurance man made a face. "She said she had to get cigarettes for Maxie."

Angie cursed and put the Galil back to her shoulder, resuming her position at the trash can, picking targets and dropping them. More staggered in from the street, from between nearby buildings and around both corners of the grocery store. A short Hispanic woman. A housewife missing most of her face. A dad still wearing an empty, dark-stained baby carrier on his chest.

The Galil cycled rounds, and they all went down.

A kindergartener with a bowl cut of black hair wearing shorts and a Hello Kitty T-shirt trudged across the lot, bumping against a shopping cart. Angie put the assault rifle's sights on her.

Touched the trigger.

Hesitated.

She squeezed her eyes tightly shut and blew out a breath, then opened them and sighted again. The little one walked with one shoulder slumped lower than the other, small sneakers scraping over the pavement in jerky steps.

Angie touched the trigger again.

And didn't fire.

She gritted her teeth and shifted to a high school kid in a yellow Polo shirt, putting one through his eye.

There was a long scream from inside the store. Margaret and Mark the insurance guy froze, each holding a case of water. Angie swore again and dropped another corpse, then ran inside. Tanya was running out, a canvas messenger bag hung across her chest and sprayed red. She was crying and had a hand clamped to her other, bloody forearm.

"She bit me! She bit me!" Tanya screamed.

Angie grabbed her. "Where?"

Tanya shook her head, her breath going in and out much too fast. "Bit me, oh, God, she bit me!"

A moan came from the shadowy interior on the left, and Angie raised her rifle, advancing as the girl ran outside. She followed the blood on the floor, moving quickly but quietly in rubber-soled boots, watching the flanks. There was a streak of fresh blood on the service desk counter where Tanya had climbed over, scattered packs of cigarettes on the floor beneath it. A dead girl in a brown smock with a name tag reading *BILLY* was on the other side, groaning and reaching across.

Angie shot her in the head and went back outside.

The lawyer's shotgun fired, and the insurance adjuster slammed the back hatch of the Excursion, calling out, "We're loaded." Margaret was already in one of the rear seats with Tanya, trying to calm the screaming girl and stop the bleeding. Hundreds of the dead pressed in across the parking lot, the kindergartener near the front.

Angie looked at the little girl for a long moment. "Drive," she ordered, and Mark went to the wheel. "Elson, we're leaving." The lawyer fired another shot, missing his target completely, and piled into the back. Angie rode shotgun.

In the third-row seat, Tanya was sobbing and wailing, "She bit me!"

The rest of them rode in silence as rain clouds rolled in from the bay.

Bud Franks was looking for Maxie. He didn't need him for anything in particular, but he wanted to know where he was and what he was doing. Normally he would have gone straight to the roof, where the man would be stretched out in a lawn chair smoking like a fiend. He was the only one in their group with the habit and had been politely but firmly told he could not smoke inside. He wouldn't be up there now, though. Maxie had run out of cigarettes two days ago and had been sullen and short-tempered ever since.

He wasn't in the kitchen. The man refused to do much of anything around the firehouse, but he had appointed himself cook, and it turned out he had some skill in that area. Perhaps, Bud thought, that had been his trade before the plague, but in the weeks since his arrival, and even with direct questions, the man had revealed nothing about himself. Margaret and Denny weren't of any help, either. They had been moving along a sidewalk together and nearly knocked the man down as he came out of a liquor store with his pistol in hand. Maxie had looked them over as if deciding whether to shoot them or ignore them, then sighed and gestured at his Cadillac parked at the curb. "Get on in," he said. Tanya was already in the passenger seat. That was only fifteen minutes before they showed up at the firehouse. When asked about the older man, Tanya shrugged and said nothing. The total lack of information bothered the cop in Bud. And then there was Maxie's refusal to do any work outside the kitchen. He wouldn't even wash dishes or clean his own pots and utensils.

Tanya had taken to him, even though he appeared to be just shy of being old enough to be her grandfather. She cleaned up after him in the kitchen, did his laundry, even made his bed. The rest of their relationship was none of Bud's business.

The one accommodation Maxie made outside cooking was to stand watch, but only at night and only up on the roof, where he could smoke. He didn't ask for a rifle or shotgun, and for reasons the ex-deputy couldn't explain, that made him feel a little better. Bad enough the man carried that .32 revolver in his waistband every place he went. Maxie hadn't said anything to indicate it, didn't have the tats or the yard walk, but he felt like an ex-con to Bud.

While he looked for their mysterious cook, Bud checked the perimeter, finding it secure. They ran the generator sporadically, usually to charge the two-way radios Bud and Angie carried, and to power up the firehouse's communication system once a day. Cooking was done with a propane stove, and Coleman lanterns provided light at night. They had covered all the windows with blankets to minimize the chance that a corpse walking by might notice movement inside during the day, or the glow of lanterns after dark. The same had been done with the glass front door, and a fat, six-foot-tall air compressor had been muscled out of the garage bay and shoved against it, then locked in place with canvas straps. If they broke through the glass, it would slow them down a little. The windows in the garage roll-up doors had been painted black except for small peepholes. There wasn't enough paint to do the rest of the windows, but it was on their shopping list.

Getting the dead away from the firehouse was Angie's job. She had retrieved a silencer from the van, fitted it to a Canadian assault rifle, and then gone to the roof, leaning over and clearing them out one at a time, front and back. The bodies were collected and hauled out to the rear parking lot over several days, and only when nothing was around that might see them. Now the only thing that would attract attention was when one of the vehicles rolled in or out, and that was done only after careful watching from the rooftop. Invariably a few would show up anyway and would have to be cleaned up with the silenced rifle.

Thank goodness for the van, he thought. Without the lethal protection of its contents, they wouldn't have survived. Additional thanks were due to the fact that Angie and Bud had happened to be out filming when it all went bad and had the van with them. They could just as easily have been in L.A. at a preproduction or script meeting, unarmed and defenseless.

Bud checked the main room, where Sophia was sitting on the floor with a circle of kids.

"Hi, Bud." Being around the kids obviously made her happy, and it seemed that taking care of them took her mind off whatever horrors she had seen before reaching the firehouse. They kept her too busy to dwell on whomever she had lost. Sophia didn't share those details, though she surely had her personal tragedies, like the rest of them, and no one pressed her about it.

"How's our new arrival?" Bud asked.

Denny, who had come in with Maxie's group, was eight but didn't seem to mind playing with the smaller kids. Next to him was a ten-year-old Angie had collected during a supply raid (Bud couldn't remember his name), and then there were the two little sisters Maxie rescued from the parking lot by letting them come in with Sophia. Each held a doll, the girls providing voices as the toys engaged in a discussion about hair and clothes. Sophia looked at a three-year-old with blond hair sitting in the circle and playing with a yellow plastic truck. He made an "rrrrrr" sound as he drove it around his knees and feet. "Ben's doing just fine." She rubbed his back. "I think he's forgotten about what happened."

"Has he said anything about his family?"

She shook her head. "I still can't believe he's alive."

Neither could Bud. One of their rooftop lookouts had spotted the boy walking down the center of the road outside, carrying a stuffed rabbit with blood on it, whimpering. The noise he was making, his mere presence, was drawing the dead from all angles. The lookout called downstairs to Angie, who was on the second floor. She looked out a window, and then a moment later came pounding down the stairs with a .45 in a shoulder holster, racking a shell into a combat twelve-gauge.

She made an animal noise as she bolted out the back door, teeth bared.

The others crowded to the windows and watched as Angie sprinted around the firehouse and straight at the child, sliding to a stop nearly on top of him, pushing him to the ground and then planting a foot on either side of him. The boy curled into a ball and covered his ears as Angie began blasting with the shotgun, turning in a tight circle. When it was empty, she cast it aside and pulled the .45, assumed a shooting stance and went to work, squeezing off steady, measured rounds, still rotating through the points of the clock. When the .45 was dry, she ejected the magazine and inserted a new one in a motion so fast and fluid that the firing didn't seem to stop.

When Bud reached her in the street, she was already on the way back, the boy in her arms as she soothed him. Twenty corpses lay crumpled in a circle behind her, all with head wounds.

"He doesn't know his mommy or daddy's name, or at least he can't remember right now. He hasn't said anything about what happened to them. He's eating okay and he gets along well with the other kids," Sophia said, smoothing his hair. Ben tilted his head into the touches. "He has nightmares, though."

Bud looked at the boy, then at Sophia. "I'm glad you're here with us."

She smiled. "Me too."

Bud went to the garage bays. Angie insisted on leading the raids and wouldn't even discuss Bud going in her place, despite his repeated offers. She was good at it, always bringing back plenty of food and vital supplies like camping equipment, fuel, clothing, first-aid supplies, and batteries, as well as toys for the kids and the occasional paperback or board game to keep the adults occupied. Bud couldn't claim he would do better, and although it still didn't feel right, he was mature enough to admit that it was misplaced, masculine pride talking. She was younger, faster, more fit, and without question a better marksman. It was the right decision.

The bays currently held three vehicles, with space for the Excursion, which was currently out. The *Angie's Armory* van faced toward the front, next to the empty slot. Facing the rear roll-ups was an extended white passenger van with six rows of seats and *Bayside Senior Care* on the side in blue letters. Parked next to it was Maxie's Cadillac.

Maxie was in here, the smell of cigarette smoke strong. The man was sitting on the rear bumper of Bud and Angie's van, legs stretched out, puffing away.

"I thought you were out," Bud said.

"I am," Maxie replied. "Found a stale one in my glove box, though. Lucky for me."

"You're supposed to smoke on the roof."

Maxie ignored him and slapped a hand against one of the van's rear doors. "Why you keep this rig locked, Mr. Bud?"

Bud walked to him slowly and folded his arms. "How do you know it's locked?"

Maxie smiled with the cigarette clamped between his teeth, flashing a bit of gold. "You afraid someone's gonna steal your guns?"

"It's safer for everyone this way. There's kids around."

The man seemed to consider that for a moment. "Don't want all that firepower falling into the wrong hands, do we?" He crushed the butt out on the cement.

"That's absolutely right, Maxie."

The man flashed a gold-capped grin and stood. "Smart thinking."

For one crazy moment Bud *knew* the older man was going to pull the .32 out of his waistband and shoot him right in the chest. Instead he started toward the firehouse door, just as the Excursion's engine rumbled up into the driveway out front. "Mama's home."

"We'll need help unloading," said Bud.

"I'll send someone out." Maxie went inside.

Tanya didn't have much longer and they knew it. She was lying on a bunk upstairs, her arm tightly bandaged, beads of sweat standing out on her face. Her eyelids fluttered and she groaned, rolling her head back and forth, trying to find a cool spot on the pillow. Margaret Chu sat on the edge of the bed and stroked her face with a wet washcloth, trying to keep her comfortable, while Sophia—wearing heavy rubber gloves and a clear plastic face shield—cleaned vomit off the floor, putting the rags in a red bio bucket.

"You can't tell me who to see, Nana!" Tanya's words were slurred. "I love him!"

Margaret pressed the wet cloth to the girl's forehead and hushed her, but Tanya was beyond noticing.

"Maybe this will pass," said Larraine, the old woman whose husband had MS. She stood behind Margaret, her lined face revealing that she didn't believe her own statement.

Angie looked sideways at her uncle. The communication equipment in the small room up front had delivered only static for days straight. Then one afternoon there was a brief transmission, a few garbled sentences where the only words they could make out were *national, evacuation centers,* and *compromised.* It wasn't encouraging. Later that day another message came through, this one as clear as if the speaker were in the same room, a recorded Emergency Broadcast

System announcement. It repeated for nearly an hour before the static took over once more, and there had been nothing since.

The message said the plague was viral, a highly contagious blood-borne pathogen transferred through a human bite. Animals appeared to be immune. The symptoms resembled flu with periods of dementia and ended in death one hundred percent of the time. The infected were to be isolated in a secure quarantine. Late-stage victims became ambulatory after death and were extremely aggressive. There was no mention of the term *slow burn* or its effect, and the word *zombie* was notably absent.

Tanya was eleven hours past her bite.

Angie and Bud stepped into the hallway and spoke quietly. They could hear rain drumming on the roof. "We know where this is going," her uncle said.

Angie glanced back inside, where the other women were trying to keep Tanya calm and cool as the fever burned her up. "So what do we do with her? Keep her in there?" she asked. They both knew that wasn't an option. She would turn, and then one of the things they were working so hard to keep outside would be inside.

"The radio said isolation."

"Where? We can't lock her in a closet."

"I was thinking about the parking lot," Bud said.

"Leave her delirious on the hood of a car? She'll be eaten in minutes."

"No, inside one of the cars."

Angie thought about it. That would be better than the roof, which she had been about to suggest. Besides, if they put her up there they would have to deal with her eventually.

Maxie scuffed up the nearby staircase and stopped, looking past them. "How's my girl doing?"

"She's dying," said Angie.

"And nothin' gonna stop that," the man said. It wasn't a question.

He went inside, and Angie and her uncle watched him rest a hand on the shoulder of each lady, taking the washcloth from Margaret and sitting down on the edge of the bed. He moved the cloth gently over Tanya's face and began to sing softly to her, something from Motown. The girl's restlessness subsided, and the women left the room, slipping between Bud and Angie and heading downstairs.

"In a car, on the street, chained in the garage bay, none of it changes what's going to happen," Bud said, running a hand through his bristly hair. "She's a danger to us, Ang."

She knew it. But the alternative . . . ? Sick people were supposed to be cared for, not put down like rabid animals, although that was most assuredly what the girl would become. Logic demanded a hard choice: either put her outside as she was and let the virus run its course, or put her down. But this was a person, someone she knew, who had a smile and a name and ideas, maybe even people left out there who cared about her.

Angie put her hand on Bud's arm. "What if we—"

A gunshot made them both jump. Maxie stood over the bed, lowering the small pistol. He had wrapped the girl's head in a towel to cut down on the mess. Angie and Bud could only stare at him as he squatted and began rummaging through Tanya's messenger bag, pulling out several packs of Salems and slipping them into his pockets. He tested the gun barrel to see if it was cool enough, then shoved it back in his waistband.

Maxie popped a cigarette into his mouth as he eased between them. "I'll be on the roof. Supper's at six."

TWENTY

Getting out was proving to be a slow, dangerous process, and Xavier had begun to doubt whether it could be done at all. The dead multiplied with each passing day as they rooted out survivors, and now they infested not only the streets but buildings as well. The once-vibrant city was a graveyard of shattered lives, a wasteland ruled by the dead. They didn't need to sleep or pause to rest, didn't get sidetracked searching for clean water or shelter, weren't forced to wait when one of their number just couldn't go on anymore. They had no need to hide, for they were the predators, relentlessly moving and hunting day and night.

The group had not seen either law enforcement or a military presence, none of the hoped-for signs of an organized evacuation. There were no more helicopters overhead, and they had only once heard a jet go by, but that was days ago. As for other survivors, there had been only a couple, as fleeting as shadows darting across streets and into doorways. The few who spotted them ran away at once.

Xavier and Alden moved cautiously through the looted pharmacy, flashlights leading the way. They passed rows of shelves swept onto the floor, their feet shuffling through everything from hairbrushes to headache remedies to packages of adult diapers. The actual drug counter would be at the rear of the store.

Alden had one of the automatics they had scavenged from the 690K hideout in his rear waistband, and he carried a fireplace poker. Xavier's AK-47 was slung over his shoulder, and he gripped a long, heavy crowbar. The handheld weapons were best, they had discovered, especially in close quarters. Several days ago both Xavier and Pulaski had used their firearms on a pair of ghouls they came across while looting a clothing store. The shotgun sounded like a cannon, and the AK was like a crack of thunder following a close lightning strike. The noise drew the dead from every direction, and the group had been forced to run, narrowly getting out the back door and down an alley.

"It's going to be a mess back there," Alden warned. "I'll have to pick through it."

"Tell me what you need and I'll help you."

Alden did: Coreg, Plavix, Coumadin, Digoxin, Lisinopril. "Don't worry about milligrams; most of them are standardized and I can break tablets if I have to. I'll take what I can get."

Pulaski complained about the time it would take to do this, but they had put it off for days, and Xavier informed him that Alden's heart medicine was more important than Pulaski's damned cigarettes. The priest was worried. Alden was pale most of the time, his breathing had become labored, and he tired easily. The schoolteacher waved it off with a smile, but Xavier knew BS when he saw it and stayed close.

The back of the store was as bad as they expected. The steel gates had been pried open, the counter door kicked in. Cabinets were forced, presumably where the controlled substances had been kept locked away, and Xavier was willing to bet there wasn't a single tablet of Oxy, Vicodin, or Percocet to be found. The world was ending, but people still wanted to get high. The shelves where the medication once stood in ordered rows were empty. The floor, however, was a wall-to-wall jumble of white and brown plastic bottles.

They started searching.

Pulaski was up front watching the street, picking through debris and looking for smokes, while Tricia and Snake searched for food and water. The girl was less panicked than earlier, the company of others seeming to keep her quiet. The boy had lost his skateboard in a run from the dead a while ago and wouldn't stop bitching about it. Pains in the ass, both of them.

He found half a dozen packs of cigarettes buried under the mess on the floor, none of them his brand, and shoved them into his pack. Flashlights deeper in the store showed him where the kids were, and more lights and rattling noises came from the back. He lit a smoke and leaned back against the cash register, keeping watch out through the broken front windows with their mangled security gates, the shotgun cradled in his arms.

The street was clear for the moment, but that could change quickly. He blew smoke at the ceiling. They were going nowhere, the walking dead so dense throughout San Francisco that it took them entire days to move a few blocks, hiding like rabbits afraid to cross the street. The dead were slow and clumsy, but still their little group crept along, jumping at every noise. Rabbits. It was bullshit, they should have been at the water by now, and they hadn't even reached the highway or passed the Bay Bridge yet. Pulaski huffed smoke out through his nose and thought about the other day at Market Street.

"There's no barrier," Pulaski said. "We can cross here."

Xavier shook his head. "We need to wait and watch."

Market Street was a wide avenue running through most of the

city, and now it cut across their path like an impassable river. It had been sealed off from the side streets by a high barrier of posts, sand-bags, and barbed wire. Official notices bearing the hazmat symbol were attached to the barrier, announcing that attempts to leave the quarantine zone would be met with deadly force. The authorities had tried to seal off part of the city, rather than go through the trouble of evacuation.

It hadn't worked.

The dead swarmed up and down Market on the other side of the barrier. Even if the group had been able to breach it, the dead would be waiting. The obstacle forced them to the southwest, down two more blocks. Both cross streets were blocked in the same way. Another day lost.

Sneaking down alleys, ducking into buildings to hold their breath and wait until a single corpse shuffled past, one that Pulaski could easily take out with the fire axe that hung from his pack, stopping so the schoolteacher could rest . . . It was bullshit, all of it. Finally they had come to where Van Ness intersected with Market, and here there was no barrier.

"What do you mean, wait? There's only a few of them out there," Pulaski said.

Xavier didn't even look at the pipe fitter before shaking his head. "We can't see very well. We don't know if there's an army of them just on the other side of those vehicles."

They were crouched in the remains of a building, little more than a shell of broken brick walls, something out of a World War II movie. Around and in front of them were the remains of a battlefield. A pair of tanks and half a dozen smaller armored vehicles were scattered in both directions along Market, and the surrounding buildings had been shattered by heavy weapons.

How had they not heard this?

Burned civilian vehicles and charred bodies were strewn across the pavement, which glittered with broken glass and shell casings. Most of the area was filmed with black soot left by incendiary weapons. None of it had done a thing to stop the spreading infestation.

"They're not bunched together," Pulaski said. "They'll be easy to run between. It's not going to get better than this."

"If we're going to be running, Alden needs to rest first."

Pulaski's face darkened. "Fuck him. He's been holding us back since this started."

Xavier looked at him. "Regardless, that's how it is."

"Oh, that's how it is?"

"That's right."

"Well I say different. I say we go right now."

Xavier made an *after you* gesture. "But if you bring them down on us, you'll pay for it."

Pulaski's eyes narrowed. "You threatening me? You must think you're back in the hood." He sneered. "Better be careful what you say, tough guy." The pipe fitter didn't notice the look on Xavier's face, that the other man was even more shocked by his own threat.

They stared at each other for a moment and then went back to watching the street. The pipe fitter thought about making the run across, screw what His Majesty said. And yet he stayed put, angry with the other man, angrier with himself. The truth was that Xavier scared him a little, and not just because of his size and strength. There was something more, a violence just beneath the surface, barely suppressed and straining to be unleashed. He didn't think the man would try to stop him if he decided to go his own way, but the other truth, the one that filled him with self-loathing, was that Pulaski feared being alone out there.

He thought about a different tactic, about making a run for one of the armored vehicles. He could lock all the hatches and drive out, rolling over anything that got in his way. He quickly discarded the idea. If it were that easy, those vehicles wouldn't still be here. He'd probably get inside only to learn it was out of fuel. It would turn into his coffin.

In the end they waited for three hours, and then Xavier nodded and they all scooted quickly across. A few corpses saw them and followed, but by the time they shambled up to the cross street the group was a block away and safely hidden inside a building. The dead lost focus and moved on.

Crossing Market, however, didn't mean they were moving any faster, and now this little pharmacy excursion was eating into the last of their daylight. Pulaski ground out his butt. Maybe he would just wait until the guy wasn't looking and put the shotgun to his head, blow it clean off. The others would fall into line, and he suspected that nice piece of tail Tricia would do *anything* not to be left alone. The idea made him smile. Whether he decided to kill Xavier or not, he would have to find a way to deal with him.

Xavier and the schoolteacher walked to the front, Alden swallowing a handful of pills with a VitaminWater. It seemed the looters had little interest in heart medication, and together they had found enough of his meds to last a month or more. Tricia and Snake showed up as well, arms loaded with crackers, Pop Tarts, canned chili, beef jerky, and more VitaminWater. It would do for a while.

Day after day they kept moving, ever careful, always watching. They killed the walking dead only when it was unavoidable, and only with handheld weapons. So far they had been lucky; no one had been bitten. One morning the fog was especially heavy and remained that way throughout the day. They didn't dare to go out in it—a corpse would be on you in seconds without you ever having seen it coming—so they spent another twenty-four hours hiding upstairs in a small office building.

Boredom led to talking. Snake's father was in prison somewhere in Arizona, and his mother was a junkie the courts had ruled unfit to take care of a little boy. He had been shuttling around the foster care system since he was five, and by age twelve he had become quite adept at looking out for himself. He spoke casually about it all and reminded Xavier of the hardened kids from his parish. Tricia was a high school dropout moving through a series of part-time, low-paying jobs. She didn't talk about her family. Pulaski, leaning against a wall away from the group and smoking in the darkness, grumbled that he didn't want to play this game.

Alden ignored him and looked at the others. "How about, 'Where were you when the world ended?'" There were shrugs. "I was getting coffee," he said. "I was on my way to work. It happened so fast they didn't have time to close the schools, and didn't warn the staff." He smiled. "I was at Starbucks."

"You mean Four-bucks," said Tricia.

Alden laughed. "Depends on what you order, I guess. What about you?"

"A bus stop," the girl said. "The bus never showed up. Then there were car accidents up the street, some shooting. . . . People started running. I ran too."

Snake was sitting on the floor, rolling a baseball bat up and down his outstretched legs. He let go and made a gesture of two thumbs wiggling back and forth. "Playing Xbox. I was skipping school at a friend's house. His mom was at work." He nodded at Xavier. "I can handle one of those guns, you know. Probably better than him." He pointed at Alden.

"I'll think about it," said Xavier.

"What happened to your friend?" Tricia asked.

Snake looked at the girl and shrugged. "He took off, said he was going to look for his mom. He probably got eaten."

"Don't say that!" Tricia said, her hands covering her mouth as if speaking the words might make them true.

"It's true. He's probably out there now, bumping into walls. What, you think it's not going to happen to you too?" The kid laughed. "We're all going to end up like them."

They were quiet for a while, and then Alden looked at Pulaski. The man shook his head. "What about you, Xavier?" Alden asked.

The bigger man was sitting with his knees drawn up, arms draped over them. He looked straight ahead and didn't speak for a while, then softly said, "I was at the rectory." The word didn't register with the two kids, but Alden nodded slowly, as if he had somehow suspected this. Xavier looked down, unsure about why he had said it, already regretting the words.

Over at the wall, Pulaski's voice: "You're shitting me. You're a priest?"

"I was. Not anymore."

Pulaski snorted a laugh. "Some priest, threatening me like he's a bad-ass or something. And knows how to handle an AK. They teach you that at the Vatican, Father?"

Xavier didn't answer. There were things Barney Pulaski didn't need to know about his life, like the fact that in order to keep him off the streets, his grandmother had gotten him involved in an Oakland boxing club. It was something for which he showed natural talent, a skill that made him strong and provided a measure of protection in a tough neighborhood. It also attracted attention. When he was seventeen, a gangbanger named LaRay Johns decided to see how tough the big Church kid was and started pushing him around outside a convenience store. Xavier shoved him back, hard enough to make the gangbanger stumble and land on his ass. LaRay, humiliated and enraged, pulled a butterfly knife and backed Xavier into a doorway, carving the line down his face that he wore to this day. Xavier had come out of the doorway with a roar, his face hanging in bloody flaps, and with his fists alone beat LaRay Johns so badly that the gangbanger's neck snapped and a broken rib was later discovered sticking through his heart.

Pulaski didn't need to know that the courts had determined that it had been a case of self-defense and cleared young Xavier Church of criminal charges. Still, the court found it necessary to give him an outlet for his dangerous ability and *encouraged* him to enlist in the Marines. The corps took him and, after boot camp and basic infantry training, decided Xavier needed to box for the Marine Corps, both within his branch and in intraservice competition. He was good, and they made him better, teaching him control. There was talk about Olympic competition, perhaps even getting him ranked. Marines, however, regardless of their assignment, were riflemen first and went where they were told. In 1992, PFC Church found himself in Mogadishu, Somalia, where everyone, regardless of age or gender, was a potential threat. It was where he learned the workings of the AK-47, the preferred weapon of the opposition.

Out on patrol with his Marine squad one morning, he heard a sudden rustle of sandals on gravel to the right. Church turned, saw two people with AKs pointed at him, and opened fire. Both went down before they could get off a shot, and while his buddies backslapped him, he walked up to see what he had done. They were boys, no more than nine years old.

Despite the manly bravado and discipline of the corps, and justified or not, Xavier Church just couldn't accept that he had killed children. The Marines quickly realized he could no longer hack it and quietly transitioned him out of the service. After a string of meaningless jobs, he found himself as a custodian in a Catholic high school, where a priest named Daniels took an interest in him. A dialogue opened, and without realizing it Xavier opened his heart as well, expressing his guilt, his feelings of worthlessness and emptiness. He needed something to fill the void. Under the priest's sponsorship he was sent to the seminary, subsequently took his vows, and was assigned to Saint Joseph's, where he could help those lost young souls on the street. There he had helped create both the youth center and the boxing club.

And, he thought, looking at the faces staring back at him, *where you pretended to be a man of God for years and murdered yet another pair of boys. Where you broke your faith and let your entire community fall into hell on earth while you ran to save your own life.*

No, there were parts of his life he simply didn't need to share.

Then why mention it? he asked himself.

Tricia crawled up to her knees and clasped her hands in front of her. "Is this it, Father?" she asked. "Is this Armageddon? Are we all in hell now?"

Xavier looked down at the floor and shook his head. "I don't have the answers you're looking for, Tricia."

She continued as if she hadn't heard him. "Has God turned His back on us? Can we still get into heaven?"

The priest looked at her. "I'm sorry."

Her face twisted, got ugly, and she pointed a finger. "You're a *priest!* You *have* to know! You can't say you don't know!" Then she started to cry and fled into the darkened office, her sobs muffled among the empty cubicles.

Over by the wall, Pulaski sat back and looked at the ceiling. "A priest." He laughed softly, and for a long time.

TWENTY-ONE

Oakland International Airport

The Air Force wanted to call it an "administrative separation." That was their terminology, a less-than-honorable umbrella for an assortment of discharges from service, which included psychological instability. Due to the highly classified nature of his work, however, the higher-ups converted it to an honorable discharge. They clearly didn't want someone who knew the things he knew leaving disgruntled.

He was disgruntled, of course. The unfairness of it all chewed on him for years.

"I'm sure you can understand why people are concerned, can't you, Airman?" the shrink asked.

"No, not really," he responded.

"You don't see how your behavior, especially considering your responsibilities, might cause others to be uncomfortable? Perhaps question your fitness for duty?"

"No. I'm good at my job."

The shrink tapped a pen against his knee. "No one doubts that. But your CO is worried you could compromise the mission."

"He's a Godless philistine. He doesn't understand our true purpose."

"And what is that, exactly?"

"Colonel Chandler says we serve our country by keeping America safe. He says it all the time. He refuses to accept that we're merely instruments of God, waiting for the day when He commands us to scourge the sinners of the world by fire."

"I see." Tap, tap went the pen. "You've been quite vocal with this opinion."

A smile. "It's the responsibility of the faithful to spread the word. No one listens, though, and they'll all burn for their lack of faith."

"But not you?"

"I'll burn too, of course. But I will be raised up."

The shrink flipped a page on the clipboard. "Have you always expressed these strong religious beliefs?" He already knew the answer. If the young man sitting in the chair across from him had given any hint of this behavior back when he had enlisted, he never would have passed the psych screening required for his highly sensitive job.

Another shrug. "Not at first, I guess. But I know now that it's always been inside me. A deep love of the Lord, untapped, waiting to be shown the light. That's what He said."

"What who said?"

"God."

"God speaks to you?"

A beaming smile. "All the time."

The shrink scribbled some notes and smiled back. "Let's meet again."

Sitting before him was a young man assigned to the missile silos in Omaha, someone who was highly trained and regularly worked up close with nuclear warheads. Someone who thought America's nuclear arsenal existed to bring about biblical destruction, and who thought

God spoke to him directly. He would be run through the standard bat-
tery of tests, as the regulations required, but the results of this single
interview would be more than enough. Airman P. Dunleavy had
touched his last nuke.

Brother Peter came to realize that he had been wrong to be angry. Being forced out of the military was an important first step toward his ministry, toward his understanding of the level of affluence and power that could be attained by someone who knew the right words and had the courage, the daring, to say them. He had made a wildly successful career by shearing the sheep with lucrative words like *charity* and *blessings* and *demonstrations of faith*. Along the way his faith had become an effective tool with which to achieve his desires, and as his empire grew, the days when he would pray on his knees with tears in his eyes, when he would joyfully proclaim his beliefs to strangers (other than when he was being paid to do so), faded with the past.

And then suddenly, the Lord announced His presence once more by sweeping away Peter's empire along with humankind. There was no question in the minister's mind that it had all been done specifically for his benefit, a divine reminder that He was real, that the pursuit of worldly goods and pleasures was a path to damnation, and that the passion with which Peter had once worshipped the Word was the only true thing. That, and God's love for him. Peter *was* special, that much was clear to him now, and the Lord had a plan in mind, something of biblical proportions, a mystery. Brother Peter was ashamed for having turned away for so long, for his many debaucheries and faithlessness, for his use of God's word as a ploy to satisfy his earthly desires, and he vowed to become that strong servant that God required. Thy will be done.

It was obvious that God had decided to forgo the fiery destruction and skip straight to the Rapture, for this was surely what was happening. Those left behind would walk the earth as lifeless shells, and the faithful would be lifted up to heavenly glory. How much longer this would take remained to be seen, but certainly long enough for His purpose to be revealed. Peter had his suspicions, his guesses, and he believed it would involve culling the goats from the lambs. He would relish the task.

But like Job, he would first be required to suffer.

And he was. He was starving.

Brother Peter looked out a small, grimy square of glass set in a metal door. Behind him was a corridor leading to another door that opened into a barnlike room of baggage conveyor belts, the metal twisted into odd shapes by the fire, a stink of roasted rubber thick in the air. There was also a stairway that led back down to their subterranean world. Four people were here with him: Anderson, a female staffer, and both of the G6 pilots, whom he had quietly begun thinking of as Thing One and Thing Two. They were all, including himself, skinny, dirty, and developing sores from poor hygiene.

"Get ready," he said, his hand on the door handle. The female staffer and Thing Two moved up close to him, each holding an empty gray bin used at security checkpoints to hold laptops, shoes, and pocket items. Thing Two had a hammer stuck in his belt.

Peter yanked open the door. "Now!" The two ran out with their bins, and the minister shut the door quickly behind them. He pressed his face against the glass, whispering, "Go, go." A United food services truck sat a hundred feet away on the tarmac, its glass shattered, tires melted, sides scorched black from the fire. The rear roll-down door was closed, though, which meant some of its contents might have survived the blaze. Peanuts, pretzels, and cookies would be a feast at this point. Thing Two and the staffer ran for it.

The dead noticed.

A dozen were in view, and they looked far different from the ones that had first forced them underground. These were burned, without clothing, charred black from head to toe like beef ribs left too long on a grill. When they bumped against objects or each other, little puffs of soot rose off them, and pieces of charcoal fell to the ground. They were hairless and without eyes, wandering blindly, but they heard or sensed the two runners at once and turned toward them.

"They'll never make it," Anderson moaned, standing just over Peter's shoulder. He smelled like a chicken coop.

"They'll make it," the minister said.

And they did, at least as far as the truck. Both arrived at the back end, and the woman kept a nervous watch as Thing Two struggled to pull up the door. It wouldn't move.

Dead, moving charcoal let out a chorus of dry croaks and closed in.

"C'mon, c'mon, put your back into it!" Peter shouted, slapping the cinder-block wall beside the door.

Thing Two heaved, but the roll-up door wouldn't budge.

"The fire must have fused the metal," Anderson said. "Maybe melted the rubber seals."

"Thank you, Professor."

Anderson shook his head. "We should have thought of that. We should have sent them out with the crowbar."

Behind them, Thing One held the crowbar close to his chest and shook his head. Brother Peter elbowed his aide away. "I can't stand your stink. And do you want to eat or not?"

Blackened corpses soon encircled the truck, and the staffer began tugging at Thing Two's shirt. They looked around and saw that there was no way back, so they went to the front and climbed the bumper, the hood, finally up to the flat roof of the cargo box. Then they knelt and looked down at the things crowding in from all sides. More began drifting in from the field and emerged from the burned ruins of the lower terminal.

"Shit." Brother Peter stomped a foot. "Shit, shit, shit." He threw his arms in the air and turned away from the door. "Well, it was a good idea, anyway."

Anderson glared at him with eyes sunken deep in dark hollows, his skin jaundiced from poor nutrition and lack of sunlight. They had been living off vending machine snacks, moldy lunches found in employee lockers, and the occasional rat. There was no shortage of those. The bold little creatures crept up on them while they slept, sniffing at faces and often taking a bite out of a lip or earlobe. They were quick, though, and difficult to catch. On those rare occasions, they offered only a little meat. There was no way to cook anything, so the animals were eaten raw.

"We can't just leave them out there," Anderson said.

"We sure can," Brother Peter replied. "Look out that window. More showing up every minute, all of them as hungry as we are. Those two are finished." He started toward the stairwell, the remaining pilot falling in behind him.

Anderson turned and opened the outside door, yelling as loud as he could. "I'll draw them away! When they start to spread out, make a run between them!"

At the top of the stairs Brother Peter spun, his hollowed face paling further. "What the fuck . . . ?"

"Hey, over here! Over here!" Anderson banged a fist on the metal door. "Come and get it!"

The charred dead began to move toward this new sound.

"Anderson, you close that fucking door right now."

"That's it! Over here, keep coming!"

"Now, Anderson. Right now!"

"They're our friends, Peter," he said, not looking back. "We can't leave them to die. It's not Christian."

"Christian," Peter muttered, reaching for the automatic in his waistband, except it wasn't there. Then he remembered he had left it behind, hidden high amid a nest of pipes. There were only three bullets left, and he couldn't risk using them or losing the pistol on a scavenging run.

Outside, the dead were leaving the food service vehicle and shuffling toward the doorway. As Anderson predicted, they were scattered, with plenty of space between them. "Now!" he shouted. "Now, go now! You can make it!"

Thing Two and the female staffer sat down at the edge and jumped. The pilot landed in a squat. The woman hit wrong, and she screamed when her tibia snapped and punched through the flesh of her leg.

The noise caused some of the dead to turn back.

"Dear Lord," whispered Anderson.

"Don't drag him into this goat fuck," Peter snarled. "This is your doing." God, how he wanted to shoot Anderson in the head. It would be worth the bullet.

Thing Two picked the woman up and put her over his shoulder, pulling the hammer from his belt and running for the door as fast as his burden would allow. He dodged and weaved, evading outstretched arms and once even shouldering a creature aside. When it fell its legs splintered, and the torso broke in half amid a cloud of ash. What was left tried to drag itself after them.

"They're going to lead them right in here!"

Anderson shook his head. "They can make it."

The pilot darted left around one of the dead, then had to swing his hammer at another. It struck at the shoulder, breaking off the arm and making the creature stagger just enough for him to get past. The woman howled with every step, her compound fracture bouncing against the pilot's chest. He didn't stop, and then suddenly he was five feet from the door, puffing hard.

Four of them fell upon him from either side of the door, lunging out of the shadows, twisted hands catching hold. He dropped the woman, who screamed when she fell. Thing Two started swinging the hammer, even as teeth bit into him. Anderson leaped outside and grabbed the woman by her wrists, backing up quickly and dragging her inside. Brother Peter slammed the door behind them as the dead took the pilot to the ground. More arrived to feed, and others pressed against the door, pounding at the thick glass and leaving black smudges.

Anderson was holding the female staffer, speaking softly to her. Brother Peter looked at them both, shaking his head. "Carry her back." He motioned at Thing One, who handed off the crowbar and helped Anderson lift her. The woman shrieked.

"You better stay quiet, honey," Peter said, wagging a finger. "Or you'll bring them down on us. I know what they like to eat, and I'll be happy to feed them." He went down the stairs.

Life underground was a trial and had become a timeless haze of unlit tunnels, dimming flashlights, and constant hunger. They found a few tools and managed to pilfer some suitcases without being eaten, which provided them with scraps of burned clothing. All of the toiletries were in trial sizes, and melted beyond use. Stairs that led to the main terminal revealed a vast haunted house of blackened bodies drifting through spaces completely scoured by high-intensity heat and flames, barely recognizable as an airport. Nothing of use there.

The network of tunnels and engineering spaces was untouched by the fire but had little more to offer other than darkness and the occasional zombie. One of the staffers, the young man who had whined about going underground, had walked straight into the arms of a hungry corpse when he opened a door without listening at it first. Brother Peter had been forced to expend a bullet to put the thing down, and then had waited patiently until his bitten disciple first died of his wounds, then arose minutes later. Peter switched to the heavy pry bar, relishing the crunch of the head when he connected. Now, after the botched raid on the food service truck, they were down to six, with one of them badly wounded.

Peter didn't want to admit it, but it had been Anderson who made the discovery that kept them alive this long: the water. What few restrooms were down here had industrial toilets with direct plumbing instead of tanks, and the water in the bowls was blue with chemicals. Juices and soft drinks from a lone vending machine ran out quickly, and the only water fountain they found sat dry and silent.

"The sprinkler system," Anderson suggested. He was right. Once the pressure in the system dropped off from fighting the unstoppable blaze, there was still residual water left in the pipes. They broke one open and caught a thin drizzle in plastic buckets and totes, repeating the process everywhere they went. It tasted awful, but it kept them going.

Brother Peter hadn't congratulated Anderson. He loudly praised God for His gift, and quietly hated his senior aide even more. And now Anderson had done something heroic and saved a life. Might the others start looking to *him* as their leader? It deserved some thought.

They had made a home of sorts in a cluster of rooms somewhere beneath the northern end of the terminal. Peter was the only one who instinctively knew north from south down here and had in fact committed the layout of the entire maze to memory. All his life he'd had an uncanny sense and nearly eidetic memory for directions, depth, distance, and spatial differences. His time in the Omaha silos had only sharpened this ability.

A small break room was where everyone but Peter slept, people curled up on makeshift beds of scorched clothing, their only light source a large, battery-operated work light that in the beginning had been a dazzling white and had now faded to an amber shimmer. The televangelist took over a small adjacent office and slept tilted back in a swivel chair with his feet propped on a metal desk. He kept the water and what little food they had in there with him, forbidding the others to touch it until he distributed it personally.

When they arrived back at their base, the remaining two staffers, a man and a woman equipped with a flashlight and armed with screw-drivers, were out hunting for food. Before they left, Brother Peter warned them not to come back empty-handed, and they had yet to return. At the minister's direction, Thing One and Anderson carried the wounded staffer through the break room and into a small locker area with a common shower at one end. They set her down gently on the white tile beneath shower heads that had been broken off but yielded no water.

Anderson squatted beside the woman and told her she would be okay, wiping at her tears with his thumb and offering a smile. She cried softly, leaning her head against his shoulder. Several minutes later he joined the televangelist in the locker area, hands thrust in his pockets. "That's a really bad break. I'm worried about infection."

Brother Peter nodded. "I don't think any of us know how to set a broken bone, or even get it back through the skin without hurting her worse."

"And it would still get infected." They were quiet for a while. "What are we going to do?"

Peter gave his aide a pat on the shoulder and walked back into the shower, Anderson behind him. He smiled at the female staffer, who tried to be brave and smile back. Then he swung his crowbar like a big leaguer in a home-run derby and caved in the side of her head, snapping her neck at the same time. She made a short noise like a newborn kitten and slid over onto the tiles.

Anderson stood with his mouth working silently, staring at the dead woman, a piece of bloody skull fragment stuck to his cheek. Brother Peter picked it off and flicked it away.

"We're going to eat her, that's what."

TWENTY-TWO

Oakland

His name was Terry Younger, a twenty-nine-year-old IT specialist who still lived in his mother's house. Single, pudgy around the middle, and with thinning hair, Terry was most comfortable in jeans, flannels, and sarcastic T-shirts, like the one he was wearing now. *WTF?* was spread across his belly in white letters.

The bites on his thighs, which had shredded his jeans along with large portions of meat and his femoral artery, were rotting and black. His skin was the color of skim milk, and his eyes a glazed yellow. He didn't know who Terry Younger was anymore, didn't know anything except to follow three others of his kind as they shuffled down the center of a suburban street. Maybe there was food nearby.

Pufft.

In front of him, the side of a corpse's head blew out, and it collapsed to the asphalt. Terry stopped and cocked his head.

Pufft.

Another went down. The sound had come from the right, soft and muffled, like a cough.

Pufft.

A third creature fell, a small hole above one eyebrow and a much bigger hole in the back of its head. Terry moved toward the sound. It meant food.

Pufft.

Something punched through his *WTF?* shirt and into his chest. He didn't feel it.

Pufft.

His collarbone shattered. Yes, up there, in that window. The sound was coming—

Pufft.

Through the M4's sight, Skye Dennison watched the last of the four go down to a head shot. Damn, three bullets to hit the mark. Unacceptable. She sat back on the bed that had been her shooting nest, lifted the M4 off the pile of pillows on the window ledge, and ejected the magazine. Taking loose rounds from a pouch on her vest, she refilled it, gave it two sharp taps on the bed frame so the bullets were well seated, then inserted it and armed the weapon again with the charging handle.

Six shots. Four tangos down. Time to move.

She shrugged into her pack and extra bandoliers of ammo, slung the padded case for the sniper rifle over her shoulder, and retreated back downstairs with her M4 ready. The first floor was as she'd left it: front door with dead bolt on, back door locked and braced with a chair, kitchen cabinets all standing open and the remains of a small meal still on the table.

She slipped out the back and crossed the yard, scaling a fence after she checked to see if anything was waiting on the other side. Moving yard to yard this way, she reached the last house on the block and peeked out at an intersection through a wooden fence. A green Prius was mashed against an elm tree, its driver's window broken and dark streaks of blood on the door. A mountain bike lay on its side near a fire hydrant. Several pages of newspaper tumbled past, a light breeze rustling through the late-summer leaves of stately trees. Nothing else moved.

Skye hurried across, rifle to her shoulder and finger resting near the trigger, immediately disappearing into the backyard of the first house on the new block. She resumed her technique of checking the fence and the yard beyond, going over, trotting to the next fence, and repeating. Midway through the block, a woman in a yellow sundress and sandals stumbled toward her through a rose trellis archway, groaning. Skye stopped, dropped to one knee, sighted, and fired. The bullet punched through one of the woman's eyes. Skye was moving again before the body hit the ground.

She traveled this way down three more blocks, with only one more encounter. Peeking over a white fence, she saw a pair of freaks on their knees, busily feeding on what might have been a dog. Skye stepped down from the fence and then walked back to a swingset in the yard, climbing the slide's ladder until she had a good angle over the boards.

Pufft. Pufft. Dammit, hit it in the back. *Pufft.*

Then she went over the fence.

At the next intersection she belly-crawled under a spreading lilac bush to scout the area. Across the diagonal was a large, two-story house with lots of windows and no big trees to block line of sight. She took ten minutes to check the area through her rifle scope. When she was certain it was clear, she took a deep breath and spent another ten minutes watching. Two freaks slouched into view from behind a minivan half a block away, moving in the other direction. She waited until they were gone before scooting across and into another backyard.

The house was unlocked. Leading with the silenced muzzle of the assault rifle—what a find that had been—she moved on the balls of her feet and checked every room, every closet, behind furniture and under beds. Then she bolted both the front and back doors, made sure the garage was empty before locking that door too, then inspected the upstairs. In a guest room she found a window overlooking the roof of a covered patio in the backyard. She opened the window as high as it would go and punched out the screen, leaving it that way. Her emergency exit.

The master bedroom in the left corner of the house commanded a nice long view of both the street in front of the house and the side street. She raised the windows, took out the screens, and found a narrow table in an upstairs hallway, dragging it in and setting it up midway between the windows, slightly back from them. A couple of pillows went on top, and she pulled a hard-backed chair up in front of it. She could now sit at the table and pivot between both windows, staying fully in the room without the barrel of the rifle ever poking outside where it might be seen.

Skye unzipped the sniper rifle and rested it on the pillows.

She took off her combat vest, liberated from an Army/Navy store, stripped down to a tank top, and with the M4 lying beside her began doing crunches. When she could do no more she rolled over and did diamond push-ups until her arms and shoulders burned, followed by more crunches. When she stayed in a house with a weight bench, she added it to the routine, pumping iron until her arms threatened to drop the bar on her chest. When she found a pull-up bar, usually mounted in the doorway of a teenage boy's bedroom, she hauled herself up and down until her arms quivered. Then she rested for a bit and did more.

Squats, lunges, jumping jacks for aerobics. More muscle meant she could carry more ammo, could run farther without tiring, could hold the shooting position for longer periods of time, and could swing harder and faster when she was in close. Her long hair didn't get in the way of her exercising, because it was gone. She had cut it all off after the zombie on the ladder tried using it to pull her to her death.

After the workout she raided the kitchen for canned veggies, fish, and meat. Tonight it was green beans and sardines, with a few crackers for carbs, and a diet Snapple. She stayed away from soda and high-sugar sports drinks, less for nutritional reasons (with the energy she spent every day, she actually could have used the calories) and more out of habits developed in a time when she was concerned about acne and attracting boys. The MREs were for emergency use only.

Then it was time to sleep, but only lightly, and not for too long.

When the sun went down she rose and spent two hours with the night scope on the big M24, hunting the street, engaging targets as far out as she could reach. Five rounds only, whether she hit or not, and then it was time to clean the rifle. One more inspection of the perimeter, another small meal, then more sleep. In the morning she would crunch and do push-ups, get her gear ready, snipe with the M4 for half a dozen rounds, clean it, and get moving.

Every day the same.

But not at first.

After her flight from the rooftop that night, Skye had gone only a short distance before hunkering down in an optical center with both front and back doors. She waited a full twenty-four hours before going back to the roof, making that long climb up the fire escape ladder and peeking over the top. They were all gone, including Taylor and Sgt. Postman. Skye collected the sniper rifle in its case and as much ammunition as she could carry. From Taylor's pack, still lying where he had set it down, she took a nasty-looking black machete in a nylon sheath. It was now strapped to her own pack. She would need it for quiet, close-in work.

Skye scavenged on the move: boots, soft dark pants with lots of cargo pockets, dark shirts, a black zip-up hoodie, a black knit cap. She gathered batteries, a flashlight, a spotting scope on a little tripod from a sporting goods store, matches and candles, feminine products, a good pair of sunglasses. Never too much of anything, always mindful of the weight.

Now, sitting at the kitchen table in the corner house, the night's sniping behind her, she nibbled on leftover sardines and crackers, sipping the Snapple. She longed for some fresh fruit but knew the fridge wasn't the answer. She avoided refrigerators. After this much time without power, they were all rancid.

On the table beside her sat her cell phone, dark and quiet. Once the center of her world, it was now just a paperweight. At first she tried desperately to find a way to recharge it, just to get at the photos of her mom and dad and sister stored within. She gave up after a while, but still carried the phone. Happier times. Smiling, living people. If she could see their faces again, would she just sit and stare, crying over what was lost?

Skye abruptly got up and carried the phone into the living room. She kissed it, and then set it carefully on the mantel over the fireplace.

In fourteen days she had not spoken to another living person. Not that there had been many opportunities, but she saw that she wasn't entirely alone out here. There had been a man with a backpack and a hunting rifle, walking alone at a distance. A week later, a band of seven people, including three women and two small children, had walked past her daytime shooting nest. Skye made no attempt to contact any of them.

Conversations led to caring. That was pain, and it was a distraction. Alone, there was no one to worry about or slow her down. Alone, she could focus.

Never stay in one place for more than a day.

Never pack more than you can carry over a fence.

Move fast.

Movement is life.

Relocate often.

Make every bullet count.

She was traveling steadily south and suspected that she had already left Berkeley behind and was now somewhere in suburban Oakland, moving deeper into heavily populated areas, doing it on purpose. It would mean an environment rich with targets.

Several days ago Skye discovered someone else's shooter's nest, set up in the second-floor street-side window of a used bookstore. It was military—she found their Humvee half a block away—and it had been overrun. One of the two bodies still in the nest, both men, had obviously turned before being put down with a point-blank shot to the forehead. The other was slumped against a wall near the shooting position covered in bites, the victim of a self-inflicted gunshot wound. The muzzle of a silenced nine-millimeter automatic was still stuck in the man's mouth, his hand dangling from it by a finger stuck in the trigger guard.

Both soldiers were in black-and-gray camouflage, but instead of the big Kevlar helmets Taylor and Postman had worn, these two had dull black helmets similar to what a mountain climber would wear. Her movie knowledge said Special Forces, not that it had helped either one of them, and however many buddies might have been here with them were no doubt out there shuffling around with the rest of the freaks.

It was like finding buried pirate treasure. She took the silenced pistol, its holster, and ammo. She took a professional-looking double-edged knife from where it was strapped to the side of one man's calf, fastening it to her own. The shooter had been using an M4 as well, but his weapon had a silencer on the end, so she swapped it for her own assault rifle and took his bandolier of magazines.

Skye drained the Snapple and went upstairs to sleep.

The moon was still up when she opened her eyes some time later, at first unsure about what had awakened her. A sound. A breaking bottle? A cough? Something outside? She padded to the bedroom door, the pistol appearing in her hand without her consciously picking it up, and listened. It was still closed and locked, the house quiet on the other side. She went to her nest and picked up the M24, turning on the night scope and tracking across the two windows.

She saw him at once. Her eyes were drawn to the movement, even as stealthy as it was, the scope showing her a nocturnal world in bright shades of green. He was creeping, trying to be sneaky. Freaks didn't do that. Hunched over and keeping to the shadows, the man moved slowly down the sidewalk across the street. He had bushy hair and a beard, wore a leather jacket, and carried an axe in both hands. A woman's head was tied to his belt by her long hair.

The man stared at Skye's house as he moved, never taking his eyes off it.

Had he seen her shooting? Seen her come in here? Did he have friends?

Shink.

The M24's silencer made a different sound than the M4. The man's head vaporized above the chin. Skye slid the sniper rifle back into its case and gathered her gear, then slipped down the stairs and out the back door. Time to relocate.

TWENTY-THREE

Emeryville

Mexico wasn't looking promising, at least not via an overland route. Things were worse than Carney and TC had imagined, the dead more numerous the farther south they traveled, thickening every day. The idea of traveling the length of California, straight into one of the most densely populated areas in the country, quickly became unrealistic.

And it wasn't just the dead. The roads were steadily deteriorating, fields of abandoned cars and trucks slowing their progress and often forcing time-consuming detours. The heavy blue Bearcat wasn't exactly economical with fuel, and they had been compelled to make frequent stops for gas. In many cases others had been there before them, the covers to the underground tanks left open and drained. The only advantage they had was that the Bearcat used diesel, and those tanks were mostly untouched.

An alternative was to head farther east and then turn to the back roads of California or even the deserts of Nevada. Traffic jams would be less common and easier to maneuver around, and the lower population would mean having to contend with fewer of the walking dead. But that solution simply created new problems, the first being availability of fuel. It wouldn't do to get out into the desolation of Nevada high desert, coasting on fumes into the only gas station within a hundred miles, only to discover the underground tanks were empty or that the entire place had burned to the ground.

They had seen plenty of that already.

The second problem with this plan was even *getting* far enough east to reach that open country. The attempted exodus from the Bay Area in the opening days of the plague had effectively clogged not only the eastbound lanes, but the opposite side as well when desperate people discovered they could use *both* sides of the road to get out. The way heading into Oakland and ultimately San Francisco was only better by a little bit.

Carney sat on the hood of the Bearcat with a scoped M14 over his knees, a durable rifle battle-tested in Vietnam and still preferred by prison guards and some special operations teams. He smoked a cigarette and watched TC play with a zombie.

They were in the empty parking lot of a Walmart, and the younger man was dancing in a circle around the lurching corpse of a young woman in tight jeans and a belly shirt. She had long blond hair, looked to be about twenty, and had probably been quite pretty. Before she was dead, of course.

"Can you believe the tits on this bitch? That's a damned shame," TC said as he punched her in the side of the head and danced away. The girl groaned and turned toward him. He hit her three times in the lower back, making her stagger, and when she spun he batted away a flailing arm and gave her an uppercut that would have dropped a grown man. The corpse's head rocked from the force of the blow and she stumbled backward but only fell down on her butt because the hit put her off balance. She started to get right back up. "Goddamn porn star, man! Look at them!"

"She *had* nice tits," Carney said.

"They're still good, man. Nice and firm. Must be implants." As she got to her feet he reached in and grabbed a handful of breast, giving it a squeeze. The creature, quicker than she looked, grabbed him by the wrist and sank her teeth into his hand.

The bite didn't penetrate the mesh-reinforced corrections gloves.

TC rabbit-punched her with the other fist, three fast blows to the face that crushed her nose and fractured an orbital socket. He ripped his hand out of her mouth and kept circling and punching. The girl rotated and grabbed, her head darting forward as her teeth snapped.

"Carney, you think I'd get infected from her cooze?"

The older man flicked his cigarette away and scanned the parking lot. Nothing else was moving. "Brother, I catch you fucking one of these things and I'll beat you like a piñata."

TC laughed. "I just won't let you catch me."

"Man, I know you're hard up, but that's sick. She's dead."

"Pussy is pussy, right?"

"No, it's not. If you can catch HIV or the syph that way, you can sure catch what she's got. Your shit would turn black and die."

The younger inmate laughed again. "Zombie dick!" He grabbed at the other breast and gave her a shove, knocking her back down. "Look at those *titties*! C'mon, man, you hold her down, we'll gag her so she can't bite, and—"

"*TC!*"

He stepped away at once, turning to face his cellmate, eyes wide.

"Goofing with them is one thing, but I'm not kidding about the sex. I *will* fuck you up."

He frowned. "Okay." The play went out of him, and he walked to a sledgehammer leaning against the side of the vehicle, carrying it back to where the corpse was struggling to its feet. The muscled inmate handled the sledge as if it were a tack hammer. He used a boot to kick the rising corpse back to the asphalt, then crushed her head with a single blow. He stood with his head down, facing away.

Carney let him stand there for a while, then shook his head. He produced a joint from a chest pocket and lit it. "C'mere, TC."

The younger man shuffled back slowly, still looking at his feet, but he caught a whiff and looked up, his face brightening as Carney held the joint out for him. He sucked in the smoke, held it, and then smiled as he hissed it out between his teeth. "Thanks, brother."

Carney grinned and slapped him lightly on the side of the head. "Asshole."

TC gave him a shy smile. "I wouldn't *really* try to fuck one. I was just kidding."

"I know," Carney said. They were both lying.

The scavenging had been prosperous. In addition to the weapons and riot gear they had taken from the training facility, the back of the Bearcat was filled with more rifles, shotguns, handguns, and ammunition collected from a gun shop that had already been looted, but not completely. They didn't even have to kill anyone to get it. An assortment of shopping centers provided them with canned food and dry goods, cases of water and soda, sleeping bags, pillows, flashlights, and tools. They had rope, a radio (it picked up only static but played CDs), walkie-talkies, a good pair of binoculars, road maps, cartons of cigarettes, toilet paper, and an impressive collection of jerk-off magazines TC took from a 7-Eleven. Spare cans of diesel, extra water, and more food were strapped to the roof under a blue plastic tarp. There was a little booze, not too much, and Carney kept a tight grip on it.

Shortly after getting into the outskirts of Berkeley, they had found a medicinal marijuana shop. TC was like a five-year-old in a toy store, but Carney held the reins, taking only a little. He maintained control over that as well. TC didn't object, just like he didn't object to being reminded to wash up and brush his teeth, being told to go easy on the Red Bulls, or the occasional sharp rebuke when he was acting like a dick.

"Finish up and let's go," said Carney. TC took three fast puffs and pitched the joint away. The Bearcat got rolling.

"You still think we're gonna find one?" TC looked out the passenger window at a trio of coyotes feeding on a body on the sidewalk. The corpse was on its back, waving its arms and snapping at the animals as they took turns leaping in, taking a bite and leaping back out. So far it appeared animals were immune to whatever it was that turned people into zombies.

"Maybe. We just need to keep looking."

TC smiled. "I've never been on one. Do you think I'll puke?"

Carney laughed. "If you do, you'll clean it up."

Despite the improbability of a cross-country journey, Mexico was still in play. Carney was looking for a boat, something small enough for the two of them to handle but durable enough to take on the Pacific as they cruised down the coast.

That was the real reason they weren't making much progress south. Carney was scouring every dock and marina he could find on his maps: Richmond, El Cerrito, Albany, northwest Berkeley. Most were empty. The few boats they found were either rotting hulks, too small (little more than rowboats with tiny outboard motors), or little sailboats requiring skills neither possessed and didn't want to risk learning in open water. They needed something like a sport fisherman, or even a small yacht. TC was optimistic, his faith in his cellmate unshakable. Carney, however, was growing more and more skeptical about his plan, although he didn't voice his doubts. It wouldn't do TC any good.

They were almost to Emeryville now, and Carney guided the Bearcat down an I-80 off-ramp, weaving in and out of cars with their doors standing open, and going around a tractor-trailer crunched against a guardrail. Ahead and to the right was the span of the Bay

Bridge, stretching out over water that was being whipped into a chop by a stiff wind. The high buildings on the peninsula looked like a graveyard.

"Check that out," said TC, pointing.

Carney braked and looked over at a Taco Bell across the street from the off-ramp. A U-Haul truck sat in the otherwise empty parking lot, surrounded by at least a hundred of the walking dead, reaching up and pawing at the sides. A man in his late sixties was kneeling on the roof, waving his arms at the riot vehicle. TC popped open his door and stood on the metal step. He could hear the old man shouting, "Help me! Help me!"

"He's fucked," TC said to his partner. "You're fucked!" he shouted to the old man.

"Don't leave me up here!"

"Why not?" A few of the dead turned toward TC's voice and began moving slowly in his direction, but not many. "What are you gonna do for me?"

"Anything!"

TC laughed. "How about a blowjob?"

The old man's shoulders slumped. "Anything."

The inmate ducked back inside. "What do you think?"

Carney looked at him. "I think you're an asshole. What's wrong with you?"

"It's fun." He saw the look on his cellmate's face. "What? We've seen people before, we never stopped to help them. Too much risk, that's what you said."

"None of them were like that." He shook his head and picked up a dashboard microphone, flicking the PA switch. His voice boomed from a speaker mounted to the top of the roof. "When they clear out, get down and get out of here."

The man nodded. "Take me with you!"

Carney keyed the mic. "No. And if you follow us, I'll feed you to them." He turned on the Bearcat's siren, a deafening *whoop-whoop* that bounced off buildings and rolled down empty streets. He let it run for half a minute, and most of the dead moved toward it, away from the truck. When enough had left, the man scrambled down over the cab and the hood, got inside the U-Haul, and drove away. Carney shut off the siren and gunned the Bearcat in the other direction.

"Why do you give a fuck about this guy?" TC asked.

"I don't. It's just a shitty way to die."

"What about the woman in Richmond? That was shitty. We didn't do anything about that."

Carney stared straight ahead. "That was different." It had been their second day of freedom, and they rolled into an intersection where a gas station on a far corner was boiling with hundred-foot-high flames, the heat marching away in waves and softening the asphalt. A woman clutching an infant and a handgun was in the road, surrounded by the dead closing in, leaving her no way out. She hugged the baby close and turned, running straight into the fire. Half a dozen corpses followed her in.

"There wasn't time," Carney said quietly. "We got there too late." He looked away so his cellmate wouldn't see his eyes tear up.

It wasn't the first time he had been too late.

And that was why he'd gone to prison.

TWENTY-FOUR

San Jose

Air Lieutenant Vladimir Yurish was flying two missions a day now, and there was talk that everyone would be increasing to three or more. The requirement was driven by a shortage of rotary wing pilots. Two birds had gone down to mechanical failures; one crashed and burned with no survivors, and the other experienced turbine trouble and was forced to land in an industrial park. When the rescue bird arrived an hour later, the chopper was surrounded by walking corpses, there was no sign of the crew, and no one answered the radio calls.

Three more birds, along with their crews, were lost during insertions or extractions in hot landing zones—LZs—when they were swarmed by the dead. Between pilots and co-pilots, this represented a significant loss of flight-qualified personnel. The order came down that all co-pilots had been promoted and given command of their own bird, including Vlad's partner, Conroy. The Russian was flying alone in the cockpit now, although he still had RJ as his door gunner.

"Ranch House, this is Groundhog-Seven, we are approaching the LZ now," Vlad said.

"Copy, Groundhog-Seven. Watch your tail, Ivan."

"*Da, da,* I am watching." Vlad brought the Black Hawk in fast to the landing zone, a helipad on the roof of a twenty-two-story office building. RJ watched the rooftop over his gun. The second the wheels touched down, eight soldiers leaped out of the aircraft, rifles ready as they hurried in a line down off the pad and toward an open doorway. As soon as the last man was out of the aircraft, Vlad lifted into the air and banked away from the building. "Ranch House, Groundhog-Seven, insertion complete. Team Bravo is moving toward objective."

"Roger, Groundhog. Bravo will extract with Groundhog-Three in zero-one hours, same LZ. Seven, I need you to come east to two-seven-zero. We have reports of survivors on the roof of a school about zero-five miles from your position. Need to confirm."

"Copy, Ranch House," Vlad said, bringing the nose to the new heading. "Groundhog-Seven en route."

Yesterday, another pilot coming back from San Jose had reported seeing a big dry-erase board hanging from a window of the building Vlad had just left, with *ALIVE × 15* written on it in bold letters. Team Bravo was one of several rescue teams working out of Lemoore tasked with searching for survivors on the ground, and they had drawn this mission. A patched-together collection of troops—regular Army, National Guard, and Air Force security police—they would go in to determine if any civilians were left alive, and if so how many. If the search was a bust, Groundhog-3 would take them off the roof in an hour. If live civilians were found, more birds would be called in to evacuate them, while the rescue team held a defensive perimeter until they were aboard.

The rescue teams lost a lot of men.

Vladimir wasn't optimistic about this mission. Before going in, he circled the building slowly at several levels and saw no messages on a board or anything else. The Russian called back that he believed the information was incorrect, only to be told that the original, reporting pilot said the building had a giant W on the side. He acknowledged that yes, this building had such a marking, but repeated that there was no sign hanging from a window. Again, Lemoore ordered him to drop his troops.

As he flew away from the tower, he brooded on the fact that office buildings were giant, dark mazes filled with plenty of places for skinnies to hide, easily a death trap for a little squad of eight men. He tried to focus on his next pointless mission, another unconfirmed sighting of survivors. It wasn't that he resented looking for people in need of rescue, and he was the kind of man who would put himself and his bird in jeopardy without a second thought if that was what it took to get them out. The problem was that each day brought an increasing number of false (or more likely, outdated) sightings.

The fuel gauge read fifty percent, enough to complete the mission and get back to Lemoore without going into the red. They reached the school in minutes and identified it easily: a flat, one-story elementary school surrounded by parking lots, playgrounds, and grassy areas. After two slow circles, both Vladimir and RJ were confident the roof was empty. Maybe people had been there, but they were gone now. Around the building, the dead drifted along in the hundreds. RJ didn't bother to shoot at them.

Vlad keyed the mic. "Ranch House, Groundhog-Seven. We have negative sightings at our location, repeat, negative sightings."

"Copy, Groundhog-Seven," the controller responded.

"Ranch House, do you have another mission in which we may burn more fuel with nothing to show for it?"

RJ glanced forward at his pilot and shook his head.

"Groundhog-Seven, stand by."

"*Da.*" Vlad put the bird in a slow right orbit and waited for orders. This was how the days went: a morning briefing, followed by either the insertion of a ground team to rescue reported survivors (which panned out only about twenty percent of the time), followed then by a grid search or a trip to validate the sightings of another pilot. They would fly back to Lemoore for fuel and a quick meal, and then go out again for more of the same. For weeks the Russian and his Black Hawk had ranged all over central California, but he spent most of his time between Fresno and San Jose. Fewer survivors were being picked up each day.

And fewer ground teams were coming back intact.

The morning briefings, conducted by a tired-looking Navy commander and several equally weary aides, painted a dismal picture, and even at that Vladimir was convinced he and the other crews weren't getting the full story. It was everywhere, and spreading. Most forms of civilian organization and control had quickly broken down, and it seemed the military was following suit. Numerous bases in the west—Naval Station San Diego, Nellis, Miramar, Pendleton—had fallen. Edwards was expected to collapse any day and was evacuating with everything they had. It was all coming apart.

Vlad didn't need the briefings to tell him that; he saw it all from the air. Highways were choked in both directions with empty cars and trucks, dotted with massive accidents. Fires had ravaged entire neighborhoods and towns. Aircraft, including some big commercial airliners, had gone down in populated areas. The San Jose International Airport had burned. There had been explosions, streets flooded by burst water mains, military roadblocks, field hospitals and refugee centers overrun.

The dead swarmed through streets littered with discarded belongings, broken glass, and abandoned vehicles. They wandered in and out of buildings, across rooftops and parking lots, more of them every day: all races, all ages, all dead. It made Vlad sad to see them, even though they were not his people. They were people nonetheless, and he had no illusions of a better situation back in his native land. Again he was thankful his beautiful Anya and Lita were already dead, far out of reach from this nightmare. He knew his gunner had a family somewhere down south, but RJ never spoke of them, and Vlad didn't ask. But RJ was quieter now, no longer cracking jokes, and he had reverted to calling Vladimir *Lieutenant* instead of his Russian nickname, *Troll*.

"Groundhog-Seven, this is Ranch House. You are cleared to return to base."

"Roger, Ranch House. Groundhog-Seven is RTB."

The Black Hawk put its tail to San Jose and headed back to Lemoore, flying low so that both pilot and gunner could watch for refugees or stray military units. They saw neither, and the flight passed with only the thump of the rotors and the vibration of the airframe to keep them company.

Naval Air Station Lemoore was a sprawling complex of buildings and runways, sitting alone in open country and ringed with a high, sturdy fence topped with razor wire. It had three primary gates with guardhouses, and several service gates. All had been reinforced and were heavily defended. The rest of the long perimeter was constantly patrolled.

It had to be; at last count, more than fifty thousand of the walking dead surrounded the base, pressing against the fence, shaking it, moaning day and night. The briefings suggested they had been drawn here by the constant noise from the airfield, the inbound and outbound choppers, and the occasional truck convoy, though there hadn't been one of those in over a week. At this point they wouldn't have been able to open the gates much less drive through the crowd, and no one was in a hurry to try either. The briefers expressed confidence in the structural integrity of the fences and the armed security measures.

Vlad laughed out loud in the briefing room at that one, drawing an evil glare from the briefer. More of the dead were arriving by the hour, adding their weight to the pressure on the fence line. The pilot understood physics well enough to see where it would end. At first, command had used the small gunships called "Little Birds" to make strafing runs outside the fence, attempting to thin them out. It was highly ineffective, consuming vast quantities of ammunition with few results. And killing them off was apparently no longer an option, because no one was flying gun runs anymore. There weren't enough bullets on base to control them, and if bombing or napalm were employed, it would only scatter them temporarily but succeed in destroying the fence.

As the Black Hawk thumped overhead and crossed the fence line onto the base, thousands of pairs of milky eyes looked upward, twice that number of reaching arms and grasping fingers clawing at the air.

Vlad set his bird on painted numbers on the tarmac, shutting it down. He and RJ spent ten minutes making sure all was secured and properly turned off, and then they walked a short distance to a truck that would carry them off the field. A small fuel tanker pulled up next to the Black Hawk. Their day was done.

In the cab of the truck, the driver gave them a nod. "Bravo was yours, right?"

"Yes. Why?" Vlad asked.

"Groundhog-Three went in to pick them up, but the ground team didn't show up at their extraction time. They circled for ten minutes until the Bravo team leader finally walked out onto the roof. He was a skinny."

A Russian in the O Club. Who could have imagined," a Navy pilot said to Vlad.

"And yet here I am," Vlad said, smiling.

The fighter jock was twenty-six, ten years younger than Vladimir. His call sign was "Rocker," he was attached to the USS *Ronald Reagan*, and the dark circles under his eyes revealed a bone-deep exhaustion. Sitting in the darkness in a rumpled flight suit while a country song played in the background, Rocker raised his beer. "To you, my friend."

Vlad tapped his own beer against the glass and sipped. He was as tired as the other man looked and should have been in bed hours ago, but there was little point to it. He didn't sleep well when he did lie down. He had bad dreams.

"What the hell is a Russian doing flying an Army Black Hawk out of a Navy base?"

Vladimir explained the Russian Federation's helicopter purchase and his training assignment. "I was stationed at Hunter Liggett, out on the coast. After the outbreak, the Army ordered every available aircraft to different locations." He shrugged. "I was sent here."

"What about your buddies?"

There had been five other Russian pilots at the training facility with Vlad, all of them close friends. "I do not know," he said.

Rocker nodded and stared into his beer. "Hunter Liggett's gone now," he said after a while. "It's bad out there."

"Yes, I know."

The fighter pilot stared at him. "No, you don't. The shit I've seen . . ." He shook his head. "L.A. is gone. We're bombing the shit out of it right now. Rockeyes, napalm, whatever we got. The *Reagan's* off Catalina right now, every pilot making three, four bombing runs a day. Hammering the shit out of the City of Angels."

"Why are you not with them?"

"I'm assigned to reconnaissance, but they've got us scattered all over. Air groups from different ships are all mixed up, orders changing all the time. No one's in charge, everyone's in charge. It's a clusterfuck."

Vlad had to agree. The briefings were becoming confusing, and he had begun to think they weren't actually withholding information so much as they just didn't know anymore. Gossip ran wild, stories changed, and there was a subtle atmosphere of growing panic among the officers. It made him nervous.

"Why are they bombing Los Angeles?"

Rocker looked up with a puzzled look. "To contain them. The skinnies are moving. Millions of them, moving out of the city, moving north. No one's told you?"

"*Nyet.* They are moving together? In a group?"

A nod.

"Why?"

Rocker shrugged. "My CO says it's like a herd mentality, they just follow each other. From the air it looks like spreading lava, only made out of people, and they don't stop for anything: tanks, rocket attacks, gas, nothing works. They just keep on rolling." He took a long pull of his beer before continuing. "The bombs and napalm don't do much. They get blown down, and get right back up. They get blown apart, and the pieces still attached to the head keep crawling. Napalm just makes them crispy, and gas doesn't bother them at all."

"And they are coming north?"

Rocker nodded. "It's a sea of bodies. Mexico, San Diego, now L.A., growing all the time. I saw them tip over a garbage truck just from their mass."

Vladimir drank his beer. He saw that the young man wore a wedding band. "What is next for you?"

"I'm waiting for orders. I might get called back to the ship, or they might send me east. Probably Salt Lake City, because both Vegas and Reno are gone." He looked at the Russian and lowered his voice. "I hear they might use nukes to keep them from getting out of L.A."

Vladimir blinked. The Americans were thinking of using nuclear weapons on their own soil? On one of their greatest cities? It was madness.

Rocker finished his beer. "I'm going to throw up and pass out, hopefully in that order. Nice talking to you, Ivan."

The Russian watched him leave, then went outside a few minutes later, breathing deeply of the night air. It was almost ten o'clock, the sky clear and full of stars. He walked past dark, quiet buildings, streetlights run by the base's self-sufficient power station throwing his long, gangly shadow on the walls. He saw no one, but from up ahead came the drone of a big, propeller-driven aircraft coming in for a landing.

He passed warehouses and hangars, and at last arrived at the edge of the airfield. Vladimir found a crate to sit on and leaned back against a hangar wall, lighting a cigarette. The field was lit for night operations, rows of red glowing orbs marching into the distance marking the runways, lights flashing atop turning radar dishes and antenna clusters.

Somewhere out there in the dark was his Black Hawk, waiting to carry him back to what the other men called the Freak Show. Closer in, he could see the silhouette of the only fighter jet on base, Rocker's Super Hornet. NAS Lemoore was normally home to an entire carrier air group, as well as a wide assortment of cargo planes, tankers, airborne radar craft, and trainers. They were all gone now, off on other missions, scattered as the Navy pilot had said. Vlad wondered if they were all still flying, if they were wrecks strewn across some mountainside or sitting empty and quiet on an overrun airfield.

The plane Vlad heard was a C-130 painted in green camouflage. It had already rolled to a stop, and civilian refugees trudged down the wide cargo ramp to climb aboard buses lined up near the plane. He wondered at the origin of this latest batch. Southern California? Nevada? Oregon? NAS Lemoore was now a refugee center, and civilians evacuated from all over had been flying in for days. The now-empty hangars had been transformed into enormous housing units, and after they filled up, a tent city was erected nearby. One of the briefings reported that there were already more than ten thousand refugees on base.

How long would the Navy be able to feed them? Protect them? Where would they go after that? How would they get there? He saw families moving from the plane to the buses: parents carrying small, tired children, and bigger kids shuffling along with the adults, holding on to shirts and pockets. How much worse was it for them? he wondered, looking at the adults. How much extra fear they must be experiencing, worrying about their young and knowing what was out there in the darkness, waiting on the other side of the fence.

Even this far from the chain link Vladimir could hear them moaning.

He smoked his cigarette and watched the refugees, wondering what would become of them all. He included himself in that question.

TWENTY-FIVE

Alameda

Both vans, the one from the senior center and Angie's Armory, were packed with supplies: food, water, sleeping bags, first-aid kits, and spare cans of fuel. It was just a precaution, and in the event of an emergency whoever made it out in the vehicles would have something of a chance, at least for a little while. The gas tanks were topped off and a map of California sat on each dashboard.

Margaret Chu, in a friendly but firm voice, had pulled Angie and Bud aside and suggested the preparation. She said it wasn't just about emergencies. She was concerned that the group had become overly dependent on the two of them, and she feared what would happen if neither was around to give direction. She also insisted that a handgun and a box of bullets be hidden under both driver's seats.

They did as she asked. Angie was ashamed that she had underestimated Margaret, considered her less important because she wasn't a shooter. A quiet strength was hidden behind those plain features, and it reminded Angie that leadership wasn't just about carrying a gun and giving orders.

Angie shut the back door of her van and hooked the Galil over a shoulder, then retrieved her pocketbook off the front seat and locked the vehicle with an electronic chirp. On her way up to the roof she met Big Jerry coming down the stairs.

"Headed up to take a watch?" he asked.

"Elson's been up there long enough. He needs some dinner," Angie said.

"I'm pretty sure Maxie has plenty of chili left." He patted his belly. "It's good. I would have gone for seconds, but no one wants a fat man in the house after a second bowl of beans."

She chuckled.

"You look tired, Ang. Why don't you get some rest, I'll take your watch."

She shook her head. "You've been working all day." The big man was a quick student and a hard worker, paying close attention to everything Angie taught him about cleaning and caring for firearms. He had sat at a table with brushes, rags, and rods until his face was beaded with sweat and he reeked of gun oil.

"I don't mind. Besides, you work harder than all of us."

"You haven't learned to shoot yet," she reminded him.

He leaned his bulk against a railing. "And whose fault is that?"

"Tomorrow," she promised. "We'll start on the basics tomorrow."

He stayed put. "I won't need a gun up there anyway, because as you've pointed out, gunfire attracts them. Come on, take me up on the offer. If anything happens I'll come get you right away."

She smiled and on impulse kissed him on a round cheek. He blushed. "You're sweet. It's okay, I could use the quiet time."

He nodded and squeezed past her, then stopped. "Thank you." When she looked confused, he took her hand and gave it a squeeze.

"None of us would be alive if it weren't for you, and we all know that. So thank you."

Angie didn't know what to say, and Jerry let her off the hook by going downstairs before she tried.

Elson was walking a slow circuit of the roof, his shotgun resting in his arms. She sent him down to get some food and sleep and then sat on the low wall at the edge of the roof, looking out at the street and the surrounding neighborhood. It was twilight, purple and pink smears peeking out between thickening clouds, the temperature dropping into the fifties. A lone seagull coasted by, and the air smelled like rain. There were no lights in any direction, the streets below silent except for the shuffling feet of the dead.

Angie opened her pocketbook. It was a heavy thing, made of fine leather, and had set her back twelve hundred dollars at Bloomingdale's in San Francisco. Only a couple of years ago she would have choked on the idea of spending that kind of money on a bag, but the money she and Dean made from the TV show made it a casual purchase. She ran her fingertips over the leather. What did any of that mean now? She took out her wallet and opened it to the plastic flaps holding pictures.

Leah smiling and hugging a Winnie the Pooh.

Dean, handsome and grinning.

The three of them together, Leah caught in the middle of a belly laugh.

She stared at the photographs as her eyes welled up. From the purse she removed a blue plastic teething ring, the kind that held water and could be frozen in order to soothe aching little gums. It was rough with tiny teeth marks. Angie closed her hand over it and held it to her breast. Was she eating right? Was Dean able to bathe her? Did she have toys to play with and her footie pajamas?

She's safe at the ranch, she told herself. *They both are.* Dean got them out, and he would destroy anything that got in their way—man or creature—in order to protect his child. Leah was safe at the ranch, with her daddy and grandparents to look after her.

Angie wrapped her arms around herself and started to cry, something she hadn't allowed herself to do until now. It was a deep, wrenching thing, and she bent over with her hands clamped to her face, her back heaving as it overtook her. She was still like that when Bud found her on the roof, and he went to her and folded her into his arms, holding her close as her body shook with sobs. He didn't talk, didn't offer meaningless noises, only held her. They stayed that way a long time, until the emotional storm passed and her body stilled. Finally she pulled away, sniffling and wiping at her tears. "What am I doing?" she asked.

He waited.

"All this. This place, these people. What am I doing?"

"You're taking care of others," Bud said.

She laughed. "Strangers. I'm running a damned orphanage."

"You can't think that's a bad thing."

She turned away, staring out at a dead world. "I should be taking care of my family, Bud, taking care of *them*, not collecting strays." She had, in fact, found two more today while she was out gathering food. One was a malnourished high school girl named Meagan who had armed herself with the type of curving blade landscapers used on high weeds. The blood on the blade and her shirt said she had used it. The other was a nine-year-old girl who didn't speak much English but said her name was Theresa. Angie had come out of a store and caught her trying to steal a jug of water out of the back of the Excursion. It took some coaxing to get her to climb in instead of running away.

"You're saving lives," Bud said.

"For how long? We can't stay here forever. I can't stay here."

Her uncle nodded. "Every time you go out alone I wonder if you're coming back."

She knew he didn't mean he was worried she'd been killed. "I'll give it another week. I'll get this place as stocked and fortified as I can, but then I'm leaving." Fresh tears sprang into her eyes. "I have to go to them, Bud. I have to know."

He nodded slowly.

"And I want you to come with me. Our family needs to be together."

The man sighed. "I don't think I could, Ang."

"Oh, bullshit!"

"I'm not sure you could, either. But if you do, it's going to destroy them. Are you telling me you don't realize that you're the only thing holding them together?"

Angie shook her head. "They'll be fine. Margaret will step up, and Jerry and Elson, Sophia . . ." She stared at her uncle. "They're not my responsibility!"

Bud rested a hand on her shoulder. "Have you even thought about what it would take to get to the ranch? It's over two hundred miles. How far do you think you'd get before you were on foot and exposed? You saw it: We couldn't even get off this damned island."

"I'll make it."

"Even if you scavenged food and water on the move, you couldn't carry enough ammo to deal with what's waiting out there."

"Two of us could."

"No, we couldn't."

She pulled away. "What do you expect me to do, just write them off? My husband and my baby are out there, and they need me. And the family needs you. What do I tell my father, that I left you behind?"

"My brother knows me a lot better than you do, little girl."

She blinked at the sharp tone.

"I know what you want, Ang. If you have to go, then you'll go, and my heart will break along with everyone else's. But we brought these people here and told them they'd be safe, that we'd protect them. It probably won't matter, I know how this will all end, but I'll make my stand with them. They're not strangers anymore."

Angie's cheeks burned with shame, and she hung her head as more tears fell. Bud took her in his arms again, hugging her tight.

"I miss them so much," she cried. "I need my baby."

"I know, honey, I know. We'll figure it out."

Neither of them noticed that Maxie had been standing in the shadows just inside the door to the roof, eavesdropping. They didn't notice him slip silently back downstairs, either.

TWENTY-SIX

I-80

They stood side by side, two armed men with binoculars at the guard-rail of a highway off-ramp, scanning the scene below. A sprawling travel plaza sat on more than an acre of asphalt: twenty pumps under a big canopy on the left, a dozen diesel pumps on the right under a higher canopy for the big rigs. There was a service garage, a car wash, space for RVs and overnight truckers, vast parking lots, and a big central building. Signs offered restaurants, a gift shop, restrooms and showers, hot coffee and a visitor's center. Everything a traveler could need.

The dead meandered among the cars in the lots, in and out of the covered fuel service areas, bumping against the main building's glass doors. The two men counted more than a hundred of the dead, scattered across the plaza.

"Do you think they know what they are?" Evan asked.

Calvin took a while before answering. "Probably about as much as a potted plant knows itself. That would be a blessing, don't you think?"

Evan agreed. "I hope they can't remember what they were. Their lives, the things they knew and dreamed about, what they loved and wanted . . . what they've lost. I hope you're right."

"Having a heart in this new world isn't necessarily an asset, my friend. But I'm glad you still have one. Hold on to it." They watched for a bit longer. There weren't any of the handwritten *NO GAS* signs they had seen over the past two days, but that didn't mean much. With their binoculars they found the concrete slab for the underground fuel tanks. The round metal covers were off, not a good sign.

"Want to keep looking?"

Calvin shook his head. "The caravan won't make it much beyond this." Three miles back, the line of cars, vans, and campers carrying Calvin's family of hippies was stopped and waiting, gas tanks nearly dry. Over the last two days they had followed Interstate 80 south through Vallejo, past the California Maritime Academy and over the Carquinez Bridge. The San Pablo Bay on the right sparkled as if brushed with gold flake, a vast expanse of empty water. They passed through Foxboro Downs and Richmond, and exit after exit found gas stations that had been pumped dry or burned to the ground.

They didn't dare stray too far from the interstate, for fear of wandering into a heavily infested neighborhood. They did add a tow truck to the column, and it led the way, pushing aside blocking vehicles when it could, dragging them away when it couldn't. The farther south they went, the more time was spent clearing obstacles, and that burned more fuel.

Siphoning became the next option, but it didn't work out very well. Almost every vehicle sitting in that great outbound graveyard had been run until its tank was dry. Now the caravan was on vapors, their spare fuel cans empty.

"If there is gas down there," Calvin said, "this will probably be our last opportunity before Oakland." He waved toward the dead. "Lots of drifters down there, but there's sure to be more farther south, more than we could hold off."

They discussed how they would do it, assuming there was fuel. Option one was to pump it out a can at a time and transport it back to the caravan. This way, only a few people would be exposed, but it was a slow process, and extremely dangerous for the pumpers. The other option attracted more attention: Roll the entire caravan in at once, keep all the guns together and form a perimeter while the vehicles were fueled, blazing away at anything that moved. More noise, more moving parts that could go wrong, but faster. It occurred to Evan that he had never fully appreciated the simple ease of pulling up to a pump, paying with the swipe of a card, and being back on the road in minutes. No one had ever tried to eat him at a Chevron station.

"First let's see if there's any fuel," the younger man said, and they climbed onto the Harley, Calvin with his assault rifle across his chest.

Without anything being spoken, Evan and his motorcycle had been given the role of scout. He could weave in and out of traffic, ranging well ahead of the caravan and spotting danger before they rolled up on it. He was happy to do it. They had taken him in as one of their own, and it felt good to be useful.

He believed, however, that they were chasing a dream with this hospital ship. Calvin's wife, Faith, said it was waiting at the Oakland Middle Harbor, once part of a naval supply base back in the forties, and since converted to commercial operations. Evan couldn't say whether the ship existed. What he did know was that every mile south brought them closer to destruction. The numbers of the dead were multiplying, as were the attacks, corpses stumbling out from between cars and trucks, coming in at night, drawn by smell or sight or God knew what. Rifles and shotguns sounded with regularity now, and last night they had lost a young man named Otter while he was standing watch, a boy barely eighteen overwhelmed by three drifters in the dark. And that was just the highway on the outskirts of the city. Oakland would be a nightmare.

He couldn't and didn't voice any of this, but he suspected Calvin knew it in his heart. Evan had every reason to leave and would have said his good-byes by now except for the one reason he had to stay. Maya.

The Harley rumbled down the off-ramp, around a Greyhound bus and into the intersection serving the travel plaza. Calvin bailed off with his assault rifle and hid between a bush and a large green electrical box on the corner. Evan took off at once, gunning the hog past the service center, between the pumps, shouting and getting their attention.

The dead moved toward him from every angle. He stopped to let them get closer.

As they neared, he throttled twenty yards ahead and stopped again, watching as they slowly merged into a crowd. With starts and stops, always aware of what was ahead and to the sides, he moved through the parking areas and toward the road that intersected the plaza and ran under the interstate.

Evan looked back and saw Calvin sprinting across the now-empty pump area. He gunned the Harley ahead once more, out into the road, and the shuffling mob followed, moaning as a single entity. They were rotten and darkening, skin drawing taut across their features, giving them a more ghastly appearance. Soiled and torn clothing hung on thinning bodies, and even at a distance they gave off a putrid stench.

He stopped in the lot of a tire center across from the travel plaza, watching them trip over the curb as they swarmed into the road, and caught movement out of the corner of his right eye. A black kid in a basketball jersey, his jeans baggy to begin with and now pooled around his feet, forcing him to shuffle, came at him from behind a nearby stack of tires. He was too close. Evan pulled a black-and-silver automatic from a shoulder holster and fired.

The first bullet punched through the boy's shoulder. The next hit him in the center of the chest. Evan swore and closed one eye. The third round hit the kid in the face, and he went down.

Need more practice, Evan thought, tucking the piece away. It was a nine-millimeter Sig Sauer, perfectly balanced and seemingly made to fit his hand. Calvin had given it to him, along with the holster and a box of rounds, after finishing Evan's handwritten book of road stories. The older man pronounced it literature and called Evan a true poet.

"Keep it," Evan said. "My gift."

"No way. You need to finish it," Calvin said.

"It is finished. The world I was writing about is finished too. It just doesn't seem to matter much, considering how things are now."

Calvin shook his head. "You're wrong. It matters even more because of what's happened. It speaks of a time when life was more than death and constant fear." He held the book out to Evan.

"I'm starting a new book about all this. Maya gave me a journal and some pens, said I needed to write about this new world. She said the universe demanded it."

Calvin scowled, but the corners of his eyes crinkled with mirth. "Evan, you don't buy into that New Age hippie crap."

Evan blushed. "It sounds more convincing when Maya says it."

"Mmm-hmm." Her father nodded, still frowning but eyes twinkling.

"Anyway, I'm on to my next project." He pushed the book back to the older man. "Please, keep that."

Calvin hugged him, even kissed him on the cheek, holding Evan's book to his chest and nodding. "This is a true gift." A while later he presented the pistol, apologizing and stressing that it was *not* any kind of trade for Evan's words, that he just wanted the writer to have a sidearm for when things got close. Evan had never cared much about handguns, but the Sig was a thing of beauty, and it felt reassuring hanging under his armpit.

A fat kid in his early teens with one arm and half his face missing blundered around the same stack of tires and galloped toward him, fat rolls bouncing in a tight T-shirt. The Sig came out again, and this time Evan hit the mark with the first bullet, blowing the top of the fat kid's head off.

Time to move.

He throttled the Harley and moved out into the intersection, making sure the horde followed: not too close, but not so far away that some might lose interest and wander back to the service plaza. He saw Calvin running back toward the green electrical box, so he roared over to meet him. Calvin hopped on the back, and Evan took them back up onto the highway.

"We're in business," Calvin yelled over the wind.

The raid worked. Evan went in first on the Harley while the caravan waited at the top of the ramp, the hippies watching through binoculars. He used the same tactic, drawing the dead together and leading them away, much farther this time, up a road he hadn't scouted, which made him a little nervous. Behind him Calvin took the caravan in fast, the vehicles lining up two by two at the underground tanks, using a pair of hand pumps to fill each one before the next two pulled up. Every gun was trained outward, watching for the dead. Finally the spare cans were topped off and loaded back onto bumpers and roof racks.

Evan ran into trouble at an intersection half a mile away. The horde from the travel plaza was closing in from behind while more of the dead staggered out from between buildings and houses. He sat straddling his bike and fired every round from the Sig. Then he unslung the shotgun that he had carried ever since he had taken it from the police cruiser in Napa and emptied that as well. With something of a path cleared, he tucked low and rocketed between reaching arms. Fingernails scraped his jacket and tore open the sleeping bag on his handlebars, but he got through.

Back at the plaza, the caravan heard the distant gunfire. Calvin and Faith saw the way their daughter clutched her hands to her chest as she stared off in its direction. Maya climbed the aluminum ladder at the back of a camper and stood on the roof watching and waiting, climbing down only when the shape of a lone man on a motorcycle appeared on the road. She was smiling, and Calvin and Faith glanced at each other, smiling too.

The caravan fueled up without losing a single member. After that, Maya rode behind Evan on the Harley.

She was born both deaf and mute, something that surprised Evan, who'd thought she was only quiet. He didn't even realize it until later that first night in camp, when he saw Maya signing with her mother. She was also very adept at reading lips.

The attraction was immediate for both of them, and coming together was as natural as breathing. There was no drama with some jealous would-be suitor or ex-boyfriend, and the other members of the Family reacted with smiles, as if it was supposed to happen. Maya started teaching Evan how to sign, used her hands to turn his face toward her when he was speaking, and communicated back by writing on a legal pad. Evan thought her handwriting was more beautiful than any angel's and wanted nothing more than to drown in those sapphire eyes.

At night they talked and scribbled for hours, asking each other about their lives, where they had been, what they had seen, what they wanted. Evan wanted to see Bermuda; Maya wanted to go to Paris. It didn't matter that they never would. They speculated about whether the government might have a secret lab someplace, where scientists were even now working on a cure. Maya's uncle Dane butted into the conversation and announced that it was precisely one of those secret government labs that had unleashed a plague of the walking dead in the first place, and they waited until he walked away before laughing. Maya urged Evan to write every day. Sometimes she brought him coffee and would sit beside him, watching in fascination as his pen raced across the pages.

One evening, Evan passed by Calvin and Faith's VW van and overheard them arguing inside.

"Her place is with us, Cal. I don't want to discuss this," Faith argued.

"Well, we need to discuss this. He can get her out of here, get her someplace safe," Cal insisted.

"No."

"Honey—"

"No, Calvin. I'm not letting Maya ride off so that we never see her again."

"He'll protect her. He's a good man, Faith."

"Our family needs to stay together."

A disgusted snort. "Isn't it enough that we're taking the other kids into this nightmare? And it's going to be bad, worse than any of us imagine. There's going to be thousands of them . . . Christ, maybe millions. And for what? A fantasy. A ship that isn't there."

"It's there! Goddamn you, Cal, that ship will be there if we just keep moving!"

A long pause, and then his voice, softer. "Please, Faith, let him take her out of here. Let at least one of our children live."

"That ship will be there," she repeated.

Evan felt dirty for listening in and did not share what he had heard with Maya. He thought about what Calvin said, though, and considered doing it on his own, just taking Maya away, making a life together. But he didn't. He stayed.

The caravan looted on the move. Any time the tow truck stopped to deal with a blockage, people with empty backpacks, pry bars, and hand weapons would fall on the trucks and cars around them like jackals, searching for food and water, camping gear if they could find it, and the rare firearm. It was a system that seemed to work, but it was dangerous. Sometimes there were drifters still in the cars, or lurking in the shadowy corridors between them. One time Maya was moving with a scavenging group when a drifter lunged from beneath a station wagon, catching hold of her foot and biting into her ankle.

Its teeth didn't get through the thick leather of her hiking boot.

The others quickly caved its head in with crowbars and pipes, and after that, Calvin insisted she not go anywhere Evan couldn't see her. Evan was more shaken up than Maya, and he took her by the shoulders and practically yelled her father's instruction. Maya giggled silently and nodded, then hugged him close.

For Evan Tucker, it ceased to be a great romantic adventure just outside El Cerrito. He and Maya were motoring slowly through abandoned cars, scouting the obstacles that the tow truck would have to handle, the caravan a mile to their rear. They stopped for a few minutes and, after a careful look around to ensure there was no immediate threat, grinned at each other and started kissing, hands exploring one another, both of them wishing they had a room, a bed, something other than the seat of a Harley.

The cry came from the right, and Evan froze. Maya felt the sudden change in him and pulled back, searching his face.

It was an infant's cry.

Ahead of them was a tangle of vehicles all facing north on the southbound lanes, those who had tried to take advantage of the less crowded side of the highway rather than sit in stopped traffic. A white uniform-service truck sat on top of a yellow Smart car, crushing it like a beer can, and behind that a beige Lincoln Navigator had apparently swerved to avoid hitting them and gone up onto a guardrail, where it became stuck. The cries were coming from there.

Evan and Maya approached slowly. Both the driver and passenger doors hung open, and as they got close there was a buzz of flies and the reek of rotting flesh. The front seats were empty, the smooth, caramel leather sticky with splashes of old blood. Flies landed there, buzzed off, and landed again. A woman's shoe was on the floorboards of the passenger side next to a pink, overturned diaper bag with a bottle of spoiled formula poking out of it. The rear passenger window was broken, fragments glittering on the road. The cry came again from inside, high and plaintive, a squeaking wail. Then there was the sound of a rattle.

Maya shook her head as Evan moved forward, but he paid no attention, stepping up and looking inside. The infant seat was secured in the center, a plastic mobile of little rattles, mirrors, and a stuffed crocodile mounted above it. The infant screeched again, and a little hand batted at the mobile, making one of the rattles spin.

"Oh my God," Evan whispered, yanking open the rear door and scrambling in before Maya could stop him. How could a baby still be alive after this long?

It wasn't.

Eight months old and wearing pink pajamas covered in dried, blackened gore, the little girl had a sizable bite of meat and fabric missing from her left shoulder. Her skin was gray and covered in dark blotches, and once-brown eyes were filmy and pale. Locked in with a five-point restraint harness, the infant saw Evan and let out a tiny screech, clumsy hands grabbing and tangling with the mobile.

Evan stared at her, and she screeched again like a tiny, wounded animal. Starving, he thought. Locked in there forever and starving.

He climbed back out and turned to Maya, signing the word *baby*. She hugged him fiercely, and he buried his face in her hair and cried. *This is the world,* he thought, *back there thrashing in a car seat.*

Eventually he pulled away and wiped his eyes on his sleeve, unable to look up. One of Maya's hands gently lifted his chin so he could see her. She held his face in both hands for a moment and then touched the butt of the pistol in his shoulder holster. She nodded and turned away.

Evan stood near the Navigator's door for a long time, the nine-millimeter in his hand, looking up at a brilliant blue September sky where mountains of white clouds drifted by at a stately, unhurried pace. Then he looked at the silent metal graveyard all around them, and back at the thing struggling in the car seat.

This is the world.

Maya didn't jump when the pistol went off.

TWENTY-SEVEN

SoMa—South of Market—was a collection of neighborhoods adjacent to the Mission District, resulting in an eclectic mixture of architecture: Victorian and early twentieth century nestled amid steel and glass. They moved through a steady rain, the sky a flat sheet of charcoal lit by flashes of lightning. Alden and Tricia had found hooded Windbreakers, and Snake wore a baseball cap, but it did little to help. They were soaked and chilled. Concrete tangles of elevated roadways loomed ahead, the point where Highway 101 from San Jose met I-80 and continued on to feed the Bay Bridge. Getting underneath and beyond would be a real mile marker on their journey.

Sneakers and boots splashed through streets strewn with trash, unmoving cars, broken glass, and the occasional motionless body. Luggage and overturned shopping carts rested near fallen bicycles and, in one case, a wheelchair lying on its side. The sight of that overturned, empty chair caused Tricia to stop and stare, frozen, until Pulaski jerked her arm and barked at her to keep moving. They saw a few cats hiding under cars, staying out of the rain, but the rats had no such concerns. Emboldened by the sudden absence of humans, they moved about in the daytime, feeding on whatever they found.

SoMa was a diverse collection of condos, nightclubs, and small parks, with galleries and trendy cafés on the same blocks as run-down residential hotels and pawnshops. For blocks they had traveled without seeing the walking dead, and it was an invitation to move into the center of the street, where they could go faster instead of creeping along sidewalks and ducking into alleys. After weeks of moving only two or three blocks a day, feeling as if they would never escape this place, finally they were making some time. It made Xavier nervous. Where were the dead?

They came within half a block of the elevated freeway, long ribbons of concrete arcing high above on thick support columns, their mass and the gloom of the day casting deep shadows on the street passing underneath. "Oh, hell yes!" said Snake, breaking away from the group and jogging toward a brick building on the left. A metal accordion security gate was pulled across the front window, but the door stood open and unprotected. An image on the window depicted a skateboard, the words *HOOD RATZ* beneath it in red lettering.

"Snake, careful . . ." Xavier called.

He wasn't.

The twelve-year-old, still carrying his baseball bat, trotted inside the skate shop without checking first, and the screaming began at once. Xavier and Pulaski started running toward the shop as half a dozen of the walking dead staggered out through the door and onto the sidewalk. A few had fresh blood on their faces and hands, and one was chewing something red.

Xavier's AK-47 and Pulaski's shotgun came up at the same time, the two men side by side as the corpses dragged toward them through the rain. Both fired, hitting chests and arms and faces, the quiet street suddenly a shooting range. Alden ran to Tricia and held on to her, his pistol in one hand as he nervously scanned the surrounding buildings.

Then it was over, the dead facedown on the wet asphalt, the last echo of gunfire fading. In its place, an odd humming sound came from above. Eyes turned upward to the shapes appearing at the edge of the elevated freeway. Five, ten, two dozen, more and more corpses gathering at the concrete guardrail, looking down at the people in the street, their collective moans gathering as a low hum. Fifty, a hundred, strung out in a line in both directions, more behind them as the dead packed the edge of the freeway, arms reaching out and down. Still more crowded in, and then they began climbing over.

Two corpses fell a hundred feet and smacked onto the road. Another dropped, then five more in succession, hitting with dull cracks.

"Run," said Xavier, dropping his empty magazine and shoving in a new one.

"We have to get Snake," Tricia said.

"He's dead," said Pulaski, trotting toward the freeway and feeding fresh shells into the shotgun. Alden tugged at Tricia's Windbreaker, but she wouldn't move.

"We can't leave him!"

"He's dead. Run!" Xavier ran toward the bodies still thumping onto the road. A couple split open when they hit, the rest crumpled as their bones fractured, but only one landed on its head and didn't move. The others pulled themselves up, limping and broken. Ten fell at once, making a rippling sound like a drumroll. The four survivors ran to the right to avoid them, and a falling body nearly landed on Alden, hitting the ground only a few feet away with a sickening crack. Tricia screamed, and the schoolteacher gripped her Windbreaker and hauled her along.

They were under the freeway, in the shadows and running. Shapes emerged from behind concrete pillars, but they were hardly worth noticing. Behind them the dropping bodies turned into a waterfall of flesh, hundreds of corpses pouring over the side of the highway above, hitting so fast their impact sounded like bursting popcorn. Hundreds more dropped, and Xavier risked a backward glance to see an unending curtain of free-falling bodies, hitting and getting back up. How many were up there? Why were they up there? Were they trying to cross the bridge and got distracted by the gunfire?

The questions didn't matter, because as soon as they emerged from the darkness of the underpass, corpses began raining down from the near side of the freeway as well, spilling over the side like a pot of water filled past its rim. The street behind them was soon filled with the ravenous dead; there were thousands, and more falling every second. Bodies appeared ahead and to the sides, walking out of parking lots and open loading bays, emerging from alleys and behind parked trucks. Xavier stopped, braced the rifle, and fired at the closest ones, Pulaski doing the same. Behind them Alden's pistol went off.

"Keep moving," Xavier shouted, leading them through gaps in the dead cleared by the gunfire. Pulaski was behind him, his shotgun going off when something got too close, and Alden pulled Tricia along at the back. They passed warehouses that had been turned into lofts and design studios, bars and workshops, fenced-off truck depots and auto repair yards where corpses stood growling and shaking the chain link. A tangle of ghouls stumbled out the door of a city bus ahead of them, and Xavier slid to a stop to unload his assault rifle at them, shell casings rattling through puddles, the crack of the rifle filling the street.

They kept running.

At Sixteenth Street Xavier led them east. A half mile away, the elevated span of I-280 stretched over the neighborhood, and if they stayed on Sixteenth they would have to pass beneath it. Another waterfall of the dead? Xavier couldn't think about that. In order to reach the water they would have to get past it, and that distance looked like forever.

"Father!" Tricia yelled.

Xavier stopped and turned, seeing Alden and Tricia farther back than he'd thought they were. Alden was bent over, his hands on his knees. Tricia was tugging at him, looking around, uncertain whether she should stay or run.

"Let's go!" Pulaski shouted, not stopping. Tricia let go of Alden and started running, passing Xavier as he headed back to the school-teacher. Beyond, only blocks back, the priest saw the street filling with a mass of the dead packed curb to curb.

"Alden, we have to go," Xavier said, resting a hand on the teacher's back, feeling the thud of the man's heart. "Do you have any nitro tablets?"

The man shook his head, his voice coming in gasps. "Never . . . found any. I'll be . . . okay . . . just . . . rest . . ."

"We can't rest here." Xavier switched his AK to his left hand and hooked an arm around the teacher's waist, helping him straighten up. Alden put both hands to his chest. He had dropped his pistol somewhere.

"Just . . . a minute . . . more . . ." His face was the color of paper, the rain pasting his hair to his forehead.

"We'll go slowly," the priest said, getting him moving. Alden started walking, shuffling like the dead around them. Pulaski and Tricia were half a block ahead of them already and not slowing. Xavier was able to move a hundred feet before he stopped to bring his rifle up, dropping a moaning vagrant that had lurched into their path. A woman dressed like a prostitute walked behind him, staggering on one broken high heel, her graying skin covered in bites. Xavier sighted on her head and pulled the trigger.

Click. The magazine was empty.

He ejected the clip and reached for another, but the pocket he carried them in was also empty. He had lost count and used the last magazine without realizing it. Xavier dropped the now-useless rifle and tore the crowbar from where it hung beside his pack, taking two steps forward and smashing the prostitute's head. The creature made a hoarse wheezing sound and crumpled.

He turned back to see Alden on his hands and knees, gasping for air. A trio of corpses closed in on him from the sidewalks, two on the left and one on the right, moving faster as they neared their prey. Xavier pulled the .44 Bulldog from his back waistband, waiting a heartbeat until they got closer. The high-caliber revolver went off like a cannon; at ten feet it blew most of a corpse's head off. The one beside it didn't hesitate and lunged. Xavier sidestepped and ducked a swinging arm, shoved it with the crowbar to make it stumble past, and then stepped in to press the Bulldog against the back of its skull.

An explosion of red and gray chunks blew across the road.

The third one was on Alden before Xavier could turn, and the teacher fought back weakly at the snarling, snapping thing. The priest leaped to them, dropped the crowbar, and grabbed the creature by the hair, jerking its head back and shoving the Bulldog in one ear. The blast left him holding a clump of scalp with a fragment of skull clinging to it.

"Get on your feet, Alden. Get up now," Xavier demanded.

The teacher nodded and slowly climbed to his hands and knees, sucking air like a goldfish out of its bowl, eyes clenched shut. The priest recovered his crowbar and helped him the rest of the way up, taking him around the waist again and getting them moving. Only four blocks to the expressway. Pulaski and Tricia were nowhere in sight.

The two men stopped moving only long enough for Xavier to reload the .44 and then moved a block, another, and soon they were at the raised mass of I-280. Thunder rumbled above and the rain kept on, a cold rain that smelled of the sea. Fortunately there was no cascade of corpses spilling over the high guardrail, and Xavier figured that if the dead had been up there, Pulaski and Tricia would have triggered them when they came this way. Assuming they did come this way. The priest moved them into the shadows under the span, Alden limping and gasping beside him, hands still clamped to his chest. The priest scanned the darkness, watching for the movement that would signal an attack. Nothing came at them, and again Xavier was struck by how surreal it was to be able to move for blocks at a time, after so many days spent creeping and hiding, making no progress.

Then they were back into the rain, still moving east on Sixteenth, Xavier watching the highway back over his shoulder, expecting to see corpses tumbling off this side. Blocks behind them, the ranks of the dead were swelling, filling the street, an army moving forward at much the same speed as the priest and the struggling teacher. Only they didn't need to stop and rest and just kept coming.

"We're going to be okay," Xavier told his companion. "We just need to go on a little farther. Stay with me, Alden."

The teacher nodded and made a grunting noise.

They passed a sprawling furniture showroom and a long warehouse that had been converted to a technology company, the streets eerily devoid of the dead. Xavier wondered again why that was but accepted it as a gift. Other than the five rounds loaded in his Bulldog, his pocket held only one squat, heavy bullet.

At the intersection where Owens Street came in at an angle to join Sixteenth, a major traffic accident jammed the road. Xavier saw that a Loomis armored truck had tipped over onto a silver BMW convertible and flattened it. A pair of taxis was piled against the back of the armored truck and had been crushed by a red-and-black Boar's Head delivery truck. A minivan had come in from the right, smashing into what was left by the taxis, and a cement mixer had somehow ended up on top of them all. The rear wheel of a motorcycle, folded nearly in half, poked out from the bottom of the pile. The whole mess was blackened by fire, and a charred corpse dangled from the rear window of one of the taxis.

Two figures crouched behind the armored truck, the bigger one peering around the side at what lay beyond. Xavier helped Alden limp up behind them, and Tricia began crying when she saw the teacher. Alden sat on the pavement and leaned back against the truck, eyes closed and breathing hard, hands pressed to his heart as if it might jump right out of his chest.

Xavier crouched beside Pulaski, who glanced at him and curled his lip. "Thought you were dead."

"We almost were."

"Still plenty of time left in the day," the pipe fitter said. His shotgun was gone, and he was holding the remaining automatic.

"Why didn't you just keep going?" Xavier asked.

"We would have." He gestured with the pistol. "But that's UCSF over there."

The priest looked out at a graduate college campus studded with buildings, open greens, and trees. Just like UC Berkeley weeks ago, the Mission Bay campus of the University of California, San Francisco, had been in its final days before classes started, the grounds crowded with students and faculty. One end of the campus was occupied by a large hospital, and now the place crawled with not only dead students and professors but corpses in hospital gowns and scrubs as well. There were thousands.

"If they spot us, we're fucked."

Alden's voice, soft and shaking, came from behind them. "Fucked . . . anyway."

Pulaski and Xavier turned as the schoolteacher pulled aside his Windbreaker and lifted his shirt, wincing at the movement as he exposed the flesh just above his hip.

He had been bitten.

TWENTY-EIGHT

Christmas. Dad lighting a fire while Mom warmed up cider. Crystal as a little girl, excited and chattering nonstop, asking endless questions about Santa. Dad in a doorway, sweeping Mom into his arms and kissing her under mistletoe.

No.

On a date with Brandon Johnson, laughing at his jokes, making out in his car after the movie. Hours of texting with Kate that night to tell her all about it. Liking the way he made her feel, wondering if she should let him go all the way.

Stop.

Mom teaching her how to make lasagna. Dad running beside her bike after he took off the training wheels. Crystal announcing she wanted to be a veterinarian. The next day announcing she wanted to be an airline pilot.

Stop it.

Hugs. Fights. Quiet times. Trips to the mall. Falling asleep in a lawn chair on a sunny day. Taking Crystal to get her ears pierced. Concerts. School.

Stop it! STOP IT!

Skye growled and gritted her teeth, crunching hard, fingers laced across her stomach and feet hooked under a couch. Up, down, up, down, her abdominal muscles burning. She forced in the vision of her father being taken down, of her dead mother lurching toward her at the head of a murderous pack. She made herself see Crystal, flesh torn and teeth snapping.

A miss is a miss.

Anything other than a head shot is a miss.

A miss is a wasted bullet that won't kill one of them.

That is unacceptable.

That is unforgiveable.

You will hit.

You will kill them.

She saw her mother being savaged on the campus lawn, saw the look of terror on her sister's face, felt her hand in her own as they ran for safety. Saw her being killed anyway. Skye screamed and flipped over, punishing herself with fast diamond push-ups.

Your family is gone.

Your friends are gone.

No one misses you.

No one cares about you.

They took the world away from you.

You will hit.

You will kill them.

All of them.

Skye cried out again and started doing mountain climbers, her thighs and buttocks aching, faster and faster.

All of them. All of them.

"All of them," she said through clenched teeth.

She collapsed, burying her face in the carpet and heaving with what might have been exertion or might have been sobs, and then forced herself to stand. Wearing black cargo pants tucked into hiking boots and a sweat-darkened tank top, she took her rifle and headed down to the basement of the house she had taken over for the night. There was a small in-home gym down here, a Coleman lantern already glowing, sitting on a weightlifting bench where earlier sweat had yet to dry. Near it was a boxing dummy, a rubberized torso and head on a spring-mounted post, secured to a weighted base. Skye pulled on her pack and rifle for extra weight and began practicing with the machete.

The first trick was to pull it from where it hung on the pack over her left shoulder, without slicing her ear off. She practiced this single move for over an hour, pulling and replacing and pulling again, slowly at first, and then steadily faster until she knew how to keep her head out of the way and still get it out quickly.

She went to work on the dummy.

Skye trained until she could barely lift her right arm, working on the singular skill of pulling the blade and landing a clean, powerful head shot in one motion. Two hours later, the dummy was a mass of shredded rubber, and the head was gone.

When she was done she washed with unscented baby wipes and toweled off. She knew she still smelled bad, and the scalp under her chopped hair was itchy and sour, but she didn't care. She didn't put on deodorant, in case they could smell it.

A meal—canned ham, canned corn, and some peaches she found preserved in mason jars in a closet—was followed by some time studying her map. She was south of the MacArthur Freeway now, in Clawson, a part of Oakland, and heading south into the city itself. The neighborhood was a mix of businesses, industrial buildings, and old, clapboard row houses with sagging porches. The dead were more numerous here, and she hadn't been able to travel through backyards as effectively as before; too much barbed wire, too many flimsy corrugated tin fences that made a lot of noise or threatened to collapse under her weight, too many yards overgrown with high weeds where a freak could be waiting unseen. Instead she jogged down alleys and sidewalks, sometimes down the street itself, rifle held ready, stopping only to shoot.

She didn't keep count of her kills.

How high did you have to count before you got to *all*?

Several hours of sleep in an upstairs bedroom was followed by late-night sniping with the M24, and instead of her normal five rounds she shot eight. Then she was empty, and she had already balanced the odds of finding more .300 ammo against carrying the added weight of a worthless rifle. She zippered it back into its case, gave it a pat, and leaned it in a corner of the bedroom before finishing her night's sleep.

When morning arrived it was raining, and a freak had found its way into the backyard.

Skye spotted it as soon as she stepped out the kitchen door, fully loaded for the day's travel. It was a heavyset black lady in a loose purple housedress, what her mother called a muumuu. The two of them used to cover their laughter with their hands when they saw someone wearing one in Walmart. The black lady was barefoot, her skin losing its pigment and her hair falling out in patches, and she groaned as she waddled forward.

Skye strode toward the freak, pulling the machete and swinging, splitting its head in half. She jerked the blade free as it fell, then realized her forehead and right cheek were wet. She wiped a sleeve at it, seeing that she had caught a few drops of dark blood.

It was something that hadn't occurred to her. Could she get infected that way? She wiped the blade on the muumuu and reseated it in its sheath, then used a baby wipe to clean her face. The weapon would be for emergencies only.

Later that morning she came upon an intersection where a pair of brown, camouflaged Humvees sat parked end to end, just like the kind Taylor and Sgt. Postman had been in when they rescued her, seemingly years ago. The nearest freaks were half a block away, and the intersection looked clear. Still, she approached with her rifle to her shoulder.

Thousands of empty shell casings were scattered across the pavement, rattling under her boots. She moved forward, finding both vehicles empty. There were no dead soldiers, but neither were there any dropped rifles or bandoliers. That made sense. Others were alive out here, and they would have immediately taken any weapons they found. She eyed the heavy machine gun mounted in the vehicle turret only briefly before discarding the idea. It was heavy and cumbersome, and even Postman's soldiers had said it was worthless for this type of combat. The thought of driving the Humvee wasn't even a consideration.

A search of the vehicle did turn up some useful things, however. A Maglite with fresh batteries was swapped out for her old one; a couple of rifle-cleaning kits provided fresh patches and gun oil; a plastic-wrapped energy bar provided a snack while she searched. In the rear seat she discovered a pair of hard plastic, cushioned knee pads and put them on at once. They would make it more comfortable to hold kneeling shooting positions.

She left the MREs she found, since she hadn't used her own yet and suspected they would remain edible for years. Skye was about to move on when she spotted a dark green metal can with a narrow, hinged lid. It was sitting on the rear cargo deck, and stenciled on the side it read, *5.56mm TRACER—DAY 500 ct.* Inside, the heavy can was filled with loose ammunition for the M4, each bullet tipped in phosphorescent green. Once again her exposure to movies and video games paid a dividend; she knew what tracer rounds were.

Skye picked it up by the handle and tested the weight. It was heavy, but not as much as it would have been prior to weeks of punishing exercise, and she could always drop it and run if necessary. She would load her magazines later. Now it was time to move.

Three blocks away her little side street intersected with the wider 32nd Street. A liquor store with bars on the windows was on her left, to her right was a little convenience and grocery store with window advertisements all in Spanish, and on the diagonal across the street sat a row house that had been taken by fire long before the plague. The dead were thick on 32nd, and she watched from a crouch behind a rusty car sitting on tireless rims. The air smelled of rot and oil smoke, and it was quiet except for the drumming of the rain on the roof of the derelict car. She watched the street. If she wanted to head farther south she would have to cross, and there were so many corpses drifting up and down it that crossing without being seen would be impossible.

Watching the dead shuffle past made her ache to pull the trigger.

Directly across the street, sitting on the corner, was a white board building with a steeply peaked roof. Narrow, arched windows of stained glass marched down the side, and from here it looked like the property was surrounded by a six-foot wrought-iron fence with sharp tips on each vertical bar. Even more intriguing was the high bell tower at one corner, rising above the main building and capped with its own peaked roof, tipped with a cross. Shuttered windows looked out from all sides of the steeple.

Skye rested a hand on the ammo can beside her, fingers drumming on it like the rain. She looked at the high steeple, at its windows, thought about the view it would command. She gripped the can's handle and bolted to her feet, sprinting across 32nd Street, weaving in and out of turning bodies and reaching arms, going through the wrought-iron gate and slamming it behind her. An open padlock hung on the bars beside the gate, and she quickly threaded it through the latch hole and snapped it shut.

The dead came to the fence, reaching through the gate.

"I'll be right with you," she said.

Holding it one-handed by the pistol grip, Skye braced the M4 against her shoulder and, carrying the ammo can in her other hand, let the rifle muzzle lead the way through the double front doors of the First Baptist Church of Clawson. There were three freaks in here, two heavy black ladies in the pews and a black man in a janitor's uniform near the pulpit. All three let out a moan upon seeing her and shuffled forward. Skye took them down quickly. A check of the rest of the church—basement filled with tables and chairs and cardboard boxes, back rooms and closets, a tiny kitchen with a rear door— showed that she was alone.

The door to the bell tower opened to a high shaft, with steep plank stairs climbing the walls in a tight square, an open space rising through the center. It had a musty smell, and the flutter of pigeons came from high above.

Skye pounded up the stairs two at a time.

Emeryville was behind them. They kept to the surface streets now, avoiding the concrete spaghetti bowl where the freeways met at the head of the Bay Bridge, all of them packed with dead vehicles and dead Californians. The Bearcat rumbled south on Hollis Street, the raised stretch of I-880, and the Nimitz Freeway, off to the right, sections of which had collapsed during the earthquake of '89 and crushed people inside their cars on the lower deck.

The riot vehicle weaved in and out of abandoned cars and overrun roadblocks, crunching over the walking dead while others pounded fists against the armored sides. There were definitely more of them now, mostly black and Hispanic as the truck rolled through a poor Oakland section of shabby houses, decaying apartment buildings, and businesses with steel roll-down gates and bars on the windows.

Trash, graffiti, stripped cars, and skinny, dangerous-looking stray dogs colored a neighborhood of auto body shops, liquor outlets and corner bars, pawnshops, check-cashing spots, and small stores selling cheap clothing.

The wipers beat steadily at the constant rain, the sky gray and puddles forming in the street. Carney looked out at the neighborhood and wondered if it looked much different than it had before the plague. Oakland, despite improvements over the past decades, was still a city known for its poverty, violent crime, and double-digit unemployment. Many of his former prison mates had come from here, and the streets were still filled with people wandering without purpose and dangerous killers. No, not terribly different, he decided.

In the passenger seat, TC had his boots up on the dashboard, drinking a Red Bull as he watched a movie. Carney had found a small portable DVD player with a folding screen and an AC adapter for the Bearcat. TC was watching a Quentin Tarantino movie, clearly having trouble keeping up with the director's style of jumping back and forth through time and locations but howling laughter at the over-the-top violence.

It was important to keep him occupied. For TC, boredom was a trigger for violence.

The Bearcat reached an intersection where Peralta crossed at an angle, a much wider boulevard of businesses and chain restaurants. Carney let the vehicle sit and idle.

TC looked up from his movie. "What's up?" he asked.

"Just thinking." So far their search for a suitable boat had been a bust. Carney consulted his map. He could angle south for a bit and then cut back west, toward Oakland's waterfront. Maybe they would have more luck.

TC went back to his movie. "Yeah! Kill that motherfucker!"

Carney stared out past the thumping windshield wipers and

listened as one of Tarantino's characters beat someone to death. TC
didn't use the earbuds for the player, and the crunch of bones and a
man screaming filled the riot vehicle. Tarantino got the sound right,
the impact anyway. But the screaming wasn't realistic. In life there
were only two or three grunts, and then nothing more.

1996, and Bill Carnes was doing okay. His parole officer was happy
that he was working, keeping out of the bars and coming up clean
on his piss tests. Out after only three years on a burglary charge,
Carney didn't plan on blowing his second chance. Cindy was working
part-time and just over two years clean and sober. Little Rhea was
eighteen months, a blue-eyed heartbreaker crawling at high speed
and starting to do a little furniture-assisted walking. She had her
daddy wrapped up tight; in his eyes she could do no wrong. Carney
was thinking about going to the community college in Sacramento,
so that maybe someday he would be supervising auto mechanics
instead of being the guy with the greasy hands and torn knuckles.

He came home from work early. Rhea, wearing yellow jammies
with a pink bunny on the tummy, was napping on a blanket on the
living room floor. Only she wasn't napping. Her face was blue, her
skin cold as Carney picked her up. She had choked to death on a tiny
blue Bic lighter. Strewn across the coffee table was a fix kit: spoon,
stretch of rubber tubing, syringe, small square of crumpled foil with
some white powder in it, all next to a cluster of empty beer cans.

Carney found them in the bedroom, naked and sleeping, Cindy
entwined with some bearded guy he didn't know. Fucking and sleeping off a high while Rhea died in the next room. He found what he
needed in the closet.

At sentencing, the judge used words like *heinous* and *depraved*,
stating that the use of a baseball bat on two sleeping people made
Carney a monster, and if the prosecution could have stretched their

case to show premeditation, His Honor would have happily supported the death penalty. The judge hadn't been interested in a dead eighteen-month-old with blue eyes.

C arney stared at the rivulets of rain sliding down the windshield. They looked like tears. He took a deep breath and started to turn right onto Peralta but then hit the brakes. Across the intersection, the street they had been traveling angled deeper into the neighborhood, and a block in that street was filled with the walking dead, more than he had seen so far in Oakland. They were all moving away from him and seemed to be converging on a small white church.

Some were falling down in the street. Quite a few, actually.

He put the truck in park and grabbed the binoculars off the center console, taking a closer look. Yes, falling down because they were being shot in the head. He scanned the area, looking for the shooter, but it didn't take long to figure the church steeple for the perfect sniper's nest. As he watched he saw a figure with a rifle moving between the open windows on all four sides, firing steadily. Even at this distance and with her lack of hair, he could tell she was female, and young.

She had some skill, and the bodies were piling up in the street. More of the dead were coming, however, drawn from all angles, emerging from houses and side streets and overgrown yards, too many of them. They were beginning to pile up around the fence, and it wouldn't take long before they forced their way over or through it.

"How long before you run out of ammo?" he murmured. TC didn't hear him. It looked like the firing was only coming from the bell tower, and he didn't see anyone else up there with her. Was she alone? Did she realize how much attention she was drawing? Did she care?

TC looked up from his movie as Carney gunned the Bearcat across the intersection. He saw the dead, saw the girl. "What's going on, bro?"

"Get your shit and mount up in that top hatch. You're going to get to kill stuff." Carney slammed the grille into a zombie, splattering it over the hood and sending the body flying as he accelerated.

"Fucking A, about time!" Then TC's face went sober and he gripped his cellmate's arm. "But why now, bro? Why her?"

Carney's eyes were hard. "Sometimes, brother, people just need saving."

TWENTY-NINE

Mission Bay

Alden looked up with a weak smile. "It's okay. I never . . . expected to . . . get this far," he said, looking past Xavier at the horde of corpses slowly closing on them, following since they had dropped from the freeway. "You should . . . get going."

Xavier shoved the Bulldog into his waistband and knelt beside the schoolteacher. "We need to get you someplace safe," he said.

"Are you fucking crazy?" Pulaski exclaimed. He pointed at Alden. "He's a dead man, and we've got to keep moving. Kill him or leave him."

"Shut up."

"He's been dead weight all along."

The priest looked at the pipe fitter and bared his teeth. "I said shut up."

"Fuck you! I'm done taking orders from you!" Pulaski pointed the nine-millimeter at Xavier. "Give me that pistol. Do it slow, or I'll blow your black ass away."

Xavier glared at him, saw murder in the man's eyes, and slowly handed over the Bulldog.

Without taking his eyes or the gun off the priest, Pulaski said to Tricia, "I'm getting out of here. We keep going until we hit Third Street, then cut north and cross the canal at the ballpark. The marina is right there. You coming?"

The girl's hands were clapped to her mouth, eyes darting between the two men, not moving.

Pulaski curled his lip. "Well, fuck you too." He spit on the ground. "Fuck all of you." Then he was on his feet and gone, running past the overturned armored truck and out of sight.

Xavier lifted Alden in his arms. "We're going to find someplace close to hide, where they won't see us. They'll pass us by."

"No! Xavier . . . this is . . . stupid." The teacher tried to resist, couldn't. "Put me . . . down."

The priest ignored him and started toward the sidewalk, away from the campus. "Come on, Tricia."

The girl didn't answer, and Xavier stopped, looking back. She was no longer huddled against the truck but was walking toward the campus, hands still pressed to her mouth.

"Tricia!"

She kept walking and then broke into a run, holding her arms wide, a rising wail coming from her that made a shiver run through the priest.

"Tricia, no!"

She crossed the curb and then was running across a lawn, straight toward a dozen corpses. They turned and moved stiff-legged toward her.

"No," Xavier whispered, still holding the man in both arms as the rain mixed with his tears. He watched her run to her death.

"She's made . . . her choice," Alden said.

Xavier watched until she reached the knot of zombies, and then looked away before he had to see what came next. He headed up Sixteenth, in the direction Pulaski had gone, but didn't see the man anywhere.

"Xavier . . ."

The priest shook his head. "Don't talk for a while, Alden." He kept walking, the horde behind them closing with every step, more of them over on the grass kneeling in a big circle and fighting over fresh meat.

Mission Bay was an odd mix of industrial area, high-rise condos, apartment buildings, and construction sites. As the terminus for both Caltrain and the city's light rail system, it was not uncommon to see luxury buildings backed up to warehouses, and neatly groomed parks adjacent to truck depots. More than a few high-rise balconies had *HELP* or *ALIVE* signs painted on sheets hanging over the sides, and many of these same balconies were occupied by corpses, bumping against the railing or wandering in and out through sliding doors.

Xavier stayed on the sidewalk, the UCSF campus slowly passing on the left, wondering how long it would be before the dead saw them and attacked, knowing he would go down swinging the crowbar, protecting a man beyond saving. But they made it all the way to where Third Street crossed north to south ahead of them. Beyond was a wall of high-rises. The waterfront would be on the other side.

"Just a little farther," Xavier said.

Alden shook his head, eyes closed and jaw clenched. "Please," he gasped, "put . . . me down."

Xavier carried him across the street, seeing corpses walking in the rain to the right and left, but none immediately ahead of them. They went into the lobby of a condo, where the gray of the day cast the room in deep shadow. Nothing came at them, and he set Alden down on a couch near the concierge desk. The teacher groaned and sagged back against the cushions.

"I'm going to find something to bind that wound."

The teacher gripped his wrist. "Stay with . . . me . . . for a bit."

Xavier crouched beside him and said nothing for nearly thirty minutes, letting Alden get his breath back. The man's face eventually relaxed, and when he spoke it was soft but unlabored. "You've been in charge for weeks," he said, "but now you're going to listen to me." He was pale, eyes sunk in darkening hollows. "I'm not going to get better."

Xavier started to shake his head, but Alden squeezed his wrist again.

"We both know what's going to happen. I'd ask you to kill me, but Pulaski stole your gun." The teacher smiled. "I don't think you'd do it anyway."

"I won't," Xavier said quietly.

Alden nodded. "I do want something else, and then I want you to leave. Give me the last rites."

"I'm not a priest anymore."

"Bullshit. I don't know what happened to you, or why you think that. It doesn't matter. Besides, I don't think that's the kind of thing *you* get to decide."

Xavier just looked down.

"Do this for me."

"You're not even Catholic, are you?"

Alden laughed softly. "Nope."

"Then why?"

"Please?"

Xavier looked into his eyes, looked at a man who had been nothing but a stranger and was now a friend. "I don't have any oils for the anointing. And you're supposed to make confession first."

"So since I'm not a Catholic, it won't matter if you take some shortcuts."

Xavier said nothing for a time, then closed his eyes and murmured something Alden couldn't hear before making the sign of the cross. "Repeat after me. My God, I am sorry for my sins with all my heart.

In choosing to do wrong and failing to do good, I have sinned against You whom I should love above all things."

Alden followed along.

"I firmly intend," Xavier continued, "with Your help, to do penance, to sin no more, and to avoid whatever leads me to sin. Our Savior Jesus Christ suffered and died for us. In His name, my God, have mercy. Amen."

"Amen."

Xavier then placed a hand on Alden's head and the other over his own heart, closing his eyes. "May the Lord in His love and mercy help you with the grace of the holy spirit. May the Lord who frees you from sin save you and raise you up." He opened his eyes to see Alden with a small smile on his face. "I don't know what good you think that did."

The teacher closed his eyes, still smiling. "It wasn't for me."

Xavier held Alden's hand until the man fell asleep, his breathing becoming labored again and his body temperature rising, beads of sweat appearing on his forehead. He started tossing a bit, murmuring words Xavier couldn't make out. The priest set the man's hands together on his chest, made the sign of the cross again, and went out into the rain.

THIRTY

Anderson James had been sulking since they'd eaten the female staffer, and Brother Peter had a black eye.

The swelling and dark smudge would go away, Peter knew. Anderson's situation would only get worse. Right after the televangelist crushed the staffer's head with the crowbar, Anderson had gone mad and rushed him, babbling and swinging his fists. One managed to connect before the pilot—Thing One—wrestled the man to the ground. Peter kicked his most trusted aide unconscious.

"What do you think, Anderson? Ribs or rump roast?" The minister was holding a Sharpie marker, gesturing with it. His last male staffer was secured to a vertical pipe by heavy-duty zip ties at his ankles and around his throat, arms held together above his head. He was naked, and covered in dotted lines, looking very much like the illustration of a cow often found in supermarket meat departments, identifying the different cuts.

In a corner of the break room, the last female staffer—Sherri, he thought—was on her hands and knees, head bobbing in Thing One's lap. She had quickly figured out how things were, and was determined to be useful, not to be eaten. Smart girl. Peter would eat her last.

Anderson said nothing.

Brother Peter poked the Sharpie at the young man's ribs. "Awful skinny. Not much meat here." The staffer wept silently, both at the pain from the zip ties and at what was to come. He, like the others, had hungrily participated in the feast (except for Anderson) without ever suspecting he would end up on the menu. Now, as his spiritual leader poked and inspected his body, he wondered how he could ever have believed he would not end up as a meal.

The Sharpie jabbed a buttock. "Lean, but still a little there. We can harvest it without killing him, make it last longer."

The boy began sobbing and shaking his head as much as the zip ties would allow. The girl with the broken leg had spoiled long before they could finish her, and they were left vomiting as their bodies struggled to reject the alien, near-toxic flesh. Her remains had been dumped somewhere in the complex, but that was days ago. They were all hungry again.

"You're insane," said Anderson.

"No, I am filled with the glory of Jesus," Peter said. He crossed the room to where Anderson was also tightly strapped to a pipe against one wall, naked like the other staffer but forced into a kneeling position. He had been there since he dared raise a hand to his minister, and stank of his own filth. He was given a little water, which he accepted, but he clenched his teeth and refused to eat any part of the girl.

Brother Peter used the marker to write *JUDAS* on Anderson's forehead. He placed a hand to his chest and spoke to the ceiling. "Traitors shall be consigned to the ninth circle of hell, encapsulated in ice in all conceivable positions." Anderson laughed at him, and Peter snarled and slapped him several times. "Stop laughing, Judas! Hear what awaits you!"

The bound man did stop, only to shake his head and smile. "That's not even from the Bible, you idiot. It's Dante, and you're quoting him poorly." Anderson looked up at him. "You're an abomination. If you want to see the devil, find a mirror."

Brother Peter clenched his fists, looking like he was about to attack, and then he let out a long breath and squatted, resting his hands on his knees and looking at his aide. "I don't know whether to eat you or feed you to the dead. What are your thoughts?"

"It makes no difference. God is waiting for me either way, and my conscience is clear."

"Oh, no, no, no. There is no heavenly afterlife for betrayers, Anderson. All that waits for you is an eternity of pain. But when the Lord lifts me up to sit at His right hand, I'll pray for you."

Anderson just stared at him.

Peter tapped his chin, then looked over his shoulder at the whimpering young man with the butcher's marks. "I'll get back to you." He looked back at Anderson. "Eat or feed, eat or feed." *Tap, tap, tap.* "Both, I think. I'm going to chop off your arms and legs, cauterize the stumps with that blowtorch we found, and toss the rest of you out into the terminal. You'll still be conscious when they rip into you. We'll dine on your limbs first, and later I'll watch the new zombie roll around on the floor, going nowhere. I think that sounds like a *good* time."

If he'd had any moisture in his mouth, Anderson would have spit on him.

A man's grunt and a gasp from the corner made Brother Peter smile and stand. "My turn. Sherri, come on over here, honey." The young woman left the pilot and approached, dropping to her knees as the minister unzipped his pants, right in front of Anderson.

Before the woman could begin, Peter noticed movement and looked past her to the hallway at the far end of the room. A rotting corpse stood there in stained white coveralls, its skin gray and sagging, hair missing from its head in patches where scalp had been peeled away. Another corpse was behind it, and more beyond that. A door left open? A way in they hadn't known about? It didn't matter. Brother Peter slipped a heavy box cutter out of his pants pocket and thumbed out the blade. He gripped the girl's hair and jerked her head back so that she was looking up at him.

"Make it loud," he whispered, and then sliced her face from hairline to chin. Her screams filled the room. Peter shoved her away as the dead tumbled in, heading frantically toward the noise. Several noticed the pilot, still relaxing against the wall with his privates exposed, and fell upon him before he could react. The rest went for the screaming girl and quickly noticed the two men strapped helplessly to the pipes.

A chorus of squeals and growls chased Brother Peter as he fled down a tunnel, a tiny flashlight leading the way with a weak yellow beam. He laughed as he ran, imagining Anderson struggling and praying loudly as they fed upon him. Meat for the beast. Funnier still was the idea that once he turned, he would spend eternity strapped to that pipe, forever hungry, forever powerless to do anything about it.

Right turns, left turns, through electrical rooms and down corridors, the darkness held at bay by mere feet in the dimming light. He sensed the way, wasn't afraid of getting lost, and he did not fear sudden teeth in the dark. God had a plan and would not permit him to be taken until that plan was revealed.

A metal stairway, a metal door, and then he was through. Even the gray overcast of a rainy day was blinding after so long underground, and he stumbled blindly out onto the grass. Yet he knew this was not God's light, and the sound of creatures around him was not that of His angels. He forced himself to squint and started to run.

He had emerged from another red-and-white-checked cinderblock building with motionless radar equipment on the roof, situated at the extreme northern edge of the airport. Twenty yards of grass led to an eight-foot fence with barbed wire at the top, an expanse of trees beyond. Peter ran for the fence as the dead came at him across the grass, some bodies blackened by fire and others dressed in the varied uniforms of airport ground crews. He hit the chain link and scrambled up and over, tearing his clothes and skin on the triple strands of barbed wire before dropping over the far side, landing on his back with a *whump* that knocked the wind out of him.

Gasping for air, he saw the dead reach the fence and hook their fingers through the links, shaking and moaning at their escaped prey. Peter lay there until he could breathe, then limped into the trees, which turned out to be little more than a screen for open, rolling green fields. Several hundred yards away stood a tiny flag next to a small white cart. He focused on the flag and forced himself to move, weak from the exertion and lack of food. He was halfway there before his brain processed the words *golf course*.

At the cart he found a sour, half-consumed bottle of beer that made him gag, and an open bag of stale pretzels that he crammed into his mouth. The cart had a dead battery, but from a bag strapped to the back he was able to arm himself with a heavy driver. Then he was moving again, with no direction in mind other than forward.

By its nature, the golf course was relatively free of the dead. Peter saw only a few of them at a distance, all male, dressed in pastel shirts and ridiculous pants. He hoped to find the clubhouse, knowing it would mean food, but after two hours of walking he came upon another fence. There was a road on the other side, and a body of water with more land beyond.

Over he went, more careful this time so as not to cut himself again, and he didn't fall. Following the road took him to a bridge crowded with cars, and he spent hours moving from vehicle to vehicle, raiding coolers and luggage and trunks and glove boxes. He found packaged food that wouldn't make him sick, and bottles of soda and water. It was a feast, and he gorged himself until he vomited on the road, then ate some more.

In a glove compartment of a Honda Civic he came across a clear plastic bag of weed—he wasn't interested—and an unlabeled pill bottle with a couple dozen capsules inside. Brother Peter recognized them at once: *methylphenethylamine*, his old friends, Benzedrine poppers. He used to gobble a few right before a stadium event or high-attendance tent revival in order to get jacked up and put on a good show for the sheep. He swallowed two and washed them down with a warm Pepsi, and it wasn't long before the speed hit him, providing some much-needed energy. A pickup truck yielded a huge hunting knife, but he decided he would also hold on to the box cutter. After carving up Sherri's face, it now had sentimental value. The cab of another pickup delivered a heavy black .45 with ivory grips and a box of shells that its absent owner never got the chance to use. It was loaded and weighty in his hand, reassuring and powerful like the sword of Christ.

He shed his filthy clothes and picked out sneakers and a black tracksuit with a hooded jacket. As he changed, Peter caught his naked reflection in the rear window of an SUV, startled at the concentration camp survivor he saw there. He was dirty and unshaved, gaunt and jaundiced, and the rain did little to wash him clean. The new clothes couldn't mask his stink.

After filling a backpack with as much food and bottled water as he could find, he crossed the bridge and entered the community on the other side. A sign read, *ALAMEDA WELCOMES YOU.* The answer to His mystery lay ahead, he was convinced of it, and he was not afraid. Breaking into a methamphetamine-enhanced jog, Brother Peter started humming "Lamb of God."

THIRTY-ONE

Oakland

Skye sat cross-legged on the dusty boards in the tower, the large bell hanging silently behind her. Rain was coming in each of the four open windows, turning the dust to sluggish, gray swirls. Her fingers moved quickly between the ammo box and the empty magazines, feeding copper-jacketed rounds in one at a time, *click, click, click* until she reached thirty, and then moving on to the next. She had been shooting nonstop for well over an hour, and the ammo can was half empty.

When the last magazine was filled she slipped them all into her bandolier and moved back to a window, arming the M4 with a snap. The area below was filled with fallen bodies. They were scattered across the intersection, down all four cross streets, on lawns, and piled against the iron fence of the First Baptist Church of Clawson. The sight of those bodies was fuel for the inferno burning within her, and she welcomed the hundreds more that emerged from the neighborhood to take their place. The silencer concealed her position only to a point, and they eventually noticed her in the tower, a powerful magnet for their primitive instinct. Good, she thought.

Sighting. Adjust for distance, adjust for wind. Squeeze. Head shot. She shifted the muzzle right. Squeeze. Head shot. A tick up and to the left. Squeeze. The bullet tore through a man's throat, and he didn't flinch. Three inches up and squeeze. Head shot. The daytime tracer rounds left a millisecond zip of bright green in the air, which helped adjust her accuracy. She wondered if soldiers switched to red tracers for nighttime, because in the movies they used tracers at night, and they were always red.

Skye stayed in the window until she emptied the magazine, then ejected and replaced it as she moved to the opening on the right. Here she leaned out, firing down at an angle so steep it was almost vertical. Fifty or more freaks had gathered at the fence on this side of the church, dead hands grasping iron bars as lifeless faces tried to push between them. Stationary targets. Five rounds, ten, twenty, thirty, the click of an empty magazine. Twenty-four more motionless bodies were piled against the fence, crumpled on a gore-spattered sidewalk. The rain was turning the nearby street gutters red.

She moved to the back window, which gave only a partial view of 32nd Street to the east, the rest blocked by the steep peak of the church roof. The last window also looked out onto a wide stretch of roof, and what slim view it offered was of the dead grass in the front yard, the street beyond the fence blocked by the leafy boughs of trees. That window wasn't much use, so she went back to the front, the best seat in the house, and returned to work.

A knot of freaks was heaving at the padlocked gate. She dropped them all, a few bullets sparking off the iron. She emptied a magazine at the creatures lurching across the intersection, used another on the front fence line, and then a third on the fence visible from the right window. Freaks went down beside cars, on the sidewalk in front of the little Latin *groceria*, near the liquor store, more at the fence, more in the intersection. The sharp tang of cordite filled her nostrils, and empty brass rattled under her boots as she moved. Skye paused only long enough to wipe the rain off her face and off her battle sights.

They kept coming, an endless infestation streaming toward the church from all directions, slumping and stiff-legged, their cries filling the street and occasionally drowned out by the rumble of thunder. How many hundreds? How many thousands? Skye didn't care, didn't think. There was only the kill.

Another reloading session, hands working in a blur, feeding bullets *click, click, click*. When she went back with full magazines, the streets were once again filled with the walking dead, a sea of them that made it look as if she hadn't fired a shot. They blocked out the pavement in places and were shoulder to shoulder along the entire fence, packed in five and six deep. Arms thrust between the bars, and broken teeth bit at the iron. Even more stumbled in to join the crowd.

Skye stood at the window gripping the assault rifle, blinking as rain streaked her face. She felt as if she had been startled awake from a dream.

"What am I doing?"

Her own voice sounded like a stranger's. What was this? She had broken every rule she was taught or created for herself, rules that had kept her alive for weeks. And for what? All those bullets hadn't made a bit of difference. She had surrendered to a killing frenzy just because she'd found a box of ammo and a good shooting position? This went beyond careless. Was this a half-assed suicide attempt? The church was about to become her grave.

"Stupid girl," she whispered. She looked down and saw that a pair of freaks had managed to get elevation at the fence by climbing up on the bodies of the fallen and were now pulling themselves over, mindless of what the spikes were doing to their flesh. Skye snapped up the rifle and sighted as they toppled over, but they shambled out of sight toward the church before she could draw a bead.

"Stupid *dead* girl," she said.

The roar of an engine caught her attention, and she looked out to see a boxy blue truck racing up 32nd, smashing zombies with its heavy grille and crushing them beneath its tires. At once she knew what that was about: friends of the madman she had killed up north, the one creeping toward her house in the night with a woman's head tied to his belt, come for payback. Okay, so this was how they wanted to do it. She would oblige. The moment they popped their heads out of that truck she would lift their skulls with 5.56 millimeters.

Skye shrugged into her gear and started down the stairs. She descended halfway before the door at the base crashed open. Looking down through space she saw a line of freaks pushing in and starting up the steep stairs. Two she recognized as those that had made it over the bars, but the others were new. Had they found a gap in the fence at the back of the church? Did the fence even go all the way around? In her hurry to get up here, she hadn't even checked. She'd just assumed, and so much so that she hadn't even bothered to secure the front or back doors of the church.

The angle was bad, and the freaks would be hidden from view at least half the time they were climbing, so there was little chance to engage them at a distance. Skye reached one of the tight little landings two-thirds of the way down and knelt, waiting for them. As soon as they came into sight, crawling up on hands and knees, she began firing across the open space. Red and gray splashed the far wall, bullets drilling neat little circles of daylight through the boards.

She reloaded and descended, hearing more coming in below. Her mind raced to find a plan. Option one: Shoot her way out of the church, clear a space at the fence, get over and sprint into the neighborhood, counting on her speed versus their lethargic movement to outdistance them, lose them in the neighborhood.

Option two: Retreat to the tower and the ammo can and go down shooting.

No, that wasn't even an option. If he could, Sgt. Postman would be kicking her ass for exposing herself like this in the first place. If she then cornered herself, it would be the final betrayal of what he had tried to do for her. She didn't have nearly enough ammo to make a stand like that, and it would indeed be suicide. She realized that she wanted to live, even if only to spend a few more days killing them. However this went down, though, the last bullet in her silenced pistol was reserved for her own temple.

More ghouls clawed their way up the stairs, and Skye descended toward them, rifle to her shoulder and squeezing off rounds, empty brass clattering off wood. The walls were painted with crimson splashes, the steps slick with blood as her boots picked their way down through the bodies. She changed magazines and kept going as more poured through the door at the base.

Outside came the *whoop-whoop* of a siren, and the staccato crash of an automatic shotgun, *boom-boom-boom* in rapid succession. A horn honked long and loud. The crazy man's friends wanted her to know they were coming, wanted to rattle her. She flexed her fingers around the M4's pistol grip. *What I've got, you don't want, boys.*

Skye focused on her sight, framing heads with slack dead faces and gray eyes, pulling the trigger as the bodies fell. A woman in bra and panties snarled only a few feet in front of her, and then the back of her head blew out. A teenager in a yellow tracksuit growled and gripped her ankle. She kicked it in the face and pressed the muzzle of the rifle to its forehead. It died in a pink explosion. Two men tried to come through the tower door side by side and got wedged. Skye shot each through an eye at point-blank range, kicked them loose, and then dropped three more out in the church beyond as she stepped over bodies and went through the door.

They were coming in from the back, a stream of freaks pouring through a doorway and moving up the center aisle between the pews. Skye went through the open front doors and leaped down the steps, into the yard.

Hundreds of corpses at the fence saw her and let out a moan, reaching feverishly through the bars. To her right, several more used the bodies of the fallen to get themselves up over the top of the fence. On her left, a gang of freaks stumbled around the corner of the church, and at her back, the first of the stream coming through the pews emerged from the front door.

Surrounded.

The rifle came up and she fired, turning left, right, back, squeezing off rounds. Bodies fell, but not enough. The trigger clicked on a dry mag, and they were too close to reload. She let go of the rifle and it fell against her chest, hanging by its strap, as she jerked the silenced pistol from its holster. *Puff-Puff-Puff.* Ghouls went down in the yard and in the church entrance, and soon that weapon clicked empty as well.

She had used the last bullet without realizing it.

Skye tore the machete from its sheath.

TC unfolded a metal bar from the ceiling of the Bearcat's cargo area, a device with two metal steps and a small platform that someone could stand on. He used it to open the armored hatch in the roof and stood there half in and half out of the vehicle. Across his chest were belts of red twelve-gauge shells, and he carried a pair of automatic shotguns with pistol grips front and back, big circular drums of ammo hanging underneath like the cylinders of a revolver, only with a much higher capacity. The wind from the speeding truck blew his hair back as he shrieked, "Get some, fuckers!" and began blasting away.

Carney drove the Bearcat into and over everything he saw, smashing bodies, sending them flying, crushing heads and torsos under the monstrous tires. Blood and rain hit the windshield as he accelerated into a huge gathering of the dead, the armored truck barely slowing as it plowed through them. TC's shotguns boomed above, blowing apart bodies and heads.

"*Get some, motherfuckers!*" TC was laughing as he screamed.

Carney used the siren and the horn, drawing the horde's attention. They shifted slowly toward this new noise, pulling back from the fence and crowding toward the vehicle. The Bearcat's grille and TC's shotguns were waiting for them.

He saw the girl exit the church and stop in the open, turning and firing. She pulled a pistol and still they came. He snatched the radio handset and hit the PA switch. "Get over that fence right now!" his voice boomed through the speaker. "I'll come to you. Climb up the hood and into the hatch!"

Carney cranked the wheel to the right, crushing more bodies, and gunned the truck at the fence. TC kept firing and laughing and screaming obscenities. Just before he hit, Carney cranked harder, roaring in along the fence and sweeping another dozen corpses off the bars and under the tires before slamming the brakes.

TC climbed out of the hatch and stood on the roof, pumping rounds at creatures in front of the truck. "Move it, bitch!" he screamed. "I ain't coming to you!" The cylinders rolled off three more shots. "Move it *now!*" The inmate swept his fire across the fence, and heads came apart like a row of melons.

Skye buried her machete in a freak's head, saw its eyes roll up, and jerked the weapon free. She sprinted for the fence. The freaks lined up before her went down in a bloody row, as a *ping* of a shotgun pellet on the iron bars left a hot crease below her left eye. She barely noticed and hit the fence at a run, tossing her machete through the bars as the tread of her boots scrambled against the metal, the muscles on her arms taut as she hauled herself up. At the top she stepped carefully so as not to impale herself, then landed in a crouch on the other side. She would use their cover to get out, but if these guys thought she would get in their damned truck so she could be raped and decapitated they were confused. She only needed a moment to slap in a new magazine, and then the asshole on the truck's roof was going down.

"C'mon, bitch, get that sweet ass up here!" TC ripped off five blasts at a cluster of ghouls behind Skye, the pellets whizzing over her head. Skye picked up her machete and—

—a ghoul caught hold of her pack and jerked her to the ground. It towered over her, teeth gnashing around flaps of hanging, rotted flesh. Another with its legs blown off at the knees dragged itself toward her, making a wet rattling noise in its throat.

Skye cried out and chopped at a leg, severing it. The creature collapsed on top of her, and Skye just managed to straight-arm its throat to keep it at bay. Its skin felt greasy as it thrashed, twisting its neck and clawing with both hands, writhing on top of her in a gruesome parody of missionary-style sex. A putrid stink of rotten meat came from its snapping mouth.

The legless ghoul reached her, fingertips scraping at the top of her head. She screamed and swung the machete at the one on top of her, sinking the blade into the side of its head at the temple, destroying an eye. The blade went deep, and the ghoul stiffened. Its head split open like rotten fruit, and suddenly a torrent of sticky black-and-yellow fluid gushed from the wound, hitting Skye in the face with a splash.

She gagged. It was in her mouth, her eyes, up her nose. She gasped and heaved the body off to the right, vomiting onto the street just as the legless creature caught her head in both hands from above. It came in with its teeth.

A black boot pinned the thing's neck to the pavement, and a rifle muzzle shoved in its ear blew its head apart.

Carney grabbed Skye by her pack straps and hauled her up, tossing her over his shoulder. She couldn't resist, could barely breathe, retching as her fingers dug at her eyes. Carney carried her to the open driver's door of the Bearcat and shoved her up and in, then climbed in after her.

TC was back inside and dragged Skye into the rear. Still she could only choke, her vision blurred. The inmate propped her against a stack of twelve-pack sodas, and sat on the bench across from her. Carney got the Bearcat moving again, driving over both walking and fallen bodies, accelerating away from the church and into the Oakland neighborhood.

TC handed Skye a bottle of water and a rag. She immediately got it wet, scrubbing at her face, washing out her eyes and nose, gargling and spitting, wiping at her teeth and tongue. TC watched her closely, saying nothing. When she was done she looked around, eyes darting. The back of the truck was filled with survival gear, food, and weapons, but no human heads. Across from her was a tattooed wall of a man with crazy eyes and a wild grin, staring at her as if she were an exotic zoo animal. She didn't know where her pistol was, and the machete was gone. The rifle, still hanging on her chest, was empty. She'd never get a magazine in before he was on her. She snatched the boot knife from its sheath and pointed the blade at the man.

"Easy. I'm TC, that's Carney. What's your name?" the tattooed man asked.

"It sure isn't *bitch*," she said tightly. She saw the door at the back of the vehicle. Could she get out before he caught her? No way. She was sure she could stick him if he made a move toward her, but he was wearing a lot of body armor and it had a high collar. She would have to get him in the face or neck and would get only one chance.

"How old are you?" asked TC, his eyes roaming over her.

She didn't respond. The vehicle was moving, the driver saying nothing. She didn't like the way this man was looking at her, like a dog eyeing a steak on a kitchen counter, sizing up whether he could reach it. She needed to know where they were, needed to get out.

Up front, Carney had other things on his mind besides their new acquaintance. The steering had a new shimmy to it, the vibrations traveling up into his hands through the steering wheel, and he had to overcorrect to keep it straight. There was a knocking in the engine too, and that worried him more than the steering. He had used the Bearcat like a bulldozer, slamming it into and rolling over hundreds of bodies. Armored and rugged as it was, the riot vehicle was still just a truck, not a tank, and he had damaged it. How badly he couldn't know until he crawled under it and got inside the hood, neither of which was possible right now. Even though the church was blocks behind them, more of the dead were emerging from buildings all around, drifting into the road, drawn by the sound of the vehicle.

He listened to the knocking. Was it getting worse? A breakdown here would be very bad. Carney slowed down, threading the Bearcat around abandoned cars and trying to avoid running over more of the walking dead, keeping to the same street. Hands beat at the sides of the truck, and some simply came right at him, impossible to avoid. They crunched under the front bumper.

Skye waited silently to see what the man across from her would do, but he just sat there, looking at her, no longer asking questions. It took less than thirty minutes. Skye's vision doubled, and then tripled. She felt sick to her stomach, felt like throwing up. Minutes later she began to sweat, the inside of the armored truck quickly turning into an oven. The man morphed into her eighth-grade science teacher.

"I forgot my homework," she said.

TC laughed.

At an intersection, Carney looked right. A block up was Peralta, the street he had crossed to get to the church, still running parallel to the street he was traveling. He saw a line of vehicles go by, led by a motorcycle, a tow truck, and a VW van. He cut up a block and stopped at Peralta, looking left, then waited until the last vehicle was almost out of sight before turning in to follow them.

Her science teacher morphed into Crystal. Her sister wasn't bitten, wasn't changed, and she was smiling. "You came back," Skye muttered, and then passed out, the knife falling to the floor.

TC picked it up and tossed it behind some boxes. Then he used the gear they had loaded from the training center to cuff her hands behind her back and shackle her feet together. He cut a length of nylon rope and shoved it between her teeth, tying it tightly behind her head as a biting gag.

The younger inmate stuck his head through the opening into the cab. "She's sick, man. I think she's got it."

THIRTY-TWO

Central California

The Black Hawk cruised south, one thousand feet above the dry central valley. RJ sat with his legs hanging out the left door, clipped in with his safety strap and draping an arm over his mounted M240. Six men in combat gear, led by an Air Force sergeant, sat in the back not talking. A few tried to sleep over the roar of wind and blades.

I-5 was a gray ribbon below, cutting through a vast open country of agriculture, quickly browning from lack of irrigation. Vladimir's eyes moved in an easy, experienced pattern across his instruments and out through the windscreens.

"Ranch House, Groundhog-Seven. Updates on our objective?"

"Negative, Groundhog. No new transmissions," the NAS Lemoore air traffic controller said.

"*Da*, Groundhog copies." Shit, he thought. More wasted time and fuel. Another hunting of the goose. Lemoore had picked up a brief broadcast from a woman claiming to be an L.A. County sheriff's deputy, who gave her position as just south of Lost Hills, a tiny farming hamlet halfway to Bakersfield on I-5. She said she was at the head of a refugee column. The woman did not respond to repeated calls from Lemoore, and there were no further transmissions. Vlad had been sent to investigate.

The highway was only lightly scattered with vehicles and remained fairly open. A few lone shapes wandered the asphalt, but they weren't refugees. He glanced at his instruments. "Coming up on objective," he said into the intercom. "Five minutes."

RJ and the Air Force sergeant, also wearing headsets, acknowledged with two clicks.

It didn't take five minutes; Vlad saw them long before he reached them, a sight impossible to miss. Ahead, I-5 was packed with a dark mass of bodies, vehicles sprinkled among them. The Black Hawk descended to three hundred feet and then swept overhead. People below began waving their arms.

Dear God, how many were there? The refugee column stretched out for more than a mile, covering both the northbound and southbound lanes and the wide grassy area between. Most were on foot carrying bags and packs and small children, others pushing wheelbarrows or shopping carts, some on bicycles with small trailers pulled behind. Trucks, cars, and buses with people piled on the roofs or hanging off the sides were trapped in the surge of bodies, the whole thing creeping along at less than a walking pace.

"Ranch House, Groundhog-Seven. We have eyes on the objective. Confirm large column of refugees on foot, moving north on Interstate Five."

"Copy, Groundhog. Can you estimate a count?" the controller asked.

Vlad shook his head. "Ten thousand plus."

The controller at Lemoore asked him to repeat the number. The Black Hawk reached the end of the column, back where the stragglers were: people carrying stretchers, a horse-drawn wagon loaded with children, others pushing people in wheelchairs, and one actually rolling along a hospital gurney with a woman strapped to it. Refugees from who knew how far south.

Vlad whispered a single word in Russian.

The dead were following, corpses from Mexico and San Diego joined by those from L.A., many of them charred from napalm strikes but still shambling forward. A wall of the walking dead covered both lanes and spread well out into the fields on either side, the closest of them less than a hundred yards behind the fleeing survivors. Vlad climbed to a thousand feet for a better view and wished he hadn't. An ocean of the dead went back as far as he could see. Though it might be only a hundred thousand or so, it could be as many as a million.

A ripple of nervous curses came from the back, the squad of troops peering out and down at the same thing the pilot was seeing.

"Ranch House," Vladimir called, his voice tight, "the column is being pursued by hostiles. Estimate they will make contact in less than two hours."

"Copy, Groundhog. Strength of opposition?"

Vlad didn't need to consult the map strapped to his knee to know where I-5 went. He stared out at a moving carpet of death.

"Groundhog-Seven, Ranch House. Report enemy strength."

Vladimir keyed the mic. "It is Los Angeles."

There was a long pause before, "Stand by."

The Russian banked and brought the Black Hawk around to the left, the men in the doorway gripping the frame extra tightly as the endless ghouls passed beneath them, fearing a fall, as if the impact from this altitude wouldn't kill them instantly. The chopper descended and came up along the side of the column again, low enough to get a good look but not so low as to buffet them with wind. They were slow, slower than the horde behind them. It was a basic math problem that would end in disaster. Vlad saw only a few firearms among them, and no military presence. The people on the ground continued to wave their arms.

"*Da*, I see you," he said quietly.

In the back, the Air Force sergeant spoke over the intercom. "Don't even think about setting this crate down, Ivan. We'd be overrun."

Vladimir clenched his teeth. "Sergeant, if I choose, I will shake this bird until you all fall out the doors. And I will fly us straight into the side of a mountain before I take orders on my own aircraft." He shook his head, instantly regretting the rebuke. The man was just scared, and with good reason. If the Black Hawk touched down, thousands of terrified people looking for a way out would swamp it in seconds. Vlad didn't descend further, simply held position off to the side of the column and waited. There was no response from Lemoore.

He could imagine why. Right now, naval officers of assorted senior rank, including the base's commanding admiral, would be in a tense discussion about the refugees. NAS Lemoore was already bursting with displaced civilians, and more were flying in daily. The dead continued to pile up at the fence line, and the repeated claims of the briefers that it would hold was getting harder and harder to believe. These new refugees, assuming a way could be devised to get them through the creatures encircling the base, would stretch Lemoore's resources to the breaking point. Vlad imagined stern-looking men debating around a table, throwing out ideas, and not all of them in the interest of the refugees. Might someone even suggest using them as bait, to draw the masses away from the fence? The situation grew increasingly dire each passing day, and frightened men made frightening decisions. Most likely, however, they would do nothing, and hope the column simply continued moving north.

The flaw in that hope, Vlad knew, was that the refugees no doubt had maps and could clearly see that the air station was the only military installation in the area. It was probably their intended destination.

He banked the helicopter so he could see the endless, hungry mass closing from behind. The dead would catch up, attacking from the rear and working forward, driving the front of the group north . . . right into the waiting teeth of the horde outside the base. And when the dead of Los Angeles reached the fence line . . . ?

"Groundhog-Seven, Ranch House," the controller said. "You are ordered to make no contact with the column and return to base immediately."

He looked once more at the people standing and waving below, hoping that his was only the first of many helicopters coming to carry them to safety. "Keep moving," he whispered. "Do not stand and wave, keep moving." He turned the Black Hawk north, climbing and staring directly ahead so he wouldn't have to see their faces as their salvation flew away.

"Groundhog-Seven copies, we are RTB," Vlad said in the mic.

No one spoke during the twenty-minute flight home.

Vladimir approached the base from the southwest, and at two miles out he could easily see the dark smear that represented the bodies packed around the fence, fifty deep. How many now? A hundred thousand? Two?

"Ranch House, Groundhog-Seven coming in at two-one-zero, two miles," Vlad said.

"Roger, Groundhog, you are cleared to land at pad seven-alpha."

The Russian was about to copy when he saw the C-130. The big green transport aircraft, driven by four massive turboprops, was lumbering in from the north, landing gear down, one hundred feet off the runway. Another load of refugees from who knew where. As he closed the distance to the base, he saw the wings suddenly waggle, the nose drifting left to right. Vlad immediately pulled on the cyclic and collective at the same time, the Black Hawk's nose coming up as he settled into a quick hover directly over the horde.

"What's up, Lieutenant?" RJ called.

"Aircraft in distress," Vlad responded, watching as the big cargo plane wobbled, began to rise as if it were going to wave off, then dropped, slamming hard onto the runway before leaping back into the air, crippled and on fire. One engine broke free and shot across the field in a ball of flaming, twisted metal, taking out a large Navy helicopter sitting on a pad, exploding it in an instant. The rest of the C-130 reared up into the sky, nosed over, and began to pinwheel through the air, pieces of tail and wing breaking free.

The doomed plane spun straight into the cluster of hangars serving as housing for refugees, streaking wreckage and gouts of burning fuel ripping through the adjacent tent city. The sound of the explosions was muffled by the Black Hawk's rotors, clouds of black and red ballooning silently into the sky.

"What the Christ was that?" the Air Force sergeant yelled over the intercom.

Vlad's eyes followed the fireball erupting from the refugee hangar. How many had been on board the plane? How many thousands on the ground? With the airspace now clear, he was about to move the helicopter forward when he caught new movement below and to the right.

The fence was collapsing.

A twenty-foot section sagged inward as tons of pressure moved against it, the dead spilling in behind it. Those creatures at the fence fell to the ground as it gave way, only to be walked over by a wave of bodies. An adjacent section folded as well, chain link torn away and metal support posts bending in half. More fence went down in a line beyond that, and the dead trudged onto the base by the thousands.

Looking out the left door in the opposite direction, RJ called, "The west gate just fell! They're inside!" The gunner watched as not fifty yards to the left of the aircraft, thousands of the dead pressed through the mangled gates and walked into gunfire coming from several sandbagged bunkers and a pair of machine gun–mounted Humvees.

Tracers lashed out at the moving wall but didn't even slow them down. They flowed over the bunkers and vehicles like high tide, burying the defenders even as they fired their weapons, their mass tipping over a Humvee. A few men in camouflage managed to break away from the breach, half of them running without rifles.

It's over, Vlad thought. There would be no putting the genie back in the bottle now.

"Get us down there," the Air Force sergeant said.

"Not a wise idea," said Vlad. "They cannot be contained."

"Goddammit, those are our guys down there! Put us down right now!"

The Russian pushed the cyclic forward between his knees and nosed the Black Hawk over the fence, over the sea of bodies, looking ahead for a safe landing spot. In the back, the sergeant was telling his men to lock and load.

"Ranch House, Groundhog-Seven," Vlad said into his mic.

No reply.

Vlad repeated the call and received only silence. He took the bird in fast and low, ensuring that his landing zone was clear of flaming debris, then flared and pivoted sideways, touching the wheels down a hundred yards ahead of the first wave of walking dead. Without a word the sergeant led his tiny squad out the door, taking off at a run toward where a small knot of men were kneeling and firing. Vlad lifted off at once and took the Black Hawk back toward the collapsed fence.

The Air Force sergeant and his squad were dead within ten minutes, and back up walking several minutes after that.

"Ranch House, Ranch House, this is Groundhog-Seven. I am taking station over the western breach, awaiting instructions." Behind him, RJ went to work with his door gun, sending long streams of automatic fire down on the heads of the crowd.

Ranch House did not respond.

The view from the cockpit revealed that the situation was far worse than Vlad had originally thought. He could see a half dozen other places where the unrelenting pressure of the dead had finally flattened the fence, and that was just on this side of the base. Reason assured him there would be many more. Fixed defenses and mobile patrols had been overwhelmed immediately, and the dead flowed in like the lava that Rocker, the young Navy pilot Vlad had spoken to, had described: slow, spreading, unstoppable, and absolutely fatal. They flowed across streets and manicured lawns, between buildings, and out across the tarmac. This was not an infantry base; there were no armored vehicles and only a small percentage of the personnel were armed.

RJ soon exhausted the ammo supply for the left gun, with little measurable effect, but still unhooked and moved across, snapping back in at the right door and getting that M240 rolling. It sounded like a chainsaw. Vlad rotated the Black Hawk to give him the best exposure as the bullets chopped into the mass below. Bodies went down in little groups, heads disintegrating under the high-power fire, but the gaps were instantly filled by more.

There was some radio traffic, though nothing from the tower. Another inbound C-130 ten miles out announced that it was turning back toward Nevada. A pair of Navy helicopters that had gone down to Bakersfield this morning transmitted that they would head south and try to reach the USS *Ronald Reagan*, supposedly now somewhere off the coast of the Baja Peninsula. One pilot reported that he didn't think he had the fuel to make it and might have to set down so the other chopper could pick up his crew.

Vlad looked at his own gauge. The trip to Lost Hills and the subsequent time over Lemoore had cost him a third of his fuel. If the *Reagan* had moved south as the Navy bird reported, it was beyond his reach. Even if the ship was still somewhere off the coast of L.A., it would be cutting things close, tight enough that an unexpected headwind could bleed off the last of his fuel right over the city. The additional problem would be finding the vessel in the first place, since the Black Hawk had no direct comms. An aircraft carrier might seem exceptionally large, but in the open ocean it was very small indeed, and every minute spent over the water visually searching for it would burn precious fuel. As a pilot, Vlad had imagined his own death many times: fire, crashes, combat. Drowning or being eaten by sharks, however, was not one of the ways he would choose. It didn't matter; the carrier was too far away.

"Lieutenant, three o'clock," RJ called.

Vladimir looked to the right across the field. He saw Rocker's lone Super Hornet still on the ground, and he wondered what had happened to the young fighter jock. That wasn't what RJ was drawing his attention to, however. Another Black Hawk sat on the deck close to a cluster of buildings, rotors turning, masses of the undead coming in at it from all sides. A small circle of men was falling back to the chopper, firing in all directions. Vlad recognized the tail number as Conroy's bird, his former co-pilot.

"Hold tight." The Russian banked hard and roared across the base toward the surrounded helicopter, while RJ loaded his last box of ammo. Ahead of them, the defenders began to fall, and two men with rifles turned and leaped through the open side door as Conroy began to lift off.

Handfuls of the dead galloped after them and scrambled aboard as well.

Groundhog-7 was almost there when Conroy's bird became fully airborne, close enough to see the side window of the cockpit suddenly splashed red. The chopper staggered and tipped sideways, racing horizontally through the air and dropping. The Black Hawk's engine made a high-pitched death whine as it streaked toward the ground, and then there was a tremendous blast as it crashed.

It hit inside NAS Lemoore's tank farm of jet fuel.

"*Shit!*" Vlad cried, banking away sharply and accelerating, pushing the turbine for all its power. Behind him there was a deep boom that he felt in his chest cavity as the first aboveground tank erupted, an enormous bomb that sent a flaming pressure wave of shrapnel in a three-hundred-sixty-degree circle. The blast set off others, the giant tanks going off like a string of firecrackers.

The pressure slammed into Groundhog-7, lifting it from behind and hurling the aircraft forward, nose down, trying to knock it out of the sky. Pieces of metal banged and rattled off the fuselage, and a frantic warning buzzer sounded in the cockpit. The helicopter dropped toward the flat roof of a barracks building, turbine intakes sucking at the superheated air, and the cords in Vlad's neck and arms jumped out as he hauled back on the cyclic.

The Black Hawk pulled out ten feet above the rooftop, low enough for the wind from its blades to scatter gravel like a dust storm. Then it was roaring across the base.

Vlad whispered something in Russian, a little prayer his mother had taught him, and slowly gained elevation. He shut off the warning buzzer—a caution that his air intakes were suffocating, though no longer—and aimed the chopper toward the tower. He circled it, calling repeatedly on the radio, and still getting no response. No one moved behind the glass. He pulled away, looking down as the streets of the naval air station filled with the dead. Many were charred black from burning fuel, civilians who had come here seeking sanctuary and found something worse than death.

The pilot made a slow, low-level inspection of the base, seeing no more firefights. "RJ, do you see anything on your side?"

The gunner said nothing.

"RJ?" Vlad twisted in his seat to look back into the troop compartment. The metal decking was slick with blood, and RJ was flat on his back, jumpsuit scorched, a blackened twist of metal jutting out of his throat. His eyes were open, staring up at nothing.

The Russian cursed softly. The man had probably been killed instantly when the jet fuel tank went off. Vlad told himself that even if he had known his gunner was hit and was able to find a safe place to land, there wouldn't have been anything he could do. Nonetheless, he felt the weight of the man's death. He could rationalize it all he wanted to, but he knew his dreams would have something quite different to say about it.

If he lived long enough to sleep again.

He continued his slow patrol across the length of the base, searching for survivors, finding only the walking dead as they continued to file through the breaches. If anyone was down there, they were out of sight, hiding in a building and beyond Vlad's help.

A howl at his right ear made him flinch left as fingernails clawed the corner of his seat. Vlad twisted to see RJ on his feet, the metal still in his neck, reaching with both arms. His eyes were filmy, and he hissed through bared teeth. The door gunner's safety line, still clipped from his harness to a ring on the floor of the troop compartment, held him back like a vicious dog straining at the end of its leash. The dead man lunged against it, coming up short, able only to touch the corner of the pilot's seat. He moaned and kept at it, jerking and snapping his teeth.

Vlad put the Black Hawk into a hover and slipped a small automatic from a zipper pocket of his flight suit, just beneath his armpit. "Forgive me, *tovarich*." He shot RJ in the face, and the gunner's body collapsed to the decking.

The pilot looked down for a moment, and then looked at the map strapped to his right knee. It showed secondary and tertiary landing zones—both military and civilian—as well as places he might find the JP-5 fuel his bird consumed at a rate of 0.74 miles per gallon. He knew that most, if not all, were out of date and already overrun.

He flew the Black Hawk north.

THIRTY-THREE

Oakland

The highway was no longer an option. It was too packed with vehicles, and the dead wandering among them numbered in the thousands now. At the head of the hippie convoy, Evan's Harley led them down into the neighborhoods of West Oakland. These would have been rough areas before the plague, dangerous and crime-infested. Now the city was infested by a new breed of predator.

Evan leaned and turned, working the throttle to scoot past clusters of the moaning dead, not stopping to use his weapons. There were simply too many of them, and they had to keep moving. Slow as they were, the creatures still had numbers, and if they managed to make a ring around the motorcycle . . . Evan didn't delude himself about their chances if that happened.

Behind him, Maya wrapped her arms tightly about his waist, leaning naturally into the turns. In one hand she gripped the nine-millimeter Evan had taken off the dead cop in Napa, and she kept her head tucked against the rain. Over the years Evan had grown accustomed to riding in all sorts of weather, but he still wore a pair of goggles he had found on the highway. His clothes were completely soaked and his hair slicked back.

The cars, trucks, and vans followed closely in a line.

Evan and Calvin had planned their route while still on the interstate, spreading a road map across the hood of an abandoned car and highlighting it in yellow. The writer committed the street names and turns to memory, and Maya watched the process closely, wordlessly memorizing as well. The map was tucked inside his jacket now, in the event their planned route was blocked and required an alternate way through.

Thunder grumbled overhead, and the flat gray above was occasionally broken by white flashes.

Evan ignored the turn onto West Grand Avenue. Although it was a wide road, with more room for the line of vehicles to maneuver, it also led to the Bay Bridge, and there seemed to be an extraordinary number of corpses coming from that direction. Were they leaving San Francisco, heading into Oakland? That wasn't a pleasant thought. There were too many of them here already. Instead he kept the convoy headed south on Peralta, watching for 7th Street, which would lead them west to the harbor.

Where their hearts would be broken when they found it empty.

Despite the growing threat around them, they had pressed on, pinning their hopes to a phantom hospital ship that would carry them all to safety and a happily-ever-after. *I'm as crazy as the rest of them,* Evan thought, *not only a part of them now but a leader.* How had *that* happened? Evan Tucker was a loner and, according to his father, a vagabond who ran from responsibility, chasing dreams. Well, Dad had been right about that last part. Except Evan suspected he was chasing a nightmare now, and he feared what would happen when he caught up to it.

The intersection where 7th crossed Peralta appeared, and Evan stopped the bike, lifting his goggles and wiping at his face. Maya patted his shoulder and pointed to where he was already looking.

"I'll be damned."

On all four corners of the intersection, large white signs had been attached to light posts, each with a big arrow pointing west up 7th. Above the arrows in tall letters was USNS COMFORT, and above this a large, red cross.

USNS . . . United States Naval Ship? Faith had said it was there, and here were the signs, pointing to the harbor. It couldn't still be here, could it? Evan was exhilarated and chilled at the same time but couldn't say exactly why he was suddenly nervous. Maya nudged him and kissed his ear, and instantly things were better. He waved to the tow truck behind him and accelerated down 7th.

Very quickly they passed back under the Nimitz Freeway and entered Oakland's main industrial center, a place of wide streets and sprawling, flat-roof buildings. Other than a lone corpse walking stiffly out of a loading dock, the dead were absent. That made a little sense, since this wouldn't have been a much populated area under normal circumstances. Still, 7th was unusually clear of vehicles, and that bothered him.

Even in the downpour the place smelled of oil and rust, and rainwater pooled in potholes and ruts in the asphalt made by the passage of thousands of heavily laden trucks. A rail line on the left followed the street as they traveled through a silent city of warehouses and truck yards, motionless freight cars parked on sidings, paved lots with rows of trailers, cranes, and greasy forklifts. Stacked ocean containers—blue, orange, rusty red, and green—rose like castle walls in vast storage yards.

Every block, the signs for USNS COMFORT directed them forward.

He wondered at the absence of vehicles. If this was an evacuation center, wouldn't it have been jammed with carloads of refugees trying to get out? He had his answer on the next block.

It had been extremely organized.

The road ahead was blocked by a pair of desert camouflage tanks parked nose to nose, a ten-foot gap between them. Several weapon-mounted Humvees stood to the sides, and a pair of sandbag gun pits had been built near the tanks. A corridor of razor-sharp barbed wire formed a funnel that would have permitted only a few people at a time to pass between the tanks. A control point.

To the left, a truck yard behind a high chain-link fence had been turned into a parking lot, refugee vehicles lined up inside in endless rows. Evan was reminded of how people were directed to park in the fields at state fairs.

Bold-lettered signs around the control point announced *NO WEAPONS BEYOND THIS POINT* and *DEADLY FORCE AUTHO-RIZED*. More signs pointed up Maritime Street to the right, past a truck weigh station. These read *QUARANTINE AREA* and *INFECTED ONLY* and had red arrows.

The tow truck idled up beside the Harley, and the VW van stopped behind them, Calvin walking up holding his assault rifle. "I'm going to be doing some apologizing to Faith," he said. "She was right all along."

Evan looked around. He wasn't so sure. The control point was abandoned, and the ground was covered in shell casings. The body of a soldier was draped facedown over the sandbags of a gun pit. Nothing made a sound here except for the engines and the rain. "Let's see what's on the other side," he said.

After a brief conversation, the tow truck driver, a long-haired, bearded man named Kyle, backed his rig up to one of the Humvees and ran out his cable. Several minutes later he was dragging the Army vehicle out of the way, creating a ten-foot-wide gap between the rear of the tank and the brick wall of a warehouse. It would be enough for the convoy to squeeze through. Minutes later they were moving once again up 7th, deeper into the industrial park.

More rail lines appeared, more rows of silent boxcars and flatbeds sitting on rails. Ocean containers were everywhere: on trains, on trucks, stacked on the ground behind walls of chain link. In one open, paved area, a huge orange-and-white Coast Guard helicopter stood as a quiet sentinel.

They came to the water. Here the road curved until it reached an attractive stone building with a sign reading *INTERNATIONAL MARITIME CENTER*, a museum of some kind. Past it, the road split in three directions. One cut back into the complex, following another rail line; one continued south along the edge of a park; the third traveled out onto a stretch of land with more train tracks and container yards, eventually coming to a long wharf with a row of high, white cranes used for offloading ships.

Oakland Middle Harbor was gray and choppy in the rain, a horseshoe of land that opened to the greater bay at the far end. Closest to them, right on the water, sat an environmental oasis among the industry, a large green space of trees and trails, playgrounds, picnic areas, and a baseball diamond. An Army field hospital occupied most of the ball field: square, green canvas tents planted in orderly rows and marked with red crosses.

But it had been overrun.

Torn and blood-splashed canvas fluttered in the breeze, empty ambulances stood with rear doors open, and people in both camouflage and civilian clothing moved stiffly among the tents. Out here near the road they saw torn fences, burned military trucks, and a California Highway Patrol cruiser so riddled with bullet holes it looked like Bonnie and Clyde's death car. The road out toward the cranes and wharf was peppered with abandoned luggage and coolers, empty wheelchairs and walkers, and dropped toys.

Evan pulled his binoculars from a saddlebag and looked out at the long white ship tied up at the distant wharf. It was the length of an aircraft carrier, boxy with giant red crosses standing out brightly against its snowy hull.

Launched as an oil tanker in 1976, *Comfort* was converted to seventy thousand tons of hospital ship eleven years later, operated by a mix of civilian and naval medical personnel. Its deck boasted a landing pad capable of handling the world's largest helicopters. Below, *Comfort* was equipped with twelve operating rooms, intensive care, obstetrics, radiology, a burn unit, dental and optometry facilities, labs, a pharmacy, and beds for more than a thousand patients. It could produce its own medicinal oxygen and distill up to three hundred thousand gallons of seawater into drinking water every day. Its proud history of service included Desert Storm in the nineties, New York Harbor after 9/11, Iraq, post-Katrina New Orleans, Caribbean and Latin American humanitarian relief, and three trips to Haiti in response to both civil unrest and the earthquake of 2010.

And now it was dead.

Evan focused the binoculars. The hospital ship was teeming with drifters, bodies lurching along catwalks and across decks. Worse still, the peninsula leading to the ship was packed with a swarm of ten to twenty thousand milling corpses stretching back from the wharf in a long tail. They had come here seeking evacuation. They had come here because they were sick, and sick people went to hospitals. Sick people.

"Oh, God," he whispered. How many were already infected when they arrived, and turned into something else? How many were still here, not just in view but herded into fenced yards and warehouses? They would have torn down the fences by now, forced open the doors. They would be loose.

Through the binoculars he saw the horde on the peninsula begin to turn and move back in their direction. At that moment a horn sounded to the rear of the convoy, long and urgent. Both Evan and Maya stood up from the Harley and looked back. The dead were emerging from everywhere: buildings, trucks yards, boxcars, coming from behind containers, streaming into the road behind them as the refugees from *Comfort* closed on the left.

Evan saw a heavy blue truck racing ahead of the warehouse swarm, passing the convoy on one side. It looked official, possibly military, and as it roared past he saw the words *California D.O.C.* on the side. The engine was knocking like a blacksmith's hammer as it went by, leaving a cloud of oily blue smoke in its wake. It did not stop, or even slow.

Evan looked into Maya's face. "Hold on!" Then he hit the throttle and chased after the armored truck, the line of hippie vehicles keeping close behind.

And the dead followed with them.

THIRTY-FOUR

Oakland

"This is about to turn to shit," Carney said, gritting his teeth and clenching the wheel even tighter.

TC nodded and went into the back, where Carney could hear him loading weapons. A glance in the side mirrors showed him that every millimeter of firepower the truck carried wouldn't be nearly enough. And now the truck itself was about to fold.

They had followed the caravan of cars at a discreet distance, and Carney was encouraged when they turned west toward the water. Maybe they knew something about a boat? It was really his only shot, because the Bearcat was shimmying and knocking fiercely now. He had done some real damage to it saving the girl. Although he said nothing, it was clear TC thought Carney was crazy for doing it, the unspoken words obvious in the younger man's expression. But TC only shrugged and smiled, his faith in his cellmate apparently still intact. It was more faith than Carney had in himself. And that smile bothered him; it went past friendly. TC wanted the girl.

About the time they passed under the Nimitz Freeway, Carney heard rustling and the tearing sound of Velcro. "What are you doing back there?"

A pause. "Just making sure she's not hiding anything."

Carney twisted around and looked through the opening into the rear compartment. TC had bound the girl earlier, but now he had removed her rifle and vest of ammo pouches—the Velcro noise he had heard—and was kneeling beside her. Her tank top was pushed up to just below her breasts, and his palm rested on her flat stomach, moving across it slowly.

He looked up with a crooked grin. "She's fit, man. Nice abs."

"TC, leave her alone."

The hand slid higher. "She's burning up with fever. It ain't fair, bro. A nice piece of ass like this . . . who *ain't* dead . . . and she's infected." His other hand moved toward her. "I'll bet as long as I don't actually touch her with my—"

Carney slammed on the brakes, throwing TC forward in a heap. He reached down and grabbed the bigger inmate by his long blond hair, wrenching his head up painfully. His voice was soft. "Touch that girl again and I'll bleed you out." He gave the hair a yank. "Fast."

"Fuck, man!" He grabbed at Carney's wrist. "That fuckin' hurts!"

"I'm not playing, TC." His voice was soft and even. "You want to stay with me, you listen and do what I tell you."

"Yeah, man, yeah!"

Another painful jerk. "Leave her alone."

"I got it!"

Carney released him and got the Bearcat moving. It was several minutes before TC climbed back into the passenger seat, and when he did he said nothing, just stared out the window. Carney didn't offer any gentle words to smooth things over this time.

Now TC was in the back again, loading up, but Carney was confident he wouldn't go near the girl. His confidence in their relationship was not so strong, and he admitted the question that had been bothering him for some time: How many times could you hit an obedient pit bull before one day it went for your throat? Not too often, but not today, he decided. TC would leave the girl alone for now, not that it would even matter for much longer. She was sick, Carney had trashed their vehicle—their life support—rescuing her, and now it was about to leave them stranded. They were all dead anyway.

He had quickly caught up to where he could see the convoy again, and stayed back while they cleared an obstacle by a pair of tanks and drove through. Carney gave them a few minutes and followed. They certainly seemed to know where they were going.

He saw the ship the same time they did, saw the destroyed vehicles and field hospital, and the army of the dead out on a peninsula near the long white vessel. And then the second army showed up, tens of thousands of ghouls spilling out of warehouses and truck yards behind them, pouring into every available inch of street and pressing forward in the rain. He remembered the signs for the infected quarantines. And now here they all were.

Carney had followed these people into a death trap.

He gassed the Bearcat down the open lane to the left of the convoy, passing vans and SUVs and sedans, rooftops loaded with gear and spare fuel cans tied to bumpers. All manner of surprised faces stared out at him as he rocketed by: families, children, people with bandannas and beards and long hair. Carney barely noticed as he passed the motorcycle leading them. He didn't know where he was going, just following a road that wasn't filled with the dead, heading south and trying to get some distance. To the right, the water of the big, semicircular harbor was only a dozen yards off the road as it ran close to the shore, lapping at the jumbles of rock and concrete slabs that formed a manmade barrier.

Ahead he could see another split coming up as the road ended at a T with water beyond, more industrial park to the left, and another stretch of land sticking out into the water on the right: another wharf, this one lined with freighters tied up lengthwise against it. A dead end.

In the mirror, the column of vehicles was hurrying to keep up.

Carney reached the T and stopped, the Bearcat shuddering. He slipped into neutral and feathered the gas to keep it from stalling. To the left, the road ran into a maze of warehouses, abandoned trucks, and rail lines with box cars lined up on them. Even as he watched, corpses stumbled into the street, only a few at first, and then crowds of hundreds swelling to thousands.

He dropped the gear and cranked the wheel to the right, up the dead-end wharf. Maybe they could make it up onto one of those freighters, lift the gangplank so nothing could reach them, deal with whatever they found on board. If he found a haven like that, would he let these other people in? More bodies potentially meant more firepower, but more mouths to feed, more trouble. He clenched his teeth. *Think about it later.*

The Bearcat bumped over cracked cement and railroad tracks, passing more rows of containers and a big black crane, weaving between a pair of forklifts. Four freighters were tied up along the short pier. Someone had spray-painted tall, yellow biohazard symbols on the rusty hull of each ship and then used some kind of tractor or bulldozer to tear down their gangplanks. Piles of twisted tubing and metal stairways were crumpled on the wharf at each vessel, and a minute later the Bearcat steered around the heavy Caterpillar that had cut off access to the ships.

He reached the end of the pier. They were out of ships.

The rumble of a motorcycle came up behind them seconds later, and then the row of cars and vans came to a stop in a line. TC popped the roof hatch and went up with binoculars and a shotgun.

"They're coming, man. Nothing but zombies as far as I can see. We're fucked, bro."

Carney pounded the steering wheel, then tensed as the Bearcat's engine hiccupped and shook. It rattled, wheezed, but then settled back into a ragged rhythm. He checked his mirrors, saw people getting out of vehicles, herding children forward while adults with firearms moved to the rear. Pistols and shotguns, mostly. It was going to be a slaughter.

He looked to the right, out at the water in front of the prow of an aged freighter with Korean lettering on the side. Carney turned the wheel hard to the right, aimed the Bearcat for that space, and hit the gas. The armored truck left the pier.

Evan's Harley followed a few seconds later.

THIRTY-FIVE

Airborne

It was a matter of mathematics now. The two General Electric 701c turboshaft engines put out 1,890 horsepower each, pushing the Black Hawk along at 170 miles per hour. When he left Lemoore, the 360-gallon internal tank was at fifty percent, giving him a maximum range of 180 miles, including his emergency reserve. At this speed, with the GEs giving him three-quarters of a mile for every gallon consumed and a twenty-knot crosswind coming in from the west, he had a little over an hour left in the air.

Vladimir kept the aircraft at a thousand-foot altitude, so when the fuel ran out he wouldn't have far to fall. The manuals called it a *forced autorotation landing*. Helicopter pilots called it crashing.

He knew the tank farms at San Jose's airport had burned, so he didn't bother going there. Instead he flew farther north, heading for San Francisco. The world passed beneath him like a stage empty of actors, occupied only by props and silent backgrounds, a theater devoid of life. He spoke to the empty cockpit, taking on both sides of the conversation.

"God, it is Vladimir."

"So now you speak to Me. Where have you been?"

"I would ask the same question of You, God. Have You seen what has become of Your world, Your children?"

"Of course, Vladimir. Now what is it you wanted?"

"I need a full tank of fuel, and I need to take a piss."

"Oh, Vladimirovich, ever the comedian. But the joke is on you, comrade. No fuel. But piss, We have plenty. Here it comes."

The Black Hawk flew into the rain, fat drops scattering across the windscreen, blown quickly away by the rush of air and rotor blades. The cockpit's weather radar showed a green mass covering the entire Bay Area, though at one thousand feet the outside world simply looked gray and dark. Patches of distant lightning promised turbulence.

"That is not what I had in mind." Vlad followed 101 north, the dead city of San Mateo passing to his left, the highway below a ribbon of vehicles frozen in place.

San Francisco International appeared in the gloom ahead, an open expanse of green crossed with paved strips, its terminals, hangars, and tower without lights, acres of cars in parking lots stretching outward from the buildings. Aircraft of all sizes, most of them commercial, stood in lines on runways and approaches. There was wreckage too, and for a moment Vlad envisioned the horror of the walking dead attacking passengers on airborne jets, biting and feeding upon people safely buckled into their seats. He saw their numbers steadily expanding as they worked their way forward, defenseless passengers unable to escape. They would force the cockpit door, come stumbling in upon the pilots, and the plane would go down—

—as that one had, now nothing more than a burned tail jutting out of the space where SF International's fuel tanks had been. There were other wrecks as well, some on the field, some that had crashed into and burned down the terminal. Vlad circled slowly, looking for a fuel truck. He found none.

The Black Hawk's fuel gauge floated one tick above the red zone. Vladimir put the airport behind him and headed north toward the city, checking his navigation coordinates and keeping to the bay-side coastline. Homes and businesses slid beneath him, and ahead the tall, darkened buildings of San Francisco resembled a cemetery in the rain. He banked right, out over the bay, and headed east.

His alternate landing and refueling sites listed San Jose, San Francisco, Oakland International, Oakland's Coast Guard Island, and Travis Air Force Base to the northeast. He knew from the briefings that Travis had been overrun, but it didn't really matter. He didn't have the fuel to reach it. He'd be able to check Oakland, and that would be that.

The bay was a sheet of slate, cold and unfriendly, waiting to swallow the helicopter. He passed over an oil tanker, adrift and without lights, and several minutes later saw a pair of dark shapes surface side by side, plumes of water vapor erupting from their spouts before mighty tails appeared and propelled them back under.

Even in the rain, Vladimir could see that Oakland International was a total loss. The Black Hawk crossed over from water to land and he simply flew straight across. There was no need to circle the blackened airport. It looked like a war zone.

A red warning light began to glow on his console, accompanied by a low electronic tone. He was into his reserves, only minutes left now. Vladimir descended, banked left and headed up the channel between Oakland and Alameda. His navigation indicated that Coast Guard Island was directly ahead.

"God, it is Vladimir."

"You again. What do you want now?"

"A fuel truck and a safe place to land."

"Sorry, fresh out of both. How about some piss?"

Coast Guard Island sat alone in the channel, accessed by a single bridge as the only way in and out, and was shaped roughly like a kidney.

A wharf ran along its left side, and the majority of the island was covered in large, flat buildings, tree-lined roads, parking lots, and parade grounds, but no airfield. A helicopter pad sat at the bottom tip, and Vlad slowed and dropped, hovering at a hundred feet while he took it all in.

The red light was now flashing, and the tone turned to a steady beep as the fuel gauge sank into the red.

There were no choppers on the pad, but no wreckage either. The base didn't have a tank farm; fuel would be delivered to aircraft with tanker trucks. None were in view, but a brick building stood to one side of the pad, four garage doors set in its face. The fuel trucks might be in there. Or they might not.

Again, it didn't matter. The area below was awash with the dead. Vlad could tell by their numbers that Coast Guard Island, like Lemoore, had been used as a refugee collection point. But it had fallen too, and now served to pack a high number of the creatures in a very small area.

There were seven rounds left in Vladimir's automatic. He wouldn't make it to any fuel trucks, wouldn't be able to safely take the time required to fill his tanks. He'd never make it out of the cockpit. He climbed and put the island behind him, moving north again.

"Thanks for the piss."

"You're welcome."

Now the warning light was flashing like a strobe and had been joined by half a dozen others, his cockpit lighting up like a Broadway show as urgent buzzers screamed that his turbines were running on vapors. NAS Alameda, the abandoned naval facility occupying the northern half of the island, was ahead and to his left. There would be no hope of fuel or anything else, but at least it had clear, wide open spaces. As the Black Hawk descended and crossed its fence line, old barracks, administrative buildings, and hangars blurring by, Vlad experienced a small measure of relief to see that there weren't any corpses wandering across the airfield.

Not yet, anyway.

Groundhog-7's wheels touched down on the center of a runway where weeds were growing up through cracks in the cement, so long untended that the sun had bleached away the tall, painted numbers indicating the runway designation. Vlad shut it all off and sat listening to the turbines winding down, the blades slowing overhead. Then he unbuckled and walked hunched over, back past his gunner's body. Once his boots hit the concrete, he had a long, satisfying piss.

The rain continued unabated. Seven bullets, a pint of water in a plastic bottle, and a granola bar in the chest pocket of his flight suit. He lit a cigarette and cupped it in one hand, shielding it from the wind as he sat down in the open doorway, next to the empty machine gun.

He blew smoke into the rain. "Thanks again, God." And this time he meant it.

THIRTY-SIX

Oakland

It wasn't open water. It was a steel ramp leading down to a rusting maintenance barge with a small deck crane and a tiny wheelhouse. A battered work truck, which might once have been white but was now so pitted and weathered that it looked brown, sat on the flat, narrow deck loaded with welding equipment.

There wasn't enough room on the barge for both the work truck and the Bearcat. The armored vehicle's grille slammed into the rear bumper, throwing the old truck forward and pushing it off the far end. It nosed over and sank immediately, and only the brakes kept the Bearcat from following it to the bottom of the harbor, tires sliding on the wet deck. The armored truck's tires stopped two feet from the edge.

Evan raced down the ramp and skidded to a stop behind the armored truck, jumping off with Maya and running back toward the pier.

"Down here! Down here!" He waved his arms. A half-dozen adults herded a collection of frightened children down the ramp, and Maya knelt on the deck, opening her arms and smiling. The children went straight to the young woman they knew so well, huddling close and hunching against the rain. Among the adults was Faith with her younger children. "Calvin's up there," she said. Rifle fire came from the pier.

Evan unslung his shotgun just as a big hand gripped his arm. He turned to look into the lean, carved face of an older man with a gray crew cut, wearing full black body armor and carrying a rifle. His eyes were an unsympathetic shade of blue. "Don't go up there," the older man said. More rifle fire. Evan stared at him a moment and then pulled away, running back up the ramp.

TC appeared beside his cellmate. "Company, huh?" He hefted his shotgun. "We gonna let 'em stay, or should I clear the decks?"

"What, kill the kids?" Carney gave him a fierce look, and TC simply shrugged and gave him that smile he had recently come to dislike.

"Just asking. What are we gonna do?"

Carney walked past the knot of children, who were clustering around the kneeling girl while the adults watched the pier, flinching with every crack of a rifle. The older con went up the ramp and stood at the top.

The shooting was constant now, and the wall of corpses had reached the last vehicle in line, flowing around it and pouring down both sides of the pier. The people from the cars and vans were backing away, firing as they retreated. Carney saw one man, the tow truck driver he recognized from earlier when he and TC had been observing the caravan, stop and look down as he fed fresh shells into a rifle. One of the dead got close and galloped at him, tackling the man and bearing him to the ground, biting at his face. The screams caused the others to break. They stopped shooting and ran back toward the head of the column.

N o!" Evan shouted as they passed him. "Keep firing! Keep them back as long as you can!"

No one listened, but Calvin appeared beside him and grabbed his arm. "You found a boat?" he asked urgently.

"A barge. I don't know if—"

"Get them on it and get it moving. Don't wait for me." Calvin slung his assault rifle, gripped the grenade hanging around his neck and gave it a sharp tug, breaking the leather thong. He pulled the pin and threw it far out into the horde, then started running at the advancing dead before it went off. When it did, the explosion was muffled by tightly packed bodies. A few bits and pieces went flying, and one body cartwheeled through the air, but the mass didn't slow.

"Calvin, no!"

Thunder rumbled overhead. "Don't wait for me!" he shouted, not looking back. Evan cursed and ran back to the ramp, passing the man with the crew cut, his boots thudding down the metal planking. Maya's eyes were wide and frightened, but he passed her by and ran for the little wheelhouse set to one side of the barge at the back end.

T C watched the man who had been on the Harley go by, then climbed into the Bearcat through the rear doors. He paused to see if anyone was watching, and then closed them behind him. Inside, the rain made a drumming sound on the truck's metal roof. He crouched beside Skye's bound form, looking her over. Her eyelids fluttered and she was muttering behind her gag, tossing her head, covered in sweat. The inmate pulled her tank top up over her sports bra and ran a hand down her body. Her skin was slick and hot to the touch, but she was so very firm. He felt a stirring between his legs.

"Maybe you'd infect me like Carney said," he whispered. "Maybe you won't." His hand paused just beneath her left breast, and he licked his lips. He could feel her heart hammering in there. "Maybe," he said, his other hand moving to his belt buckle, "we'll just have a little party, and then I'll cut your throat and throw you overboard, tell them you started to turn, that there was nothing I could do. Who would know?" His eyes gleamed, and he smiled. "Yeah, that works. You're gonna die anyway, right?" His hand moved across her skin. "Let's have a party."

Outside, Evan yanked open the wheelhouse door and stared at the greasy controls. They looked simple enough. Years ago he had driven a friend's boat while waterskiing on a Virginia lake. How much different could this be? He searched for keys, didn't see any. His eyes roamed the small control board, seeing the empty ignition, and what looked like the steering wheel from a 1970s Buick. Keys. Keys, Goddammit!

There they were, attached to an orange flotation key ring, hanging from a small hook screwed into the plywood ceiling. He stabbed the key into the ignition and turned. It cranked slowly, and he wondered if the engine for that same 1970s Buick was what powered this heap. It died. He tried again, and it made a *huh-huh-huh-huh* sound before coughing out again.

A heavy rifle up at the pier let out a string of quick shots.

He spotted a knob that reminded him of something from an old lawn mower engine, a choke. He pulled it out and turned the key once more.

Huh-huh-huh . . .

The small diesel caught, and black smoke belched from a rusting pipe mounted outside the wheelhouse. Evan examined the simple forward-backward control and the throttle stick. He stuck his head out of the wheelhouse. "Untie us from the dock!" he called out.

Faith and a woman called America nodded and ran to the ropes tethering the barge to the pier. Hippies with rifles and pistols ran down the ramp, crowding onto the tight, narrow deck.

U p on the pier, Carney watched the man run at the dead. *Stupid way to commit suicide,* he thought. *Asshole.* He heard the barge's engine start and started to sling his rifle, turning away. Just before he did, however, he saw the older hippie stop at a VW bus a mere twenty feet from the head of the oncoming horde, yank open the side doors, and lean in.

A pair of corpses stumbled toward him.

The man emerged a moment later with a red-and-white metal cooler in his arms, a car charger cord dangling from one end. He started back, just as one of the corpses caught him by the shoulder.

C alvin jerked away, and another clutched at the back of his arm. He pulled, but the first grabbed the back of his leather vest, hauling him close. The crack of a rifle and the hum of a supersonic bullet passing his ear came at almost the same instant, and one of the ghouls fell in a bloody spray. The man in black armor with the crew cut shifted a bit and fired again. Another close hum, and the corpse gripping his vest went down. Calvin ran, the horde close behind, and he reached the ramp in seconds as the man kept firing past him.

"Big risk for beer," Carney said.

"My kid's insulin," Calvin gasped, his heart racing. "But I could sure use a cold one."

They went down the ramp together as the wall of corpses swallowed up one car after the next, a wave of hungry, mindless flesh swarming like angry ants.

Free of its bonds, the barge slid away from the pier. The old diesel chugging, Evan eased the vessel backward, and the metal ramp fell into the oily water. The swarm arrived moments later, and without hesitating stumbled right off the wharf and into the water by the hundreds, like monstrous lemmings. They kept coming, kept walking off the edge, and soon the water was filled with bobbing heads. They quickly sank.

Evan continued backing the barge away as Maya joined him in the wheelhouse, hugging him from behind and pressing her head against his wet shirt. He watched the dead, thousands more arriving and crowding onto the wharf, many still falling off into the water, arms outstretched even as their prey drew farther and farther away. He looked right, past the end of the pier toward a stretch of land on the far side of the channel. The rain and the deepening afternoon cast everything in charcoal tones, and the sky was darkening, promising a more severe storm. He patted Maya's hand, and she came around to look at his face.

"Look," he said, pointing.

She did. Out there in the rain, past the channel, a helicopter with a tiny, winking light on its tail was slowly settling onto that far stretch of land.

Evan shifted the drive forward and turned the wheel. "That's where we're going."

THIRTY-SEVEN

Alameda

It had been a piece of luck, at least for Angie, not for the people who had been here. Cruising alone in the Excursion on the south side of town, she came across a street filled with emergency vehicles. There was a pair of fire trucks (from her firehouse, she wondered?), an ambulance, and two police cars. The burned-out shell of a city bus was buried in a storefront, and the building itself had clearly been on fire. The flames were out, but there was no saving the people on the bus.

They must have quickly spilled out to overwhelm the first responders.

Now a few charred corpses lay in the street, victims of lucky head shots by the police, but everyone else was gone. The passing weeks and the current rain had washed away all other traces of gore. The scene was untouched by scavengers, so Angie left the Excursion in the middle of the street and set immediately to work.

The ambulance and fire trucks provided a supply of oxygen

bottles, which the elderly couple would need. All carried mobile medical kits and other emergency supplies, and she took the fire axes from the trucks as well. Although the police officers were gone—along with their sidearms—their squad cars still carried a pair of shotguns, ammunition, flares, and full-sized spare tires and jacks. She even took the car batteries. It all went into the Excursion.

As she worked, Angie remained aware of her surroundings. Getting too involved and focused on a project out here was a good way to get jumped and bitten, so she stopped regularly to look and listen. A San Francisco Giants cap kept the rain out of her eyes, and the Galil hung in a sling across her chest so she could keep her hands free to work, but still reach it quickly if needed. The dead didn't seem to be around at the moment, though.

On a corner across from the burned bus stood a Walgreens, and it took her a moment of staring before she realized the windows weren't broken. The Galil came up, her finger curling around the trigger. She checked the street right and left, saw it was still empty, and advanced toward the front of the store.

The dead electric doors pushed aside with a little effort. Gray light from the front windows penetrated a short distance in, leaving the aisles and back half of the store in shadows. She stopped and held her breath, listening.

Nothing.

Angie pulled a small, powerful flashlight from a cargo pocket and held it in her left hand, along with the front grip of the Galil, keeping the muzzle in line with the beam. Everything was still on the shelves; there was no sign of looting. She checked behind the register counters to be certain nothing was lurking back there, then moved sideways across the front end, pointing the light and the rifle down each aisle as she passed. Every one of them had full shelves, and no walking dead. At the far end of her beam, at the back of the store, she could see the pharmacy counter. The security gate was down, but it was intact.

Her mind raced. National chain drugstores like this were at least one-third grocery store these days: nonperishable food and beverages, along with batteries, first-aid supplies, vitamins and remedies, even cigarettes to satisfy Maxie's foul habit. The stockroom would hold more of everything, and there was a full pharmacy at the back, all of it untouched. This one store could keep the firehouse group going for at least a year.

The flashlight fell upon an end cap loaded with packaged diapers. The image of a mother looking tenderly at a swaddled infant stared back at her, and Angie felt her chest tighten. And suddenly her decision was made. Her uncle's argument made complete sense, and she carried most if not all of the responsibility for the people she had rescued and gathered together. But Angie had a daughter, a husband, and that was that. She would mark the site on the map for the others, deliver the treasures she had already found today, and that would be her final service to them. She would make one last appeal for Bud to come with her, but whether he agreed or whether she went alone, Angie West was leaving in the morning. Leah was waiting.

An unusual noise came from behind her, out on the street. Angie held her breath again, straining to identify the familiar sound, but then a rumble of thunder blotted it out. Frustrated, she waited until it came through again. Something distant, not right outside. She started slowly toward the doors, and then she had it. A helicopter. Angie bolted for the entrance, just as blocks away, the firehouse siren went off.

Bud Franks was on the roof when the helicopter passed by, flying low and following the channel, a white light blinking at its tail. He watched the Black Hawk with his mouth slightly open, feeling like a caveman seeing a spaceship. It headed north, then banked and slowed, dropping from view. Landing.

At the old naval air station.

Thoughts tumbled through his head as he raced for the stairs: rescue, a working government, safety for the people hiding in the fire station, maybe even a way to get home. "Helicopter!" he shouted into the top-floor hallway as he went down the stairs two and three at a time. "Helicopter!"

Sophia Tanner and Margaret Chu emerged from a doorway, startled by the yelling, fearing the worst. Bud slid to a stop. "A helicopter just landed out at the old Navy base. I think it's the Army."

"We're getting out of here!" Sophia hugged him, and Bud grinned.

"We can be on the road in five minutes," Margaret said. "The vehicles are ready."

"Angie's still out," Bud said, his smile evaporating. The mate to the two-way radio she carried was downstairs. "I'll track her down."

"And I'll get them packed and moving," Margaret said.

Bud was almost to the main room when the siren on the roof of the building went off, a long, piercing howl that would carry across the entire island. And draw the attention of every corpse within miles.

"Son of a *bitch*!" The radio was in the little front office, but Bud ran past it. The button for the siren was in the garage. Who the hell would set that thing off, knowing what it would attract? He already knew the answer.

"Bud, what's happening?" Jerry and Mark Phillips were in the main room as Bud went by. He didn't stop to answer and moved quickly down a short hallway, hitting the door to the garage on the run.

Maxie was waiting. He shot Bud in the chest the moment the man filled the doorway. The former deputy staggered to the left, clawing for his shoulder holster. Maxie shot him again, and Bud fell into the side of a metal storage locker with a crash. Holding the .32 revolver, Maxie walked to him and pulled the big automatic out of his holster, shoving it into his waistband. Then he crouched and patted Bud's pants pockets until he found the keys to Angie's van.

Jerry and Mark came through the door to the firehouse. "What the—"

Maxie turned and fired three times. Two bullets splintered off the door frame, making the heavyset comic leap back inside. The third caught the insurance adjuster under the chin, and he went down with a gurgle.

It was hard to breathe, and it felt like someone was standing on his chest. Bud wanted to sit up, wanted to grab Maxie by the throat and choke him until his eyes rolled up, but instead he slid further down the side of the locker. He was cold, too tired to do anything but lie there.

". . . why . . . ?" he managed, looking at Maxie and trying to lift his arms.

The man stood and tossed the van keys into the air, catching them, laughing. "I got to take care of myself." He shook his head. "It don't have to make sense to you, and besides, I never liked you much, anyway." He smiled with that one gold tooth. "Some folks is just bad people, Mr. Bud." He chirped the door locks and walked to the front of the bay, hitting the switch not only for the garage door in front of the Angie's Armory van, but also for the door in front of the empty space where the Excursion was usually parked.

"I expect they'll be in here directly," he said, gesturing at the dead that were shuffling in from all directions, drawn by the wailing siren. He laughed again, and then he was climbing in, starting the van.

Margaret Chu came out of the firehouse racking the pump of a shotgun with Jerry close behind her. *"Bastard!"* She blew a hole in the side of the van as it started forward, racked the shotgun again, and blew another hole. Maxie gunned the engine, the rear tires squealing on the polished cement before roaring out onto the street. Margaret sent another blast after him and tore a ragged hole in a rear door as he turned left, knocking down half a dozen of the walking dead as he accelerated away.

"Mark is dead," Jerry said behind her. He went to the fallen deputy. "Bud's still alive." Elson and a crowd of frightened faces filled the door to the firehouse.

Margaret racked the shotgun and moved to the roll-up doors. "Elson, drag Mark out onto the driveway. I'll deal with him when he turns. Jerry, get everyone loaded."

The men hurried to their jobs, Elson grabbing the dead insurance man by the ankles and pulling him across the floor, leaving him just outside the bay doors. Margaret went to the controls, shut off the siren, and lowered both roll-up doors at the same time, standing ready with the shotgun. By the time the doors connected with the ground, the dead arrived and began piling up, pounding on the metal and glass. Their friend Mark Phillips soon rose to join them.

Jerry got the senior van loaded with as many people as it would hold, then herded the rest to Maxie's Cadillac. He let out a relieved breath when he found that the man had left his keys in the ignition.

Margaret faced Elson and Jerry. "They're not going to go away, and they're going to force their way in. We have to leave. We're heading to the Navy base, and we'll hope that helicopter is still there." She pointed to the men and the vehicles. "Elson, you drive the van; Jerry, take the Cadillac. The base is on the maps."

As they moved, Margaret went to where Bud was slumped. His chest was rising and falling with irregular hitches, and his face was colorless. Too much blood covered the floor, and Margaret bit her lip, knowing there was nothing she could do. Bud seemed to know it as well.

"I'm so sorry," she whispered, kneeling in front of him, tears filling her eyes.

". . . yours . . . now . . ." He took a shallow breath and closed his eyes. "Do it."

Margaret nodded, kissed the man on the cheek, and then stood and pressed the muzzle to his forehead. In the vehicles, the adults made the children look away. When it went off, the shotgun sounded like the world exploding.

Sobbing, Margaret went back into the firehouse and retrieved the walkie-talkie that would connect her with Angie. Before she climbed into the senior van, she opened both rear bay doors, and the two vehicles rolled out the back a moment later.

Angie reached for the radio on her hip as she ran for the doors, then remembered it was on the dashboard of the Excursion. Outside the siren was much louder, even though it was many blocks away. In normal times she probably wouldn't have heard it at all over the street noise and the airport traffic flying overhead, but Alameda was quieter now. The world was quieter.

The dead were responding to the siren. They emerged from doorways, appeared at second- and third-floor windows. One even crawled out from under a fire truck, right where she had been standing a short while ago. It couldn't have been there earlier, she thought. It would have tried to bite her ankle.

Angie raised the Galil and fired. A man in a sport coat went down. A woman in a meter maid's uniform and another in a bathrobe collapsed with head shots. Turning left, she dropped a high school student, an elderly man, a fireman, and the rotting corpse of a teenager limping toward her in a thigh-length cast covered in signatures and lipstick hearts. More appeared.

She trotted to the big SUV and tossed her rifle onto the passenger seat, climbing in and locking the driver's door behind her. Bodies thumped against the vehicle as she fired up the engine and reached for the walkie-talkie. "Bud, what's happening?" she asked.

No reply.

"Bud, come in. Do you copy?"

The siren cut off abruptly, and at that moment she caught a horrible, sour stench coming from the backseat. She glanced at the rearview, already reaching for her shoulder holster, and saw a scarecrow seated behind her wearing a hooded sweatshirt. His eyes jittered, the pupils so big and black that they looked like twin bullet holes. The muzzle of a pistol pressed against her right temple, and her hand froze on the butt of her own automatic.

"Hello, beautiful," the man said. "I'm Peter."

THIRTY-EIGHT

Mission Bay

It was only three blocks, but Father Xavier's journey from the building where he'd left Alden to the waterfront was the longest and loneliest time of his life. He moved down the center of a street that was like a canyon, the high walls of condominiums rising on the left and right. Cars sat parked in silent rows along the curbs, many of their owners banging rhythmically at windows high above, dead and trapped within their homes.

A rat that appeared as big as a housecat strutted insolently across the street in front of him, its gray-black hair slicked flat by the rain. A solitary corpse, a woman in tight jeans and a torn blouse, one hand so chewed it looked as if she had stuck it in a lawn mower, hobbled after it, not seeing the man in the street. They quickly disappeared between a pair of buildings on the left.

The rain drummed on the hoods and roofs of cars, creating puddles on the asphalt and plastering the priest's clothes against his chest. It was a cold rain.

I saved no one, Xavier thought. *I protected no one.*

He suddenly wondered why he was going on at all. To what purpose? To stay alive in a world where only he existed? To perhaps encounter another handful of desperate, frightened people, only to fail them as well?

It was then he knew Tricia had been right. He was already in hell, and this was God's punishment for his unforgivable sins. Did he deserve less? If this were a movie, he would cry to the heavens, "God, why have You forsaken me?" But he already knew why. God had turned his back because Xavier Church was a killer, and one who masqueraded as a man of faith, perhaps an even greater sin. He had taken lives and, in doing so, broken his covenant with God. Now he was condemned to walk among the dead, a man without hope.

And yet he kept moving toward the bay.

Eventually he came to a final cross street, Terry A. Francois Boulevard. Beyond was a large park that led to the water. Xavier turned left and kept going, staying close to the park side of the street, watching for movement in the rain and still wondering why he bothered. Near Mission Bay Boulevard South, the park ended at another industrial area on the right: small garages, fenced yards where boats rested elevated on metal racks, repair facilities, and a few shops specializing in sport fishing equipment. Xavier moved into this area, still heading for the water, and soon found himself at the edge of a long wharf. Off to his left was a large building with many windows and umbrella tables outside. To the right was a commercial fishing pier and docks, where small cranes sat waterside near ice houses, ready to receive the day's catch. The air reeked of oil and salt and fish, but there were no boats in the water. A dirty gull stood on a piling not far away, watching him with small black eyes.

The priest stared out at the gray day, at the storm clouds passing slowly across the sky, at the water, choppy and cold. He knew its temperature could get down into the forties, even in September. It wouldn't take long before the water sapped him of heat and strength, pulling him under and quickly silencing him.

Suicide meant immediate damnation.

But he was already in hell, wasn't he?

It took a moment before he realized he had been watching the small shape of a helicopter far out across the bay, moving slowly along Alameda Island. He blinked. Helicopter. That processed for a moment, and then he began to wave his arms and shout, demanding it see him, demanding it come. And then he dropped his arms and shook his head, feeling foolish for the unthinking reaction. Did he really think he could be seen or heard at this distance?

But he did get a response. A chorus of moans called out behind him.

Xavier turned to see a hundred or more of the dead coming at him in a crowd. They had approached steadily, quietly, while he stared out at the water. Now they were less than ten yards away.

The priest ran, heading into the commercial fishing area. The crowd followed, and he didn't get far before more corpses staggered out onto the wharf in front of him. He cut left, running down a floating wooden dock that bobbed beneath him, threatening to throw him off balance and into the water. It was a short dock, and he reached the end in less than a minute, angry with himself for coming this way, not thinking, knowing he had obeyed a primitive instinct to run, run, run. He turned and saw the dead streaming off the wharf and onto the wooden planking, bumping against one another as they came on in a wave.

Xavier looked at the crowbar in his hand, looked at the water. A few of the dead lost their balance on the bobbing dock and fell off the sides, but the rest kept coming, their moans rising. Fifty feet. Twenty-five. Mouths dropped open and the creatures in the lead began lurching faster.

The priest planted his feet and raised the crowbar, the beginnings of an Our Father coming out in a whisper without him realizing. He tensed to swing.

A spotlight framed him from behind, and he heard the sound of an idling motor. He turned to see a San Francisco Police Harbor Patrol boat drifting fifty feet away, silhouettes of people moving behind the light.

"Swim!" someone shouted.

Xavier dropped the heavy tool and dove. The water took him in a frigid grip, and when he broke the surface he gasped, trying to breathe. Dozens of splashes came from behind him, and he forced his arms and legs to move. The boat seemed miles away.

"Faster!" the voice yelled, and then there was the boom of a shotgun. Xavier pulled himself through the water, forcing himself to take even breaths, not to give in to the stabbing cold. Another shotgun blast went off just overhead, and then one of his hands rapped hard against the fiberglass hull. He pawed his way down the side, finding a narrow metal platform half submerged at the stern. Xavier hauled himself out of the water and tumbled into the rear of the boat.

A man and a woman sat on a bench seat, keeping close together and huddling under rain ponchos. The woman was pregnant. Another woman in blue camouflage and a ball cap stood at the helm, gripping the wheel and already throttling the patrol boat away from the dock. Xavier slumped to the deck, shivering as a man stood over him. He wore sneakers, khaki jeans, and an expensive caramel-colored raincoat. His skin was a light mocha, and he wore his hair in tight, necklength braids with a few shells and colored beads woven into them.

He was pointing a shotgun at Xavier. The priest thought he looked terrified.

"Helicopter," Xavier said, his teeth chattering.

The man with the braids ignored him. "He's shaking," he called to the woman at the helm. "I think he's got the virus."

She didn't look back. "Then kill him."

Xavier raised a hand and shook his head as the man pointed the muzzle of the shotgun and pulled the trigger.

THIRTY-NINE

On the deck of the barge, the hippies sheltered their children as best they could, pulling on hoods and hats, staying close together. There was sadness over the few they had lost on the pier, but a quiet joy that Calvin had safely returned to them.

Inside the tiny wheelhouse, with Maya tucked close against him, Evan guided the barge out of Oakland Middle Harbor and across the western tip of what someone had shouted was Alameda, the old Navy base. From the water they could see only a rocky shoreline with a high fence fifty feet in, tall weeds growing along the chain link as it stretched away in both directions. Beyond the fence stood a line of tall metal-frame towers with airfield landing lights mounted atop them, and a high red-and-white radio antenna, but from this angle the actual field could not be seen, and thus there was no sign of the helicopter. The shore was jagged stone and uninviting to boats, so he stayed well off, following the land and looking for a soft place to beach.

The surface was choppy, and the barge, designed for flat harbors

and never intended to withstand even the relatively calm waters of
the bay, swayed dangerously, forcing people to widen their stances
and hold on to whatever they could. Maya kept one arm locked
around Evan's waist and braced a palm against the plywood wall of
the wheelhouse. The young writer had too much imagination for this
as he envisioned the barge rolling over to the left, dumping screaming
people into the cold water, and the armored truck over on top of them.
It made him tighten his grip on the wheel.

O ut on the open deck, once he was certain his wife and children
were accounted for and after he checked with the others to see
who was missing, Calvin headed for the cab of the armored truck
parked at one end of the barge. Carrying the small cooler of insulin
in both hands, he nodded in satisfaction when he saw that the vehicle's
engine was still running. Using an elbow, he opened the passenger
door.

"You're so beautiful, baby," someone crooned from within.

Calvin hesitated, then stepped up onto the metal running board
and leaned into the cab. There was sudden movement in the back,
and then a face was looking at him through the opening between the
cab and the rear compartment. It was a muscular man in his early
thirties with long blond hair and tattoos, wearing black, military-style
clothing. His face was flushed, and he glared at Calvin, quickly buck-
ling his pants.

"I just need a place to plug this in," Calvin said, waving the adapter
cord for the small cooler. He looked at the dashboard, then unplugged
a portable DVD player from the cigarette lighter, switching it for the
cooler cord. He didn't see the man behind him bare his teeth when
he did it.

A groan came from the back and Calvin turned to see that, among
the stacks of supplies and piles of weapons and body armor, the

younger man was crouched over a girl. She was gagged and bound tightly, lying on the floor partially undressed. Her eyes were closed and she was breathing rapidly, her body slick with sweat. Calvin recognized the fever at once.

"What are you doing?" Calvin whispered, redness creeping up his whiskered neck. The girl was Maya's age.

TC's lip curled as he bared his teeth. "None of your fucking business, old man."

Calvin stepped between the seats and removed his hat, bending slightly at the knees as he smoothly drew a large, bone-handled knife from a sheath at the small of his back. He held the knife low and looked TC in the eyes. "It's my business now," he said, his voice little more than a growl.

TC sized him up. No stranger to close-quarters prison combat, he recognized an experienced knife fighter when he saw one and wasn't fooled for a moment by the man's age. He was hard, and the inmate could tell that the man was ready to go all the way.

"You sure you want this, old man?" TC asked, giving him a smile that didn't reach his eyes.

Calvin simply said, "Get out." There was no bluster, no threats, only the tiniest, snakelike wave to the tip of the big blade and the man's steady gaze.

TC nodded, smiled more broadly, and slipped out onto the deck through the Bearcat's rear double doors, then slammed them closed behind him. Calvin sheathed his knife and crouched beside the girl, pulling her clothing back into place. *What kind of sick bastard . . . ?*

The truck rocked as someone climbed into the cab. "What are you doing?" said a voice.

The hippie turned to see the man with the crew cut and black body armor, the one whose rifle had saved his life earlier on the pier. He was dressed just like the man Calvin had chased off, and he immediately made the connection; they were together. Calvin's hands shook. "Your buddy was about to . . . if I hadn't come in . . . She's sick, for God's sake." Calvin finished covering her and put the back of his palm on her forehead. "She's burning up. Is it the virus?"

Carney put it together quickly. "I don't know. Probably. She got a face full of fluid. Where did the other man go?"

"Out the back." Calvin was still crouched over Skye, as if this new arrival might also attempt to defile her. He eased his hand back toward the big knife.

Carney shook his head slowly. "You need to relax. Come on out of there."

Calvin looked at him, seeing they were both about the same age, each toughened in his own way by different lives. This man's eyes were different than the younger man's, though. They lacked the crazy he had seen in the would-be rapist. Calvin climbed out and stood beside Carney in the rain. After a moment, they gave their first names and shook hands, never taking their eyes off one another. Both had solid grips.

"Who is she?" Calvin asked.

"I still don't know her name. She's someone who needed help out of a tight spot, and you can see what good that did her."

Both men looked forward, picking out the mass of TC Cochoran walking slowly through the crowd to the front of the barge. He stripped off his armor and shirts until he was bare-chested, revealing his broad, deeply chiseled upper body and canvas of ferocious tattoos. He sat and dangled his legs over the water, the auto shotgun resting beside him.

Calvin faced his new acquaintance. "If he goes near that girl again . . ."

Carney didn't like threats, and his eyes narrowed just a bit, but he had warned TC about the girl and he would have to deal with the situation. Now was not the time, however. "You want to stay clear of him, man."

"He doesn't scare me," said Calvin.

"He should," Carney said.

Up on the bow, TC threw his head back into the wind and rain and let out a long howl. The gathered hippies and their children jumped at the primal noise.

"Is he going to be a problem?" asked Calvin.

The con stared out at his cellmate. "If he is, then he's my problem."

The two men looked at each other for a long moment, coming to an unspoken understanding of the situation, and each other. Then Calvin extended a hand, Carney shook it firmly, and the hippie made his way back to his family.

Evan continued to pilot the barge along the shore and fence line, coming to a literal corner of land so squared-off it had to be man-made. Just beyond the fence, rising out of tall grass, was a cement airfield tower that looked as though it had been unused for half a century. In front of the tower, standing with rotting fingers curled through the chain link, was the corpse of an old man in baggy khakis and a dark blue jacket covered in military patches, one of those elderly vets who donated their time at military museums, sharing their stories with those who would listen. Strands of thin hair were matted to his head, and his skin had a greenish hue. He rattled the fence and peeled back his lips as the barge chugged past.

The writer brought the vessel around the corner to the left where the shore and fence continued on as far as he could see, still rocky and unfit for landing. The expanse of the bay spread out to the right, San Francisco in the distance, a gray shadow behind a curtain of rain. The corpse turned its head to watch them go by, and then it disengaged its fingers from the fence and began to trudge through the high weeds, unable to keep pace, but keeping steadily on.

Evan knew that if he stayed on his course, eventually he would find a way into the base, and from there they would seek out the helicopter. After that? He had no answers, but at least they were together and safe for the moment.

Behind him, the old man's corpse followed, as relentless as time.

FORTY

Alameda

"Angie, come in, it's Margaret. Angie, can you hear me?"

The radio sat on the Excursion's dashboard untouched, Angie sitting very still behind the wheel, fingertips resting on the grip of her automatic. The muzzle of the pistol was cold against the skin in front of her right ear, and her eyes were locked on the mirror, on the man in the backseat.

"I'm sorry," said Peter. "I . . . I can't take any chances."

"I understand," said Angie, surprised at the calm in her own voice.

"I've been watching you gather supplies," said Peter. "Are there others? Other people alive?" His voice was reedy, and Angie could see he was trembling. "I've been alone . . . so alone." He suddenly removed the pistol from her temple and sat back. "I'm sorry if I scared you. I didn't know if you would try to hurt me."

Angie still didn't move. The gun was out of sight, but a spot between her shoulder blades itched as if she could feel the big .45 pointed at her through the seat.

"I won't hurt you," she said quietly. "You scared me pretty good, but it's okay."

"It is? I just . . ." The man trailed off.

"There're other people out there, a place where you can be safe. What's your name again?"

He hesitated. "Peter."

"Okay, Peter. I can take you there, but if we're going to be friends, I need you to hand me that pistol, okay?" She watched him in the mirror. His eyes darted and he chewed his lip.

"You're not mad? You won't hurt me?"

Angie shook her head slowly. "No, Peter. Will you please give me your gun? Then we can be friends."

And just like that he passed the weapon over the front seat, butt first. Angie immediately ejected the magazine and the bullet in the chamber, dropping it all on the floorboards, jerking her automatic from its holster. She first buzzed down the passenger window and then the driver's, shooting a trio of corpses in the face at close range and clearing them off the SUV. Peter ducked and covered his head at the explosive crash of the nine-millimeter within the confines of the truck. Then Angie jumped out the driver's-side door, yanked open the rear door, and leveled her weapon.

"Get the fuck out of there! Move! Now!" she demanded.

Peter scrambled out, hands raised.

"On your knees! Put your hands behind your head!"

The minister did as he was told, dropping to his knees on the wet pavement, head down. "I'm sorry. I told you I was sorry!"

"Shut up!" Angie stepped to him and rammed the muzzle against the crown of his head, her body shaking. "You son of a *bitch*!"

"I'm sorry," Peter whined. He began to cry.

"I said shut up!" She pushed his head with the handgun. "I should blow your head off right now. Or gut-shoot you and leave you for them." Gunfire and human activity on the street was continuing to draw attention, and more figures emerged from buildings and alleys, shuffling into the street, mindless of the pouring rain. They began to moan.

"Please," Peter cried, "I was just scared. I don't know you, and there are people out there who . . . I've seen such horrible things . . . I didn't . . . I wanted . . ." His body was trembling and he began to sob. "Please don't kill me."

Oh, how she wanted to do just that, apply a little pressure on the trigger and spread his brains on the asphalt. He had frightened her, made her feel powerless, and she hated being helpless. But now she was doing the same thing to him. She snatched the weapon away with a disgusted grunt and retrieved the walkie-talkie from the dashboard, eyeing the approaching dead. Margaret's voice had been coming across every few seconds.

"Margaret, it's Angie."

"Thank God! Are you okay?"

"I'm fine. What's happening? I heard the siren."

There was a long silence before she said, "Angie . . . Bud's dead."

Angie didn't say anything, just stood in the rain holding the radio. She stared at the whimpering figure still on his knees beside the Excursion.

"It was Maxie," Margaret said. She told her how Maxie had set off the alarm and opened the doors, trying to let in the dead. She explained how he had ambushed Bud and killed Mark Phillips too.

"Where's my uncle?" Angie's voice was flat.

"At the firehouse. I . . . I made sure he wouldn't come back."

Angie thought about what that meant and didn't reply.

"I shot at Maxie, tried to stop him, but he got away. He took your van and all the weapons." Margaret told her about the helicopter, about how even now she and the others were packed into the remaining vehicles, approaching the gates of the naval air station.

"Keep moving," Angie said, finally. "I'll get back to you." She

tossed the walkie-talkie back onto the dashboard and retrieved her
assault rifle, propping it against the center console between the seats.
The dead were closing in on the Excursion, feet sliding through puddles, damaged throats letting out hungry, rasping noises. A coldness
settled over her that had nothing to do with the rain.

"Peter." She prodded the man hard with the tip of her boot, but
he refused to look up. "This is simple. I'm still pissed at you. I should
leave you for the dead, but I'm going to give you a chance." Angie
looked up at a long groan from twenty feet away, raised her automatic,
and shot the creature in the head. Peter flinched. "I don't have time
to screw around. If you come with me, you do what I tell you. Do you
understand?"

He nodded.

"If you don't do what I tell you, I'll feed you to them. Do you
understand *that*?"

He nodded again and wiped tears and snot on his sleeve.

"Get in the truck, front passenger seat." Before she let him stand,
she pulled the hunting knife from his rear waistband and tossed it
onto the floorboards next to the empty .45. When they were inside
with the doors locked, Angie turned toward him, her automatic resting on her thigh and pointed at his belly. She wrinkled her nose at
his smell. Outside, a handful of the dead had reached the SUV and
were now beating at the metal and glass. Angie ignored them.

"You sit there, and put your hands in your jacket pocket. Keep
them there. If you move wrong, you'll be dead before you know you
made a mistake, and I won't feel bad about it. Are we clear?"

"Yes." He slid his hands into the front pouch-pocket of his hooded
jacket, his right hand closing over the friendly, familiar shape of the
box cutter that had opened up Sherri's face only this morning. He
suppressed a smile. Like the many sheep of his flock, this woman
would be easy to fool too.

Angie backed over a corpse banging on the rear window and then took them through the streets of Alameda, glancing frequently at her passenger. He kept still, staring out at the dead city and only speaking once to ask her name. Evening was falling rapidly, the storm demanding headlights, and fifteen minutes later they revealed the firehouse ahead on the right. Angie slowed and let the Excursion roll up to it, ignoring the corpses in the street that slowly turned toward the sound of the engine. Beyond the thumping wipers she could see shapes moving behind the garage windows, saw curtains moving on the upper floors, and even a few shapes staggering along the edge of the rooftop.

"Was this your safe place?" Peter asked.

Angie didn't reply, and grabbed the radio. "Margaret, Angie. Where are you?"

"We're on the base. There was a locked gate, but we found a construction entrance a hundred yards down the road where the fence was taken down for the trucks. We drove right in."

"You're all okay?"

"Yes. We've seen some wandering around, but only a few and always at a distance. Jerry thinks we can get out to the airfield in ten or fifteen minutes."

"Okay, get to that helicopter and let me know what you find."

There was a brief silence. "Did you see the firehouse?" Margaret asked.

Angie stared at the building for a while, imagining her uncle on the floor in there, being fed upon by those abominations. She pictured Maxie smiling with that single gold tooth and gripped the walkie-talkie so tightly her knuckles turned white. "Let me know about that helicopter," she repeated.

Margaret's voice was alarmed. "Aren't you coming? Where will you be?"

Angie keyed the radio, her voice soft. "I'm going hunting."

FORTY-ONE

CLICK.

Xavier jumped at the hollow snap of the trigger pull, expecting a flash of light and death. Instead the black man in the overcoat and braided beads made a startled face and struggled to work the shotgun's slide. Xavier didn't give him a second chance. He came off the rocking, slippery deck with a roar and snatched the weapon out of the man's hands, straight-arming his chest and sending him flying backward into the open wheelhouse.

The woman at the helm drew a black automatic from a flap holster and turned, one hand on the wheel, the other pointing the pistol at Xavier's face. Her eyes were dark and unblinking, her body swaying easily with the motion of the boat.

Xavier checked the chamber of the shotgun, then tossed it back at the other man. "It's empty," he said, not taking his eyes off the woman. "And I'm not sick. That water's cold."

"Strip," she said. "Right now."

Xavier peeled off his wet shirt and shrugged out of his pants, raising his arms and turning slowly, revealing that he was unbitten.

The woman nodded and holstered her pistol, turning back to the wheel. The man in braids reached into a coat pocket and started to feed a shell into the shotgun's chamber, then stopped, staring at the muscled, mostly naked man with the fearsome scar splitting his face. He tried to speak, but nothing came out.

Xavier pulled his pants and shirt back on and stepped toward the man. "Don't ever point that at me again."

The man shook his head rapidly. "I'm sorry, I thought . . . I'm sorry. My name's Darius, I'm a professor at UC San Francisco, I—"

Xavier ignored him and brushed past, stepping into the wheelhouse to stand beside the woman. He pointed through the Plexiglas windshield. "A helicopter landed over that way a few minutes ago."

"I saw it."

He looked at her. The woman was in her late twenties and light skinned, not too tall with black hair tied up under a blue military cap. She was the kind of pretty that turned heads. In the soft instrument glow from the patrol boat's dash he couldn't quite make out the name on the tag sewn over her left blouse pocket.

They rode in silence for several long minutes, their adrenaline slowly subsiding. "I'm just being careful," she said at last.

"I know."

"Don't make me regret saving your ass."

"A few minutes ago you told someone to kill me."

"It's still an option," she said. She talked tough but couldn't hide a thin smile. "Darius isn't good with weapons." She glanced back at the braided man, who had now taken a seat along one side of the rear deck, the shotgun across his knees. He looked green and clearly wasn't enjoying the weather or the ride. "He couldn't hit the side of a barn if he was standing inside one."

Xavier stared through the windscreen. "Well, we're all learning new things these days, aren't we?"

The woman said nothing but nodded slowly. She had the patrol boat aimed straight into the San Francisco Bay, the bow pointed at a distant landmass. Finally she glanced at the big man standing beside her. "Who are you?"

After a moment he said, "I'm Xavier Church." Then he took a deep breath. "I'm a priest."